Copyright © 2013 by Russell Cruse
Cover design and Photography Copyright © 2013 by Russell Cruse

Russell Cruse asserts the right to be identified as the author of this work.
All rights reserved.
No part of this book may be reproduced in any form or by any electronic or mechanical means including information storage and retrieval systems, without permission in writing from the author. The only exception is by a reviewer, who may quote short excerpts in a review.
Russell Cruse

First Printing: 2013
Special thanks to Oxfam for permission to use their brand name.

Note on the Crossword:
The author is not Colin Dexter. Nor is he anything approaching a professional crossword compiler. The crossword at the end of the book is just to give readers a flavour of the *"Luscinia"* puzzle, by which Arthur and Bracewell stumble upon the code. The author is also aware that some of the clues are, frankly, not terribly good and that there are many "unchecked" solutions (or "unchies" as the aficionadi refer to them). If the reader is likely to be upset by the deficiencies evident in the crossword, the author respectfully suggests that he/she should not attempt it.
In addition, the author would like it to be known that he is not a professional composer of serial music and that if he has offended in his construction of the piece, *"Limns"*, offendees will not feel compelled to instigate a hate campaign against him.

## The Rothko Room

There are secrets and then there are *secrets*. *Secrets* are kept secret even from the people who keep the greatest secrets of all. That is how secret they are.

# PART 1 MONDAY
# Rome

'*I'm* Stephen Mosley.'

That was a lie. The man seldom used his own name and emerging from the Arrivals Lounge at Aeroporto da Vinci Roma, he had spotted this one on a sign. It was being held by a particularly agreeable-looking young woman in a smart wine-coloured business suit. Even the fearful vulgarity of a wide felt pen could not disguise a fine hand; an English hand. He had no way of knowing that the previous night she'd had too much to drink and had gone to bed far too late. But then he'd always been lucky.

'Oh!' she said to him, 'we were expecting a ... more... that is a...'

'Younger man?' he said, raising an eyebrow and offering his hand.

'I'm sorry,' she said, lowering the sign and clearly flustered. She took his hand. 'You must think me terribly rude.'

'Not at all,' he said with a smile. She returned it with some relief and he gestured towards the exit. 'Shall we?' As they left the building neither noticed the real Stephen Mosley, a young man not renowned for his patience, cursing the idiots running the Italian arm of his father's company for having failed to pick him up.

'I didn't catch your name,' the man said, as he opened the driver's door for the young woman.

'I'm Vanessa Aldridge,' she said, settling herself and bringing down the driver's window, 'your... father's Personal Assistant.'

'And how is the old boy?' he asked her.

'Erm... extremely... well.' She looked at him more closely. '...In the circumstances. You're not Stephen Mosley, are you?'

'I'm afraid not, Vanessa,' he said, leaning in the window. 'Now, I do not wish to kill you but please believe me; I shall if you don't do as I say.' The small automatic pistol was not pointed at her; it was held lightly in his hand as he spoke. Her stomach lurched.

She might have a chance were she able to get the car started... No she wouldn't; she saw it in his serene face. If this plan didn't work for him, she observed, he would fashion another without missing a beat. He must have recognised the face of submission for he smiled and moved unhurriedly around the front of the car to the passenger side.

'What do you want?' she asked.

'I'd like you take me into Rome, if you wouldn't mind.'

'Whereabouts?'

'The British Embassy.' She looked at him. He raised both eyebrows this time, nodded and smiled once more. Vanessa started the car, selected a gear and pulled away from the curb.

'Are you going to tell me what's going on?' she enquired.

'Ooh shouldn't think so, Vanessa,' he said. She was doing her best to remain calm but her vodka headache had returned with a vengeance and she could feel the blood draining from her face. She had to ask.

'What happens when we get there?'

'Well, so long as you behave yourself, I get out and you go on to have a long and happy life.'

'You'll have to tell me where it is.'

'No problem.' He pointed forwards. 'It's that way.'

Once out of the airport and onto Coccia di Morto, she stole a glance at her passenger. He was early to mid fifties, she reckoned, with greying temples, clean-shaven and handsome. She noticed gold links on the cuff of the silk shirt that jutted a couple of centimetres from the sleeve of his extremely well-cut grey suit. He was certainly not Vanessa's idea of a desperate fugitive. She faced forwards once more. As traffic filtered in from the right, she pulled over, glancing in her mirror and stealing another look at the man's face. It betrayed no sign of anxiety, no tell-tale bead of sweat.

'Do you think you're behaving yourself, Vanessa?' he asked without looking at her. Vanessa snapped her head forwards immediately.

'I... I'm sorry,' she said, feebly.

'Oh, it's all right. You're curious. Perfectly natural in the circumstances. My name's Geoffrey, by the way, Geoffrey...'

'Please! Don't say any more! I don't want to know.'

'Really? Why ever not?'

'Well, if you tell me your name, I'll know who you are and then... well, you know.'

'Oh!' he said, 'I see! Mmm...' He sounded thoughtful. 'You know, I hadn't considered that. Oh dear. Now I shall have to shoot you.' She felt sick and looked round, anxiously. He was grinning at her. It took a brief moment before she realised that this was his idea of a joke. Her laughter was practically hysterical.

'I'm sorry,' he said. 'That was unkind. I realise this is terribly disturbing for you. Believe it or not, it's happened to me once or twice so I know what you're going through.' Vanessa dared to look at him once more.

'Are you in some kind of trouble?' she asked.

'Trouble? No, not really. There was someone at the airport I didn't want to bump into.' Although he was being civil – almost flippant, something told Vanessa that she'd better not press him.

'Take the next exit,' he said.

She turned onto the A91. She became aware that he was studying her face and she began to feel uncomfortable. She wondered if she ought to say something. Under normal circumstances she would have done. He himself said nothing for several kilometres and then she heard,

'Tell me a little about yourself,'
'Why?'
'I'd like to know.'

She thought it best to comply.

'Where do you want me to start?'
'What do you do for a living? I suspect this isn't your car.'
'Oh God,' said Vanessa.
'Belongs to your boss, eh?' the man said. He sounded almost sympathetic. 'Oh dear. He'll not be happy about this, will he?'
'You could say that,' Vanessa said. 'And I expect his son will be fucking livid. Oh! Sorry!''
'Ha! No, I expect he will.' She took a deep breath and blew it out then stretched her neck a little, concentrating on remaining calm. Noticing, he said to her,

'If it's any consolation Vanessa, you're handling this very well.' She took a risk and turned to look at him again.

'You do this sort of thing a lot, then?' she asked. He smiled and said,
'You know, I haven't needed to in a while but it's been a funny sort of day.'
'You don't say?' That was way too flippant but to her relief, it seemed to please him. She actually heard him chuckle and she joined in.
'That's better,' he said. 'I think everything's going to be just fine.' Vanessa snorted.
'You've never met Andrew Mosley, have you?' she said.
'Can't say as I have. But I'd venture he's a complete bastard. Any man who can't find it in himself to forgive a beautiful woman is a villain of the first order.' Vanessa screwed up her face.
'Oh please!' she said.
'Ooh!' He sounded hurt. 'A cynic. And so young.' He laughed, evidently pleased with himself. 'Anyway come on; what's a nice English girl like you doing in Italy, driving for a monster like this Mosley chap?'
'It's a long story.'
'Well, the traffic's terrible; I suspect we have plenty of time.' She glided the Mercedes up against the rear bumper of a Punto that was trying to insinuate itself into the melee of tail-lights and car-horns that was the intersection. She looked at him again. He didn't seem to object, which should have worried her but didn't. He smiled. Despite his age, Vanessa had to own that he was an extremely attractive man. In other circumstances... She blinked and said,

'Oh, I was stuck here when the company I worked for went bust. I managed a hotel for a while and then Mr. Mosley gave me a job.'

'How jolly decent of him.'

'Yes, jolly decent.' When Mosley had first suggested she might like to come and work for him, Vanessa had actually believed that her true worth had been recognised. Less than a year down the line, she had been under no illusions as to why she'd got the job.

'Are you happy in your work?'

'Well, the money's outrageous,' she answered.

'Does that mean too little or too much?'

'Way too much! You wouldn't believe.'

'Oh, I think I might,' he said, touching the lapel of her suit. 'Versace, if I'm not mistaken; beautiful colour, by the way. Burgundy, would you call that?' Despite herself, Vanessa was impressed and not a little intrigued. She gazed at him and did not react as he let go her lapel and placed his hand gently upon hers, as it rested on the steering wheel.

'Tell me, Vanessa, do you have many friends in Rome?'

'Yes. Yes, I do, as a matter of fact.' She began to feel uneasy again. Where was this going? The man was looking at her intently.

'No, I don't believe you do. You have one or two people you enjoy going out with occasionally but I don't expect Mr. Mosley allows you much time to yourself. Not enough time for real relationships, eh?' What concerned her about this observation was not simply that it was true and nor was it that he'd deduced it so easily; it was the fact that he seemed to care.

Suddenly, he released her hand, sat back in his seat once more and directed her attention forward. She became instantly aware of the cacophony of car-horns and the fact that a number of scooters and mopeds were weaving into the gap in front of her. The Punto was now about ten yards ahead.

'Shit!' she said, and pushed the Mercedes into gear. Her ears were ringing and her headache was getting worse.

'So impatient, the drivers in Rome, don't you find?' he said. 'Look at that. All that energy and anger and stress and for what? A couple of yards of tarmac. If it weren't for their Mediterranean diet, they'd all be dead of coronaries by the time they're forty. Anyway, you were telling me about yourself.' Vanessa's sense of unease, gone for a few moments, began to reassert itself.

'You know, there's really not much to tell.'

'Oh, I'm sure there is. Everyone has a story.'

'Not me. Not one you'd be interested in anyway.'

'You'd be surprised what interests me, Vanessa.' She thought for a moment. There was more, of course but she had the feeling that the less she shared with him the better.

'All right,' he said, 'what about before you got stuck in Italy?'

'I worked at Asda.'

'What is that, aeronautics?' She laughed.

'Good Lord, no! When were you last in England?'

'This morning, Vanessa. You were meeting the flight from London.' She suddenly felt very stupid and for some reason, ashamed.

'Oh… yes. Silly of me. I'm sorry.' She really wasn't herself this morning.

'Don't be.' Then, almost wistfully, it seemed to Vanessa, he said, 'No, I'm afraid I'm sadly ignorant of most things English these days.' Almost immediately, he brightened.

'What about your school,' he said.

'Eh?'

'Where did you go to school?'

'Uckfield. In Sussex.'

'Ah. Beautiful part of the world. Corehampton Girls?' Vanessa frowned.

'St.Philip's Grammar.'

'Oh,' said Geoffrey, 'grammar school.'

'Is that a problem?'

'No, no. I suppose one makes judgements. Never a good idea. One of my dearest friends is a grammar school boy. Nothing wrong with it at all.' He reached into his pocket and Vanessa eyed him, nervously. He must have noticed, for having retrieved the item, he held it up for Vanessa's inspection. 'It's one of those sprays you can use to cool yourself down. They gave them away on the aeroplane. Would you like me to…' He held the little atomiser up to her face. Certainly, she was extremely hot, climate control or no but she held up her hand in front of her face.

'No thank you,' she said. 'I'm fine.' The man placed the little object in the moulded dip next to the handbrake.

'You might need it later,' he said.

Within half an hour, they were within striking distance of the Embassy. The traffic, of course, was ghastly and the general standard of driving… well, Italian. She was having to concentrate and was aware that several times she had tuned the man out and had settled into conveying him as though that were her job, handling the alternating car-parks and racetracks that are the streets of Rome with some aplomb.

'I really don't like this town,' her passenger said. 'It's quite beautiful of course but... ossified.'

Vanessa was surprised at herself. She was utterly calm and had quite forgotten the circumstances of the journey. Indeed, it was the fact that she was feeling so relaxed that helped to make what happened next so shocking by comparison.

With a start, she realised he had grabbed the wheel and as if it were a standard manoeuvre, had jabbed his left foot onto the clutch pedal, shoved the car into reverse and gunned it. There was a sudden and substantial impact and the small Cinquecento behind them disappeared in a cloud of steam and exhaust-smoke.

'In the back,' he said, quietly. Then, as if to himself, 'Silly idea to move the engine to the front in those little 500s. Modern ideas, eh?'

Without a sound, Vanessa did as he asked. He slithered with practised ease into the driver's seat and the car lurched forwards, as the pillion passenger on the Vespa in front turned, gun in hand. The scooter buckled as the Mercedes rammed it and the passenger tumbled onto the bonnet. Geoffrey's left arm was out of the driver's window in an instant and the man on the bonnet convulsed three times and rolled off. Vanessa smelled gunsmoke for the first time in her life and Geoffrey spun the car to the left. Another shot, this time through the passenger window and a second helmeted figure slumped against the car and slid down the back window.

An inch from her face, Vanessa saw the neat, smoking hole in the black visor and put her hand to her mouth to stifle the scream. She was thrown against the door then pushed back hard into the rear seat. When she could bring herself to look once more, she saw that they were hurtling along Viale Enrico de Nicola to an ostinato of car horns. She heard him say,

'Vanessa, please could you do me a favour?'

Less than two minutes later, in the shadow of Santa Maria degli Angeli, Vanessa Aldridge was standing in the middle of the road and watching her boss's surprisingly unscathed Mercedes tear off around the Piazza della Republicca. No-one else was watching it; they were watching *her* and most had cameras.

It doesn't take much to stop the traffic in Rome, but if you want to be really sure of doing it, it helps to have at your command an attractive woman partial to La Perla underwear and high heels. And a gun.

## Vauxhall Bridge Rd.

As Arthur Shepherd walked across Vauxhall Bridge, he realised his mind was wandering. In his line of work, such a thing was unusual, to say the least. In his line of work, a mind has to stay very much on the straight and narrow and so his reveries (which were becoming more and more frequent), had been a cause for concern. In darker moments, he wondered if it might be the onset of dementia but when reasonably equable (as he was at present) he supposed it might be simply his brain's chosen method of ignoring the noise of the traffic. The moment this thought entered his head, he became aware of the din; so all-pervading that he could not imagine how it had not registered long before.

Grafton, one of the Engineers at the Council had told him that the ambient volume of the traffic on the bridge is 97 decibels rising to 163 whenever the lights on Wandsworth Road change and everyone rushes to grab a decent lane. Grafton had said that the noise of the traffic in London was approaching the pain threshold and that something should be done. He hadn't said what.

Although occasionally called upon to drive in London, Arthur possessed no car and hadn't for some twelve years and since he could bear the company of cab drivers for only five minutes at a stretch (a period of time which, when translated into distance was worth less and less with each passing year), he had also stopped taking taxis. No, he always tried to walk whenever he could and take the tube when necessary.

His preferred mode of transport was the bus. Now that there was no smoking, a seat on the top deck at the very front was a pleasure to which he actively looked forward. It was like watching a travelogue of London in Cinerama or IMAX or whatever it was called. Like most Londoners, he had a soft spot for the old Routemaster but he realised it was more enjoyable on the outside than on the inside. All those who'd campaigned for its retention had, (likely as not) never had to travel on one. Arthur was prepared to lose a little London quaintness in favour of a great big fuck-off window that didn't steam up every time there was more than one person on-board and seats with a bit of legroom.

A tourist boat glided beneath him through the central arch of the bridge. The bow wave spread, like a white-edged tear along a mottled blue-grey silk screen. Even above the roar of the traffic, he caught the pre-recorded commentary announcing to the company that to their left, should they care to look, they would see the Tate Gallery, founded in 1887 by the sugar magnate, Sir Henry Tate and which until the year 2000, housed one of the finest collections of Classical and modern art to be found anywhere in…

'Mind yer back!'

To his left and on the pavement, a cycle courier spandexed by at speed.

'Watch it!' the rider yelled.

Notwithstanding the fact that he had just been presented with the perfect view of a perfectly bound and muscular behind, Arthur seethed.

The sense of injustice was still simmering on his moral hotplate as he gained the North bank. He pressed the button on the lights and stood waiting for the steel and glass deluge to dam. He had been told that the buttons didn't actually work for pedestrians at all; the traffic flow was far too precariously balanced to allow for that. It was simply for the look of the thing; to give people a sense that they retained a modicum of control over their environment. Arthur refused to believe it. Eventually – not that long, really – the green man relieved his red counterpart and to an electronic, monotonic accompaniment, Arthur Shepherd crossed Milbank. Only then, of course, did he realise that he would have preferred to have walked along beside the river.

He never used to get distracted like this, especially not on the job. Perhaps retirement really was on the cards, after all. He'd started thinking about it after he heard that Jeavons had copped it in Berlin a couple of months ago. Then Bartholomew, who had joined the same week as Arthur, had gone down in Vienna and there'd been rumours of others. The idea of packing it all in had somehow wormed itself into his consciousness. So he hadn't been as put out as he thought, when summoned to an interview last week at the Ministry of Truth.

The woman who'd conducted it couldn't have been more than twenty-two if that and even she had some poor sod of an intern carrying her bag for her. Arthur could only mutter vaguely in response to her anodyne questions, since the only words his mind seemed capable of forming were, "patronising" and "cow". She was one of those sharp-faced little pieces who turn up from time to time in their black suits and ruched blouses, clacking down the corridors on improbable heels, Blackberry supported between hunched shoulder and cocked blonded head, trying to hold their papers and look at their watches at the same time. Busier than thou.

Human resources, they called it. Human resources? He supposed that sharp-faced women would argue that it made people feel more valuable - to be a "resource". Double-plus value. He was certain that the sharp-faced woman had no idea of his real value for he had been interviewed under what he called his "stage name": Arthur Henley. This was the name, with which Arthur Shepherd had been lumbered at M.I.6. He had mentioned at the time that Arthur was not a common name and might it not be advisable to alter it to say, Dirk or Rock or some such? But no-one was having any of it.

He caught a glimpse of the Ministry of Truth through the sparse planting of trees on the opposite side of the road, looking for all the world as if some Danish architect had just knocked it up out of Lego.

Practically everyone he knew adored its uncompromising linearity and its neo-brutalist simplicity. So did Arthur, as it happened. He still hated it, though. The fact that the move there from Lambeth had coincided exactly with the loss of the Rothko Room never ceased to swim to the surface of his thoughts whenever he saw it; and he saw it at least once and often several times a week. The move back to Lambeth, surprising and very clever, had been one of the masterstrokes of the Council.

The companion thought to this one (yoked together like a pair of plough horses) was that just seven of his twenty-eight years of service had been spent actively engaged in the task for which he had been originally recruited and trained. Perestroika and glasnost had seen to that - although there was still the odd aftershock for which he was grateful. This thought should have effectively closed the parentheses upon his musings. That it didn't was testament to the force of the distraction.

He smiled as he remembered another interview. It had been with a man from Sandhurst– Captain Davidson – who had visited Arthur's school in about 1967. Having spoken to a selected group of boys, it had been his pleasure to interview each one individually. Arthur had sat outside the headmaster's office awaiting his turn and wondering why it was that the great military academy was having to plunder his grammar school for suitable candidates. Had the public schools finally succumbed to the inbreeding that had threatened the upper classes ever since congenital idiots had stopped dying in infancy?

Were there no longer Featherstonehaughs or Cholmondleys with the requisite number of un-webbed digits to hold a swagger-stick?

'Your headmaster seems to think you might have what it takes ...' (looks down at paper) ... Shepherd.'

'Can't imagine why,' Shepherd responds, all slouching uninterest.

'He says you have a mind of your own. We need people like you in the Army, these days'

Arthur used to tell this story, in the days when he had friends and this line would always elicit a huge roar of laughter, especially when Peter Cooked to perfection. Yet Davidson had not been "establishment" to any large degree. In fact, to Arthur, he'd seemed very down-to-earth; a good sort and of course terribly good-looking. Arthur had always known that this had been the deciding factor. Queen and Country, my arse. It was good joke but he'd never had anyone to whom he could tell it and rather resented the fact.

## The Tate

A few more yards and Arthur had reached his destination. He paused, as he invariably did, to spend a few seconds admiring the portico. The great entrance to the temple of art had been designed, contrary to the wishes of its patron, to be intimidating rather than inviting - a silent interrogation in Portland stone. "Should you be here? Are you truly ready? There is still time to turn away." These days, of course, few understood the language. To any who still bothered to venture this far away from her upstart namesake - her ungrateful offspring four miles downriver, this was just another pompous white building that could have been anything from government offices to a secretarial college; a hotel; a bank; a restaurant.

But Arthur spoke fluent Portland and always did her the courtesy of at least seeming to hesitate before springing up the unnecessary steps – another test of commitment - and entering her cool vestibule. The phrase elicited from Arthur a slight, involuntary shudder.

Inside, his pace slowed once more. Whilst the commands of the façade might go unheeded, within, few could fail to miss the signals. As the traffic noise (so wearisome to the gossamer-thin membrane of the eardrum but no match for four and a half feet of calcium carbonate), fell away to a mere murmur and the light and warmth of a bright autumn day yielded to the cool adumbration of ancient stone, most visitors would pause under the pretext of needing to acclimatise to the gloom. They might fool their conscious brain, but the primal hind-brain (where the Old Fears still abide) would know that here was a place in which it would be unwise to exhibit ego without attribute to support it.

He frowned as he watched the foreign tourists crowding around the desk, eager to hand over their "suggested donation". More Newspeak.

Were he to ever have loved a woman, it would have been the current guardian of the vestibule. Tall, imposing even; and confident beyond her tender years. The upper frames of the black glasses that perched upon her long nose were angled towards the middle so that she appeared to wear a permanent frown, like a bird of prey. Dressed as she was in the customary black, her dark hair wrapped up tightly behind her head, she would have been more than a match for anyone who prevaricated over their "suggested donation". He could tell that she would show no mercy to the hesitant, the weak. She would pounce on them like a great black heron; spike them with her beak, these minnows.

He could afford to pay; he could have put it on expenses for that matter but it was the principle of the thing. This building and its contents had been a gift to the nation, his nation and its people. A gift. To hand over money for the privilege of entry would amount to little more than an insult to the bewhiskered benefactors who had dedicated their time, effort and (all right) wealth to educating and enlightening the hearts, the minds, the very souls of the British people at a time when others of their ilk saw the working man as mere factory fodder – a human resource - to be exploited and depleted in the crucible of capital. Tate (and many like him) had lifted him; helped him to peer over the fence that divided him from his cultural heritage that he might strive ever harder to tear it down.

'Saatchi? My arse,' muttered Arthur.

Although it was now subsiding, Arthur Shepherd was proud of the anger he had felt at the passive-aggressive charges being made for entry to Tate Britain. He hadn't changed. The idealist was still in there somewhere.

By this stage in his reverie, he realised that his feet had been taking him unbidden towards Room 28. It was almost as though they hadn't quite got the message his brain had received ten years ago. Room 28 was no longer the Rothko Room and whilst not quite Room 101, it still frequently contained some of the worst things in the world.

Today, it was host to some particularly dreary pieces by that frightful old queen, Hockney. Now Arthur had to admit that he had rather admired him in his youth (not for his paintings, of course – they were largely crap) but for his working-class origins and his open and flamboyant homosexuality and he was still impressed by the extent of his generosity towards good causes. But as a painter, Hockney possessed little more depth than one of his beloved Hollywood swimming-pools.

They were, he supposed, trees. Bleak, wintery trees on a huge canvas constructed from a mosaic of smaller canvasses that he guessed were meant as some sort of valedictory for the artist. How bleeding obvious could art get? Well, pretty bleeding obvious, it would appear.

At least this work was devoid of writing. Arthur had noticed that too many contemporary artists seemed incapable of understanding the difference between art and literature.

Kadlec was already waiting.

'Vaclav,' Shepherd said, sitting down next to him on the far-too-soft seat provided for patrons who wished to study the work more closely.

'Arthur. It's good to see you again,' said Kadlec. 'You bring me news?' Kadlec had made Arthur's acquaintance on several occasions over the years. He believed that Arthur was a trusted servant of Her Majesty but it would be a week or two before he came to realise he might have been wrong. Arthur said nothing, but leaning forward slightly and with the smallest gesture towards the enormous Hockney, asked,

'What do you make of that?' He heard Kadlec inhale deeply through the nose and a moment later, heard him say,

'It's all right, I suppose.'

'If you like that sort of thing, eh?' Arthur smiled.

'Yes, yes. Exactly. If you like that sort of thing.' There was a silence. The attendant, poised on her uncomfortable, stay-awake stool, stared into the middle distance. She was a small, pinched-looking woman whom Arthur found it impossible to believe wanted to be there.

Monica was long gone, of course. He'd got on rather well with Monica in a visitor/attendant sort of way. A studious ignoring for a few weeks, followed by pleasantries when each had finally acknowledged the other's existence and when eventually the subject of the paintings themselves was raised, it became apparent to Arthur that Monica in many ways understood.

In fact, she was pretty sound on Abstract Expressionism in general and that had been enough for Arthur to value her company from time to time, but he had to admit that it was largely the look of her, her shape; broad and squat; her face, wide and chestnut brown; her hair black and frayed at the edges and her uniform; a deep dark maroon, which had intrigued him from the outset. She was so perfect for the Rothko Room that once, Arthur even found himself doing the maths to try to work out if she could possibly be old enough to have been recruited for her post by the wilful and idiosyncratic Rothko himself. She couldn't have been though, which somehow made her presence even more serendipitous.

Arthur also knew that she *saw* the Rothkos and for that he had admired her.

'I don't like it.' Arthur said, at last.

'The painting? That is a pity. It will be here for another four months.'

'Four months?'

'So I understand.'

Arthur was silent for a full minute, then said,

'He calls it *Bigger Trees Near Warter*. Do you suppose it to be referencing his earlier work? You know... *Bigger Splash* photo-montage sort of thing?' Kadlec sighed.

'I have no idea,' he said 'I know very little about art. Where is the water? I see no water.'

'No, it's "Warter" with an 'r'. It's a place, apparently, in Yorkshire.'

'Oh. Like I say, I know very little about art.' Arthur turned to look at Vaclav Kadlec. He looked tired and sad. Arthur realised it was no use.

'Mint Imperial?' he ventured at last. Kadlec peered at the crumpled paper bag in Arthur's hand.

'Imperial?' he said, suspiciously.

'For goodness sake; it's just a name, Vaclav. Made for Queen Victoria, I've always believed. They liked their grandiose appellations in those days. Nothing to worry about.'

'I never thought it was. Your people still like their grandiose names, even today, with their "Emporio Armani" and their "Buick Regal" and their "Burger King".'

'Burger King?' said Arthur, frowning. He shook away the thought. 'Anyway, all those things are American.' Kadlec shifted to face Arthur and raising an eyebrow asked,

'Even "Armani"?'

'Well, yes. The Emporio bit, anyway.' Arthur didn't know for sure but it sounded like something they might do. Kadlec faced forward again.

'Well, you are all the same,' he said, dismissively, 'you and your "Special Relationship".' He said the phrase as though it were poisoned.

'And in any event,' Arthur continued, 'isn't it to do with "Emporium" rather than "Emperor"?

'I have no idea,' Vaclev said, 'It's your language, after all, not mine.'

'Look, do you want a Mint Imperial or don't you? Just think of it as a big Tic-Tac. Nothing grandiose about that is there?'

Kadlec paused, extended a forefinger and thumb and pinched one of the shiny, hard sweets. He lifted it slowly from the bag and brought it to his mouth. He held it, an inch from his lips and barely turning his head, caught Arthur's eye. Arthur pretended for a moment not to understand but then gave in. He smiled, picked out a mint and popped it into his mouth. A second later, Kadlec did the same.

'You don't honestly think we still do that sort of thing? We're all friends, here, aren't we?' Arthur said.

'For now. But you British are fond of your… what do you call it…*long game*?' Arthur turned his gaze upon Hockney's painting once more and after a moment or two, said,

'I'll miss you, Vaclav. Good luck.' He placed his newspaper on the seat and stood up. The attendant, optic nerve stimulated by the movement, glanced over before slowly averting her gaze once more.

As soon as Arthur had left Room 28, Kadlec picked up the newspaper and despite his many years of experience, could not resist stealing a peek at what it concealed. Airline tickets to Prague; in the name that he and his wife now used. He allowed himself a smile and sucked on his Mint Imperial.

'Nothing but sugar,' he mused.

Arthur was with the 16$^{th}$ Century English Masters when he saw Kadlec leave, the newspaper under his arm.

Half an hour later and feeling strangely empty, Arthur too made for the exit. It had been the first killing he'd carried out in several weeks and it had left him...unfulfilled. Had it been too easy? Well, yes. A little distraction, a soupçon of legerdemain, that's all - but that wasn't the reason.

The Bird Goddess was still there as he padded through the cavernous vestibule and so he slowed to admire her once more. She caught him looking and returned his gaze. He fancied that she knew he had donated nothing and felt a frisson of anxiety. It passed in a trice, however. She must also know, he reasoned, that there are some over whom she has no power. No minnow, he. He smiled. She didn't and he turned his head and strode, blinking into the sunlight once more.

## Art and Reason

Arthur would not be likely to hear about Vaclav Kadlec's death, though he had no doubt that it would occur; probably in about a fortnight's time. He'd be feeling a little queasy even as the plane landed but would put it down to airline food. It would be a number of days before the thallium had worked its irreversible magic.

He imagined the truth dawning on Vaclav - where? In his apartment? At the theatre? Surely, he'd know before he checked into the hospital? Arthur would have quite liked to have been there to tell him that it was just business. Nothing personal. Then he remembered hearing that platitude somewhere before (*The Godfather*?) and felt a little disgusted with himself. Ideally, of course, he would have liked to have given Vaclav a little more time at the Tate.

Cleaners are not mere killers. They are craftsmen – and women, of course – whose job is to... make the environment a little more pleasant for all concerned and the best are able to command an array of skills in pursuit of that aim. They are not, strictly speaking, "spies". The Council designates such people (with its own peculiar nomenclature), "Social Workers" and they are the nearest thing the Council has to actual spooks. Naturally, for them, killing can sometimes be a part of the job but for a Cleaner, it is the entirety of the job.

In the social hierarchy of the Council, Cleaners rank fairly highly; but that doesn't mean they are told more than anyone else about its workings. The fact that Arthur knew as much as he did was down entirely to his length of service and the indiscretion of (usually late) colleagues.

The disposal of unsightly and possibly hazardous waste is a key accountability, of course, but a good Cleaner will always consider the possibility that renovation rather than annihilation might be a more cost-effective option. It is in the nature of the Council that certain Cleaners are allowed discretion in such matters and Arthur had occasionally managed to convince himself and his superiors that like deftly-applied French polish upon a severely scratched table top, a few well chosen questions in sympathetic surroundings could result in a severe liability being transformed into a valued asset. A quiet conversation could decide the issue and what could be more civilised? But he just couldn't bring himself to do it that time. Not there. With that. That Hockney. How could anyone reveal his secret self anywhere near the thing?

Arthur consoled himself with the fact that Vaclav really didn't understand art at all and (unfortunately for Vaclav) art was Arthur's favoured reagent, revealing more about a person than any C.I.A. refined interrogation technique ever could. Not so messy as bladder-charging and quieter than a nail-gun in the kneecap, a soft leather seat in an art gallery afforded the ultimate in stress positions.

When the Rothkos went and Tate Modern's hanging committee betrayed him, Arthur had experimented. Sharp-faced women would have approved of how he transformed a setback into an opportunity and he'd tried, he really had and had indeed achieved some success with the odd Malevich (a *Carre Noir* worked a treat on a Russian oligarch who, it turned out, understood more about decadent painters of his homeland than he had realised.) Arthur had happened to be in Paris when the job came up and the Pompidou had been very handy. Arthur ended up killing him anyway but he'd proved a point.) De Kooning was another favourite and surprisingly, a late Moholy-Nagy at the Guggenheim in New York. It was this, which provided S.I.S. with one of its more effective and very much extant double agents.

But Paul Klee was the only one who came close to rivalling Rothko.

Like trying to glimpse one's own profile in a mirror, the full explanation of why this should be would always seem tantalisingly close but would disappear when confronted. Evidence, perhaps of a quantum explanation for the power of art that Arthur had several years before explored and rejected, once the mathematics had begun threatening his sanity.

But Arthur knew himself well enough to recognise that this altruistic excuse was only part of the reason he preferred to work near art. The fact was it put him in a better place. Oh, he could kill anywhere and pretty much had and to have been unable to do so would have counted as an unforgivable weakness on his part. It had been many years before he'd realised why some jobs just simply went better than others and he'd concluded that the reason was art. It need not be painterly or even a matter of artifice at all. Occasionally, a random ordering of shapes – the overlapping corners of nearby buildings, the drift of a landscape, reflections, even the pattern on a client's shirt – all these things had taken him to a level of consciousness where he could perform best.

What it was about Abstract Expressionism, he never quite knew. He had first encountered it in reproductions in a number of the more unsuitable art books in his school library. The art teacher had, so legend had it, sneaked them in and with the help of a sympathetic librarian had been able to put them on the catalogue.

Being reproductions, their effect on young Arthur had been slight but enough to make him realise that there was something going on in these pictures; something that he had hitherto not recognised in others. It wasn't until he saw them in the flesh for the first time that their true impact became apparent to him.

The sensations ranged from mild euphoria to (he was now unashamed to admit) pure orgasm and ran a gamut, which included a variety of sensations for which he believed there was not even a name.

It was when he'd finally realised this, that he'd begun to choose his places and there was no place like the Rothko Room at the Old Tate.

Arthur had been to the Rothko Room at Tate Modern only twice: once to see the paintings and once to kill a right-wing Dutchman. The first time, he'd thought it would probably be fine. After all, wasn't it the paintings themselves, rather than the space? Well no, not really. It had not been long before he'd realised that of course the whole thing had been about the space. The Seagram paintings were conceived in order to enhance a space, not to merely hang on a wall.

He'd actually been physically sick in the lavatories shortly after experiencing the "Rothko Room" at Tate Modern and had not returned until the Dutchman arrived. But it was no better. He'd had to leave without even making contact and had eventually shoved him in front of the Eastbound at London Bridge Station. Most unsatisfactory.

## Republicca to Nazionale and Beyond

Standing in her underwear outside a convent in Rome was not a circumstance in which Vanessa Aldridge had ever expected to find herself so she could have been forgiven for not being too sure of her first move. Having up-ended her bag all over the passenger seat and relieving her of all other possessions, the killer had actually handed back her phone, telling her she could use it to call for help as soon as he was out of sight. Bastard. He'd taken the battery out whilst she'd been undressing.

Cursing, she flung the useless mobile phone into her bag and was surprised to hear it hit something solid and now that she came think of it, rather heavy. Reaching into the bag, her hand closed around a gun. It was still warm. Scarcely able to believe it, she drew the weapon from the bag and stared at it. It was a few moments before she realised that she had inadvertently managed, if it were possible, to draw even more attention to herself. Eyeing the gathering crowd, she slowly replaced the gun and summoning up as much dignity as her situation would allow, she shrugged her bag further up her shoulder and set off for Via Nazionale.

Before she'd landed a job that allowed her to shop in the Via Borgognona, she had often browsed in the shops along Via Nazionale. Nowadays, of course, she wouldn't touch it with a bargepole, unless of course she was naked (apart from her blood-red lingerie, Gucci shoulder bag and six-inch heels) in the streets of a major European capital city.

There are very few places where the Italian male stereotype is more stereotypical than in Naples but Rome comes a close second. The men weren't exactly pursuing her but they weren't exactly coming to her assistance, either: just enjoying the show. She knew she had to be her own saviour when a clutch of men called out to her asking her to slow down whilst they got their mobile phones out. They were caribinieri.

Vanessa Aldridge, humiliated as she was, was not going to run. She'd just faced down a man whom she'd watched kill two people not five minutes previously; she could certainly deal with this.

With a shock, she realised (as she turned at long last into Nazionale) that the shame she would feel entering one of these shops would far outweigh any discomfort her journey from Republicca had caused her. She actually walked past three stores that would have suited her needs both then, when she was a mere chambermaid, and now.

Shuddering slightly, she turned into a branch of Bata. A small number of bemused customers turned towards her. The sales desk boasted one rather bored-looking teenager and a middle aged woman.

Vanessa, determined to brazen it out, stood with her arms folded and said to the woman,

'I need some clothes.'

'Yes, you do.'

'I have no money. I was robbed.'

'Evidently.'

'Well?'

The woman shrugged, sighed and moved over to a rack. She looked at Vanessa, fingered a number of hangers out of the way and tugged out a pair of jeans. Vanessa looked unimpressed but the assistant was having none of it. She took the jeans over to another rack, eyed Vanessa once more and selected a top. It was, if anything, of even poorer quality than the jeans. The assistant stood by a changing cubicle, tugged back the curtain and held the items out.

Biting her tongue, Vanessa snatched the clothes and strode into the cubicle.

Having changed, she had just fastened the straps on her shoes when she became aware of the commotion. Drawing back the curtain, she studied in a sort of detached way, the scene that greeted her. It wasn't real; it couldn't be. Surely there couldn't be half a dozen Italian policemen shouting, gesticulating and aiming a bewildering number of small arms at her, could there?

Then she was on the floor. Her bag was wrenched from her grasp and her arms jammed up her back. She cried out but no-one paid any heed. So she simply cried.

## The Crawthorne Beasley Affair.

Arthur stood waiting for the lift. Another job already? Something must be up. Nightingale hadn't even wanted to see him this morning and it had been his secretary who'd sent Arthur down to Floor D.

Floors D and K would not be found on any plan of Vauxhall Cross and it would have taken a very sharp-eyed observer to notice that there were actually more storeys in the building than it appeared. When the building was first unveiled, great play was made of the fact that the architect had very cleverly designed the building to appear as though it was far taller and grander than it actually was. Architecture students marvelled at the forced perspectives, the foreshortening and the trompe l'oeil effects supplied by niches and false windows and admired the designers who had come up with such a revolutionary technique. The real trick, of course was that there were none of these things at work. The building simply had two lettered floors between two of the numbered ones and even those who worked there at "Box Standard" (as some at the Council insisted on calling it) had no idea. But people often complained about the slow lifts.

Floors D and K are exclusively reserved for Council Workers and Floor D was where Arthur would learn what his superiors wanted him to do. It's all very lo-tech and that suited him very well indeed, being little more than a pigeon-hole, a shredder and a chute to an incinerator.

The lift doors opened and in he stepped. He was alone, of course. He had summoned the lift with his security card, as everyone had to do but as soon it was detected that the card was Lambeth issue, the lift would be certain to arrive empty and it would go automatically and directly to Floor D unless overridden by the same card. Anyone looking at the card would have been surprised that a Co-op Dividend Card could gain access to one of the most heavily secured buildings in London.

The lift came to a gentle stop and the doors opened. Waiting to enter, a woman; grey hair; late middle age accompanied by a much younger woman holding an armful of papers. He stood to one side, automatically and unnecessarily holding the door to prevent it from closing.

'Arthur!' said the older woman. 'It's been an absolute age. It's fine, Jacqueline. You go on ahead and we'll meet at St. James's later on.' The young woman smiled pleasantly, nodded politely to Arthur and stepped into the lift. In moments, he and the older woman were alone.

'Jennifer, how good to see you.' They pecked each other on the cheek. 'Working?'

'Afraid so. Abroad.' She said the word as though it carried with it the stench of corruption.

'Oh bad luck.'

'Only a day, though. How about you?'

'Nothing for a few weeks and now my second in a couple of days. I think they must be mopping up some cold-war dinosaurs.'

'I know a couple of cold war dinosaurs, Arthur. You shouldn't be so disparaging.'

He laughed. 'You're being too hard on yourself. Aren't we always being told we're living longer these days?'

'Ah, that's so they can keep putting back the retirement age for *ahem* civil servants such as ourselves. By the time young Jacqueline retires, she'll be gone eighty.'

'God!' said Arthur. 'I'm already looking forward to having nothing to do but the Telegraph crossword.'

'Ah, you're just a spring chicken, Arthur. I've got three or four years on you at least. Arthur suddenly looked grave.

'Are you sure you're O.K. to be back at work? he asked.

'It was bullet in the thigh, Arthur. I've had worse,' she said.

'Perhaps a stick would help?'

'Not fucking likely,' she said. It's bad enough being an old woman without looking like one. 'Besides, they've given me young Jacqueline there to mentor. She seems very promising; already taking some of the strain.'

'All the same, take it easy. This job you're on: not too taxing, I hope?'

'Just a bit of light dusting. I'll be back by this evening.' Arthur nodded and said,

'Erm...and I was sorry to hear about your father, Jennifer. My condolences.'

'God's teeth, Arthur, he was a hundred and four. It wasn't entirely unexpected.' She swiped her card to draw down the lift.

'Private funeral?'

'Oh yes, he didn't want anything... too flamboyant. I hope you can come.'

'Thursday week, St. James's? It will be an honour.'

'Go away with you, Arthur. You are so full of shit.'

Arthur was a little put out. He'd always had deep affection for Jennifer's father and with good reason. Sir James Carlisle it was, who had founded the Council in the dying days of the Second World War.

Sir James, Arthur had always believed, was the reason that the Council had withstood efforts by various interested parties to "modernise" it. It wasn't that he was stuffy and dictatorial – far from it. On the very few occasions Arthur had met him, he'd found him to be a very forward-looking individual. So forward-looking that he was able to see quite clearly where adherence to current fads and fashions would inevitably lead. In that sense, Carlisle had been a true innovator.

Retiring at the age of eighty-two, he'd managed to outlive and out-work a good many deputies to the extent where no-one was at all certain who was the current Leader of the Council. But it didn't seem to matter, as Sir James' presence continued to permeate the Council long after he'd left the building. Now he had really left the building and Arthur was saddened.

'I know. But he was a great man.'

'So they tell me.'

Arthur felt the sting of embarrassment.

'I take it,' he said, 'there was no deathbed reconciliation?'

'No. In fact, there were a couple of times when I had to stop myself putting the pillow over his bony old face.'

Arthur sighed. It was an open secret that Jennifer and her father had had a falling out. Over what, no-one knew but it was suspected that it was over the issue of his successor. Arthur decided that it would be politic not to say more in praise of Jennifer's father.

'I'm sorry to hear that,' he said.

There was a ping and light flooded into the dingy corridor. Jennifer placed her hand across the open doors, holding them open.

'You think you're over these things then...' She smiled a bitter smile and stepped into the lift.

'Nice seeing you again, Jennifer.'

'You too. Take care. Let's have a proper chin-wag at the funeral.'

She swiped the card again and the doors closed. Darkness returned.

Alone again, Arthur walked down the passage and into Room 9. He could see the envelope sticking out of his pigeon hole before he even got there and upon opening it, it wasn't long before he realised that this was not your run of the mill cleaning.

Crawthorne Beasley was himself a Cleaner. Or rather, he had been. Arthur had heard the name on occasions but had never met the man. This was not unusual. The Council was a very, very secretive secret organisation and he was glad of the several photographs paper-clipped to the instruction sheet.

What was unusual, however, was the order to off a Cleaner. It wasn't unprecedented of course. Any organisation – particularly one that had been around virtually unchanged for nigh-on seventy years – would be likely to have nurtured its fair share of naughty boys and girls but the only other time Arthur had been involved in disposing of a fellow Cleaner was old Leslie Wintergreen back in '79 and as he recalled, there had been a meeting, which he had attended, followed by a higher level one, which was itself, he understood, followed by an extremely lofty one before word had come directly from somewhere above the clouds that the job was to be carried out. And Wintergreen had even been given a chance to explain. He couldn't, but that was neither here nor there. He'd been given twenty-four hours to get his affairs in order and then he'd gone to Regents Park Zoo, where Arthur had met him.

It had been a fine spring day and the tulips had looked particularly splendid. He and Wintergreen had sat together on a bench watching the penguins and chatting about this and that until at one point, Arthur had turned around to find that Wintergreen was dead. He had bitten down on a cyanide capsule.

Arthur had been grateful for that for although a hardened professional killer by that time, he'd not been looking forward to Cleaning old Wintergreen and a similar frisson of unease trickled down his back now, as he read the details of the job, such as they were. Considering the import of bumping off a fellow Cleaner, the despatch came with the minimum of rubric. In fact, it was downright perfunctory.

Name:
BEASLEY Crawthorne Stanley.
Circumstance:
N/A
Current residence.
1 LONDON, BLACKHEATH PARAGON.
2 HUNTINGDON, CARDAMOM COTTAGE
Whereabouts as of:
THIS AFTERNOON 3:15 : FESTIVAL HALL.

It could not have been simpler. Arthur didn't know whether Beasley knew what he looked like or not but this instruction made it clear that he should make no contact whatsoever, other than by means of something long and sharp. It need not look accidental.

'Poor old Beasley,' Arthur said to himself. There was something… distasteful about this. A Cleaner deserved a reason and a chance to explain. Perhaps he'd been wrong about the name. Mind you, not many Crawthorne Beasleys kicking about the place and after today, even fewer. It must be the same fellow. For no other reason than professional courtesy Arthur felt that he'd quite like to know more about the circumstances before committing to it.

Of course, it would mean having to speak to Sir Auberon Bloody Nightingale but there was no help for it. He chucked the photos into the shredder but the missive he slipped into his jacket pocket and made his way back to the lift. On the way up to the 4$^{th}$ Floor, Arthur practised what he would say. He wasn't afraid of Sir Auberon – far from it – but he was an awkward sod when he wanted to be and he wanted to be rather a lot of the time. Their relationship was an extremely complicated one so it was entirely possible that Sir Auberon knew nothing of the Beasley thing.

'What can I do for you, Shepherd? Only I am extremely busy.'

'Yes, that paper is unlikely to push itself around.'

Sir Auberon removed his glasses and sighed.

'…And, as the laughter fades…' he said.

'I've been given a job.'

'So they have yet to see the light. What does that have to do with me?'

'On the off chance you may know what goes on around here, I wondered if you could throw some light on it.'

It had been a relatively new development, the first inklings of which had emerged some five years or so earlier. Agents, even Council Workers, had always had cover stories at some time or another but it had been decided somewhere that since S.I.S. was now a more open organisation, expecting agents to adopt cover personae was a bit old-fashioned and frankly a bit suspect so the idea was set to be dropped. Someone pointed out, however, that there were still a few people (how could they put this) for whom anonymity might possibly still be required. It was then suggested that as M.I.6 was no longer a "secret" secret service, it would itself be able to provide such operatives with all the cover they would need.

This system was now pretty much taken for granted and new recruits, who had known no better, accepted it without question. To people like Arthur, it was utterly insane but someone, somewhere thought it was a good idea and so he had found himself being dragged, kicking and screaming, in from the cold; but still with plenty of snow on his boots.

So Sir Auberon Nightingale had become Arthur Henley's immediate superior at M.I.6 but he should have known, of course, that his role as Arthur's boss was titular and that Arthur was very well thought of in circles that spun many leagues above his own. However, he seldom gave the impression that he knew anything of the sort. So much so that Arthur had wondered on occasions, if he oughtn't to have a word with someone on the Council about the zeal with which Nightingale kept up the pretence. For a while now, it seemed as though he had been chucking his weight around a little more than was necessary. Arthur was prepared to let himself be bossed around, up to a point - he sort of felt it was part of his duties – but Nightingale seemed to be really pushing his luck.

'Now, what do you suppose I'm likely to know about the shady goings-on at Lambeth, Shepherd?'

'This is rather unusual. I wonder if you've been told that I'm to… I don't know, attend a meeting or something?'

'Attend a meeting? How wonderfully grown-up. You must be terribly excited.'

'You know, Nightingale, I long for the time when I see your name smiling out at me from one of these little slips. It's the only thing that keeps me going.'

Sir Auberon replaced his glasses, sighed again and held out his hand. Arthur gave him the envelope.

'No file?' he asked as he removed the slip of paper and commenced reading.

'Just that. Seemed a bit… brisk.'

Nightingale turned the paper in order to check there was nothing on the back. He replaced it into its envelope and returned it to Arthur.

'Those who live by the sword, I suppose,' he offered.

'You've heard nothing?'

'Shepherd, you of all people will know that I understand only a modicum of what goes on in your little world. I get a message; I let you go. That's how it works. Frankly, I thought you preferred it that way. God knows there's plenty of proper work you could do about the place.'

'I'm disinclined to take this job.'

'Oh? Is that an option, then?'

'Not really, no.'

'Then I would suggest that you had better pop over to the South Bank and get it over with.'

'It doesn't seem right. He should be given a reason. A few years ago, I'd have just handed him a cyanide capsule on the concourse at Waterloo and he'd have done it himself.'

'Have you considered that might already have been tried?'

'I have. However, in such a case, there'd be some tracking down to do. But they know where he is and where he'll be at quarter past three this afternoon. He knows nothing about this, I'm certain. It's bloody sneaky is what it is.'

'A sneaky assassination? Heaven forefend.'

'You know, what really annoys me is the fact that against all previous evidence and experience, I had thought even if you couldn't do anything, you might at least understand.'

'I *do* understand, Shepherd. I just don't *care*. Now, will that be all?'

Arthur shook his head and made for the door.

'Oh,' Nightingale called over, 'and if it's not too much trouble, please would you leave your mobile switched on?'

'My... "mobile", as you call it, is my own affair. Besides, if I leave it switched on, the batteries go flat and I can't use it if I need to.'

'And the fact that no-one can contact you doesn't bother you?'

'Should it?'

'Actually, yes.'

'Well, there may come a time when I'm sitting by the telephone waiting for someone to bring a little light into my dark and joyless existence but it's likely to be a long time hence.'

'They tell me you have an I.Q. of 142.' said Nightingale. 'Unusually high for an idiot.'

On the bus down to the South Bank, Arthur had come to a decision. Technically, the instructions left no room for discretion in this case but he was buggered if he was going to off a Cleaner without so much as a by-your-leave. No matter what Beasley had done, he deserved to make his case; or have it made for him in some way.

As usual, the Festival Hall was hopping. Arthur (like all Cleaners) could pick a target out of a crowd with relative ease, and after only three circuits of the foyers, he spotted him. Behind a low table, upon which were neatly arranged a variety of leaflets, posters and compact disks, sat a white-haired party wearing slacks, desert boots, a navy jumper and sporting a cravat. To his right on a low dais, stood four chairs and four music stands. A 'cello rested on the floor beside one of the chairs. Wandering over, Arthur approached the table and picked up one of the CDs.

'That's one of their finest,' said Beasley. 'The Beethoven 14 in particular is marvellous.'

Arthur looked up.

'C sharp minor is such a tragic key,' he said.

'Indeed. It sets up the Milton Babbit wonderfully. There's a Cage on there, as well.'

'Milton Babbit,' said Arthur. 'Odd name, isn't it?'

'Oh, not as odd as some,' smiled Crawthorne Beasely.

'I'll take it.' Arthur took out his wallet and handed over the requisite tenner.

'Thank you very much. They'll be starting again soon but I'm sure I could get it signed for you, if you'd like. My daughters, you see,' he said, shyly. 'First Violin and Viola. I'll only be a moment.'

Beasely stood up and walked over to a table where the musicians were relaxing before tackling, (Arthur glanced at the music stands), Samuel Barber. Beasley pointed over to Arthur and the musicians turned to smile at him so he favoured them with a little wave. A moment or two later, Beasely returned, placed the CD into a small plastic bag and handed it over.

'There you are. I hope you enjoy it. As I say,' he said, 'they are about to begin. Will you be staying for the Barber?'

'Why not?' Arthur said, with a beaming smile. He went to the bar, bought himself a bottle of Guinness and sat down at a table that would offer him the chance to study the man he was about to kill. People nearby lapsed into silence but foyer performances are always subject to extraneous noise and, so the Quartet No 2 by Samuel Barber for two violins, viola, 'cello and various punters began.

Arthur knew the piece but he wouldn't have said he was familiar with it. As the first movement unfolded, he began to recall the odd passage. By the time it was over, he had received enough bites from the dissonances to cause him to wonder why he hadn't given the piece a more favourable hearing in the past. The jarring excitement of the second movement had him beating his index finger on his thigh – the closest Arthur ever came to dancing. The final movement was long and languorous and Arthur decided, rather dull. He realised why he had failed to return to the piece more frequently. Still, the playing was competent and for youngsters, the musicians imbued the piece with a vigour that it possibly didn't deserve.

Throughout the performance, of course, much of Arthur's attention was devoted to Crawthorne Beasley, who was seated behind the table holding his walking stick. Arthur noticed that the stick was braced against the dais and Beasley's chin rested on his hands. Noticing that there was no rubber tip on the end of the cane, Arthur began to develop a theory.

After the encore, the second movement of Barber's First String Quartet, (chosen, no doubt, for the sake of those who had merely wandered in out of the rain) the musicians and their CD salesman began clearing away. Arthur stepped up behind Beasley.

'Beasley,' he said. There was no response. Beasley continued to pack unsold CDs into boxes. 'Crawthorne Beasley,' he said, a little louder this time. Again, there was no response. Arthur had seen Beasley throughout the performance, reading from a score. Only during the louder second movement, did he turn his head to one side and cup his hand behind his ear.

Arthur tapped Beasley on the shoulder and he turned around.

'Excuse me,' Arthur said. 'Is there a CD with the Barber on it?' At the name, "Barber", Arthur engineered an itchy nose for himself so that his hand would obscure his mouth.

'Oh, hello again. Sorry, did you say "Britten"?'

'No, the Barber. The one they just played.'

'I'm afraid they haven't recorded that one as yet. I do have one with Barber's *first* quartet, if that's any good?'

'Not really,' said Arthur, 'but thanks anyway.'

'You enjoyed the performance, then?'

'Yes I did. Did you?' Arthur hadn't forgotten that Beasley was a Cleaner and therefore likely to be a lot cleverer than he looked. Hubris had led him to try such a ploy. There was no response from Beasley other than a genuine,

'Oh yes, indeed. But then, of course I am biased. Mind you, there was a moment in the third movement when I was a little anxious about the phrasing. Did you notice it?'

'I'm afraid I didn't.'

'Annabelle will be very cross with herself. She will require a little soothing, no doubt.'

'It's jolly good of you to do this sort of thing for them,' Arthur said, indicating the boxes of CDs and posters. Beasley returned to his task of arranging the boxes into a tower on a small hand-truck.

'Oh not at all. It gets me out of the house. I've been retired for a couple of years now.'

'Very nice,' said Arthur.

'Oh, it all sounds wonderful when you're working but the reality of retirement can be rather a let down. My wife died, you see, shortly after I left the Civil Service. Hit and run. It doesn't always pay to make plans.'

'I'm sorry.'

'But listen to me going on. That's what happens, you see.' Beasley chuckled. 'You find yourself sharing intimate details of your life with total strangers. Still; one step up from talking to yourself eh?'

'What did you do in the Civil Service?' Arthur was unsurprised that Beasley's face revealed absolutely nothing.

'Oh, nothing special. Troubleshooting, I suppose you might call it.'

'Sounds exciting.' Beasley stopped stacking boxes.

'You know,' he said, 'it was. It was.' He paused for a moment, wiped his hands on his jumper and said, 'Well, that's me done. Jolly nice to have met you Mr...?' He held out his hand.

'Henley. Arthur Henley.' Arthur took it.

'Mr. Henley. Beasley is my name.' Beasley indicated the musicians. 'They're here every Monday about this time. Different programme every week. Hope we'll see you again.'

'I hope so too,' said Arthur. 'Take care.'

'Oh I always do, Mr Henley; it's the curse of the Civil Servant.' Arthur watched as Beasley led the hand-truck for a few yards before it was wrested from him by one of his daughters. She took his arm and together they made for the Waterloo exit.

Was he simply being sentimental? He wasn't sure but on balance, he would have said not. Of course, Beasley could have been onto him from the outset and might have been playing him like his daughter's fiddle. Arthur doubted it. No Cleaner would expect another Cleaner not do his job simply because he felt sorry for his victim. Yet Beasley lived and Arthur had no regrets.

Beasley's deafness was clearly profound and it must have begun to manifest itself whilst he was still working for the Council. Arthur had looked for evidence of a hearing aid or cochlear implant, but had detected none. Beasley had certainly been lip-reading for some time, since his proficiency was undeniable and Arthur suspected that with the aid of the score and by watching the hands of the players, Beasley had managed to appreciate the performance exactly as he had said. Arthur realised he would have had a little help from the laws of physics via the hollow dais and his walking stick but he was always impressed by the way musicians, even profoundly deaf ones, did not need to hear the music to experience it.

Arthur found no fault in the man. Had the rubric given a reason (as frequently it did,) he might even have done for Beasley without hesitation but he couldn't get over the feeling that he was simply being asked to do someone's dirty work. Dirtier than usual, that is. Arthur wondered what the Council had against Crawthorne Beasley.

He wouldn't find out much over at Legoland. Nightingale had been a dead loss and there was no-one else there who would know anything. Fortunately, the home – both spiritual and actual - of the Council was a few streets away from the Festival Hall. Century House, Lambeth had been the headquarters of M.I.6 from 1964 to 1995. The Council had occupied the top five of the twenty floors in those days. Arthur remembered his initiation into the arcana of the Council as though it were yesterday.

Denholm Flinders, the fellow had been called and it had been he who had greeted Arthur as he'd stepped out of the lift on the sixteenth floor. He hadn't known what to expect but whatever it had been, it hadn't been what he'd got.

## 1974

The lift doors juddered open only part way and Arthur was obliged to force them apart so that he might step out. The place smelt bad. Damp, mostly although mould of various species was also apparent in the nose of the place. The floor was thick with dust and the corridor was lined with broken desks, chairs and fittings of all kinds. The lights were broken and a number of ceiling tiles were missing.

'Good morning, Shepherd,' Flinders said. 'I'll show you to your desk. Watch your step.' Arthur followed Flinders down the dingy corridor. Doorways – some even with doors – ranged down each side. Arthur glanced into one or two and saw much of the same. Clearly, this entire floor had been abandoned some time ago. At the end of the corridor, there was a stairwell and a flight of stairs going up but none going down. At the top of the stairs, there was a door. They walked by this and up the second flight. Flinders stopped outside the door on the seventeenth floor, pulled a key out of his pocket and unlocked it. He opened it, stepped through and held it for Arthur.

The contrast was jarring. He found himself in a wainscoted and Morris-wallpapered room, which contained two leather-upholstered high-backed chairs and a desk, behind which sat a young woman. She stopped typing for a moment and said,

'Good morning, Mr. Flinders, Mr Shepherd.' There was a buzz and a click and the oak panelled door on the far wall swung open. This time, Flinders walked through ahead of Arthur. This room was bigger – longer, certainly, than the first, with one door at the far end and one in the middle of the wall to his left. To his right, he had calculated, should have been the outside wall of the building but there was no sign of any windows. Arthur figured that there must be a corridor running the length of the room.

'Good morning, everyone,' Flinders said. The low murmur and the clatter of typewriter keys, which had been the only sound in the room, died away and all eyes turned towards Arthur. 'May I introduce Arthur Shepherd. You've all been briefed so I'll leave it to you to make yourselves acquainted. Perhaps someone might get him a cup of tea?' He turned to Arthur, indicated a dim corner to his right and said, 'Your desk is there. Thank you very much, everyone.'

And that was it.

Arthur sat down without a clue as to what his job was. He'd been given a designation, which he found, frankly, rather puzzling. What on earth an "Assistant Cleaner" did around the place, he couldn't begin to guess; and how that fitted into what they were pleased to call his "Startout" –the training he'd had following his stint at Sandhurst, he could not fathom.

He knew after his first year at Military Academy that he had been singled out for special attention but his next two years passed without any of his expectations being met. The final two years of his training had been unusual, apparently. It was only whenever he ran into a contemporary who would explain, breathlessly, that they were off to some far flung corner of the Empire to shoot the natives, whilst he was in a Nissen hut in Andover, sitting through lectures called things like "Major Organs: the effects of poisons on." and "Know Your Enemy: the Forensic Scientist in today's police force." that he realised something might be up. He was wondering what to do next when a box-file landed on his desk. He looked up to see the back of an extremely expensive suit, shrouded in cigar smoke, moving away from him and towards one of the three doors that graced the walls of the room.

'He always likes to get a look at the new bugs.' Arthur glanced up to see the man of his dreams sitting on the edge of the desk and offering him his hand. 'Wittersham,' he said. 'Geoffrey. That was Sir James Carlisle. He runs the place.'

'I thought Maurice Oldfield ran it,' Arthur said. He heard a number of snorts and looked over to see the colleagues nearest him smiling and shaking their heads.

'Oldfield runs M.I.6 – for the moment. Read the book, Shepherd. All will made clear; well, clear-er at any rate,' said Wittersham, tapping the box file. He winked at Arthur and said, 'Read the book.' He stood, once more and followed the trail of cigar-smoke out of the room.

Arthur opened the file and took out a small bunch of keys, followed by a red, leather-bound portfolio. As he opened it, a mug of tea appeared at his elbow. The bearer of the offering was a woman, slim and petite. She appeared young but was not dressed, Arthur noted, in what passed for fashion at that time.

'I see you caught Geoffrey's eye,' she said.

'Did I?'

'Hmm. Pity. He's off clockwise tomorrow.'

'Clockwise?'

'Yes; South Face.' She pointed at one of the doors down the far end of the room. It's how we progress: one side of the building at a time, usually every couple of years and then up a floor and it all starts over again. Geoffrey's not been here that long. He must have impressed someone.'

*He certainly impressed me*, Arthur thought. He lifted the tea and smiled.

Thank you,' he said.

'Don't mention it. You've come straight here from Sandhurst, then?'

'Yes. Is that unusual?'

'Oh, it's happened before,' she said. 'And it's always nice to have some young blood round here.' She smiled archly and glanced around the room to a chorus of ribaldry, in which she seemed to revel. She walked slowly towards her own desk, glancing coquettishly back at Arthur.

'You're wasting your time, Jennifer,' someone called. 'Didn't you read his file?'

'I think he's got his eye on Geoffrey,' called another.

'Oh, I've never been one to resist a challenge, Michael,' Jennifer called back.

## Century House

Arthur had anticipated ragging of some kind but his experience of women had been slight indeed and he had to admit he'd been rather embarrassed. However, he smiled at the memory, as he waited the second or two for his implanted chip to do what was needed to allow him entry to Century House.

Nowadays, it was apartments. Very expensive apartments, all the way to the top floor. The residents were the sort of people who had other people who arranged the purchase of property and those people would assure them that there was a single sub-basement and certainly no sitting tenants. And they would be wrong on both counts. After M.I.6 shifted over to Vauxhall Cross, the Council began some renovations of its own. Five levels of sub-basement were hewn out of the London Clay beneath the tower and the top five floors were transferred below ground. The work was completed in less than eighteen months, after which and much to the relief of all parties, the Council returned to Century House, leaving only a small force over at Vauxhall Cross. At that time, M.I.6. would occasionally take advantage of the Council's Cleansing services, so Despatch and a couple of other departments had remained.

Perversely (or quite logically, some believed), the floors retained the same designation as before but were now inverted so that one entered by the decoy Floor 16 – the first sub-basement – and continued down to Floor 17, thence to Floor 18 and so on until the deepest floor of all: Floor 20. Apart, of course, from the fact that filing cabinets typewriters and telephones had all been replaced by I.T. equipment, anyone who had seen the place in the late sixties and as it is today would be hard pushed to tell the difference. However, there aren't that many of those people left.

The Council still thrived, though and Arthur noted with satisfaction that it seemed to run much as it always had; in spite of that pantomime with the cover story and the fact that a number of the faces were rather younger than had often been the case (Arthur conveniently failed to recall the fact that apart from Geoffrey Wittersham, his had been the youngest face the Council had seen since its inception in 1945.)

This afternoon, there were a dozen or so people going about their business on the two floors with which Arthur was most familiar. It had taken him less than a year to move clockwise, almost two years for him to gain access to Floor 18 and since then, he'd gone on to add a few more keys to his fob. Not literally, of course. The Council used a wide variety of access arrangements and Arthur was privy to several of them. This allowed him entry to rather more of the Council than most but he remained several keypads, card-swipes, fingerprint recognisers and possibly even a retina-scan away from those who made the decisions.

'Shepherd! Don't see much of you in Clerical. Something up?' A thin man, arms clasping papers to his breast, beamed at Arthur.

'Afternoon, Mulberry. Is Ricketts around?'

'Sorry. Everyone seems to be out at the moment; 'cept muggins, o' course and you know how much they tell me. Marginally less than they tell the media. And they don't tell *them* anything.'

'Any idea when there might be someone about?'

'Ricketts is due back later this afternoon. Kirkwood's not been seen for days, Armitage is over at the Ministry of Truth and Rackham is at a funeral.'

'Apart from Ricketts, I never heard of any of 'em,' Arthur said.

'Oh couple of them've been around a while. Armitage is one of the newer chaps. They've taken on a few in Accounting, recently. No-one in Filing, though. Funny, that.' Mulberry's voice was heavy with irony.

'Well, to be fair, it's not exactly "filing" any more, is it?' said Arthur. 'I mean all it needs is you and a computer and a knocked off version of Access and things'll run as smooth as you like.'

'Yes, Arthur. Just like all you need is a blunt instrument and a nearby water-course.' Mulberry glanced down at the huge wad of paper that was attempting to escape his clutches. 'I mean, does this look like a paperless office to you? Arthur smiled.

'Point taken,' he said.

'Cup of tea?' Mulberry asked him.

'Is there one on?'

'Is the Head of M.I.6 a Mason?'

'Go on then.'

Mulberry took himself off into a side office and Arthur followed.

'Chuck that lot on the floor,' he said, indicating a chair that was doubling as a filing system.

'You really that short staffed up here?' Arthur asked, as he tried to find a space to put the armful of paper he now found himself holding.

'Sorry, Shepherd, I must be a bit stressed at the moment. The urge to resort to sarcasm has never been so hard to resist as it is right at this moment.' A thought occurred to Arthur.

'Are you finding... and please don't take this the wrong way, that... mistakes... are creeping in?'

'Mis...takes?' It was as though Mulberry were trying out a new word in a foreign language. 'Shepherd, have you been sent to torture me?'

'Nothing to be ashamed of, Mulberry. We all make mistakes. Thanks.' He took the proffered cup and saucer from Mulberry, who said,

'Yes. A lot of us haven't really forgiven you for Elvis.'

'Blimey,' Arthur said, 'that was years ago. Some people just can't let go, can they?

'Anyway, as to your main point: so far as I know, there have been no errors emanating from this department. Perhaps if you could tell me what's bothering you?'

Arthur had nothing against the Clerks. They had all undergone the same training as any other Council Worker and were subject to identical rules and sanctions, but Cleaning – particularly if the subject were another Council Worker – was something he was reluctant to discuss.

'Best not,' he said.

'Suit yourself. Digestive?' He held out the packet and Arthur pinched one. 'Only... you know... professional pride and all that.'

'No, no. You needn't worry.' Arthur decided to change the subject. 'So your lot and Accounting still on speaking terms?'

'Just. Mind you, it was always a sort of uneasy alliance at the best of times.' In any organisation, those who spend and those who don't want them to are likely to be at loggerheads much of the time, but like everything else, such things always seemed a little more amplified at Century House, where contact between departments even a few doors apart from one another was perforce, limited.

'It doesn't help, you know Arthur,' Mulberry said, 'when the pain isn't shared evenly.'

'Pain?'

'Yes, Arthur: the recession.'

'Oh, that.'

'Yes, "that". Accounting does seem to have escaped its maw rather better than most, it appears.'

'Well, they can't sack anybody, can they? And don't forget the *Two-Twenty Rule*: one person leaves, another takes his place.'

'*A* place, Arthur,' Mulberry corrected. 'Some departments are growing at the expense of others. In fact, Ricketts has even been seconded to Accounting. He's asked for the move to be permanent. I'm pretty much on my own up here now. Hence, the tip you see before you.'

'Crikey. Ricketts deserting, eh?'

'Aw, he's been after it for a while. It's just the inequity of it all that I find so galling. I put in a request for help a few days ago but nothing, of course. Actually, I haven't really got time to be sitting here drinking tea and chewing the fat like this but what the hell,' said Mulberry, taking a long swig. 'What doesn't get done, doesn't get done.'

'That's the spirit.' Arthur's phone rang. It was a text. He read it and said, 'Bollocks. My own fault for switching the bastard thing on.'

'Oh dear. What's all that about?' Mulberry asked.

'Another flaming job. Nothing for weeks and then three on the trot. They're having to bloody text me. I don't know what they're playing at.'

'I don't even know who's playing,' Mulberry said.

'That's half the problem, as it happens.'

'What?'

'Oh, nothing, Arthur said. 'I've been doing a lot of thinking out loud lately. I reckon I need a holiday.' Mulberry sipped his tea. 'They've got a big Cezanne exhibition at the D'Orsay this autumn.'

'Really?'

'Yes. Mind you, Cezanne is probably not really your cup of tea, is he?'

'Borderline abstract, Mulberry. On the cusp of styles; heralding a new dawn and all that bollocks. No, I'm quite partial to Cezanne.'

'Yes, there's certainly a wonderful two-dimensionality (to his later works especially) but he's hardly Malevich is he; or Rothko?'

'Who could be?' said Arthur.

'Ah, yes I remember your obsession with the loony yank,'

'Yank, I'll grant you, Mulberry even possibly a touch on the loony side but I am not, nor have I ever been "obsessed" as you put it.'

'Oh come on,' Mulberry chided gently, 'I remember you telling me you'd never set foot in Tate Modern again until they rehung the Rothkos properly.'

'Did I?' Arthur asked, airily. 'You must have misheard.'

'You must have been over the moon when they finally did so.'

'What?'

'When they re-hung all the Seagrams together, Arthur. It must have been a few years ago now…'

'Re-hung?'

'Yes! Come on, Arthur. Surely you must have seen them. Room 6; third floor?'

'Erm… Oh yes,' Arthur said, his pulse beginning to race, 'yes I'd clean forgot. You see I'm not that obsessed.' He laughed. It was a pitiful sound, which he knew had fooled Mulberry not a jot. Sensibly, however, Mulberry chose not to press him on this blatant lie and changed the subject. Eventually, as they chatted, Arthur began to feel rather more equable until, in a slight hiatus, Mulberry asked him,

'This little problem of yours: does it have anything do with this plethora of jobs?'

'Might do.'

'Where do you normally pick 'em up?'

'Floor D over at Vauxhall Cross. Why d'you ask?'

'I could divert it over here, if you'd like. Save you a shlep, at least.'

'Hmm,' Arthur said, noncommittally.

'P'rhaps you're right,' Mulberry said. 'Just a thought.'

'Hypothetically,' Arthur said, 'how might one go about such a thing? Hypothetically…'

'Well, hypothetically, one would log into the despatch computer under an admin name and redirect it from the machine that prints them out there to a machine that could print them out here, provided the encryption and the system get along.'

'Thing is, it's probably already been printed and sent and then, as I understand it, deleted from the system.'

'Ah, hard-copy only job eh? I like that.' Arthur looked around the room at the Alp of paper that rose from each marginally flat surface in the place.

'I can see why.'

'Of course,' Mulberry said, '"deleted" is such a misnomer, isn't it?'

'I don't follow you.'

'Well when something is deleted from a computer, all it really means is that it's a bit harder to get at, doesn't it?'

'Does it?'

'Of course! Come along, Shepherd, where have you been for the last fifteen years?'

'Deleting people,' Arthur said. 'Anyway, how come you know so much about it?'

'Well, it's practically common knowledge. No offence. Stuff is encrypted, of course but there's always a way in if you've got enough time and patience.'

'So why on earth do people use computers if they're that easy to break into?'

'Because no-one can quite believe how vulnerable they actually are,' Mulberry said. 'Amazing faith in technology, your average punter, Shepherd and that's what the villains rely on.'

'I can't believe the Council would lay itself open so easily, particularly when it comes to despatch. The ones ordering them are not going to be far away.'

'Perhaps they destroy the hard-drive after every despatch,' Mulberry said. Arthur was considering this possibility when Mulberry said, quietly. 'I'm joking, Shepherd. Bloody hell, you really don't know much about I.T. do you? Mind you, it would explain why they're so strapped for cash that they can't spare an extra bod round this place. No, we've got some pretty good geeks working for us up in Cheltenham – best in the world, I reckon. Chances of hacking M.I.6 without getting collared, (never mind the Council) are vanishingly slender. Still, where there's a will, eh. Best not to commit anything to cyber-space you wouldn't want your mum to read. I'm even thinking of ditching my smartphone. Far too sophisticated if you ask me.'

'Eh?'

'Well, you have a phone decrypter, don't you – for hacking into other people's phones?'

'We all do. Don't use it much, as it happens.' Arthur used his as a key-fob.

'That's as may be. But if you did, you could read a phone as though it were your own, right? That's why the Council still uses enigmatic texts and codes and what have you. Nothing is safe. Now, the older the technology, the less opportunity there is for data to get lost down the back of the sofa, so to speak.'

'Eh?'

'Look: your average smartphone is no different from a computer. It treats you as though you are an idiot and makes it difficult for you to lose anything – even if you want to. It's full of fail-safes, cookies, cache-stores, swap-files and goodness knows what. You really need to read up on this stuff, Arthur. Mind you, not using your phone is also a pretty sound strategy and one which you appear to have been employing for some time.'

Arthur pulled the slip of paper on which Crawthorne Beasley's fate was writ and held it out.

'Take a look,' he said.

'Are you sure? Ricketts will be about eventually. He may even be down the corridor, Room 189, if you'd rather…'

'An idea has just occurred, Mulberry. And as it's based upon the intelligence you've just favoured me with, I think I'd like to run it past you, if you don't mind. Besides, why would I want an accountant to check this for me?' Arthur smiled and Mulberry accepted the compliment.

'Would I be placing myself in terrible danger?' he said, affecting a worried air.

'Naturally.'

'Oh well, I do that every time I use a bloody light switch down here. Lets have a look, then.' Mulberry took the slip of paper and opened it up. He stared at it for almost a minute, whilst Arthur poured some more tea and helped himself to another digestive.

'Christ,' Mulberry said at last, 'It's no wonder you're still alive after all these years, Shepherd. You really are a clever sod, aren't you?'

'Am I?' Arthur said, even though he knew exactly what Mulberry was talking about.

'It's not a bloody computer printout at all, is it?' Arthur beamed at Mulberry. 'It's a bloody teleprinter message!' Arthur's face fell.

'Oh,' he said, flatly. He'd thought they'd used a typewriter.

'That's why there's no possibility of tracing a despatch. Once it's left the source, an R.O. teleprinter chugs it out. They get it to you and there's no record of it anywhere. Brilliant!'

'But I thought you could intercept teleprinter messages with a bit of copper wire and a tin can. Arthur said.

'Well, you could, pretty much but nowadays, who's going to be looking for a sodding teleprinter message? I haven't even seen one in about forty years. This is bloody genius. Hundreds of spotty-faced nerds poring over hot terminals and there's stuff like this flitting about down the old G.P.O. lines. Ha! Makes you proud to be British.'

'Forgive me, Mulberry. I don't wish to cast aspersions on your deductive powers but how can you be so sure it is a teleprinter message?' Mulberry turned the paper towards Arthur.

'See there? Bottom left-hand corner?'

'They've always had things like that on them as long as I can remember. Just a reference of some kind isn't it?'

'It's a teletype source-code.'

'Is it really? Well, I never. Does it… er… tell us anything?'

'Not much, I'm afraid. Except that the sending machine is likely somewhere in this very building. 5E could be anything (I'd have to look it up) but the L-A-M is definitely Lambeth. The receiving machine could be anywhere but if you pick 'em up at Vauxhall Cross, I'd imagine that's where it is.'

'Is it possible to find out more? Like who sent it?'

'What, just based on this? Don't think so. Are there ever other odd numbers and letters on these things?'

'Well, yes' said Arthur, 'I never really paid any attention to them.'

'Never paid attention? Is this what the security of the realm depends upon? I thought you chaps were supposed to be observant.'

'Well, Mulberry, there's observant and then there's anal. Procedural details and instructions, I can commit to memory almost instantaneously but when it comes to strings of numbers and letters, well those I leave to the anal. Hence my presence here. In your office. With you.' Mulberry smiled and said,

'Well in my anal opinion, with just a teletype code, the only way you could even trace this machine would be if it were actually sending at the time. And what good would that do you unless you plan to run in and catch 'em at it? Anyway, this all sounds a bit naughty to me, Arthur; questioning orders.'

'You're probably right,' Arthur said. 'I was just a bit put out by this one, that's all.'

'Any particular reason?'

'I suppose it didn't ring true as a bona-fide Council job, that's all. Anyway, forget all about it, Mulberry. And I mean, forget all about it…'

'About what?'

'Thanks for the help, anyway; and the tea of course. I'll show myself out.' The door closed and Mulberry grabbed at a piece of paper, which the draught had put in flight. A split second later, the door opened again and Arthur popped his head round.

'Were you serious about that smartphone thing?' he asked.

'Well, the old ones did a lot less and that meant there were fewer ways to compromise them.'

'Hmm,' said Arthur and left.

Mulberry watched in dismay as the closing door kicked up a zephyr, which sent a landslide of paper tumbling to the floor.

'Bollocks,' he said.

## The Police Station

She heard Signor Nesci hang up. Her boss's right-hand man, his English was not good, although he knew enough to get by in business. Phrases like, 'Speak to Mr. Mosley's Personal Assistant' and 'I'll have the Chablis' and oh yes… 'You're fired' tripped faultlessly off his tongue.

Getting that job had been her big break. On leaving university with a Desmond[1] in Business and Human Resources, Vanessa had been eager to pursue those career opportunities that the course had promised. After twelve weeks working on the complaints desk in Asda, she took what she believed to be a step up, becoming a press officer for a cryogenics company – Don't Fear The Reaper Ltd – which, one Thursday afternoon, went the way of all flesh.

She'd studied the concept of receivership during her course but couldn't remember the part where an employee of a failed business, (who happens to be in Rome on behalf of the company) arrives back at her four-star hotel to find her bags in reception, along with a demand for immediate payment of the bill. In cash. Nor had she any recollection of the part where said employee goes to A.T.M. and finds her company cards are no longer valid. And any discussion about how the fuck she gets to the airport with six euros in her purse, even in the unlikely event of her being able to persuade the hotel to release her luggage must have passed her by completely.

The manager of Hotel La Domina, who had (as men often did) taken a shine to her, offered her a job as a chambermaid. Vanessa, out of ideas, had clutched at this passing straw of combined act of Christian charity and attempt to get laid and had taken up the offer. Within six months, Italian (at least in the somewhat restricted argot of the hotel business) improving, she had found herself working in Reception and making a pretty good fist of it. The salary, however, barely covered her expenses and she was desperate to move on.

When Andrew Mosley, looking to extend his hotel chain, arranged to examine the potential of La Domina, it was Vanessa who, on the strength of her nationality (and it had to be said, effect on male clients), was given the task of showing him around. He was impressed. He bought the hotel and hired Vanessa as his P.A. at a ridiculous salary. She had told him that she wouldn't let him down.

Had she simply been conned into picking up the wrong man at the airport, she might just have got away with it but losing a ninety-seven thousand euro car and oh, she'd almost forgotten, involving said car in a double homicide on the streets of the Italian capital; well, that pretty much sealed it.

She stared absently at the police officer's mobile phone as she idly tumbled it end over end on the desktop until he reached out a hand. She

---

[1] Second-class honours as in: 2:2 : as in Tutu.

held it up for a moment, not quite understanding and then placed it in his hand.

'Thank you,' she said, quietly. 'Could I have a pen and paper, please?' The policeman tossed her a ball-point from his top pocket and tore off a sheet from his pad. 'When may I leave?' she asked.

'Very shortly, I would imagine,' said the officer, 'It would appear that your account of the events tallies with what the witnesses have told us. You were very lucky.'

Vanessa considered for a moment just how lucky she had been but her Italian didn't really run as far as advanced sarcasm.

'So you have no idea what happened to the car?' she asked.

'No. You tell us he was trying to get to the British Embassy but no-one there has any idea who he was or what he wanted. The car was probably driven straight into a meccanico. Knock out the dings, new paint, new plates and down to Ostia to the ferries before the afternoon rush hour.' He was writing something down on the form attached to his clipboard when he asked, without looking up, 'Why didn't you call us straight away, as soon as you found the gun?'

The abruptness of his question threw her for a moment.

'I was half-naked and he'd pretty much taken everything I had – including the battery from my phone, if you remember,' she said in disbelief. He struck a full-stop with some finality.

The door opened and another policeman entered. He walked over to the officer and whispered something to him. Vanessa couldn't catch the reply but thought she heard the word, "*ambasciata*" – embassy. About bloody time. Both men left the room and a few minutes later the officer returned, accompanied by a stranger. He gestured towards Vanessa and left.

'How do you do?' said the newcomer, presenting his card, 'My name is Christopher Maytham.' Vanessa made no response but continued to doodle on the paper she'd been given. She was, she supposed, trying to give the impression that she was both angry at being kept there so long and yet blasé about the whole thing. She soon realised that she was just giving the appearance of being a sulky teenager. After an awkward moment, Maytham placed his card into his top pocket with his left hand and held out his right. 'I'm from the Consular Service at the British Embassy,' he said. Finally, Vanessa unfolded her arms and reached out to accept his greeting.

He was everything a consular official should be, with his tailored suit, expensive shoes and attaché case. And whilst he appeared younger than one might have expected, after the brusqueness of her Polizia experience, his assured manner was welcome. But she wasn't going to let him know it.

'May I sit down?' he asked. An arched eyebrow and her hand lifting momentarily from the table, told him it was a free country so he scraped the plastic chair towards him and sat. 'Well,' he said, after a pause, 'they tell me you've had quite a day.'

'I've had better,' she said. 'When can I leave?'

'Soon, soon. Of course, I must ask you a few questions first.' Vanessa sagged and resumed her doodle. Noticing this, Maytham continued, 'I mean, incidents of this sort can be very embarrassing…'

'I can imagine,' Vanessa said flatly.

'Look, I promise it won't take very long. Would you like another coffee?'

'No. It's piss, frankly.' He smiled and said,

'Right. Let's get started then, shall we?' He placed his case on the desk and clicked the latches. 'Now, can you describe the man who abducted you?' She certainly could; she could even recollect the scent of his after-shave and was enraged that even now she remembered the attraction she had felt towards him. However, all she offered Maytham was:

'Medium height, medium build; greying, well dressed. Mid fifties. I've given all this to the police.'

'Sometimes,' Maytham said, 'things do occasionally get lost in translation.' He reached into his case, took out a photograph and span it over to her. 'Is this him?'

The photograph was blurred and clearly had been taken with a telephoto lens at a great distance from its subject who, even though younger in the photograph was definitely the man who'd abducted her. To her surprise and discomfiture, the sight of him made her stomach flutter.

'The police said you had no idea who he was,' Vanessa said. It appeared to be confirmation enough and Maytham recovered the photograph.

'Yes, oddly we don't tell the Italian police everything.' Vanessa, cross at her own naiveté, said nothing. 'His name,' Maytham continued, 'is David Swanson. He's done this sort of thing a number of times, I'm afraid. Interpol have been after him for some time…'

'…Geoffrey,' said Vanessa.

'I beg your pardon?'

'He said his name was Geoffrey; Geoffrey…*Wittersham*… I think. I told him I didn't want to know his name but I suppose he must have told me anyway.' Maytham was silent and after a short while, Vanessa glanced up. 'Something wrong?' she asked.

'No, not at all,' Maytham said. That's one of his aliases, we believe.'

'Why was he trying to get to the British Embassy?'

'We don't know. We think he was probably just trying to mislead you to keep you from making too much of a fuss.'

'Who were the others?'

'Others?'

'Yes, the ones he killed today.'

'A couple of very unlucky carjackers called Agresta and Frati. The police tell me they've been looking for them for months.' Vanessa was thoughtful for a second or two then asked,

'Why would he do that? Wouldn't it have been more sensible just to have run off to try his luck elsewhere?'

'One can't always understand the criminal mind. Anyway, the important thing now,' he went on, 'is that we try to get you sorted out. We can organise a new passport for you and if you wish, get you home... to England, I mean.'

It was the first time that it had truly occurred to Vanessa that she may not be able to stay in Italy. She had a few euros saved up but that wouldn't last long and she had no idea whether or not she was entitled to benefits. There was nothing really keeping her here but then again there was nothing much to go back to England for, either. She blinked, as she realised that Maytham was still speaking.

'So, in the meantime,' he was saying, 'we're here to look after you.'

'How?' she asked.

'Well, I could begin by taking you home.'

'Shit!' she said.

'Well, it was only a suggestion. I imagined in the circumstances...'

'No. No, it's not that. It's just. Well he took my keys, of course; flat, car, the lot. I just keep forgetting. I don't know what's the matter with me.'

'Well, you've been through a traumatic time. A little disorientation is only to be expected...

'Bugger it!' she said. Then, relaxing a little, she sighed, 'Oh, I'm sorry. It's just that I've not been moved-in above a week and I've already lost the keys. Bastard landlord will probably take my deposit.'

'Now, now, not to worry. We'll pop round to your landlord's and I'll explain to him what happened to you and I'm sure he'll give you a spare key.'

'He didn't look the forgiving type.'

'Don't underestimate the power of the British Consular Service,' he said, smiling.

The door opened and two policemen entered. One of them was familiar to her, the other, clearly of higher rank, was not. Vanessa looked anxious and Maytham, noticing, held up his hand, discreetly. The gesture clearly said, '*Let me handle this*.' He rose and approached the officers.

Vanessa couldn't hear what was being said but the gestures made it clear that her getting out the police station was far from a foregone conclusion. Maytham appeared to be handling the situation well and she admired his poise and cool demeanour throughout, even as the officer became more agitated.

Finally, the officer sagged, held his hands up in supplication. He didn't say, 'Oh, just do what the hell you like!' but his body language said it for him. Returning to the table, Maytham smiled, picked up her bag and held it out, the chain at full stretch, so that she had only to place her arm through the loop. It was a small gesture but she appreciated it and together they left the police station.

'He seemed a bit cross.' Vanessa said, once they were outside.

'Oh, he had nothing. It was all bluster,' Maytham said. 'I think he was hoping there might have been a kickback in it.' He directed her to a sleek, black, embassy car, which was parked almost directly in front of the station.

'Handy,' Vanessa said.

'Well, as they say: it has its privileges.' He held open the passenger door and she climbed in.

'Very nice,' she said, as she sank gently into the leather.

'Make the most of it.' Maytham said.

'Oh? Why?'

'Cutbacks, Miss Aldridge. We're already replacing these with Toyotas.' He smiled at her and shook his head in a gesture of resignation. 'I don't know,' he continued, 'we'll all be on scooters soon, I expect.'

Maytham held her gaze for a moment and then asked,

'Have you eaten?'

*Here we go*, thought Vanessa. 'Not since this morning,' she said.

'I know a splendid little place near the Trevi,' he said.

I'll just bet you do. 'I thought we were going to get me a spare key.'

'Well, yes, of course... I just thought that afterwards... well, I thought you might like some dinner. That's all.'

'Will they let me in looking like this?'

'Like what?'

'I mean these clothes; they're not exactly...you know?' Maytham looked nonplussed. 'What I mean is...oh, never mind.'

She felt just a tug of shame, small but noticeable. There was a time when her thirty-seven Euro outfit from Bata would have been a source of delight to her. Had she changed so much? Yes she had, she decided and so what?

## PART 2 TUESDAY
## The Apartment

As she turned off the light, Vanessa had to think for a moment. Yes, it was only just yesterday morning that she'd gone to pick up Stephen Mosley from the airport.

Earlier at the restaurant, Maytham ("Do please call me Christopher") had been a charming companion.

'I practically go to dinner for a living,' he'd said. And it had showed. 'How about you?' The question had almost jarred loose her fillings as she bumped back down to earth.

'After today, I don't really know,' she'd told him, resting her chin on her hand. She'd known that she had been punching above her weight even as a P.A. and had already realised that her refusal to put out for Mr. Mosley had numbered her days in the post but now that the axe had actually fallen, she really wasn't sure what she could do.

'Erm, did you say something - back in the police station - about a passport?' she'd asked him.

'Oh, yes; we can get you another one of those, easily.'

'How long will that take, do you think?'

'A day; two, at the most. So long as you're not an international super-criminal, or something.'

'Well... if there's an opening... I'll take anything.'

He laughed.

'Jolly good. Don't lose your sense of humour, that's the ticket.'

She had begun to feel that he could be relied on but just to be on the safe side, she'd decided to add a little catalyst to the chemistry.

'So does your wife like it... here in Rome, I mean?'

'Oh, I'm not married. Goodness me, no.'

'Really?' she had asked, running her finger around the rim of her wine glass, 'a man like you?' Maytham had said nothing but had smiled in a disarming way, tilting his wine glass towards him and looking downwards, swirling the contents. 'I'd have thought you'd be quite a catch; young, urbane, good-looking, sophisticated...,'

'...Gay,' he'd said.

It had been easier after that. She knew that men found her attractive and had used the fact to her material advantage a number of times throughout her career. To her credit, she seldom did so without a twinge of guilt but she nevertheless found it difficult to believe that people embarked on relationships without an ulterior motive. With Maytham immune, she'd decided that it had been a complicated enough day as it was and had simply settled in to enjoy a free meal. And enjoy it she had.

Maytham had driven her back to her apartment at around eleven and had even walked her to her door. He'd told her to make sure all her doors and windows were secure and to sleep well and things would seem better in the morning. She rather liked him.

It was two-thirty before she finally decided that she wasn't going to sleep. It was one of those times, when a combination of exhaustion, over-excitement and a bloody inane tune going round in her head had conspired to deprive her of sleep. She had just made the decision to go and pour herself a glass of whisky, when she heard a faint *click*, followed by an equally faint creak. She held her breath. Shuffling? Footsteps? Was someone there - in her apartment? Oh Christ! Could it be Wittersham?

For a fleeting moment, she felt a sense of excitement at seeing him again. *What the bloody hell was up with her?* Irrationally, it seemed, Christopher's innocuous comment about locking her doors and windows began to take on sinister significance. Why had he said that? Did she have something to fear? Oh God; what if he'd come to finish her off. He'd taken her bloody keys, hadn't he? But then again, perhaps he'd come to fetch her - to whisk her off somewhere warm and safe.

What!!?

She shut her eyes and tried to breathe steadily.

What's wrong with you? This man, charming as he might be, actually kills people; and he dumped you in your underwear in the middle of Rome! He is not a very nice man, Vanessa!

She began to think more clearly but as her mad fantasies melted like snow, into their place flooded the awful reality of her situation. She lay there and actually wondered how he'd do it; this killer. Would she hear the faint *pfut!* of a silencer before oblivion engulfed her; feel the cool smoothness of a silken cord as it wound around her neck; or the slender penetration of a stiletto?

Well, she'd be buggered if she was going to wait to find out.

Silently, she got up and tiptoed over to her bureau. It was amazing that only when you wanted silence, did you realise just how noisily even the most innocuous of things operate. She'd have sworn that the bureau opened with barely a whisper and yet there they were: not just one but several distinct creaks. She opened it as much as she dared. Of the intruder, there was no longer a sound. She reached inside the bureau and allowed herself a breath as her hand closed around a pair of scissors. She removed them gingerly and then wondered whether it would be wiser to close the bureau and risk the creaks she already knew lay in the hinges or whether to risk opening it further and gamble that all the creaks had been used up. She stood there, holding the bureau lid at half-mast and feeling like an idiot. Decision made, she gently let gravity take it and to her relief, it yawned open with no more complaint. Again, she breathed and she listened. Nothing.

It was at this point that Vanessa began to wonder if she'd actually heard anything at all. She hadn't got used to the place yet. It would have its little bumps and creaks and groans and soon she would get used to them. Or perhaps she'd been nodding off and in that shadowy half-land between wakefulness and sleep, she had imagined the whole thing. For what seemed an age, she stood with her ear at the bedroom door during which time, she thought about alternatives. She might arrange her pillows to look as though she were still in bed, wait behind the door and then, as he stood over pillow-Vanessa with his Uzi nine millimetre or whatever, poised, she would jab the scissors into his kidneys – which would be messy: and besides, she wasn't sure where kidneys actually were. Or she might just nip out, lock the door and get away. That was a good plan in all but one important feature: the bedroom door had no lock.

She glanced at the window. One floor up – not too bad. Wasn't there a drain pipe or something out there? How far was it from the window? Was there some sort of ledge? God! Why hadn't she thought about escape routes? Her friend, Jessie, always had escape routes. "It's the first thing I do when I go into a strange room; plot my escape routes," she'd told Vanessa. Neurotic cow! Still. Hearing nothing, she inched the door open. In the gloom beyond, she could discern only shadows but (she supposed afterwards), because she had heard no further sound from the "intruder", began to believe it was no more than her over-active imagination.

Emboldened, she stepped into the hallway and switched on the light. Rationality flooded in and she shook her head at her foolishness. What the hell was she doing? She ran a hand through her hair. She giggled.

'Idiot,' she said aloud and sighed. Still, now she was up... a wee dram would go down a... And then a hand was round her mouth and an arm around her waist, pinning her hand and the scissors to her side.

The breath had left her body so she couldn't have cried out anyway, but still the hand pressed hard on her face. She knew the game was up and indicated her submission by relaxing. Then, she was dragged back to the bedroom. The hand on her waist took the scissors from her now-unresisting fist and the one on her mouth slowly released pressure. She felt it gently pull her head around. Her eyes had filled with tears and in the gloom, it took her a moment to realise who her assailant was.

She'd never been one to go quietly and as she inhaled to scream abuse at him, Maytham put a finger to his lips and widened his eyes to emphasise the urgency of the gesture. For some reason, Vanessa acquiesced. She found her voice but something told her it had better be a whisper.

'What the fuck...!?' she hissed.

'We must get you away from here,' he said, urgently. 'I'm afraid I may have placed you in some danger. You must do exactly as I say.'

'Bollocks.'

'No, Vanessa, not "bollocks". Please listen; we need to move quickly.'

'I'm not going anywhere with you, you tosser; what are you doing in my flat?'

'I'm here to warn you.'

'Oh, I see. You're here to warn me, are you?' 'Oh, thank you! What would I do without you?'

'Please, Vanessa.' He seemed exasperated. 'Look, I'll try to explain but we have very little time.'

She looked hard at him and said,

'Go on, then.'

'Well, after I dropped you, I returned to the Embassy…'

'At gone eleven? Why would you do that?'

'I had to return the car, of course.' Somehow, it didn't seem plausible but Vanessa decided not to argue at this point.

'All right. Then what?'

'Look, can we go? I'll explain on the way…'

'No. Explain now.'

'Vanessa. If we don't leave right now, there is a strong possibility that neither of us will be alive by morning.' Maytham appeared as afraid now as he'd appeared confident a few hours before but perhaps that too, was all part of the training. He said, 'Look. What have you got to lose?' Movements in her face heralded what would have been a magnificent oratorio of venomous abuse had Maytham not hurried on. 'I have you already. I could just grab you and manhandle you down stairs…'

'I'd like to see you try.'

'…or kill you where you stand.' A pit opened up in Vanessa's stomach.

'What?'

'Well, if I meant you harm, I could have done it already. Please believe me: I want to help you. Here…' he said, handing back the scissors, '…you can jab these between my ribs any time you like.' She snatched them from him and waved them under his nose.

'And don't think I won't, you bastard.' She considered her options and decided that Maytham was right: she didn't really have any.

'I'll need to get dressed,' she said.

'You're fine as you are.'

'No, I'm not fine, Christopher. I'm wearing boxer shorts, fluffy pink slippers and a t-shirt that says, *The Girl All the Bad Guys Want*. On no planet in any universe is this "fine". I'm going to get...'

Maytham picked up the black Gucci bag he had seen her with earlier that evening and from her bedside table, he scooped up her phone.

'Hey...!' Before she could say anything more, Maytham asked,

'Did you have anything else with you when Wittersham dropped you at Santa Maria degli Angeli?'

'I was in my underwear!' she hissed. 'Wait: *what?* You said his name was *Swanson*!'

'Where is it?'

'Where's what?'

Maytham dashed into the bathroom. Vanessa's clothes were on the floor, where she had flung them before stepping gratefully into the shower, a couple of hours ago. He went down on one knee and gathered up the clothing.

'What the hell...' she began.

'Anything else?' asked Maytham.

'What. ?'

'Shoes?'

'Well, yes but. ?'

'Where are they?' Without waiting for an answer, Maytham rushed back into the bedroom and returned with the red Louboutins dangling between his fingers. He stood before her.

'Vanessa; I know we've only recently met and that I have broken into your apartment. I know that you are in your sleeping clothes and your hair is a mess but I'm begging you: please, please come with me.' He bundled his burden so that he had a free hand, which he held out to her. She looked down at it and then back at him.

'My *hair's* a mess?' she said.

He smiled and with a shake of her head and a whispered, 'Oh Christ...', she took his hand and together, they left her apartment.

At the street-door, Maytham bade her stand still whilst he stood in the shadow of the porch and looked up and down the dark street. Clearly satisfied that the coast was clear, he tugged gently and she followed him across the road. As she scuttled after him, she became aware, by virtue of the cool breeze on the back of her neck, that she was drenched in sweat. Maytham pointed and clicked and a twitter and an orange flash showed her that she would be riding in a Toyota. Maytham caught her expression.

'I told you,' he said. 'Actually, it's rather fortunate. Far less conspicuous. We might just get away with this if we're lucky.' He settled into the driver's seat.

'And if we don't,' said Vanessa, sitting down alongside and brandishing the scissors, 'you'll be the first to know.'

'Oh, Vanessa,' Maytham said, smiling, 'you wouldn't really stab me. You're not the stabbing kind.' She tried to look determined. 'No, far too messy. Now poison – that I'd believe. Here.' He dumped the clothing, bag, shoes and all into her lap and turned the key. As the car sprung into life, he turned to her, nodded at the clothes and said, 'You really oughtn't to chuck your clothes around like that you know. A bathroom floor has more grit lurking in it than you'd ever imagine. And the colour in that cheap top will almost certainly run after being on that damp floor.'

With only a slight squeak of tyres, Maytham turned the Toyota into Via Garibaldi and they sped away through darkened streets.

## The Autostrada

'You should try to sleep,' he told her. All manner of pithy responses were brushed away by Vanessa's smarter self and instead, she said, simply,

'Christopher? Please tell me why we're having to do this.'

'I'm not sure that I can.'

'Look, you've got what you wanted. I agreed to leave with you in the middle of the night, I'm sitting here in my night clothes with… with dirty laundry on my lap and driving God knows where. I think it's pretty much the least you can do, don't you?'

'I don't think you'll be very happy.'

'Oh. Right. Because, at the moment, I'm so deliriously overjoyed, I don't think I can stand it. How much more unhappy do you think I can be?' Maytham's expression hinted that she might well not yet have reached her full unhappiness potential. And he was right. He took a deep breath.

'After we spoke at the restaurant, I reported back and told the intelligence chaps that I was certain you were…'

'Hang on.' Vanessa's voice remained dangerously calm, as she turned to him. 'Intelligence Chaps? *Intelligence… Chaps*? 'What "Intelligence Chaps"?'

'They initially said I should find out what you really knew about Wittersham…'

'Oh, did they? Did they, really?'

'Look…'

'No! You look!' Vanessa's eyes blazed. 'I thought you were looking after me! All British Embassy and consulate and diplomat and shit! Bloody hell! You were just trying get me to drop my guard. You were no better than those bastard police!' This was no feigned anger. Vanessa was furious and once more, afraid.

'You don't understand…'

'Oh, I think I understand perfectly!' That was foolish; she hadn't a clue.

'Vanessa, I'm most terribly sorry about all this.' She tore her eyes from him, pulled her knees up to her chin, placed her feet on the dashboard and stared ahead at the red, white and occasional orange lights that constituted all she could see of the autostrada.

'Bastard,' she whispered, just loudly enough.

'Perhaps I ought to start at the beginning,' he said.

'Bastard,' said Vanessa

'A few days ago,' Maytham went on, 'a small group of intelligence officers arrived from the UK – some sort of liaison thing; it happens occasionally and usually, I don't have a great deal to do with such things. This time, however, I was assigned to work with them.

'Well, as far as I could make out, it was just routine stuff: the odd file, the occasional phone call, a little bit of translation; nothing too onerous but there was something not quite right about them. I couldn't really put my finger on it – still can't but at one point I contacted my superiors in Whitehall only to be told that the Consul was bound to afford British Intelligence every convenience and if that meant my being seconded to a small unit for the duration of the operation then I was to do exactly as I was bloody well told… or words to that effect. I wasn't happy about it, I can assure you.'

'My heart bleeds.'

'Please, Vanessa. Do hear me out. I know this all seems… odd…'

'Ha!'

'…But I promise you, this situation is as alien to me as it must be to you. I'm in way over my head as well and now that I've helped you, I'm in every bit as much trouble as you, I assure you.'

'I should bloody well hope so,' Vanessa said. 'Of course, I wasn't in any trouble at all until you turned up at my flat.'

Maytham ignored her.

'There was definitely something up but of course, they told me nothing. It wasn't until they asked me to interview you at the police station that they told me that they believed you and he were working together.'

'Eh?'

'Wittersham. As far as they were concerned, you'd arranged to meet him and to them, it meant only one thing. They got a description of the car from the chap he avoided at the airport and sent two of their men to intercept you.'

'The men Wittersham shot.'

'The same. News came to the Embassy that three British agents were dead at the hands of this man, Wittersham.'

'Three?'

'He'd already done one of them in before he picked you up; between stepping off the plane and entering the arrivals lounge.'

Vanessa said, 'Fuck.'

'Indeed,' said Maytham. 'He wasn't coming from London, by the way'

'Oh?'

'No. It was an internal flight: he'd been in Italy about a week. Anyway, the next we heard was that a young woman had been picked up by the police, apparently after having been abducted by a man at the airport. I checked up on you and told the spooks that you were clearly an innocent party - wrong place wrong time, sort of thing. They weren't so sure; particularly as it was reported that you were armed.'

'So they told you to find out what my involvement was?'

'At first. However, it was clear they mistrusted both me and my judgement even then. Remember, as we were leaving, the pugnacious little policeman who made such a fuss? He told me that the embassy had called to say that you were to be held overnight. I've never known the service seek the help of the police in such matters. I was extremely worried but fortunately, you had already been released into my custody. I told the officer that if he wanted to keep you there, he'd have to re-arrest you and by that time, there might well be a full-blown diplomatic incident on the cards. The police frankly didn't want anything to do with it so they didn't take too much convincing.

'It was when you told me that Wittersham had told you his name that I became a little confused. Frankly, it crossed my mind that you were trying to draw me into some kind of trap. I thought it politic to try to find out a little more about you.'

'So even the offer of dinner was a ploy, eh?' Maytham looked a little ashamed but went on,

'After I dropped you, I reported back. I knew they'd be angry but I didn't realise just how furious they would be. For a start, they were livid that I'd let you return home and they made all sorts of noises about my career and so forth. I've never responded well to threats so I told them what I thought of them. That was when Hermione said that if I wasn't careful I'd get it as well.'

'It?'

'These people were most peculiar, Vanessa. It was almost as if they were actors in some appalling B-movie. They must have thought they'd cowed me into submission because they quickly lost interest in me. I knew by then that not only must they have been exceeding their authority, they were unhinged enough to do something very bad indeed. They really wanted you, Vanessa.

'Anyway, I decided I had to help you. Fortunately, the address they'd tracked down was the one you'd recently left. I reckoned that by the time they'd worked out that they'd made a mistake and had managed to get the right address, I could slip out, warn you and get you away. Which, happily, I was able to do.'

He seemed so genuine that Vanessa had to remind herself quite forcefully that he had misled her from the moment they had first met. She decided to let him know that she wasn't convinced. She produced what she hoped was a wry smile and said,

'That's quite a story, Christopher. Our escape seems almost miraculous in the circumstances.'

'Look,' Maytham said, 'I don't blame you for being suspicious of me. Pretence; lying if you like, is simply part of what I do. But so is protecting British Subjects. I promise you; you have nothing whatsoever to fear from me.' Vanessa pulled out the scissors.

'I know I don't,' she said. It sounded foolish and flippant, which it was. There could be no hiding from Maytham just how anxious and confused she really was. 'So who *is* this Wittersham, then?' she asked him. It was some time before he answered.

'He is an assassin. He works for British Intelligence.'

## Florence

'Where are we?' Vanessa's words were distorted by a yawn and strangled by a stretch.

'Surely you recognise Florence?' said Maytham.

Vanessa tugged her sleeve over her hand, wiped the condensated window and eventually scraped into existence some dirty daylight and the offside door of a Fiat Panda. A metre beyond the Fiat, an eighteen-wheel truck barred her view of a half-chevron row of eighteen-wheel trucks, which stood in the way of the clump of trees two hundred metres from Autostrada 42, three kilometres beyond which might be glimpsed the spires and domes of Florence – were it not for the Pirelli factory.

As lay-bys go, she'd seen worse and at least this one had a toilet. There are few things better at staving off the memory of an unforgettable night than tangled hair and a full bladder so it wasn't until Vanessa had washed her hands, her face and whatever else she could manage to reach without drawing too much attention from the lady truckers, that she began to recall the events of the night before. So well did she recall them that on returning to the car to find that Maytham had embarked on his own ablutionary enterprise, she cursed as she noticed that although the car was open, he'd taken the keys with him. Would she really have ditched him, given the chance? It was but one of many scenarios she was beginning to sample. The sleep had helped and she was thinking more clearly.

As Maytham settled once more into the driver's seat, she asked him,

'What's on the menu today, then?

I intend to head north and try to cross into France. Of course, they'll be looking for us so…'

'Hold on! "*Try* to cross into France"? What "*try*"?

'Vanessa, you must remember; you have no passport,' said Maytham, patiently.

'Well, I know but surely…? I mean, we're in a car… European Union… entente cordiale… and all that? There aren't even border posts any more, are there?'

'In much of Europe, no. But between Italy and France and Italy and Switzerland and Italy and Austria and Italy and Slovenia…? Well, yes. Not that the Italians have the monopoly on paranoia, of course. Crossing the Alps will be a doddle compared to getting into the U.K. But I'm hoping we can have you a passport by then.' Vanessa half wondered if she should ask how but decided that she didn't really care. Instead, she asked,

'Who'll be looking for us, then; the police?' Maytham chuckled.

'Oh dear me, no! That's the last thing the Foreign Office would sanction. Can you imagine the scandal?' She couldn't but the thought seemed to amuse him. 'No, it will be M.I.6, I'm afraid.'

'I think we should go,' she said.

'Yes,' Maytham agreed, 'but first we should get some coffee and a bite to eat. Not on the autostrada; they may well have alerted the service stations.'

'I still have no money.'

'Never mind about that.'

'I need a battery for my phone.'

'I'll get you one but I don't think it would be a good idea to try to ring anyone at the moment.'

'Do you think we could have the radio off?'

'It isn't on.'

'Oh.'

## Villa Sangone

With numbers on the roadsigns to Turin now in single figures, Maytham turned west onto what was the first truly major road they had encountered all day. They'd taken on supplies in a small town quite close to Florence and had stopped only once since then. Even so, his estimate of six hours had been out by over two and the early evening sunlight was full in Vanessa's face as she opened her eyes once again. She had the now-familiar headache and her back protested each move as she straightened. In spite of her best efforts, she had slept for almost four hours. She'd had strange dreams and had woken occasionally but drifted off again before much had registered. Maytham, frankly, looked awful. He noticed her stirring.

'How are you feeling?'

'O.K. ' she managed. 'How about you?'

'Last legs, I'm afraid. But we're almost there.'

'Where?'

Maytham pointed towards the wooded slopes to their right. She could see only one building; one very big building looking like a painting in a frame of trees.

'It's called Villa Sangone. Belongs to an old friend. We'll be safe there and we can rest.'

'How old a friend?' asked Vanessa. She surprised herself by how suspicious she appeared to be becoming.

'Oh, I've known her as long as I can remember. I suppose she counts as some sort of cousin or something. I used to see her quite frequently when I was a child. Called my mother "auntie" even though neither of my parents had brothers or sisters. Some dark family secret, I expect.' Maytham looked at Vanessa and gave a mock shiver of intrigue, which, whilst she knew it to be facetious, nevertheless heightened her unease.

'She's English, then?'

'I believe so,' Maytham said. Now... it's around here, somewhere. Ah!' Maytham swung the car right, through a gap in the trees and a few yards further along, pulled up before a set of gates. He leaned out of the window as a speaker, bound to a post, crackled. He said, in Italian,

'I should like to see Mrs. Gagliardo-Patricelli, please.'

'Oh, very English,' said Vanessa. Maytham ignored her and after the next crackle, said,

'Christopher Maytham. From the Embassy in Rome.' There was a pause and then the intercom crackled once more. This time, however, the sound appeared to be far more modulated, almost musical; as though the intercom were picking up a foreign radio station broadcasting Wagner.

'Linny!' Maytham said. 'Yes... yes, I'm sorry, it wasn't exactly planned...' He gave a bright laugh. 'Of course, yep; see you in a mo.'

Vanessa heard the clank of the gates, as they swung open. The sound drew her gaze to a long driveway, the avenue of trees on both sides of which drew the eye to a portico. As the car approached, it became apparent to Vanessa that either the avenue of trees was far longer or else the building far larger than she had imagined.

'You've got to be kidding,' she breathed, gazing upwards as they rounded the flower bed, with its low box hedge. A well-built young man in livery was hurrying down the steps and as the car crackled to a standstill, he opened the door, held it and stood aside.

As Andrew Mosley's personal assistant, she had seen her fair share of grand houses. She had attended receptions, dinners and a ball or two and though a little overwhelmed at first (her preferment had been rather rapid after all), she had watched the other beautiful women who surrounded their own corporate caliph, had learned and had soon come to expect and yes, enjoy the gloss, the flummery and the trimmings associated with the world of big business. But this was very different. This was the real thing, not some corporate chimera. And although she hoped it was because she was tired, aching and a little smelly or because she merely wasn't dressed for it (although it was more likely because she knew it to be true), she felt as though she did not belong.

As a young woman of seventeen, she and two friends had gone to a rock festival in Scotland. It had of course, rained. And rained and rained. So much did it rain that the organisers, on the orders of the police, had been forced to abandon the event and evacuate the revellers to higher ground. She remembered huddling under a plastic sheet, caked in mud, water dripping into her brand new pink wellingtons, looking down at the campsite in which wallowed their tent, sleeping bags and most of their food.

Fiona, the friend whose idea it had been, had mentioned that a member of her Scottish family lived nearby and almost wordlessly, they had decided to seek them out. Two hours later, they were squelching up the steps of a grand house on the edge of Kirroughtree Forest and presenting themselves to Fiona's mother's cousin's wife. It had been Vanessa's introduction to the life of the other half.

As a child of lower middle-class parents, she could only gaze in wonderment at the splendour and opulence in which this family had lived. Not only had they spare rooms for each of the friends, they'd also given them clothes belonging to the daughter of the family (away at university) and had offered, without a moment's hesitation, money for train fare home and food for the journey. She had never forgotten that sense of being so much out of place, terrified lest she make some faux pas, even to the point of wondering if she were being looked on with amusement or even pity by her host.

That sense was upon her now. Vanessa Aldridge, Charity Case. Well, she didn't care if she was on the run from M.I.6 (*oh fuck*), she'd be buggered if she'd let Caroline Quatro-Fromaggio (or whatever her name was) play Lady Bountiful with her. Food and a wash and that's it! *"Thank you and we'll be on our way."*

'My *darling* Christopher!' Caroline Gagliardo-Patricelli embraced him. 'How marvellous to see you but why on earth didn't you phone? And how is your poor mother?'

'Oh, if I know her, she's already back on her feet.'

'Well do send her my love when you see her, won't you? Mrs. Gagliardo-Patricelli's accent was not just cut-glass; it was Murano crystal, engraved with a coat of arms and Vanessa tensed, as she turned to face her.

'And who is this, Christopher? Don't tell me you've seen the light at last?'

'You are wicked, Linny. This is… a friend of mine. Caroline Gagliardo-Patricelli; Vanessa Aldridge.' Vanessa knew that protocol demanded she acknowledge her own pleasure first so whilst smiling, she said nothing. Maytham's face fell slightly and to Vanessa's surprise, Mrs. Gagliardo-Patricelli said,

'I'm delighted to meet you, Miss Aldridge. Please, both of you.' She gestured them up the stairs. 'Gianfranco will take your luggage.'

'Erm, we have no luggage, Linny.'

'Oh. How mysterious,' she said. 'Do come in and explain all!'

## The Terrace

Vanessa knew that no matter how hard she tried or how much she might pretend, she could never hope to emulate the effortless grace of Caroline Gagliardo-Patricelli. Her age hard to determine, tall and slim, auburn hair (surely not genuine?) piled into a loose bun on the back of her head she had the manner, peculiar to the genuine aristocrat, which made Vanessa feel in every way inferior. It wasn't arrogance but pure self-assuredness and an honest desire to make everyone feel at ease; and unlike those staggeringly wealthy and powerful people she'd encountered in the course of her employment, this woman would expect nothing in return, save courtesy. Vanessa herself had been an early beneficiary. Struggling to recall her hostess' name and probably showing it, she had been relieved to receive the exhortation,

'And do call me Caroline, please, Miss Aldridge. Mrs. Gagliardo-Patricelli is such a mouthful. Now, drinks first, I think.'

As she and Maytham were led through the conservatory, Vanessa couldn't take her eyes of Caroline's clothes. Although the cheap jeans were holding up pretty well, her top was creased and crumpled beyond anything she had worn in two years and looked worth every cent of the fifteen euros it had cost. Walking behind Caroline (who was gliding along in an embroidered housecoat, silk pantaloons and sandals), Vanessa felt so dowdy, she could have wept until, with a start, she realised how little she had cared until now.

Caroline ushered them out onto the terrace and towards a table, where three gin and tonics already glistened and tinkled in the evening sunlight.

Gianfranco came over and whispered to Caroline, who beamed and said,

'Splendid! Signora Anna, my cook, has agreed to stay on this evening to prepare a meal for us.' Vanessa tried to banish the image of some poor wizened old peasant in tattered shawl and apron being made to toil an extra three or four hours so that Domina could entertain. *"Agreed" Ha! And what if she hadn't?* 'Usually, I'll just make myself a sandwich in the evening,' Caroline explained. 'Signora Anna just hates it when I rummage through the refrigerator so I expect she'll be quite pleased.'

Maytham smiled broadly and Vanessa wondered why she'd never given the cooks who had prepared Mr. Mosley's meals a second thought.

'Now,' said Caroline, 'tell me what brings you all the way up here, Christopher.' Vanessa was all ears. How would Maytham explain their presence? He was, she believed an expert liar and was looking forward to a master-class in mendacity. She was disappointed.

As Maytham finished the story, Vanessa could not identify a single missing detail. Throughout it all, Caroline Gagliardo-Patricelli listened intently, interrupting only twice, the first time to express sympathy to Vanessa for her ordeal and the second to tell Maytham that he had done the right thing to have driven there on minor roads. Who was this woman whom Maytham trusted to this degree? More than "a cousin of some sort", that was for sure.

'And old Sir Edward knows nothing?' Caroline asked, as she stood and stepped into the conservatory.

'I'm certain of it. To the extent where I think he might even have been in danger had I told him. In fact, I don't think any of the embassy staff have a clue about any of this. The intelligence bods played their cards very closely.

'And who were these "Intelligence bods" as you call them?' she asked on her return, notebook and pen in hand.

'I knew them only by their first names, I'm afraid. The one with whom I had most dealings, was called Hermione. The other two were

Harry and Ron.' Vanessa and Caroline glanced at one another and Caroline said to her,

'Poor Christopher doesn't get out nearly so often as he should.'

'What?' said Maytham.

'Never mind, darling.' Caroline suppressed a smile.

'Oh. They were not their real names, were they?' Then, almost to himself, he said, 'I really don't like Intelligence, you know. They've always been a blooming sneaky lot but nowadays they seem… well, downright untrustworthy. No offence, Linny.' Caroline smiled, almost indulgently.

'Come along,' she said, 'it's starting to get cool and our supper will be ready.' She rose and then stopped, suddenly. 'Just one more thing…' she said.

'Yes?' Maytham asked.

'How did your "spooks" refer to themselves?'

'How do you mean?'

'I mean, did they describe themselves as "M.I.6", "British Intelligence" or what?'

'They always spoke of "S.I.S." – Secret Intelligence Service. Is it important?'

'I shouldn't have thought so,' said Caroline. 'Now; come: you must be famished.'

At supper, there was no mention of Rome, the Embassy or S.I.S. Instead, the conversation turned to mundane matters of family, friends and gossip. Vanessa learned that Caroline was indeed English, although her parents had both been diplomats living abroad for most of her childhood. She had gone to Roedean and from thence to Cambridge. Her familial relationship to Christopher was not made clear but her "Auntie Sam" (Maytham's mother) was a relative of her father's. From the stories they recounted, Vanessa did some sums and reckoned that she must have been Maytham's senior by some twenty-five years or so, making her what… mid fifties?

She was careful to include Vanessa in the conversation, of course.

'Oh, my. A sweet shop? How marvellous for you!'

'Yes. Yes, it was,' she said, remembering her father saying that if ever she felt the urge to help herself to any sweets from his shop, he would cut her fingers off with rusty scissors. She had believed him.

'And tell me, how on earth did you end up in Italy?' Vanessa told most of the sorry tale although not the bits that made her look foolish.

'A Personal Assistant? How glamorous!' Anyone else and she would have thought they were taking the piss.

After supper and despite coffee, Christopher Maytham dozed off in an armchair by the fire and as she studied his face, Vanessa began to believe that he might just be genuine.

'He's a sweetheart. Not too bright but good at his job, by all accounts.' It was Caroline. She was sitting at a desk in the enormous drawing room, surrounded by books and papers and had turned in her seat to speak to Vanessa. Removing her half moon glasses and allowing them to hang around her neck, she smiled.

'So how *was* Geoffrey?' she asked.

## The Walsingham

To most people in London, the large green and white building overlooking the Thames at Vauxhall is the M.I.5 building but to those who know it best, it is known as Vauxhall Cross. People could be forgiven for not knowing the official name of the place and Arthur had always found it amusing and apposite that most don't realise that it is, in fact, the M.I.6 building. Known variously by those who work inside as *The Birthday Cake* or *Legoland*, its bold and striking riverside façade seems at odds with its intended purpose as the home of British Intelligence.

But Arthur understood this perfectly. M.I.6 had come in from the cold a long time ago. It had since settled itself on the sofa with a nice cup of tea and had become known as S.I.S.: Secret Intelligence Service. Bloody stupid name. What sort of "Intelligence Service" would it be if it wasn't "Secret"? He was debating with himself the wisdom of his having failed to send yet another missive from Despatch down to the incinerator. Logic and training told him he was being stupid to hold onto it but curiosity told him he had little choice.

It was as convoluted a bit of work as he'd come across in a long while. Whereas the Beasley thing had been a triumph of brevity, this one appeared to have been written by Leo Tolstoy. The directions and timings were complex and very precise but it wasn't that which led him to hang onto it. It was that, at the bottom of the first page, in the opposite corner to what he now knew was the teletype code he'd spotted a second alphanumeric string. Then, at the top of the second page, another. It was unusual for despatch notices to run to two pages.

He guessed the codes were little more than page-break instructions but Mulberry might find them useful.

This thought brought to mind the conversation he'd had with Mulberry the day before. Not the one concerning work, but the far more important one concerning Mark Rothko. His first thought had been to get round to Tate Modern as soon as but was surprised to discover that on considering this, a nervous flutter had begun to tickle his stomach. The more he thought about it, the more nervous he became. What if it wasn't right? What if it was another awful disappointment. He wasn't sure that in his present state of mind, he could cope with it. No, perhaps better to wait until he was feeling a bit more settled. Yes; build up to it slowly. Perhaps a Pollock or two and a Barnet Newman; and only then, the main course.

This was becoming distracting and he couldn't afford distractions on this complicated job.

'Ah well, least said, soonest mended,' said Arthur.

'Sorry, old man?' Rupert Stainforth crumpled just enough of his Telegraph to allow him to peer over it. The pair were sitting in the oak-panelled splendour of the Walsingham Club off Piccadilly, a hideaway popular with those who liked hiding away.

'Oh, just musing; that's all,' said Arthur.

'Oh? What about?'

'Nothing really. It's just that…'

'Yes?'

Arthur was unwilling to share his current thoughts with Stainforth so he responded with the other thing that had preying on his mind for a couple of days.

'Stainforth, have you ever wondered what you're going to do when all this gets… you know: too much, as it were?'

'Eh?'

'I mean, we all have to pack it in at some point, don't we? Have you ever thought about what you'll do, when the time comes?'

Stainforth lowered the rest of his Telegraph and gazed out of the window over St. James's Park.

'Well, I'm a little *over* retirement age, as it happens, Shepherd. Two years, to be precise. I'm quite happy being a Postman though and frankly, the job's not over-taxing. So as long as they're prepared to pay me, I'm happy to turn up when needed and do what must be done. But I'd imagine that Cleansing gets a bit hairy at times. I should think you chaps have probably had enough by the time you're sixty.'

'Hmm,' Arthur said. 'No pressure to leave, then?'

'None at all. I have an interview every six months; do some sums; sleep on it for a day or two and so far, I've always decided it's worth staying on. But I dare say, there'll come a time and then… well, who knows? Probably Suffolk. By the sea. I have a sister lives in Felixstowe. You?'

'Only just beginning to think about it.' Stainforth seemed to ponder a moment then said,

'Hate to think what'll happen when our lot finally all retire.'

'What do you mean?'

'Well, we and to a large extent, the generation who followed us into the Service are pretty much up to the mark but I do worry about the next lot coming along.'

'Oh?'

'Yes. I mean the pool's a bit polluted now isn't it? Anyone looking around for Council Workers from the recent recruits to M.I.6 are going to have their work cut out finding the right sort. I mean, advertising in newspapers and on the internet! How can they hope to attract the right calibre of person? They're probably barely competent Intelligence Officers, never mind Council Workers. Still. Best be on your guard anyway, if you'll forgive me.'

'Oh?'

'Oh, yes. Very ambitious these days, young people, Shepherd. All a bit distasteful but there you are. Progress, I suppose.'

Arthur sighed. 'Yes, it's sad, isn't it? They think it's like working in the City. All bonuses and promotion.' He smiled at Stainforth, who didn't reciprocate.

'You operate in rather a more, shall we say *rarefied* atmosphere over at Lambeth, Shepherd. I'm afraid you may be, if you'll forgive me, a little... out of touch... with the way things tend to be done, nowadays. Brown-nosing works, now, you know.' Arthur looked aghast. 'Oh yes. It's a veritable shitocracy, these days. I mean if you or I had tried to ingratiate ourselves like these youngsters seem to do, we'd both probably have ended our careers like poor old Spooner.' Arthur winced.

The Reg Spooner episode was one of which practically all Council employees were aware and served as a salutary lesson for those with ideas above their station.

Stainforth leaned forwards a little more and Arthur cocked his head as his companion, (having glanced around the room) said, 'Some of the new bugs aren't even military, you know.' He gave Arthur no time to express the astonishment this revelation produced. 'Oh, no. I was talking to a chap just this morning who told me that his liaison officer had once been a Parliamentary Press Officer! Mind you, he'd been a naughty boy, apparently. So perhaps not to read too much into it – but there it is. To the dogs, old man. To. The. Fucking. Dogs. Another Cognac?'

Arthur nodded and Stainforth beckoned a waiter, who arrived with two fresh glasses, which he placed on the small table that sat between them. He was beautiful but Arthur seemed not to notice.

At the time of his own recruitment, he'd had no inkling of how the Secret Service actually functioned. Oh, he'd read the novels and seen the films and he'd even followed one or two of the more prurient newspaper stories but he could never have said that his knowledge was any greater than that of the Man on the Clapham Omnibus. He had known nothing of the Council before he studied the book he'd been given on the first day, even after four years of prior training.

The Council makes Black Ops look like the Co-op. It considers itself a cut above M.I.6 and with good reason.

To begin with, M.I.6 is now designated S.I.S. and its workings are a matter of record. Scrutinised by public bodies of every description, its leaders are all but household names, answerable to Parliamentary Select Committees, compilers of Reports and Royal Commissions. Some operatives have Facebook accounts, for God's sake. No self-respecting Council Worker – even someone like Stainforth, stationed in the Sorting Office on Floor K at Vauxhall Cross – would dream of doing such a thing.

'But surely, Stainforth, these sorts of fellows don't become Council Workers, do they?' Arthur asked.

'That's just my point. At the moment, one would hope not but eventually… It's only a matter of time; mark my words. Don't forget the *Two-Twenty Rule*.'

Arthur hadn't. In fact, it had popped into his thoughts several times since his chat with Mulberry the day before. The rule had been a feature of the Council since its creation. When Sir James Carlisle had come up with the idea, he had decided that the optimum number of agents in this elite branch of the Secret Service would be two hundred and twenty people: no more, no fewer. The *Two-Twenty Rule* had always been seen as a *limit* on membership; it had never occurred to Arthur that the number of agents might ever drop below that figure.

'You mean,' he said, 'that as people retire or drop off the twig, the number of suitable replacements may not be enough to keep to the *Two-Twenty Rule*?'

'That's exactly what I mean. And if there are not suitable candidates then all they'll be left with to fill the places will be the unsuitable ones.'

Arthur leaned back in his chair and cradled his cognac. He had warmed to Stainforth years before, after learning that he had faked his own death and taken up a permanent residency at the Walsingham just to get away from his wife. He was good sort, if a little stuffy and it was nice on occasions to chew the fat with someone who was on the same page as it were. And he'd been right as well: there were precious few around now who knew what it had been like in the old days. Which reminded him.

'You ever heard about teleprinters being used round the place, Stainforth?'

'Teleprinters? Bloody hell, you're talking stone-age now Shepherd. Bloody noisy, I remember. All disappeared now, though. Can't say I've seen one for… ooh, thirty, forty years. And as I recall, it was mostly boffins and secretaries that used 'em, wasn't it? Everyone had their own job to do in those days. Not like now. Most of my chaps do all their own typing. Bloody degrading, if you ask me.' He returned to his paper. Arthur looked over, as a strange sound emanated from Stainforth.

'You all right, Stainforth?' asked Arthur.

'What? Oh, yes, yes. It's just this photograph in the paper. You wouldn't appreciate it but she is a little cracker. Some feller chucked her out of a car in Rome wearing her undies.'

'Why was he wearing her undies?'

Stainforth smiled.

Feeble, Shepherd; feeble. Are you staying here, tonight?'

'Er, no. I have a job and then I think I'll toddle off home.'

'Anyone I know?'

'Shouldn't think so. Some Saudi prince who's been making noises about embarrassing us over nuclear weapons sales.'

'Well,' said Stainforth, smacking the creases out his Telegraph, 'give him one for me, eh?'

## The Al-Nimrah Hotel

His napkin delicately dabbing at his false moustache - greyer than the last one he'd used - Arthur pushed his still-half-full plate to one side, his lip curling perceptibly. Astonishingly, the Al-Nimrah Hotel, Knightsbridge (Arthur could scarcely believe it) boasted five stars.

'None of them are for the bloody cuisine, that's for sure,' he muttered.

Prince Muffarim had eaten in his suite and Arthur sincerely hoped that the Saudi's final meal had been rather more memorable than the one he himself had just half-eaten.

He looked at his watch. If the prince expected to get to the theatre in time, he'd have to get a wiggle on, that was for sure. Even a prince's limousine (whilst it might be entitled to park for a good hour and half outside his hotel) has to stop for traffic lights and there are a shitload along Knightsbridge, the Brompton Road and Piccadilly. Then it could easily take fifteen minutes to negotiate Shaftesbury Avenue. It was a good job that Arthur was going to kill him well before he got there.

The traffic, as it happened, formed an integral part of Arthur's plan. Once he'd offed the prince and his bodyguards, he'd simply abandon the car between C.C.T.V. cameras, in traffic with the hazards on. It would be at least half an hour before any plod dared to approach it and by then, Arthur would be well on his way back to Harrow Gardens. Or, (why hadn't he thought of this earlier?) he could do it outside the Ritz and then pop in for a bite of proper supper. Oh yes, that sounded like a plan.

'Driver!'

Arthur bit his lip. That supercilious twat of a desk-clerk had been treating him like shit all evening. Arthur hated doing things in disguise and to be fair, he seldom had to but it still got up his nose, and when he was disguised as someone of even lower social status than a hotel desk-clerk, it really rankled. Nevertheless, he stood up, put on his cap and walked over to the desk.

'His Highness' aide is on his way down, now.'

'His what?'

'His aide; his assistant.'

Arthur was concerned at how much he felt affronted. For a start, he was disguised as a driver so why on earth would he expect to be treated otherwise? But the fact was that he felt affronted on behalf of all drivers, real or imagined, everywhere. And the very fact that the desk-clerk felt the need to announce the imminent arrival of someone who was merely employed by the person for whom he had been waiting, pissed him off, mightily. Nevertheless:

'Good-oh,' he said, cheerfully.

'I do hope he won't be late,' said the desk-clerk. Arthur affected a puzzled frown.

'Lift a bit slow, is it?' he asked.

The desk-clerk sneered as only a desk-clerk can.

'Of course,' he said with exaggerated patience, 'I was referring to His Highness' arrival at the theatre.'

'Oh, I think he is going to be late. In fact, I'm fairly certain of it.' Arthur hated it when he couldn't boast about a pun.

'I shall telephone the theatre.'

He fucking will, as well, thought Arthur. He pictured the theatre manager pondering his dilemma. Should he delay the start and risk upsetting the punters who'd been arsed to get there on time or let the show begin without the prince who, Arthur was aware, had made a big show of promising The Shaftesbury Theatre a donation amounting to three years' funding? In these straitened times it was never a wise move to piss off a potentate. He almost felt sorry for the theatre manager. Whatever he decided to do, it was going to be one of the worst evenings of his life.

'Driver!'

This time, the voice came from the direction of the elevator. The prince's aide beckoned Arthur over.

'I am authorised to give you this when you return, provided his Highness arrives on time.' The aide held out a little flap of banknotes. 'Two hundred pounds.'

Arthur really should have just nodded his assent. Instead, he said,

'It wouldn't matter if it was two thousand. There's nothing I can do about traffic.'

'His Highness dislikes being late.'

'He should get his finger out then, shouldn't he? Tell you what; keep the two hundred and buy him an alarm clock, eh?' Arthur closed the aide's hand around the little fold of notes. The aide trembled a little.

The second elevator binged and three figures from central casting emerged: Prince Muffarim and his two bodyguards. Clearly realising that it was too late to find another driver, the aide addressed Arthur through gritted teeth.

'This will be the last time you drive His Highness,' he hissed. A forefinger waggled beneath Arthur's new moustache. 'In fact, I shall see to it that you do no more driving for this or any hotel in London ever again.'

Right, that was it.

'I need the toilet,' said Arthur.

'What?'

'I. Need. The. Toilet.'

'You...? But... His Highness.' The aide gestured towards the exit where the doorman was already bowing and scraping as he held the door open. The prince wafted outside, the meat in a bodyguard sandwich. Arthur tossed the keys to the aide who stared at them in horror.

'Shan't be a mo',' he said and disappeared into the Gents. It was only whilst he was in mid pee, that he realised what hubris might have done.

'Bollocks!' said Arthur, as he tried to hurry. 'Bollocks!' The aide had the keys and it was likely that at least one of the guards could drive. Mind you, he'd read somewhere that Saudi driving tests were a bit of a joke and was hoping that it would be unlikely that one would prepare you for Central London in the rush hour. But could he be sure?

'Bollocks!' said Arthur once again, shaking furiously. His zip barely missed his scrotum as he yanked it shut and although it pained him beyond measure, he ran out of the toilet and into the ante-room corridor without washing his hands.

## Knightsbridge

For anyone close enough to experience, yet not be killed by an explosion, the chief sensation is one of blinding light. It sears the retina and for some time afterwards, the world is viewed as if through bird shit on a greasy window. The light is followed (physics being what it is) by heat, pushed ahead of the blast-wave. The wave itself is what normally kills you, the pressure of it compressing, collapsing and tearing the vital organs, before dismembering you. If you can survive that then all you need worry about is being deafened and lacerated by debris.

In a five star hotel, you'd expect the door leading to the lavatories to be pretty solid and Arthur was grateful that the prince had chosen the Al-Nimrah over say, a Motorlodge.

He'd endured a number of explosions in the course of his career, but this one was a right bastard. Fortunately, apart from the eight-inch square, wire-reinforced glazing panel (which had lit up nanoseconds before the door flew inwards), the door was intact. He crawled from beneath it and acknowledged his new status as deaf and partially blind, almost immediately. Both disabilities would of course, be temporary but they might hinder his escape. He knew that he would have to try to find an exit other than through the remains of the foyer.

The restaurant where he'd just half-eaten his nasty meal was devastated and he was doubtful that he would even find the kitchen door, let alone be able to clear the debris from in front of it. The flames had the stairs firmly in their grip so there was only one chance left. His knees and his forearms had taken a good deal of the force of the door as its hinges succumbed so he was forced to limp to the inner sanctum of the Gents' toilet. Here, he was able to see that his uniform was still intact, apart from small holes in each knee, a ripped pocket and a torn seam on one sleeve. The inside shouldn't be too bad. His hat had skittered away down the corridor so it was relatively unscathed.

He supported himself on a basin and chanced a look in the mirror. Blink. He peered hard through the grey mist, as black blotches rose and sank before his eyes. Blink. He could make out only a shadow of his face. Blink. Blink. As far as he could see (which wasn't very) he looked all right and then...Bugger! No false moustache. A sudden thought struck him and his hand flew to his torn pocket. Shit! The despatch note had gone.

The Met are, by and large, lazy bastards and he could have reasonably hoped that the shooting of a Saudi might not have engaged their attention to any great degree. They would have passed it straight to Special Branch and made a bit of a show of helping track down the driver but in all probability, no-one would have really given a toss. Now after this little lot, the Counter Terrorism Command would be all over it. And they don't fuck about. There could be no loose ends – particularly not carefully-trimmed and surprisingly expensive polyester ones and *definitely not* bits of paper detailing with anal exactitude how to go about assassinating a Saudi prince.

Arthur set about arguing with himself. With luck, he reasoned, the fire would see the moustache turned into a nasty blob of charred goo. But without luck, C.T.C. would find it and every surveillance tape within a fifteen-mile radius would be gone over like a week-old kipper until the bloke who'd entered with it on his face was traced back to where he came from – in this case, the lock-up behind The Cut where he'd picked up the car. Even so, he might manage to cope with that but if the despatch was found, he would find himself afloat in such a sea of sewage that death would come as a kindness. He girded himself, took a breath and opened the door of his lavatorial sanctuary.

Out in the corridor, smoke tinged with the lurid orange of the fire that propelled it, was now billowing through the shattered opening to the foyer. Arthur lay down and pressed the side of his face flat on the carpet and sighted along the corridor. At the point of focus, there was just a grey shadow but some peripheral vision was returning. Suppressing the almost overwhelming desire to hurry, he methodically scanned every inch of ground before him, allowing his brain to concentrate only on the very edge of his vision. Though dusty, the dark blue carpet was undamaged and even with the smoke and the darkness and the fact that he was pretty much blind, Arthur had to try. All the oxygen in his first breath was now dissolved in his blood stream. There was no help for it but to draw in a lungful of the hot, carbon-rich stuff that now surrounded him. He wouldn't be able to do that again without doing himself some lasting damage.

And then, in the ring of light, which for the time being served as Arthur's field of vision, he fancied he could detect a slight embossing of the dust; a little extra shadow on the skirting board. A shape where none should have been. He edged forwards, reached out his arm and gently stroked the anomaly with his fingertips. His hand closed around the moustache. OK, minor problem solved; but the chances of finding a couple of folded A4 sheets in this lot, were slim.

Entering the toilet once more, Arthur lay against the door, heaving against the counter-thrust of the hydraulic door-easer, a superb piece of British engineering, which was currently enabling thick smoke to pour into his refuge. He pushed against it with all his might. He could feel the hot draught blasting through the slowly-narrowing gap, bringing all manner of charred detritus along with it. One particularly substantial bit caught his eye and, as the door finally succumbed, Arthur let out a shout along with the carbon-dioxide, which had been sustaining him for several seconds. He dived on the floor – thank God it was five-star toilet – and sucked in surprisingly fresh air. He opened his eyes and, as he had expected, in front of his face he saw the blackened despatch, both sheets still folded together.

He thanked the God of Assassins and clutched the dry, crackling sheets to his chest before stuffing them inside his shirt.

With the door now closed and the window open, the smoke began to dissipate. There was time - just. He removed his suit and turned it inside-out. This gave him a chance to wash his hands and face and dab at his bloody knees with a wet towel. Soon, his dark-grey driver's uniform transformed into a dark–blue jacket and light-grey trousers. The knees of the trousers were torn and bloodstained but he guessed there would be worse sartorial tragedies for most of the people in the vicinity of the Al-Nimrah so he wasn't over-concerned. Taking the shiny plastic brim off the hat and sticking it in his pocket, he turned what remained into a very passable flat cap. Right: time to get out and away to Mrs. Jempson's on the hurry-up.

He combed his hair and winced as his plastic comb encountered a solid obstruction. Gingerly, he removed the shard of glass from his skull. There was blood so Arthur balled up some toilet paper, pressed the bundle against his head and replaced his cap. Carefully checking his appearance and hoping he didn't look so damaged that some kind soul might try to thrust him in the back of an ambulance, he decided it was time to leave.

He had climbed through many a toilet window in his youth but seldom in quite so much discomfort. The wire mesh had taken some shifting and so, even as he hoisted himself onto the radiator, he saw the paint on the inside of the toilet door blacken and blister. He should have lowered himself but on a point of principle and as a two-fingered salute to sharp-faced "human resources" women, he opted to jump from the ledge. He grimaced as he hit the ground and with not a little difficulty, straightened himself up, taking in his surroundings.

Alleyway. Excellent.

Arthur limped slowly towards Knightsbridge.

Ahead of him, as if on a screen edged by brickwork, figures ran, cars didn't and the noise of sirens and screams increased as he approached. A copper rushed past and glanced down the alleyway. Each man caught the other's gaze. Arthur tensed for a split second but the policeman hadn't even broken stride. He was off-screen in an instant.

Emerging from the alleyway, Arthur felt the shards of blasted brickwork and the practically powdered glass grinding beneath his feet. Dust and smoke scraped his windpipe and he put his handkerchief over his face. He slalomed between the stationary cars, and was soon standing on the south side of the road. He headed west as far as he could go. Many of the buildings around the Al-Nimrah were standing but he could clearly see fading daylight through some and in the innards of most, fires blazed. He could not get close to the front of the hotel since, even though most people had got away as quickly as possible, some remained, doing what they could for the victims.

From what he could see, it was much as he'd expected. Where he'd left the car was... nothing, actually. All right, so there was a huge indentation in the tarmac but of the limo itself, there was no sign amidst the tangle of metal that nad once been the vehicles parked on either side of it. There was nothing he could see that might have been body parts but he was in no doubt that anyone who had been within twenty metres, inside or out would be dead and the enormous blast radius would certainly have caused many and massive collateral injuries.

Arthur had no doubt that this was a crude terrorist bomb but the size of the explosion was far greater than a single target warranted. This had been designed to kill as many innocent bystanders as possible. He had never been a mass murderer and the thought of it was as distasteful to him as pies at half-time would be to a master chef. It was… disgusting. As he left the scene, Arthur found himself musing once more and once more, it irked him. A thought kept grabbing his elbow, exhorting him to look more closely but he determinedly thrust it away. It was some crap about good luck, fate and that sort of bollocks. No time for introspection; time for Oxfam.

## Gloucester Rd.

'Ooh dear, Mr Shepherd. Was that one of yours?'

'No, it bloody well wasn't!' Arthur instantly regretted being short with Mrs. Jempson, who was a good sort and had worked for the Council for a very considerable amount of time. She looked at Arthur exactly in the way he deserved and he looked at the floor.

He hadn't been due to drop off his chauffeur's uniform until Wednesday morning but had decided, in the circumstances, to do it immediately. The Oxfam, of course, was closed at that time of the evening and he'd been extremely grateful when, in response to his hammering, Mrs J. had appeared in the frosted glass in the side door and even more so when she had led him through to the shop itself. Even here, off the main drag and a quarter of a mile away, there was the noise of dozens, perhaps scores of sirens negotiating the gridlocked streets around the Al-Nimrah and yet the silence hung heavily in the little shop.

'I'm sorry, Mrs J. That was uncalled for. I've had a bit of a rotten time of it so far this evening. I would have phoned ahead but I'm afraid my phone battery is flat as a witch's tit. That's what you get for leaving it switched on, I suppose. I need a change of clothes.'

'Yes, you do. I'm surprised at you wandering about in that state.'

'I didn't think I looked too bad in the circumstances,' said Arthur, his professional pride singed, along with his eyebrows. 'You should've seen me before I cleaned myself up. D'you know? It blew my flaming moustache off!' Arthur opened his hand to show her.

'Well, I think you probably got away with it,' she conceded. 'Bit of a mess but I doubt anyone would have noticed. Still, can't be too careful.

Sounded from here, like one for the C.T.C. and they don't hang about. Here, try these on.' She handed Arthur a suit and a shirt. He took them, and made for the changing room. 'I take it you avoided the C.C.T.V.?'

'Absolutely,' he said, over his shoulder, whilst flicking back the rough red curtain, which was to be all that stood between Mrs. Jempson and his Y-fronts.

The modesty screen was worn, moth-eaten and paper-thin, yet for some reason, Mrs. Jempson raised her voice when she spoke.

'So if not you; who?'

'I have no idea,' Arthur called out. 'But they can't have just been after the prince. The thing took out half of Knightsbridge.'

'A prince eh? I expect that pleased the anarchist in you.'

Arthur's head appeared, cradled by swag of curtain, which he grasped tightly to his neck.

'There is no "anarchist" in me,' he said.

'Chance would be a fine thing eh?' she muttered, folding a yellow acrylic jumper and laying it neatly on a shelf.

'What?'

'Nothing. How's the suit?'

'Give me a minute, for goodness' sake! My back's giving me absolute gip!' Mrs Jempson busied herself with tidying and muttered something about the feebleness of the male gender, which Arthur didn't quite catch. Eventually, he stepped out of the cubicle. Mrs. Jempson looked him up and down for a moment, made a face, then said,

'Mmm... it looked better on the hanger, frankly. But never mind; any old port in a storm, eh?'

'You're too kind, Mrs. J. How much?'

'Fifteen for the suit, seven for the shirt and you can have this for 50p.' She tossed him a light blue tie. Arthur returned to the cubicle and fished out the crumpled chauffeur's uniform. He began to fold it... badly. Mrs. Jempson tutted and whisked it away from him.

'You know,' she said, 'for a homosexual gentleman, you really are not much of a one for clothes are you?' Arthur tried to look affronted.

'I shall treat that piece of blatant homophobic stereotyping with the contempt it deserves. Just because a fellow veers towards the distaff side, it's no guarantee that he will have a way with fabrics and the like, Mrs. J.'

'No, indeed Mr, Shepherd.' She rang up the ancient till and the drawer crashed open. 'Twenty-two pounds and fifty-pence, if you'd be so kind.' Arthur stroked a twenty and a ten from his wallet and handed them over.

'We'll call it thirty, shall we?' he said and pointing at the now neatly-folded uniform, asked, 'You'd better give me that. If the C.T.C find it here, there could be trouble.'

'What do you take me for, Mr. Shepherd? I've been at this game a good long time and if and when they turn up, this will be a freshly dry-cleaned and invisibly-mended doorman's suit complete with linen lining. We'll get eighteen quid for it, easy.' Arthur smiled and shook his head.

'Forgive me, Mrs. Jempson, for underestimating you,' he said.

'You're not the first, don't worry. That's how I've stayed alive so long. Right, will that be all, sir?'

'Yes, thank you Mrs Jempson.'

'Sure I can't interest you in a nice overcoat? A book, perhaps? Ooh, we've just had a bunch of CDs in this morning.'

'Er, no thanks,' said Arthur, eyeing the pile of grubby jewel cases.

'Are you sure? Classical: not your usual rubbish.' Arthur sighed and took the first one off the pile.'

'In what universe, Mrs. Jempson, is James Last considered a) "classical" and b) "not your usual rubbish"?'

'I never said I was an expert, Mr. Shepherd.' Arthur smiled and was about to toss the CD back where it had come from, when his eye fell on the second in the pile. He picked it off.

'This looks a bit more promising,' he said. It was a compilation of modern music. A glance at the back told him there were two with which he was unfamiliar. 'How much for this, Mrs. J?'

'Eight pounds.'

'Bloody hell! I was only being civil by even looking through the pile! I could probably get it new for that.'

'You do that, then. Take food from the mouths of the needy. I'm sure they'll be very happy you got a better deal elsewhere.'

'Bloody hell,' he said again, fishing in his pocket. 'I don't know,' he muttered, 'Fellow gets blown up for his country and all he gets is shafted by a charity shop.' He gathered together the necessary and handed it over. Mrs Jempson brightened.

'Pleasure doing business with you. Right. The back way, just to be on the safe side and I'd go straight back to Lambeth now, if I were you. They're bound to be worried about you.' She and Arthur looked at each other for a full five seconds before both of them began to bellow with laughter.

'You are, Mrs. Jempson, what we used to call "a card".'

## Linny

It took Vanessa several seconds to realise what Caroline was asking. She thought about making a run for it but decided in short order that it wasn't going to happen. For a start, she hadn't a clue where she was but there was also something about Caroline that made her think it would be a bad idea; a really bad idea.

'Who are you?' she asked. Caroline pretended to frown and said,

'Why, I practically told you my life story over dinner.'

'All right then; what are you?'

'A much better question. What are you?'

'I told you. I'm...' Vanessa was going to have to say it. She'd worked so hard to convince herself that it wasn't true but it was, wasn't it? 'I'm... nobody,' she said.

'Well, I've never known a better judge of character than Geoffrey Wittersham. He wouldn't have trusted you lightly.'

'He didn't trust me. He just used me to get away from whoever was after him.'

'Oh, Geoffrey would have managed perfectly well without you. If he let you go, he had a good reason. Also, he appears to have spoken to you at length and believe me, he is not one for small-talk.'

Vanessa realised she was feeling faint. Caroline obviously noticed because she stood up and walked to the sideboard. She poured golden liquid into two glasses, sodaed both and walked back towards the sofa, one glass held out before her.

'Here,' she said quietly. Vanessa took the glass from her, trying not shake. It wasn't any use.

'I wonder,' Caroline continued, her eyes narrowed, head moving gently from side to side. Her vowels remained liquid and her consonants razor sharp but her voice was low and mellifluous; gentle, soothing. In perfect contrast to the words she was saying.

'How much can I tell you, Vanessa Aldridge, without having to kill you afterwards? I mean, I'd rather not kill you, of course. Geoffrey wanted you alive so I suppose I ought to respect that.'

Vanessa's head was spinning. She feared she might throw up. Caroline sat on the sofa beside her.

'Tell me, apart from the gun, did Geoffrey give you anything yesterday morning? And Vanessa? Do, I beg, think very, very carefully before you answer.'

Vanessa was terrified. All that bravado had been easy with Maytham but it wasn't going to work on this woman. She knew that she really was staring death in the face. When she heard her own voice, she barely recognised it.

'No, I swear to you. All he did was take stuff from me.'

'Apart from your telephone?'

'What?'

'Your telephone.'

'My mobile?'

'Yes, your... "mobile". May I see it, please?' Without taking her eyes off Caroline, Vanessa leaned down and took up her bag.

'Gucci,' said Caroline, approvingly. 'And genuine. You weren't doing too shabbily were you?'

'No,' she replied but forbore to add that had it not been for Geoffrey bloody Wittersham, she still would be. She reached into the bag and removed the phone. 'Hang on,' she said handing it over, 'you'll need this.' She gave Caroline the blister pack containing the new battery.

More deftly than she'd ever seen it done before, Vanessa watched Caroline remove the battery from its packaging and set it into place. She switched the phone on and it binged into life.

'Will I be needing a password?' Vanessa mumbled something in reply. Caroline angled her head.

'Forgive me, I'm afraid I didn't catch that,' she said.

'Puddleduck' said Vanessa. 'It was a... nickname I had... for someone.'

'As it sounds?' asked Caroline with a sigh.

'Yes.'

Vanessa saw Caroline make a couple of passes over the screen and then smile, broadly and genuinely.

'Looks like we're not going to need it,' she said.

'Eh?'

'I don't believe this is your SIM card.' She turned the phone around so that Vanessa could see the screen. Instead of her background photograph of Lady Gaga, there was... some sort of pattern. No, not a pattern. More like a couple of bands of brown or grey with sort of a black splodge.

'What are you playing at, Geoffrey,' Caroline said, looking at the handset once more. She ignored Vanessa for the next few minutes whilst she explored the phone. There were no facial expressions to give anything away. Finally, she walked over to the desk and flipped open a laptop. She turned to Vanessa once more and asked,

'And you are certain he said nothing nor gave you anything else?'

'I'm not certain of anything any more,' she said.

There was a murmur from Maytham and both women looked over to see him open his eyes.

'Christopher,' said Caroline, expansively, 'we thought you were out for the count, didn't we, Vanessa?'

'Yes,' Vanessa managed, feebly. Not for the first time, she wondered if he was for real.

'I'm sorry, Linny,' muttered Maytham as he heaved himself upright, 'you must think I'm...'

'Not a bit of it, darling,' said Caroline, rising to her feet and pulling the cord that hung by the mantelpiece. 'You must be utterly done in. You're welcome to doze as long as you wish but should you prefer to turn in, Gianfranco will have already prepared your room. You'll find everything you need there. We won't be terribly long ourselves, I shouldn't think.' She smiled warmly at Vanessa, who felt her own mouth give a weak upward turn.

Maytham stood up and buttoned his jacket.

'I think,' he said, his speech a little slurred, 'I'd better turn in for the night. Caroline, I apologise.'

'Nonsense.'

He favoured each of them with a slight bow as Gianfranco came and stood by him. He smiled and turned to leave.

'Christopher...' It had occurred to Vanessa to try to get him into her conversation with Caroline but she suddenly thought better of it. He turned to face her. 'Thank you. For everything,' she said. He smiled, turned and followed Gianfranco out of the drawing room.

Vanessa stood, turned to Caroline and began a sentence.

'Actually, I think I ought to be...'

'Do sit down, Vanessa. Won't you? It wasn't a request. Vanessa lowered herself onto the sofa once more. 'Geoffrey has used your telephone to send me a little message. Isn't that nice?'

'But how could he...?'

'He is a very resourceful chap, Vanessa. Oh, it's terribly unsafe to put anything important onto these things,' she said. 'But I think we have enough here to move us a little further along.

'Will there be anything else, Signora?' It was Gianfranco, who had re-entered the drawing room unnoticed.

'I think that should be all until the morning, thank you. I shall show Ms. Aldridge to her room. You can go up yourself anytime.' Gianfranco bowed courteously and withdrew and Caroline returned to Vanessa once more.

'Now, Vanessa,' she said, 'I should like you to try very hard indeed to remember everything; and I mean everything that Geoffrey Wittersham said to you yesterday morning.'

## Harrow Gardens

There wasn't, of course, a taxi to be had. The C.T.C. had gone into full terrorism mode and had closed the tube stations. Within half an hour of the blast, the buses had all been ordered back to depots and hundreds of thousands of Londoners were wending their way towards the outskirts of the metropolis and the edge of the cordon sanitaire, where they hoped that friends and loved ones might be able to pick them up and drive them home. Arthur had decided, rather guiltily, to ignore Mrs. Jempson's doubtless sage advice and instead go home for a little lie down. Fortunately, his flat was only about a mile and a half away.

Although he may have had the appearance of a slightly bemused and balding estate agent, physically, few men of his age were more fit. He often affected a slightly shambling gait for business purposes but he thought, in the circumstances, he might pick up the pace a little. However, it was not long before he began to notice that the pains in his back and side were causing him to catch his breath; his left leg and his wrist, where the heavy oak door had smashed into him were beginning to bruise; and his limp was becoming harder to disguise. Still, the door had almost certainly saved his life so there was little resentment on his part.

By the time he arrived at Harrow Gardens, it was quite dark so even here, blue lights could be seen striking distant buildings and tinting the low grey cloud that had descended over the capital. He let himself in and noticed that the air tasted stale and there was a definite, almost damp chill about the place. His position carried a high salary and the grace and favour was all part of the deal. In fact, Bloomsbury was so full of Secret Service agents, that some mornings the bus resembled a works outing.

Arthur went into the sitting room and switched on the gas fire. He winced over to the sideboard and obtained for himself a large tumbler of Talisker 12 year old single malt, which he brought back to the heavy, brown leather armchair by the fire. He sat down with a grunt and a grimace, took a long drink and placed the glass on the chair arm. Arthur Shepherd folded his hands in his lap and bathed in the glow, smell, pop and hiss of his twenty-eight-year old Belling gas fire, he fell asleep.

## Part 3 WEDNESDAY

Next morning, the pain was thunderous. For a full ten minutes, Arthur moved as though he were wearing spiked shoes (with the spikes on the inside) and barbed wire underpants (which, curiously, he once did in Tangiers). He was certain there was no serious damage but he'd be slow for a day or two. John Humphrys explained to him that a massive car-bomb had gone off in Knightsbridge the previous evening and so far, there were eighteen confirmed dead with many more injured. It appeared that the target was Prince Muffarim ibn Abdallah, a prominent member of the Saudi Government with links to a number of moderate organisations, themselves connected to Israeli and U.S. counter-terrorism services. There was some speculation that his bodyguards may have been responsible. London was pretty much inaccessible by road from the west but tubes were again running.

Arthur realised that he'd been listening to "Gary with today's sport" for several seconds before his thoughts caught up and when they did, the first one was, *why the boiling fuck did no-one tell me that this was on the cards?* Closely followed by, *... and who will I have to kill to find out?*

Of course, he'd heard about this sort of thing happening before. Crossed wires, the odd message missed. There had even been an occasion when two Cleaners turned up for the same job at the same time. Unfortunately for one of them, the other had been Geoffrey Wittersham. There'd been bit of a to-do about that, Arthur remembered and procedures had been, as they say, tightened up.

After what Stainforth had told him about the quality of new recruits, he believed the likelihood of more of these little problems occurring could only increase. Arthur, of course, had no idea who had ordered the Muffarim job but found it hard to believe that it could have been someone so inexperienced as not to know that the prince was being targeted by terrorists. But these days it seemed, one never could tell.

'Hello?' Arthur winced as the heavy Bakelite receiver contacted the swelling inside his ear.

'Ah, glad I caught you in, Shepherd. I take it you'll be along to Vauxhall Cross some time today?'

Arthur said nothing.

'Only we have one or two things to chat about. I'm going to have a Parliamentary Under-Secretary of State with me. As far as he knows, you were just one of our bods on surveillance. Wants to pick your brains. All right?'

Sir Auberon would have known only too well that it was far from all right. In the first place, he would have known that Arthur would be wondering (and planning to ask about in a robust manner) who told a

Parliamentary Under-Secretary of State that he had been there and in the second place, he had just been blown up and was likely to be a little tetchy. Wisely, Sir Auberon gave Arthur no time to respond.

'He'll be arriving around twelve. See you then.'

Arthur listened to the purr for a second or two then replaced the receiver with a sigh. He would have to report in, there was no getting away from it. It was all a bit of a complicated and not atypical situation for a Council employee to find himself in but it was bloody irritating.

Although he had no power over Arthur Shepherd, Nightingale could ask Arthur Henley to do pretty much anything he liked. Thankfully, from Arthur's perspective, a call from the Council trumped any hand that M.I.6 proper might have wanted to play but his day-to-day job as Arthur Henley was carried out at the behest of Sir Auberon Nightingale.

Hang on... Parliamentary Under-Secretary of State for what? Ah well, it didn't matter. They were all much of a muchness but it would have been nice to have had a name.

## Amazas and the Foothills

'This one is yours,' Caroline said, as she heaved the saddle across the back of the Haflinger. 'She's called Abri. She'll accept English and American aids.' She placed a bridle in Vanessa's hand and walked away, leaving her looking at the tangle of leather and shiny steel.

*She's trying to make me look foolish*, Vanessa thought. *Well screw her.* The little horse stood quietly as Vanessa fitted the bridle. The curb bit, always tricky, was accepted with barely a toss of the head. Within three minutes, the saddle was secure and Vanessa was adjusting the stirrups when she became aware of Caroline standing beside her.

'Gianfranco will do that for you once you're up,' she said.

'Thank you but I prefer to do it myself.'

'As you wish.' Caroline walked over to her own horse and Gianfranco crouched down, presenting his interlocked hands to receive Caroline's boot. She touched his shoulder and as he stood upright, she whispered to him. Vanessa saw him glance over in her direction and their eyes met for a fraction of a second before he turned and nodded to his mistress. Caroline swung herself easily into the saddle and Gianfranco looked up at her, shielding his eyes with his hand.

Vanessa was determined to do this. The horse was small enough but somehow, she couldn't find the strength to hoist herself onto its back. She felt a strong hand close around her booted calf and another around her knee. As Gianfranco gently bent her leg, Vanessa applied a very little pressure and was able to swing her right leg across Abri's back.

'Thank you,' she said. Gianfranco didn't even look at her but began to loosen the stirrups.

'You will need more length in the straps than may be normal for you. Please. A moment,' he said, in English.

Vanessa could see that the stirrups were far too high. She felt stupid for not checking and surrendered to Gianfranco. For good measure, the servant gave a tug on the girth straps and notched them two holes further in. He then released one of Abri's ears from beneath the crownpiece, patted her cheek and squinting against the bright, early morning sun, he smiled at Vanessa. She returned it and said, 'Thank you,' once again.

Gianfranco moved across the yard to where Christopher Maytham was sitting atop his own sturdy little Haflinger. He raised his hand in salute as he caught Vanessa's eye. Gianfranco turned his own mount and placed his foot in the stirrup. As he did so, Vanessa could clearly see the stock of a rifle, jutting forward from a saddle-holster.

She had never heard of Amazas before this morning and why would she have? A half-dozen miles to the north-west, the peaks of the French Alps glistened in the golden sunlight, though the slopes remained in deep shade. There were, she knew, several miles of rough terrain before the climb would begin and her earlier anxieties began to surface once more.

It had been five-thirty in the morning, when Gianfranco had knocked on her door to waken her. Feeling astonishingly and unwarrantedly refreshed, she had opened the door to find him dressed in a thick cotton shirt over which was stretched a pair of braces, these in turn attached to short breeches, buttoned below the knee. He had handed Vanessa some clothes, told her to bundle her own together and had said that she was expected in the kitchen in fifteen minutes.

Even before she had showered and dressed, Vanessa had had an inkling of what might be on Caroline's mind and had hoped that she was just being fanciful. But as she'd stood outside the kitchen, the air thick with its promise of coffee and pastry, she had counted four pairs of leather riding boots and had known that she wasn't.

'Hang on. Hang on,' she'd said to Christopher. 'Are you serious? We're going to ride across the Alps?' It was Caroline who answered her.

'Vanessa, you are in tremendous danger. These people want you and they will do their damndest to get you. Either they will kill you to stop you passing on any information they think you possess or they will take you, torture you until you tell them what they want to know and then they will kill you. This way, we have a chance of getting you back to London in one piece.'

'But I don't know anything! He never told me a thing. I thought I explained all that last night!'

'And most helpful it was, Vanessa. But for now, you will do as I instruct.'

'But won't those bastards from British Intelligence work it out sooner or later, anyway?'

'Yes,' Maytham had told her. 'But as long as it's later, we should be fine. Look, there'll be no sightings at any of the border crossings, ferries or airports and they'll believe we're still in Italy for at least a couple of days, if not more. They might not even be aware that you don't have your passport so it could be even longer. I would estimate that we can be in Paris within two days, three at the most. I can arrange a passport for you there and we can be on the train to London on Saturday morning.'

'And that's a worst-case scenario,' Caroline said. 'If I can swing it, we may be able to get there even sooner than that. But you have to trust us.'

And that was the point, wasn't it? At the back of Vanessa's mind was a very dark patch that had been making things difficult to work out. She was certain it was anxiety and she didn't want to scrub away at it in case it ended up being a slightly lighter patch of pure, blind panic. So she'd decided to go along with the mad scheme.

'Right!' Caroline called out. 'Is everyone set?' Maytham tapped his riding hat with his crop and Vanessa shortened her reins and nodded. Caroline, in turn, nodded towards Gianfranco who then mounted his own horse. 'If we make good time, I shall ride with you as far as Pont Sacre and then I'm afraid I must return; however, Gianfranco knows the way. He'll take good care of you. Right. Line ahead; Vanessa behind me and Gianfranco will bring up the rear.'

Slowly, the horses threaded their way through the deeply morning-shadowed village streets, their shoes setting the cobbles ringing, echoing off pink and white stucco walls. The village of Amazas was waking. Already, the sound of stiff bristles on stone was hissing around the square as they rode through it and the smell of coffee drifted and tantalised. A first-floor window opened a few metres in front of Vanessa. As she passed, an old woman appeared. She smiled as the party rode by and "*ciaos*" were exchanged. Vanessa turned in her saddle to see the old woman lift a small boy in pyjamas up to view the spectacle. She saw Gianfranco smile and give a little wave at the boy, who flapped his own hand in vigorous reply. Vanessa had always wanted a life in the fast lane but today, on this bright morning, she envied the ordinary little two-stroke lives that puttered along around her.

The houses began to thin and before long, the village was behind them. Ahead, the southern slopes of the Western Alps lined up like solid, gigantic waves in front of them. Caroline held up her left hand and wheeled her horse in that direction.

'Watch your legs!' She called out. As Vanessa followed through a narrow gap in the low stone wall, she felt her boots scrape against the posts that stood on either side. Abri stumbled a little and Vanessa tensed.

'Just let her find her own way, Vanessa,' Maytham called over to her.

The track was little more than a scrape in the mud and in places, a mere darkening of the green scrub. Vanessa tried to follow it with her eyes but lost sight of it a couple of hundred metres ahead, as it rounded one of the immense granite boulders that were strewn over the valley floor. Within minutes, Vanessa realised that she was leaning forwards and became aware that the track was becoming steeper.

'You must stand in the saddle and put your weight over the forelegs,' Caroline called down to her. As she rounded a tight bend, she could see, to her right and some three or four metres below, Maytham and Gianfranco, high in the saddle, urging their mounts forwards.

'Lean over her neck!' Maytham called to her. Vanessa had never liked taking advice. The last couple of days had brought home very forcefully the fact that perhaps she might need to do so once in a while but she was beginning to tire of being told how to ride.

'I have done this before, you know!' she called back. 'I do know what I'm doing.' She saw Maytham glance at Gianfranco, who raised an eyebrow. Turning forwards once more, she saw Caroline looking intently at her. After a long moment, the older woman smiled and turned to face the hill. She tugged at the back of her cap and Vanessa saw a thin piece of white fabric drift out to cover the back of her neck. Vanessa realised that beneath her own riding helmet, she was beginning to sweat. She unclipped it and pulled it off, shaking out her hair.

'Put it back!' It was Gianfranco. 'It is very dangerous to remove the hat.' Vanessa did as she was told but not before removing her jumper and tying it around her waist. The warmth of the sun on her back was mitigated by a gentle breeze and as Vanessa sucked on the water bottle that hung over her saddle, she actually began to enjoy the experience. Casting a glance behind once more, she was able to see the roofs of Amazas. Although she knew the village must be at least a kilometre behind them and many metres below, she could clearly hear voices. The sounds of hammering, of motor scooters and the crackle of an idling chainsaw drifted up the valley. Ordinary lives. And here she was; riding over the Alps on horseback to avoid passport controls between two major European countries. Vanessa breathed deeply and tried to convince herself that everyone had her best interests in mind. That she didn't succeed and yet continued to follow Caroline Gagliardo-Patricelli up a mountain, was a credit to her capacity for self-deception.

## The Ministry of Truth

It was a small room filled mostly with table but with a very nice view out over the river. At one end of this table three men stood as two others entered. The shorter of them thrust out a hand in a practiced manner as he strode across the floor. Arthur recognised him at once. His name was Ashley Sullivan. Arthur could remember little about him except that he was a New Zealander and that once upon a time, as a Junior Minister in Agriculture, Food and Fisheries and shortly after a nuclear submarine had gone down off Rockall, he'd appeared on T.V. and eaten a herring. Must have gone down well with Central Office, Arthur supposed.

'Sir Auberon,' Sullivan said, 'How good of you to see me at such short notice.' Whatever accent he had once possessed had long since succumbed to the upper-middle-class drawl of the rising Tory.

'Pleasure, sir,' said Nightingale and turning to Arthur, 'please allow me to introduce Mr. Henley. He is one our most experienced operatives: a very valued and valuable asset to the service. You expressed a desire to meet him.'

'Indeed I did. How are you, my dear chap? Must have been frightful. Frightful.' The Minister shook Arthur's hand vigorously. 'Do, please sit down.' Arthur knew enough about politics to know that this seemingly innocuous request would have annoyed Nightingale and he wondered if that had been the Minister's intention. Nightingale, however, barely missed a beat.

'Yes, do please, Arthur and you too, sir.' Arthur knew that the minister would kick himself later for saying, 'Thank you.' Against all his instincts, Arthur found himself admiring the way Nightingale had turned the tables.

'My secretary, David Henderson,' said the Minister, indicating his companion. 'He will be taking notes.'

'I wonder, Sir,' said Nightingale, 'if you have been advised that minutes are not taken at these meetings,'

'I said, "notes", not minutes, Sir Auberon.'

'Yes, sir but' (he indicated his own secretary) 'we keep our own notes…'

'Yes, and we keep ours,' the Minister said with some finality.

*Aye aye*, thought Arthur. One-nil to H.M. Government. He treated Nightingale to a warm smile.

'Let's begin, shall we?' the Minister didn't ask. 'Now tell me, Mr. Henley, whilst you were at the Al-Nimrah, yesterday, did you note anything that may be of interest to the Government?'

'Apart from a fucking great explosion, do you mean?' said Arthur. Mr. Sullivan smiled.

'Very good, Mr. Henley; very good indeed. You are right, of course. It was a foolish question. I am rather new at this and I'm still, as it were, finding my feet. I shall simply listen to what you have to tell us about the incident. Please.'

Already warming to the Minister for his treatment of Nightingale, Arthur found himself impressed by this admission and resolved to give the little twerp as full an account of events as he could manage, leaving out the fact that he had gone there to do the very thing the terrorists had done; (a lot less noisily of course but the effect would have been much the same). Well no, not the same because he wouldn't have left bits of forty-odd people spattered all over the countryside.

Sullivan listened in silence and when Arthur had finished, said,

'Tell me; is it usual for agents such as yourself to work alone on such assignments?' Arthur said,

'What makes you think I was alone?'

'Well, you didn't mention anyone else so I naturally assumed…'

'It's unwise to assume anything, round here,' Arthur said.

'Er, what Mr. Henley means, Minister, is that we don't discuss operational matters'

'Of course, of course but,' Sullivan forced a laugh, 'I am Parliamentary Under-Secretary of State. Surely, that carries some privileges; else, what would be the point? Ha Ha.

*You might well ask*, Arthur thought.

'Nevertheless… Minister,' Nightingale said.

'Mr. Henley?' said the Minister.

Both men were now looking at Arthur. Clearly, there was history between these two. Finally, Arthur said,

'Gentlemen, I am more than conscious that each of you is reluctant to give way in this matter. However, Minister, I'm afraid you are not at present in possession of the level of authority needed for me to override the wishes of my immediate… I suppose the term is "superior". You strike me, though, as the sort of chap who, should he turn his hand to the matter, might manage to come up with something but alas, as I say, not at present.' As he saw Nightingale's demeanour re-establish its usual frustrating equilibrium, Arthur made a mental note that Sir Auberon owed him one.

'Well, Mr. Henley,' the Minister said at last, 'I must say that I admire your candour and indeed, your loyalty… to the Service. The government is of course, fully committed to supporting the Intelligence Services and you may be assured that you and your colleagues will always have our enduring gratitude for keeping our country safe, as you do. I trust that you'll now be taking a little time to yourself; to recuperate, as it were? Recharge the old batteries.'

'Shouldn't think so.'

'Oh?' The minister appeared surprised. Sir Auberon said,

'Er... no, Minister. Policy is always to get the operative back in the saddle as soon as possible. In fact, I understand that Mr Henley has a little task to perform later today.'

'Goodness me,' the minister said. 'If only all employers felt the same way, the country might be back on its feet a lot sooner.' He stood up and offered his hand, which Arthur accepted. 'I'm jolly pleased to have met you and perhaps I may have the pleasure again; who knows?'

Arthur smiled.

'Possibly,' the Minister went on, 'when I have garnered sufficient authority, eh? Good-day to you as well, Sir Auberon. It has been most... enlightening.' With that, the Parliamentary Under-Secretary of State for... Arthur still had no idea... left.

'That went well,' Arthur said, cheerfully. Nightingale stood up, raised an eyebrow and shook his head. Arthur went on. 'Why do you think he came here?'

'I suppose he just wanted to be kept abreast of matters.'

'Why do you reckon he wanted to know if Arthur Henley was there on his own?'

'I have no idea,' Nightingale said, dismissively. 'He's new at the job; probably just wants to be seen hand on the tiller and whatnot. Perhaps he's just nosey.'

'How did he know that Henley was anywhere near the Al-Nimrah?' Arthur said.

'How should I know?'

'Oh, I don't know. Aren't you some kind of M.I.6 commander or something?'

Sir Auberon's face remained impassive. He said,

'Oh, do be careful, Shepherd. I have only so many ribs.'

'Someone told him. Doesn't that worry you?'

'Should it? The job was logged as "surveillance" for S.I.S. records. I suppose even the Parliamentary Under-Secretary of State for Foreign and Commonwealth Affairs might have found himself in the loop.'

'Foreign and Commonwealth Affairs!' Arthur said, snapping his fingers. Then he murmured, 'I don't know. You eat a herring on T.V. one day and the next, you're a guardian of the nation. Isn't politics marvellous?'

'Actually, his full title is "Parliamentary Under-Secretary of State responsible for Afghanistan, South Asia, counter-terrorism, proliferation, North America, Middle East and North Africa, F.C.O. finance and human resources",' said Nightingale.

'They spread 'em a bit thin nowadays, don't they?'

'The Government is no doubt conscious of the need to get the best possible value out of its Public Servants.'

'That must be why you're so busy.'

'That sense of humour never lets you down, does it, Shepherd?'

'It wobbles occasionally,' said Arthur. 'For instance, when someone who should know better goes around telling government ministers the name, fake as it may be, of a Council Cleaner and invites said ministers round for tea with him.'

'Oh come now, Shepherd. Even you must realise one has to expect this sort of thing, nowadays. I can't say like it any more than you do, I'm sure, but information is far more readily available than it used to be and it's far more difficult to keep things secret...' Nightingale picked up his folder and tucked it under his arm. '...even, I'm afraid, for the Secret Services. You need to go down to Floor D. They have your next assignment.' He turned, signalled to his secretary and the pair of them made for the door.

## A Probe Or Two

Arthur was at home. If anything, he hurt more now than he had earlier. An abstemious man, he was reluctant to dose himself with booze before it even got dark so he sucked down a couple more painkillers.

After the meeting with the Minister, he had, as instructed, collected the job from Floor D. It had comprised a single sheet. Apart from the obvious variations in the details of the task, it had appeared to be a job much like any other. He'd decided there was nothing out of the ordinary, so he'd sent it to its shreddy, fiery fate. He still had the Beasley one and the one from last night's disaster and frankly, Beasely had paled into insignificance. He still wanted to find out who'd cocked up the Knightsbridge job so he'd thought he might pop round to Century House and see if he couldn't shed a bit more light on the matter.

Mulberry had been extremely solicitous.

'Crikey, Shepherd, that was a close one and no mistake. Are you all right? You still look a bit singed, truth be told.'

'You know,' Arthur had told him, 'it's a good thing we work for the Secret Services, else everyone and their mothers would know what happened to me yesterday.'

'Well, you must admit, it's bound to be a bit of a talking point. Someone's going to be in shtook for that. Thank God it never came across my desk.'

'Did it not? Pity. I could have done you and Ricketts in and been home in time for lunch. Oh, I was forgetting; Ricketts has abandoned ship, hasn't he?'

Mulberry's face suddenly became earnest and he stepped over to the door to make sure it was firmly shut.

'Arthur, you know me: I swear to you, I said nothing about that little tracing thing you were asking about on Monday but the damndest thing…'

'Oh?'

'…Yes, when I got in this morning, Ricketts was back here, messing up the bloody place again. I didn't say anything because he had a bit of a face on. Anyway, long story short, he goes off for a pee and I happen to glance over. He's only going through a great pile of ancient missives dating back, as far as I could see, to the year dot.'

'Not unusual for you chaps, I shouldn't wonder,' Arthur had said.

'No,' Mulberry had countered, 'but these missives were teleprinter messages.'

'Eh?'

'Shitloads of 'em, Arthur. He was definitely looking for something. He'd scribbled down a bunch of codes – mostly L-A-M and a few J-A-M (from when M.I.6 lived at St. James Street). I didn't get far before I heard him coming back, though. What do you think?'

'I think,' Arthur had told him, that I would very much like you to take this…' He'd handed Mulberry what was left of the despatch concerning Prince Muffarim, '…and do everything you can to find out where it came from, who sent it and where I can find the fucker.'

'Blimey!' Mulberry had said, looking at the heat-dried sheets, 'Is this the job they sent you on last night? I'll bet whoever despatched you on this is feeling a bit sheepish today.'

'He'll feel a lot more than that if I find him. Someone should have known that the prince was already under threat. This is one cock-up too many, Mulberry and I'm beginning to lose faith in my employer.'

'I don't blame you, Arthur. By the looks of this,' he said, turning it over, 'there's not much more here than there was on the other one but I'll have a look at it for you. Odd though, that Ricketts is fishing about as well.'

'Yes,' Arthur said, 'I wonder what he's playing at? I'll make sure I catch him in next time.'

'Don't be too hard on him, Arthur. He's a good sort, really.'

'Mulberry, the world is full of good sorts who go and do bloody silly things. And doing silly things around here is what usually gets folk killed. Still, if it'll make you feel better, perhaps a little gentle probing on your part might yield something before I have to deploy a probe or two of my own.'

'Have you got my mobile number?'

'Fucked if I know.'

'What's yours?'

'My what?'

'Your mobile number.'

'Why do you want to know that?'

'So I can give you mine, of course,' Mulberry said. 'Are you sure you haven't got concussion or something?'

Arthur fished in his pocket and removed his phone. He tossed it over to Mulberry.

'Do what you have to,' he said. Mulberry fiddled around a bit then said,

'I think I'd better start by charging it up.'

## Pont Sacre

'Right. We can rest here, for a while,' said Caroline. They had been in the saddle for some five hours and the sun was high in the sky. The horses had been walking beside and occasionally in a swift-moving stream for about five kilometres before the terrain had flattened out considerably, the narrow pass opening onto a wide valley. They were now approximately half way across that valley in the direction of the next pass and had halted beside a steeply angled, stone bridge.

'Pont Sacre,' announced Caroline.

'Does that mean we're in France?' Vanessa asked.

'I'm afraid not. Lots of names for things in these mountains and in a variety of languages. Borders were much more fluid in the old days. The Romans built this bridge; no-one knows what they called it.' She dismounted, removed her horse's saddle and led the animal to a rock with which she was obviously familiar. There was a hole right through it and Caroline tethered the little Haflinger there.

Close by the track, was a circle of small boulders, which had clearly been arranged on purpose; although when, was anyone's guess. Roughly in the centre of the circle was a dark patch of earth, which had (it appeared) been the site of many a fire. It was to this spot that Gianfranco carried a small disposable barbeque and lit it. Vanessa clambered down from her mount and immediately her legs gave way. She tumbled to the grass. Within moments, Maytham was beside her.

'Here, now,' he said. 'Take it steadily. It's been a difficult ride and you're probably not used to this kind of terrain. Take my arm.' Vanessa held on to Maytham for dear life. There was no sensation in her lower limbs and it was only by going through the motions that she was eventually able to loll against one of the boulders. She saw Gianfranco whispering to Caroline.

'Perhaps,' Caroline said, 'but we needed to get a good start. I think we've made excellent time. We can probably afford an hour here and then I must return. You should make Capanna dell'Aquila long before nightfall, now.' She raised her voice: 'Right. Sausages!'

'Hooray!' said Maytham and Vanessa fell asleep.

She awoke to find that everyone had already eaten but the aroma of sausages still drifted over to her.

'Ready for a bite, now?' It was Maytham.

'Thanks,' she said, hauling herself into a sitting position, as Maytham held out a paper plateful of lunch. 'How long...'

'About an hour.' He pointed over at the horses. Caroline was already mounted and appeared to be giving Gianfranco some instructions. 'Linny's about to head back,' he said.

'Why does she have to return?'

'She's going to drive to Alberges and meet us there, tomorrow.'

'Doesn't it seem a bit odd to you? To come out all this way and then just leave us and go back.' Vanessa shovelled sausage and potato salad into her mouth.

'No. It's what any host would do. Besides, she loves riding these mountains.'

Vanessa wondered if she wasn't becoming a little paranoid but she decided to give herself a break - she'd had plenty to be paranoid about in the last few days. She looked across at Caroline and her servant. A strange pair, Vanessa decided. He was clearly devoted to her and she treated him very well but there was a formality, which in her day to day life, Vanessa had never really encountered. Gianfranco was fussing with the pack that was tied on behind the saddle of Caroline's mount when, suddenly, his head whipped around and he scanned the peaks. No-one else had noticed and so Vanessa was the only one to follow his gaze.

She could see nothing but became aware of a deep-throated, drilling note, pummelling down the mountain. A helicopter. Somewhat to her surprise, she managed to spot it whilst it was still half a mile distant and several-hundred metres above the valley floor, which it seemed to be following. It was heading towards them. Gianfranco gave a shrill whistle and made a single, urgent gesture towards the old Roman bridge. He gathered the reins of his own and Caroline's horse and tugged the animals into motion. Caroline herself moved no less swiftly. She dismounted, ran to the centre of the stone circle, kicked earth into the barbeque and flung the paper plates and plastic forks into the stream where they bobbed and bucked for a few moments before disappearing into a cataract. Gianfranco, still holding both horses, scooped up his saddle in his free hand and led the animals unhesitatingly into the water. Caroline followed and all disappeared from sight beneath the Pont Sacre. A moment later, Caroline's head re-appeared.

'I think you should get out of sight,' she said.

Vanessa and Maytham looked at one another and then at Gianfranco who, rifle in hand, was now striding across to the rock to which their mounts were tethered. He grabbed a saddle and swung it onto Vanessa's horse. Maytham did the same with his and within seconds the entire party, human and animal, was huddled beneath the ancient stone bridge.

The swift-flowing water was much, much colder than Vanessa could ever have imagined and within seconds, discomfort was turning into real pain. She found it difficult to get a purchase on the slippery pebbles and more than once, she staggered and almost fell. Caroline noticed her struggling.

'Hang on to her mane,' she told her. Vanessa twisted the Haflinger's thick golden hair around her hand and grasped its bridle. She was almost actually and certainly metaphorically completely out of her depth.

As it came nearer, the drone of the engine developed into a stuttering chord that sang until it was overwhelmed by the thud of rotors. The fact that she could feel the pulse right through her body and could see a curtain of water sizzling upwards on either side of the bridge, told Vanessa that the aircraft was passing right overhead. It had seemed higher further up the valley but she realised that was because its height was relative to the valley bottom. Now it was no more than forty metres above their heads.

All the oxygen seemed to be forced out of the small space in which the little group was huddled and she could see that the others were struggling to draw breath. It was over far quicker than it seemed. The battering of the rotors diminished, to be replaced once more by the engine note, falling in pitch as the machine carried on down the valley. Had anyone on board known they were there, they clearly hadn't cared.

Vanessa was the second of them to emerge. Ahead of her, on the bank, Gianfranco stood, his head lowered and one hand behind his neck, the other beating his sodden hat angrily against his sodden jeans. He glanced at her and quickly looked away. Caroline scrambled by and pulled herself easily onto the bank. She walked straight past Gianfranco, whose head remained lowered and stood a little beyond him, gazing after the helicopter, one hand shielding her eyes, the other in the small of her back. She stretched a little and placed both hands on her hips. By now, Maytham had clambered out and he came to Vanessa's side. Vanessa looked at him. He looked anxious. Then Caroline spoke.

'What must we have looked like?' she said and Gianfranco's head fell even lower. Then they heard her laugh.

She turned around, walked over to Gianfranco and laid both hands on his shoulders. 'My brave little soldier!' she said teasingly and shook him gently. A shy smile played on Gianfranco's lips as he looked up. She touched his face, gently and said, 'It was the right thing, Gianfranco.' Christopher and Vanessa almost laughed with relief themselves.

## St Pauls And The Bucking Bridge

Arthur had jumped off the bus by St. Paul's before it had even come to a halt. It was his way of telling his body that he didn't care what it thought and he wasn't going to let being blown up by a terrorist bomb annoy him any more than was strictly necessary. He winced and said fuck, but for the most part, he got away with it.

As the bus pulled away, he felt the almost gravitational tug of the massive building in front of him. He tried so hard not to look but the lure of seeing stone and marble performing so confidently could not be ignored. Not without some trepidation, he presented his neck to her as he gazed upwards. She had been the avant-garde marvel of her age. Talk about a statement.

Actually, Arthur had never really liked the cathedral; however, he was a little afraid to think about that standing so close. As he made towards the river and the building stopped staring, he turned once more and allowed himself to consider her outmoded pomposity. Once, she would have been magnificent; soaring even in repose, like a lion guarding a kill. All nonchalance so long as nothing approached. But she had long ago allowed herself to be encroached upon; intimidated by hyenas whose agenda had been written by Mammon, not by God. Now, she seemed... cowed and Arthur felt a little more secure. He turned and strode towards the bridge.

The last time he had set foot upon the spindly sliver of steel that was the Millennium Bridge, it had been swaying and bucking like the floor of the Crazy House on Southend Pier. How delightful it had been. His fellow "passengers" (as he had thought of them) had laughed and talked and grabbed onto to one another as they had staggered across and once safely on the opposite bank, had turned and gone back for more. Now that was subverting the paradigm. A bridge, which not only impedes one's crossing but which one immediately wants to re-cross in the opposite direction! His faith in architecture had received a minor fillip. Then he'd read in the Guardian that it hadn't been intentional. The architect had miscalculated and so they (who?) had stopped people crossing for a few months, had "repaired" it and now it was merely another, not-terribly-attractive footbridge.

Few of the pedestrians (for that is what they had become) were smiling and even fewer were talking. Most wore the intense frown of the commuter or the vacant stare of the Londoned-out tourist. Some of them must have been coming from Tate Modern, surely? Arthur decided to leaven his dull walk by trying to detect which had done so. Those carrying gaudy carrier bags or souvenirs didn't count, of course, it being an indicator that they had been there as customers and not as visitors.

He spotted just one of whom he could be reasonably sure. A gamine blonde who wore a man's shirt (not tucked in), a short, black and white checked skirt, black tights and low boots. She carried a large, canvas bag, which no doubt contained her sketch-pad and her charcoal. As she came nearer, he smiled at her approvingly, nodded politely in her direction and ignoring her sneer and extended middle digit, congratulated himself.

## Tate Modern

Even now, Arthur was thinking it was a bad idea but he had chosen to take it as some sort of a sign when the despatch told him that Darlington would be at Tate Modern. Darlington was pure Box Standard: a minor functionary who'd apparently been a little indiscrete with a group of Christian Zionists. There was no question of options, of course; this was a straightforward Cleaning job and as far as Arthur was concerned, he'd just as soon have done him like the Dutchman.

Naturally, Darlington had no idea that he was to die. He would have been told that a chap from S.I.S.; Henley by name, was bringing him a fake passport so that he could go on assignment in Pakistan. What better place to drop it off (they must have told him) than in plain sight in a public place? Actually, there are far better places; like out of sight in a dark alley or, better still, inside a wardrobe that's inside a locked room in the basement of a deserted house. Darlington had probably been brought up on Jason Bourne and so he'd fallen for it.

Arthur wasn't going to. Yes, co-incidences happen all the time but this really was pushing credibility to the limit. On Monday, Mulberry had told him that the Rothkos had been re-hung. He had made a note to visit and now, on Wednesday, he'd been given a job, had contacted the target and the target had suggested Tate Modern as a meeting place.

No-one had tried to do away with him for years now. Most of his old enemies were dead and his skill and experience had prevented him from acquiring new ones. However, as soon as he stepped off the bridge, he began to feel uneasy again. Nothing to do with the job – everything to do with the Tate.

This was no Art Gallery; it was a Tourist Attraction. No purpose-built Temple of Athena but a converted power-station, an expedient, a compromise; post-fucking-modern. He could feel the bile beginning to scald his oesophagus as he negotiated the knots of people congealing around the entrance. He looked around, expecting to see some sort of reinforced glass ticket booth (no doubt employing some species of microphone and speaker arrangement via which he would tell the lobotomised twat within that he had no intention of donating a brass-farthing) and a queue snaking away from it. But to Arthur's astonishment, no-one, tacitly or otherwise suggested, as he entered, that he donate. Why such a very small thing should have so profound an effect struck Arthur quite forcibly, as it crossed his mind that he may have been wrong.

As is often the case in such situations, one of the less ghastly memories of that first visit now presented itself. In spite of the trauma of his Rothko experience, Olafur Eliasson's sun had amazed and overjoyed Arthur as he had entered the Turbine Hall, a fact that he had quite forgotten until now. The work was quite remarkable – unashamedly two dimensional (as all the best art should be) yet touching the viewer in a truly physical manner – photons bounced off him and were absorbed by him and he was delighted. The memory lightened his step as he made his way there.

He cursed his naiveté as he emerged into the vast space.

No sun. Oh no. Not even close. He'd thought that the squeals and shouts, which had grown louder as he'd approached, might have been part some sort of installation. They weren't. They were part of children being happy. It took him some time to figure it all out. He wondered for a moment if he'd wandered into the place (he understood such things existed) where parents could leave their brats to play whilst they themselves went off to do something more interesting. He was wrong. This was art. But those things snaking away above him were exactly what they appeared to be.

Slides. Bloody children's slides; complete with queues like some ghastly theme park. What, he asked himself in bewilderment, were these playground toys doing here? A helpful leaflet told him that "a daily dose of sliding" could be beneficial in helping us perceive the world and asked whether slides might not become part of our "experiential and architectural vocabulary." Arthur exasperated, said,

'Fuck me...'

He forced himself to read on and then finally replacing the leaflet in the rack from whence he'd taken it, turned to find a heavily-set young man, small child in tow, peering menacingly at him. Arthur looked over his shoulder, just in case. Satisfied that he must indeed be the object of the fellow's attention, he turned to face him once more.

'Erm...may I help you?' Arthur asked.

'My daughter says you just swore at her,' said the man. Arthur, understanding at once, relaxed and said,

'Oh? Oh, no, you see, I wasn't swearing *at* her, I was merely swearing *near* her, so to speak. That is, she must have been near me...when I swore. Well, technically, it wasn't swearing at all; no names being taken in vain, you understand. It was more of a profanity.'

'A what?'

A profanity. An obscenity.'

'You used obscenities near my daughter?'

'Well, I suppose I did. But in the circumstances...' Arthur gave a little laugh and gestured towards the slides.

'People like you shouldn't be allowed in places like this,' said the man.

'Oh?' Arthur was nonplussed.

'No; you shouldn't be allowed anywhere where there are kids.'

'Well, usually, I'm not.' Immediately realising how the man was already interpreting the comment, Arthur hurriedly continued, 'where there are kids, I mean... I mean, normally, I don't go where there are children. I didn't expect there to be any here, as a matter of fact but I suppose that's what happens if you fill an art gallery with fucking slides.'

His training took over instantly and the man's punch not only missed but the momentum of it caused him to pitch forwards into Arthur's arms. A sharp, four-fingered jab to the sciatic nerve and the fellow was in spasm, unable to move, speak, or breathe properly. He stared at Arthur in blank astonishment.

'Whoops-a-daisy!' said Arthur, taking the man's weight, as two or three faces turned towards him. 'They keep these floors rather shiny, don't they? Here, let me help you. Goodness, a chap could do himself a mischief here couldn't he? Now, sit yourself down. Will you look after daddy? Good. I expect he'll be fine in a minute or two.'

'More like a day or two,' mused Arthur, as he made for the lifts. He'd gone in a bit hard; a fact that he put down to his rather fragile condition – some sort of over-compensation thing, he imagined. 'Ah well,' he said to himself as the crowd swallowed him up.

## The Purgatory of Paintings

Alone in the lift, Arthur, warmed by his exertions, divested himself of his jacket and was folding it when the doors opened with the customary ding. He stepped out and practically walked into his victim.

'Darlington,' he said.

'Henley! I thought you weren't coming.'

'I was... delayed.'

'Right. Well, where would be a good place to... you know...'

It really was a gift.

'Room 6, Third Floor. It's a very... quiet room.'

'Good,' said Darlington. He began to look around and as his eyes fell on a member of the gallery staff, he called out,

'Excuse me!' And wandered over.

No wonder Box Standard wanted rid of this twerp. Arthur followed, shaking his head. Then his eyes fell upon the attendant. It was her: the glasses, the nose, the hair dragged backwards and upwards, held this morning by a what looked like two ebony chopsticks. Arthur's Bird Goddess from the Old Tate

Darlington said to her,

'Please could you direct us to Room 6 on the third floor.'

'Certainly,' she said. 'However, I'm afraid that room is closed at the moment. The paintings are being taken down in order to be moved for an exhibition in Paris.' Arthur, detecting the merest whiff of a European accent, stole a glance at the attendant's name-tag and noticed that she was not an attendant at all. Her name was Carina LaSalle and she rejoiced in the title of "Gallery Assistant: Permanent Exhibits".

'I can understand your disappointment,' she said. I found out from my supervisor only today. Apparently they are to go on display at the Pompidou next month.'

'Pity,' said Darlington, I'm off to Pakistan in a couple of hours.' He indicated his carry-on bag. 'Ah well, never mind. Anyway, Mr. Henley, do you think...?'

'Hmm? Yes. Yes, better get on, I suppose,' he said, absently.

'I shall be sorry to lose them myself; even temporarily,' Miss LaSalle went on. They are most remarkable paintings, aren't they?'

'Yes,' said Arthur. 'Yes they are.' After a moment of silence, Miss LaSalle shrugged and said,

'I am most terribly sorry.'

'Really, it doesn't matter,' Darlington said. 'We'll be on our way...' Miss LaSalle turned to him.

'Well, it does matter,' she said firmly. 'Art always matters.' She turned to Arthur. 'As I say, I'm most terribly sorry.'

'Is everything all right, Miss LaSalle?' Arthur turned to see a short, stocky, woman in a cheap suit. Her name-badge said, "Mrs H. Yardley: Supervisor: Permanent Exhibits".

'Oh, everything's fine, Mrs Yardley. I was just explaining to these gentlemen that the paintings in Room 6 are no longer on display and that they are bound for Paris.'

'Indeed they are.'

'Only this gentleman in particular appeared quite keen to view them.'

Mrs Yardley peered down her nose and through the glasses that were poised on the end of it. To Arthur, her eyes appeared huge.

Mrs Yardley studied Arthur's face and said,

'I tell you what; if you would care to wait here for a moment, sir, I may be able to help in some small way.' She left them.

Arthur had no idea what rights the position of "Supervisor: Permanent Exhibits" conferred upon its tenant but a tiny glimmer of hope ignited in his chest.

'What does she mean?' Arthur asked Miss LaSalle.

'I'm not sure. She's new. She has… "*ideas*".'

Darlington looked at his watch and Arthur caught him doing it.

'I hope you're not going to try to rush me,' said Arthur, with a smile.

'Not at all,' he said, returning the smile. Within a short space of time, Mrs Yardley returned.

'I thought as much,' she said. 'The paintings are currently waiting to be crated up. We usually require an appointment for this sort of thing but… well, I think we could pop down and take a look at them. What do you say?' In truth, Arthur wasn't sure. To him, the hanging was as important as the painting but any old port in a storm and he had rather psyched himself into it.

'If you're sure it's no trouble'

'None at all. It's always a pleasure to meet a visitor who has a passion for art.'

Arthur wondered if she was making some kind of a joke.

'Oh, that's marvellous!' said Miss LaSalle. She actually clasped her hands together.

'Miss LaSalle?'

'Yes, Mrs Yardley?'

'You are needed in "Energy and Process".'

'Oh,' she said. Turning to Arthur and Darlington she said, 'Enjoy your viewing.'

'I'm sure we shall,' Darlington said, smiling and practically bowing. He turned to Arthur and whispered, 'Actually, do you think we could get this over with quickly?'

Time was pressing but not for the reasons Darlington might have imagined. Arthur did the sums. If it took five minutes to get down to the paintings, he could easily afford fifteen minutes with one of them. Five minutes back up: Kill Darlington; out by midday. Spot of lunch at Greville's in Fleet St; not been there for a while. Wonder if the duck's...'

'Shall we?' said Mrs Yardley.

The two men followed her into the lift. As the doors closed, she handed each of them a piece of paper. It was a form. Arthur was always very careful about forms anyway but even the greenest operative would have known that the last thing you wanted to do was to write all your details down, signed and dated, a few minutes before you kill someone. Mrs Yardley must have sensed his concern.

'Oh, don't worry about the details,' she said, 'just write your name there, fold it and pop it in here.' She handed him a little plastic wallet with a clip on it and a bookie's pen.

Arthur, arm full of jacket, hands full of paper and plastic wallet, shifted things around so he could write on the form. He filled it in, folded it and as instructed, stuffed it into the plastic wallet. He clipped the wallet to his tie and Mrs Yardley straightened it for him. He glanced over at Darlington.

'What about him?' Arthur said.

'What about me?'

'He hasn't filled his in.' Darlington screwed up his face.

'What?' he said.

'Why haven't you filled yours in?'

'I...'

'Now come on, Mr Darlington,' said Mrs. Yardley, 'It'll only take a moment.' Darlington sighed and did as he was told. As Darlington stuffed his own form into the plastic wallet and affixed it to his jacket, there was a tiny jolt and the doors opened. Arthur ushered him out between himself and Mrs Yardley.

There was a surprising number of people at work beneath Tate Modern. What they all did exactly, Arthur couldn't be certain but they scurried hither and thither, looking busy. Occasionally, someone would pass, smile and nod at the three of them as they made their way through the labyrinth.

Eventually, Mrs Yardley stopped by a set of large doors. She swiped a card through the waiting mandibles of a reader and Arthur was gratified to hear a good, old-fashioned whirr and a click, followed by a buzz, at which she pushed one of the doors open. Overhead lights tinkled on automatically as they entered.

The room was big, white and sterile both metaphorically and literally. Climate controlled and bristling with sophisticated dust and bio-filters, it began sucking London out of them even as they entered. Arthur donned his jacket against the chill. Ranged along both sides of the room were roller racks. Each system appeared to consist of twenty enormous mobile shelves, each of which could be separated from its neighbour by enough distance to allow the canvasses they no doubt contained to be withdrawn with ease.

Mrs Yardley walked purposefully over to one of the racks at the far end of the room and turned the hand wheel. Gears and chains did what they do and two shelves moved apart. Arthur of course didn't see her right hand closing around the handle of the gun in her inside pocket but then, after that performance in the lift, he hadn't needed to. By the time she turned around, he already had his own out. She stopped dead. A second later, Darlington shifted his gaze from the roller shelves and he too stared at Arthur.

'Mr. Shepherd!' gasped Mrs Yardley. 'What are you doing?'

'Who's Mr. Shepherd?'

'What?'

'My name is Henley and I don't even recall telling you that.'

'Mrs. Yardley laughed, weakly.'

'I… I must have been mistaken. I… must have misread your badge,' she stammered. Arthur plucked it off and threw it over to her. She looked at it. Arthur had written, "Dame Maggie Smith".

'I wasn't going to write my name on that; especially as you appeared to know Darlington's over there, even before he filled it in.'

'What?' said Darlington.

'She knows who we are, Darlington. I don't suppose you recognise her?'

'Never seen her before in my life.'

'Search her.'

'What?'

'Search her. She must have a weapon. I'll keep her covered.'

Gingerly, Darlington approached Mrs. Yardley. Wincing and looking decidedly uncomfortable, he began a standard pat-down. It was really not very long before he stopped, a hand on her ample bosom. He opened her jacket and said,

'Bloody hell!' From inside her left breast pocket, he removed a pistol, complete with silencer.

'Bring it over here,' said Arthur. Darlington walked over to stand beside him. Arthur held out his hand and Darlington placed the gun into it. Arthur looked at the weapon.

'Glock. Police issue? How singular,' said Arthur. 'Now what would a "Supervisor: Permanent Exhibits" be doing with one of these?'

'We get a lot of rats down here,' she said.

'I'm sure you do,' he said. Arthur knew that bravado was not common amongst people caught in such situations. She was too confident.

'Who organised this?' he asked.

'Oh please, Mr Shepherd!' she laughed. He knew he wasn't going to get anywhere. She must have a back-up plan of some kind.

'Right, Darlington,' he said, 'let's get her down to the Council Offices and see if we can't shed some light on this.'

'You'll never get me out of the building, let alone down to Lambeth.' she said. Arthur knew she was right. He had to find an edge.

'Darlington,' he said, 'put her in there.' He indicated the gap between the roller shelves. There was flicker of concern on her face – but no more; and it was gone instantly. Darlington guided her into the tiny space and as he did so, Arthur released the safety catch on the hand wheel. A quick spin and Mrs Yardley was pinned between the shelves, not too hard, but firmly enough to ensure she could not get away. He took out a Swiss army knife – modified, of course – and worried away at the safety catch until it came loose. Within seconds, it fell away.

'Shocking workmanship; Health and Safety will have a fit. So,' Arthur said. 'Names?'

Mrs Yardley said nothing. In the dim recess, all Arthur could clearly see of her, were the whites of her eyes. Her mouth remained clenched shut. 'I didn't think so.' Arthur said. He pushed lightly down on the hand wheel and the shelf drew an inch closer to its neighbour. A grunt escaped her.

'You were perfectly content to be taken to Lambeth,' Arthur said to her. 'I wonder why? I ask again. Names?'

'You'll destroy the painting!' she gasped, sounding just panicked enough to make Arthur realise he might just get somewhere with this. He glanced at the label on the rack – David Hockney.

'I really don't care,' he said.

'Henley,' Darlington said, 'what the hell's going on? Who is she?'

Arthur ignored him.

'Mrs Yardley,' said Arthur, 'you must surely know that I will kill you if you don't tell me what I need to know.' He turned the handle another notch.

'Help me!' Mrs Yardley screamed. Then, 'All right! I'll tell you! Just let me out of here!' Her earlier confidence had unnerved him a little and hearing that it had clearly evaporated, he felt comfortable enough to press home (ha ha) his advantage.

'Tell me; then I'll let you out.'

'All right,' she breathed.

'For God's sake, Henley,' Darlington said, 'let her go.' He reached for the handle. Arthur tightened his grip and braced himself against any attempt Darlington might make to release Mrs Yardley. But Darlington, idiot that he was, had got it wrong. He took hold of the handle but instead of turning it against the pressure Arthur was exerting, he did the exact opposite.

There was a choking scream and a muffled crack.

'Oh, Lord,' said Darlington. 'Oh my God!'

'Oh well done, Darlington!' Arthur slapped him away with the back of his hand. The mobile shelf had locked in place. Even if he could have opened it, there was little chance that Mrs Yardley would be anything other than a fleshy sack of broken bones and crushed organs.

Sprawled on the floor and holding the side of his face, Darlington said,

'I'm sorry! Oh God, I killed her! I thought... I'm so sorry!'

'Get up, we're leaving.'

A surprisingly small trickle of dark blood was flowing down the runners of the roller shelves as Arthur and Darlington left the room. A moment after the door closed, the room became dark, quiet and still, once more.

## A Bit Potty

In the lift, Darlington wouldn't shut up.

'Who on earth was she, anyway? How did she get so deep undercover in this place? She was going to kill us, wasn't she? So who was she working for?'

'I don't know the answers to any of those questions, I'm afraid,' Arthur said. 'But I might do, if you hadn't killed her.'

Darlington took a number of deep breaths and straightened his tie as they approached the first floor. The lift halted and the doors opened. Arthur held out his hand as a signal that the little tribe of visitors would not be allowed in. He pressed the button for the third floor.

'What are you doing?' Darlington said. Arthur was looking thoughtful.

'She thought someone was going to help her; right up to the very end, she didn't expect to die.'

'You'd better give me that passport now and let me get...'

'Oh, come on, Ted. For fucks sake!'

'What on earth are you talking about, old man?

'You know what?' Arthur said, 'I'm insulted; I really am. Whose idea was it to meet here?'

'What? I don't know! I thought...' Arthur grabbed Darlington's lapels, pushed him against the side of the lift.

'No,' said Arthur, 'I'm afraid you didn't. That little charade down there proves it. She wasn't afraid, because *you* were there. She was expecting you to rescue her. You killed her on purpose as soon as it looked as though she might talk.'

'You're insane...' Darlington managed.

'Tell me,' Arthur said. 'Why didn't you finish the job, down there, when you had the chance, before I suspected you?' Darlington held Arthur's gaze but said nothing.

'I think,' Arthur went on, 'that once you knew Mrs. Yardley had been rumbled you decided to play along with me. She let you in the hopes that you might be able to despatch me before anything too messy happened. She'd have had to have been pretty green or pretty thick to put her trust in you, eh? Who set this up?'

Darlington evidently decided that there was no point going on with the deception.

'I'm not going to tell you anything,' he said.

'Really?' said Arthur, 'That would be a shame.' The lift stopped and Arthur bundled Darlington out onto the third floor landing.

'Anyway, you can't do anything in here,' Darlington said, looking around at the hundreds of visitors. Arthur followed his gaze.

'Oh, it might be tricky but they must have told you that Cleaners are very well trained.'

He studied the look on Darlington's face as his words registered. There was both anger and fear. He clearly realised there was no way he could get out of this and it was not unknown for Cleaners to learn a great deal from defiant last words. He might be able to goad Darlington into revealing something. It worked.

'Cleaners,' said Darlington with contempt. 'You people.'

Arthur's satisfaction with this response quickly gave way to feeling strangely offended. True, the Council had always been a ... singular organisation. Each department treated freedom of information in much the same way as an American doctor might treat an uninsured patient. That is, as if it did not exist. Arthur wondered how Darlington even knew about Cleaners let alone felt emboldened enough to mock them.

'Move,' he ordered.

'Or what?'

Arthur removed a ball-point pen from his pocket.

'Do you see this?' he asked.

'Don't tell me. It shoots laser beams,' Darlington said.

'Eh?'

'Or it's a tactical nuclear weapon or some such ridiculous "Cleaner" shit.'

'*Cleaner shit*?' Arthur was bewildered. 'No, Edward. It's a biro.'

'So?'

'So if you don't do as I say, I'll ram it into your heart, sit you down on that little bench and bugger off. Darlington's smile wavered and he began to walk. Arthur steered him towards the entrance to the slides.

'Look at these bloody things,' Arthur said, conversationally. 'Now what do you suppose any of this has to do with art?'

'How would I know. Read the leaflet.'

'I've read it. Trust me, it's not much use. Have you heard of Carsten Holler?'

'Who?'

'The artist. Apparently, he does this sort of thing all the time. Do you know…?' Arthur chuckled, 'he came up with something he called "Frisbee Room". Yes, you heard me. It was a room… full of Frisbees. Haven't a clue what he calls this one. Do you want to try it out?'

'What?' said Darlington.

'Try it out.'

'Fuck off.'

'Oh, come on!' Arthur said, 'He's gone to all this trouble. There must be something in it. Or else it wouldn't be here, would it, in this hallowed place?'

'You've gone a bit potty, Shepherd,' said Darlington. 'That's why they want to get rid of you.'

'Gosh,' Arthur said, noting that Darlington had used his real name, 'is that what they told you? No, I don't think it was, was it? In fact, I don't think anyone told you anything much. Just stick with the woman and follow her lead, eh?'

They were close to the entrance to the slides, which from the look of them, seemed to be able to take the punters three floors down in a matter of seconds. This was the point at which Arthur reckoned Darlington would try and run.

Almost on cue, Darlington slammed his carry-on bag into Arthur's chest and was off, demolishing the orderly queue as he made for the gaily-coloured maw of the slide. He flung a small clutch of children aside and leapt into the tube. Too late, he realised that he should have grabbed one of the plastic trays. His descent was slow and fitful.

Arthur arrived at the entrance without drawing any attention to himself. The pandemonium in the wake of Darlington was keeping attendants, parents and children sufficiently occupied to let him through unmolested. It had crossed his mind to allow someone else to follow

Darlington into the art but even he balked at allowing six-year-olds to die in his place. Now, had they been teenagers... He took a tray from the abandoned pile, fell on his belly and was off, head first.

The mark of a good operative, Darlington would have been told, was to turn setbacks to advantages. At the speed he was travelling, it had been no trouble at all to brace himself against the side of the tube and bring himself to a complete halt. He fumbled in his pocket and pulled out his own Swiss Army knife. He turned out a tool, a device of indeterminate purpose and pulled the tip of it. The tool extended, telescopically until it was about two feet long and very sharp. It locked into position. He might cop a kick in the teeth but he could ignore that and ram this thing right into that loony's vitals. He braced himself against the walls of the tube. A rumbling sound above him grew louder. And then Arthur Shepherd was upon him.

The first thing to contact the spike was Darlington's own carry-on bag, which Arthur was holding in front of him. The impact deflected the spike and Arthur felt his weight thrust Darlington's arms downwards, bending them at the elbow and wedging his body fast in the tube. Darlington grunted as he tried to break free but he was lodged tight.

'Who?' said Arthur.

'I... can't... breathe...,' Darlington said.

'Try,' Arthur said.

'Selam,' Darlington gasped. 'I know him only as Selam'

'Where did you meet him?'

'I've never met him. He sent a message. Now... get me... out of here!'

From above, there came a rumble and the tube began to sway slightly. Someone was on the way down. Was a name enough? Not really but...'

'Here, old chap: let me help you,' Arthur said. Darlington relaxed and Arthur placed a hand on Darlington's temple and with the other, reached down and hooked him under the chin. Darlington knew then what was going to happen. But not for long. Arthur tugged and twisted. As Darlington went limp, he pulled on his arms until the body came free and there was enough room to clamber over it.

A moment later, Arthur Shepherd tumbled out at the bottom of the slide onto a welcome pile of crash-mats. He stood up and dusted himself down, settling his thin and thinning hair across his scalp.

'Goodness,' he said to the attendant, 'how exhilarating! There's more to modern art than meets the eye, isn't there? Well, good afternoon to you and thank you for a most enjoyable visit.'

He was a few yards away when he heard the scream and good thirty yards away and making for the exit when Darlington's body was slowly shat out of the slide. An hysterical teenaged girl tumbled out on top of it.

It had been an odd sort of morning.

An hour later, sitting (as he had planned) at his table at Greville's, the tattered remnants of an excellent duck cooling on his plate, Arthur was thinking. Two British agents (albeit not terribly good ones) had tried to kill him and that simply wouldn't do.

Arthur had actually allowed himself to feel flattered that someone had gone to such lengths to bump him off until he realised how improbable it all was. Certainly the Council – even M.I.6 - had laid more elaborate traps in the past and establishing a new supervisor for a few weeks and priming the gun as it were, was not outwith the realms of possibility. However, it occurred to him that Mrs. Yardley might have been placed there for some other reason and that she just happened to have had the perfect opportunity to lure Arthur into a trap.

Suggesting the Tate had of course, been deliberate but to get the Rothko Room closed and come up with that plan to get him into the basement would have had to have relied a good deal on an understanding of Arthur's predilection for Rothko. He was on the brink of blaming Mulberry, when something occurred to him.

From the time he entered the building to the time he left, the name of Rothko had never been uttered. Arthur felt Co-incidence poke him in the ribs and say, "Told you!"

His telephone rang and with a sigh, Arthur slumped back into his chair. It was Mulberry.

'Ah, well done, Shepherd!'

'What?'

'Your phone's switched on.'

'We all make mistakes.'

'You're a Luddite, Arthur. Anyway, can you get over here this afternoon?'

'What's up?'

'Come and see what I've found in a room on floor 16.'

'Actually Mulberry, I'm not feeling a hundred percent at the moment. Can it wait?'

'Oh, I reckon so. It's jolly intriguing though. I don't know what you've stumbled on but it's shaping up to be quite interesting. Just call me when you're feeling a bit better.'

'Very civilised of you Mulberry. Goodbye.'

Arthur slipped his phone back into his jacket pocket and immediately felt it tickle his left nipple. He tutted and withdrew it.

'Bollocks,' he said, noticing who was calling.

'Ah, Shepherd. All done and dusted?'

It was Nightingale.

'Yes,' he said to the telephone. Nightingale would know nothing more than that Arthur was on a Council job and Arthur was happy to keep it that way.

'Good, good. We'd like to have you back here, this afternoon, if poss.'

'Oh?'

'Yes. Sullivan again, I'm afraid.'

'What has that to do with me?'

'We thought you'd like to be here.'

'Really? Well, sadly I think you are wrong on this occasion.'

'Shepherd, you misunderstand. We'd like you to come to Vauxhall Cross. At once.' Arthur sighed. He really needed to speak to someone about Nightingale.

'Do you know an Edward Darlington?' Arthur asked.

'No,' came the reply, 'should I?'

'He just tried to kill me.'

'Did he, indeed?'

'He was certainly S.I.S., although in what capacity, I didn't have the opportunity to determine.'

'You killed him, then.'

'I did. However, he managed to blurt out a name.'

'Oh?'

'Selam. Ring a bell?'

'No. Was this Darlington alone?'

'Does it matter?'

'Not really.'

'There was a woman.'

'There always is.'

'As far as Darlington knew, I was Arthur Henley; however, they both knew my real name.'

'Fame is a two-edged sword, Shepherd.' Arthur was losing patience.

'Who told you that the job was waiting for me?'

'As I recall, it was a memo from Floor D. Oh dear, don't tell me you fell for a ruse of some sort?'

'I think, in the circumstances,' Arthur said, ignoring the jibe, 'I might just pop home. I'm still a bit sore from yesterday and I think I may have done myself a mischief in the slide.'

'What slide?'

'Never mind. Anyway, I think I've suffered enough so if it's all the same to you, I shan't come over to Vauxhall Cross today.'

There was a slight pause at the other end of the line then Nightingale said,

'I suppose having two near-death experiences in as many days is pushing it, even for a Council Worker.'

'Yes, it is. Mind you, I remember once, in Beirut…'

'…Tomorrow then. I have you down for 2pm,' said Nightingale and hung up.

Arthur switched off his phone before putting it back in his pocket.

## Poor Old Mulberry

On his way from Blackfriars, intending to take the Northern Line from Embankment and the Piccadilly from Leicester Square, Arthur realised that what with his discomfort and the rush hour, his journey home was going to be a bit of a chore. A night at the club began to appeal as an alternative. A shave, a sauna, a massage and a hand or two of Bridge, followed by a late supper and few Cognacs would remind him why he still carried on doing this ridiculous job at his age.

As he stepped onto the platform at Embankment station, he noticed signs for the Bakerloo Line. Century House was only a stop away. He pulled out his phone and turned it back on, intending to tell Mulberry he'd decided to pop round after all. As it binged into life, a buzz told him he was in receipt of a text message. If not a job, Arthur's text messages generally concerned some feeble offer from some feeble company casting a very wide net over a very shallow sea. This one, however, was from Mulberry. He opened it and, puzzled, closed it again after a moment or two.

A bunch of numbers; that was all it was. No explanation, no clarification; just digits and the odd letter. It was clearly a code of some kind. What was Mulberry playing at?

He found Mulberry's number somehow and dialled it. Mulberry's cheerful voice told him to leave a message and he'd get back to him. Oh well, it was only one stop. If Mulberry had gone home, it wasn't the end of the world.

There was no reply to his courtesy knock so he opened the door to Mulberry's office and poked his head in. He knew immediately, of course, that Mulberry was dead. He didn't need to check for a pulse but he felt he owed him the courtesy. Opening his phone, he checked the time of the message. It had left Mulberry's phone eighteen minutes before. Arthur had never been one for "… if onlys…" so he set about trying to deduce what might have happened, muttering to himself the while.

'Very mucky. Not planned, that's for certain. What do we have…? Three, four bashes on the bonce? With the stapler, for fuck's sake…?

Now, if you'd had one of those plastic pieces of crap, you might have survived this lot but you had to opt for big old shiny steel job with the knob on the end, didn't you? Bloody hell. The bastard must be covered in blood and I'll wager you got a few lumps of DNA down your fingernails before he did for you, eh? Yes, I thought so; and a scrape or two on those knuckles as well? Well done, Mulberry! Now, what was it you found up on Floor 16, eh? Just piles of crap up there to disguise the place, aren't there? Tell you what: that'll just be our little secret eh? Right; I really need to find that despatch I left with you. Sorry about this, old man.'

Arthur was as expert as anyone could be when it came to searching corpses discreetly. No-one would know he'd done it. To his disappointment, however, he found nothing of interest. It is a good deal harder to search beneath a body without leaving signs but again, Arthur had got his badge for that about thirty years before. Although the mess was indescribable, Arthur was reasonably sure he hadn't missed the despatch.

Arthur called the Constables – he really couldn't put it off any longer – but continued his search for as long as he dared. Eventually he had confirmed to his satisfaction that the despatch note was nowhere to be seen and that it was likely whoever had killed Mulberry had taken it.

The usual team of three – a Sergeant and two Bobbies - turned up to do a preliminary survey of the scene. The Bobbies set to work at once, filming, photographing and recording the entire scene. Their Sergeant approached him.

'Arthur Shepherd? My name's Evelyn Bligh.' She shook Arthur by the hand. 'I understand you found him?'

'Yes.'

'You touched nothing, of course?'

'Of course.'

'Are you sure?'

The Constables are the least tractable, the most suspicious and amongst the most intelligent of Council Workers. Their job is to not only tidy up after any unplanned, spontaneous "incident" of the terminal variety, but also to get to the truth as to what had led to said "incident" occurring, with a view to collaring the party or parties who had been responsible. They are, in their own way, scrupulously fair but their adherence to procedure is legendary.

Being found by Constables in the vicinity of a fresh corpse is seldom an uncomplicated matter – even if you have been the one to call them. However, when you have something that you might not feel sanguine about sharing with them, it can be a very uncomfortable affair. Arthur knew he had to be on the ball.

And he most certainly could not get away with any sarcasm.

'Absolutely certain,' he said.

'Did you have an appointment with him or did you just happen to stumble upon him?'

'We had arranged to meet.'

'With what purpose?'

'He had some information concerning a case.'

'What sort of information?'

'Technical stuff, you know: numbers and such.' Another of the team handed Sergeant Bligh a slip of paper.

'It says here that you and he spoke on the telephone a short time ago and he sent you a text shortly after that. We will need your mobile.' Arthur handed it over without complaint. Sergeant Bligh held it as though she had recovered it from a building site portaloo.

'This is your mobile?' she asked.

'My telephone, yes. Is that not what you meant?'

'How long have you had this?'

'A few years, why?' She looked at him in the way his mother used to do if he sat down to the table without washing his hands. She called for an evidence bag and dropped the offending article into it.

'Sign here,' she said. 'And here; and here. We'll have it back to you as soon as poss.'

He had, to the best of his knowledge (admittedly limited in this area) made it appear as if the message from Mulberry had not been read. In a way, he had Mulberry to thank. The previous Monday, having been enlightened as to the parlous nature of secrecy in modern communication, he'd returned home, and had put his woefully underused smartphone in a drawer and fished out the old brick he'd given up using years before. Secure in its lack of sophistication, he had been using it ever since.

After marking the text from Mulberry as unopened, he'd switched the phone to silent mode. Ms Bligh's chaps would report that it was perfectly possible that he had not known a text had been received by his phone. And hadn't he handed it over without any fuss? There was no way the Constables would be able to prize much from its feeble memory.

Sergeant Bligh's questions and Arthur's answers bounced back and forth for some time until, apparently satisfied, she suggested they take a look around. Constables are not the police. They do not have to provide evidence in court and the concept of "burden of proof" has no meaning for them. They simply have to gather as much information as possible before making it appear as though nothing ever happened at all. They pass the information on to group of workers known as Inspectors and if further action is needed, someone (frequently someone like Arthur) is despatched.

'So then, Mr. Shepherd, anything seem... out of place?  Arthur surveyed the devastation.  Even though it was an open goal, it would still have been unwise for him to answer anything other than,

'I can't really tell.'

'Time to move him, Evelyn,' one of the Bobbies said.

'Right, Neville. Thanks. Lets see if he's hiding anything, shall we?' As Mulberry's body was lifted, Ms. Bligh knelt down and surveyed the paper-strewn surface beneath him. She stood up.

'By the look of things, the first blow did for him.'  Arthur had surmised as much.

'And yet, he said, 'they saw fit to hit him another three times.'

'Nervous,' said Sergeant Bligh. 'Not done this sort of thing often, if at all. Likely to be a bit on edge at the moment. Might give himself away before we even close in. I don't really think this will take that long.' She spoke to her colleagues. 'Every bit of paper within a yard of the body will need to be bagged. Sorry, chaps. Either of you come across his phone?' Both Bobbies shook their heads.

'Killer may have it,' said Ms. Bligh. 'Right, one each end and I'll get underneath. Try not to let him drip on me.'

Arthur gazed around the room and said quietly to himself,

'Poor Old Mulberry; you died as you lived – in a right old fucking mess.'

## A Bloody Big Number

'Haven't the foggiest,' Stuart Bracewell said, without looking up.

'Come along, Bracewell, Arthur said, 'you haven't even looked at it, for fuck's sake. I mean, what the hell do you lot do all day if not this sort of stuff?'

Before the Constables had arrived, Arthur had written Mulberry's message down exactly as it had appeared before marking it as unopened. He had brought the result to what in Council terminology was known as "Engineering". It was where phones were hacked and bugged and where messages were intercepted and deciphered.

'We encrypt and we decrypt, Shepherd: we do not track parcels.  I expect the Post Office is nearer your man on this one.'

'It's not a parcel tracking code, Bracewell.'

'Then what is it?'

'I can't tell you'

'Then I'm afraid I can't help you.' Arthur held it out and pointed to the first set of digits, and although Bracewell still refused to look, said,

'Look: Get rid of the letters in this first series: couldn't that be a phone number?'

'Good Lord!' gasped Bracewell, plucking the paper from Arthur's hand and waving it in the air, 'I think you could be right! Grafton! Grafton, get over here! Looks like Shepherd's cracked this one!'

'You haven't forgotten that I'm a trained assassin, have you, Bracewell?' Arthur said, as Grafton came over.

'Is he buggering you about, Arthur? Here, let me have a look.' Grafton snatched the paper from Bracewell. Upon it was a series of numbers and letters, which to Arthur appeared purely random. Mulberry had died soon after sending it and judging from the fact that there appeared to be no clue as to what it was, it may well have been *very* soon after sending it.

'Bracewell may be a tiresome sod,' Grafton said, glancing at his beaming colleague, 'but he's right about this. Unless we know what the purpose of the code is, we can't even begin to come up with a meaning. Context is extremely important. Where does it come from?' Arthur sighed, took back the piece of paper and slipped it into his pocket.

'I'm sorry,' he said, 'I can't tell you that. But thanks anyway, *Grafton*,' he said, pointedly and made to leave. Grafton's slightly raised voice stopped him.

'The last two numbers in the first 12 digit sequence are often a check-digit of some kind and coming out as two-zero might mean it's an internal memo either aimed at or coming from, one person.'

'Oh? Why's that?'

'I'm sorry, Shepherd,' Bracewell said, 'we can't tell you that.'

'Don't mind him, Arthur,' Grafton said, 'he's getting a bit antsy at all the changes round here.'

'He's not alone,' Arthur said.

'Yes, too much work and not enough people. We're down to just the two of us now. Let's have another look.' Arthur handed the paper over. Grafton scratched his nose and said,

'The two-zero thing: it's nothing but a convention. All internal memos check out at two-zero. That's the good news. The bad news is that if it represents anything as specific as, let's say, an individual, then it's likely to be untraceable. Twelve character alphanumeric – one or more characters of which are probably irrelevant depending on the day of the year – denoting one department; one Worker; one week and, if you're unlucky, one day. Randomly selected. The odds of hitting it just right come out at...' Bracewell was there ahead of him.

'5,591,320,323,850,000 to one,' he said.

'Billiard,' said Arthur, accusingly, 'is not a number.' Grafton laid his hand on Arthur's shoulder.

'It is, I'm afraid and take it from me: it's a bloody big number. Many factors of a billion greater than the number of people in the world,'

'Ha! If it is an individual, it'd be easier to go round everyone in London and beat the shit out of them until they told you if was them,' said Bracewell.

'I wonder,' said Arthur, looking at Bracewell, 'who I might begin with?'

'Come on, Shepherd, tell us where it's from. I'm actually beginning to be intrigued,' Bracewell said.

'No. But perhaps if you decipher it for me, you might find out for yourself.'

'All right, then. Just leave it here and I'll see what I can do.'

'Hang on,' Grafton said, hurriedly. 'We've got more than enough to do round here without that – sorry, Arthur. I mean he's forever complaining about short-staffing and workload and what have you. You don't have time for puzzles, Bracewell.'

'And you don't have the brains for them,' Bracewell said. 'Give it here.'

'I can handle it. You've got enough to do,' Grafton said, taking the paper from Arthur and lifting it out of Bracewell's reach. Arthur shook his head.

'Shit and corruption,' he said to himself. This may have been a mistake. Still, it was worth a try. The two were still bickering as he closed the door. Possibly anticipating that he might not have been able to show Arthur in person, Mulberry had chosen to send that little bunch of numbers to him and if he wanted to discover why, those clowns were his best hope.

He made his way back along the warren of corridors that comprised Floor 18 and called for the lift that would take him up to floor 16, the dummy floor that served as a firebreak between the Council and the outside world. To anyone coming down to Floor 16 for the first time, it was as dark, smelly, damp and dusty as it had been back when Arthur joined the Council – except of course, instead of being sixteen floors above ground, it was now one storey below.

Arthur took out a flashlight and picked his way through the chaos. Broken chairs, smashed water-coolers, even bits of garden furniture and old gym equipment – there had certainly been nothing like that in the old days.

He had thought that something so evidently important to Mulberry would make itself apparent relatively quickly but the longer he stumbled in and out of various rooms the more it began to dawn on him that whatever it was that Mulberry had found, unless he knew what it might be, Arthur Shepherd hadn't a cat in hell's chance of finding it.

## The Road to the Capanna

In the saddle once more, Vanessa waited. She had donned a thick duster coat to try to keep warm.

'Now, you should still make it to the Capanna by nightfall but it's going to be a much colder climb than you may have been hoping for,' said Caroline. 'There's little chance of you drying off much and the temperature will begin to fall rapidly after about five p.m. Even at the height of the Capanna, you're unlikely to freeze to death at this time of year, but you should keep those blankets around you and don't stop again until you get there. I'll see you all tomorrow on the other side. Gianfranco knows where and when.' She nodded at her servant, smiled and with a wave, she pushed her mount straight into a gentle rising trot.

They saw her again a couple of times after that, although only when Gianfranco pointed her out. Once, as she skirted a ridge about a mile distant and again, as a small speck far below, riding across the strip of marshy terrain they had encountered some four hours before.

Three further hours of climbing had been endured since that last sighting and Vanessa now believed she might die. Long ago, her feet had lost all sense of feeling unless, as she occasionally did, she bent her toes slightly and then, strangely reassuringly, excruciating pain knifed across them. Her hands were frozen, although several fingers still operated. However, the wind had dragged the last remaining excited molecules out of her skin and through the still-wet membrane of her shirt and fleece. Wherever the duster laid its weight on her frame, an icy compress scraped at her skin. But this was nothing compared to the discomfort elicited by her jodhpurs. Cold, wet and chafing, with each uncertain step that Abri took, another microscopic yet nerve-filled layer of skin felt as though it had been abraded from her thighs. She feared she may weep at any moment.

She had stopped looking upwards and now simply stared fixedly at the sliver of mountain track that bobbed and swung between the Haflinger's ears.

As the little group gained a low ridge, the last rays of the sun jumped from behind it and caught her. But any heat was long ago spent and as the riders edged slowly forward, the wind that had also been using the ridge as a hiding place, clutched at them with fingers of blistering cold, dragging and shaking their garments this way and that. Through water-filled eyes,

Vanessa took in the new vista and a moment later was startled by Gianfranco's cry.

'There!' he yelled above the piping of the wind and Vanessa followed the line of his outstretched arm. The sun was still teasing some of the higher peaks and valleys and far off, beneath a jagged pink and red tooth of rock surrounded by snow, Vanessa saw the cabin.

'Two hours. No more,' called Gianfranco.

Vanessa's heart sank. Gianfranco had sounded triumphant but two more hours of this was impossible to contemplate. What the hell was she doing here? At the time, she'd been convinced that going along with this mad thing was the only way out. Now, swaying in the saddle, dragging thin, freezing air through gritted teeth and shivering uncontrollably, she had the sense that the last couple of days had not happened to her at all.

To Vanessa, it appeared that her life was being taken apart, brick by brick and being reassembled in a manner she didn't recognise. It was an image she could not shift, even when she realised that she was pretty much hallucinating. Her thoughts became... blocks, like one of those little square puzzles where you have to push the numbers around to get them into sequence but every time you push a square aside, you realise it's blocking another that must be moved. Nothing seemed to fit. When a square of her old life seemed like it was about to fit into place, she would find it blocked by a bit of this new life. Suddenly, she realised that she was nodding off.

Ahead of her, the two men in whom she had placed her trust and her life were themselves slumped and rocking from side to side with each step. The inane tune, which had been playing in her head for a couple of days, took on the rhythm of their movement. It became a kind of children's song whose lyrics consisted of apparently random words like; "clip", "clop", "sway", "swish". In order to stop it, she had to speak to it quite sharply.

A great gash had been widening and deepening along the side of the track for the best part of the afternoon and evening. At this point, she reckoned, it could probably be defined as a ravine. She looked up, blinked and shook her head. Falling asleep, she realised, would be a really bad idea. But in spite of her efforts, again and again, the world, her horse, the mountains, the cold and the pain, would fracture and collapse and it would take her every ounce of willpower she possessed to keep sleep at bay. At one point, she looked into the ravine and imagined her life, now transformed into the blocks in a game of Tetris, drifting down into the blackness. She began to think she was losing her mind.

One hour and fifty minutes later, across a snow-covered stone bridge over the chasm, the three horses with their burden of frozen and weary travellers made their way and shortly thereafter came to a halt beside a singularly uninviting-looking timber building.

It looked as dark and cold as the surrounding rocks and Vanessa made no attempt to dismount.

'Vanessa?' It was Maytham. 'Vanessa, are you all right?'

She wanted more than anything to climb down from the horse and to get out of the cold wind. With great effort, she opened her hands, placed them on the pommel and made to dismount. After a moment or two, she realised that it wasn't going to happen.

'Vanessa?'

'I don't think I can move,' she said.

'Wait there, I'll come and help.'

With some apparent difficulty, Maytham dragged his right leg over the haunches of his horse and hung himself over the saddle for a few moments before sliding, heavily to the ground. She heard an involuntary moan escape him as his feet hit the stones. Even Gianfranco was moving slowly and carefully as he came towards her. Between them, the men took her weight and lowered her to the ground. She could not stand.

'Keys,' Gianfranco said to Maytham, tossing them over

Gianfranco swung Vanessa up into his arms and climbed the small flight of steps to the front door of the cabin. Maytham bustled past and undid a number of padlocks before finally turning a key in the front door. It swung open easily and they entered.

## Capanna dell'Aquila

Gloomy and damp, the only advantage that the cabin appeared to offer was proof against the wind and now, ten minutes after Gianfranco had lowered her into this battered armchair, even that benefit was beginning to pale. Gianfranco had disappeared and had returned with a rough blanket, which was now draped around her shoulders. Her legs and feet remained numb with fatigue and cold.

The only light was a torch, which was beside Gianfranco's knee as he worked on getting the wood-burner started. It was, he had said, their only source of heat for cooking and it would be a good hour before it was ready for any kind of service. Meanwhile, Maytham was on his knees beside the grate, making a small stook of kindling over a solitary firelighter. Three false starts and it began to glow. The kindling took and Maytham began to add some larger pieces of wood. Eventually, the fire began to draw and with a grimace, he stood up and began to arrange a number of pieces of metal in the fireplace. As he moved away, Vanessa saw an arrangement that was clearly designed for hanging a pot over the fire. She saw him turn and wink at her. He disappeared and returned with a kettle.

Twenty minutes later and the three of them were clutching hot mugs of tea. Vanessa took a first, grateful sip. The cold was slowly beginning to succumb to the combined efforts of the stove and the fire. Tilly lamps hissed away quietly on the windowsill and table. In their glow, Vanessa was able to see her surroundings more clearly.

'Cosier than I was expecting,' Maytham said.

Vanessa drew her feet onto the chair. They were tingling, on the cusp of pain. She winced.

'Are you all right?' Maytham asked.

'You know, I can't understand it. I mean, I know it's been years since I was on a horse but I didn't think it would affect me like that. I think I was actually hallucinating.'

Maytham smiled. 'It was a very hard climb; and that dip in the river didn't help, either. I was pretty done in as well.' He lowered his voice and nodded in the direction of the small scullery where Gianfranco was ministering to a large pan of frying meat and noodles. '...and between you and me, I think it even caught him out.'

'I'm going to be fit for nothing, tomorrow,' Vanessa said. 'Is there far to go?'

Maytham looked thoughtful. 'Not sure,' he said.

'But we'll be OK once we're on the other side of the mountains, right?'

Maytham cast a quick glance at Gianfranco and shrugged. 'Well, not necessarily. Alberges is in France, of course but the mountain borders are, shall we say, sometimes a little flexible.'

'How flexible?'

'Well, it's always seemed to me that it depends who built the dams,' Maytham said, with a smile. Vanessa smiled back but looked puzzled.

'Hydro-electric power,' Maytham said. 'There are lakes and reservoirs all over the place and each country uses them to provide cheap electricity. There are always disputes about who has rights to the meltwater and once an agreement is reached and a dam built, that pretty much becomes the notional border. Occasionally, there's even joint ownership and then it becomes really confusing.

'During the war, there were border controls on all the passes and they still remain on the main roads of course but frankly, no-one really knows exactly where the borders are and even if they did, it probably wouldn't matter to anyone up here. So the answer to your question is that we won't be truly in the clear until he tells us we are.' He nodded towards Gianfranco.

Vanessa said nothing. It wasn't the answer she'd wanted. The whole thing was just mad and again she became aware that she had no point of reference from which to draw up any kind of a plan. She'd tried to think things through on the way up the mountain before the cold had got the better of her. She'd try again once she'd rested and eaten. She really needed to make sense of it for the sake of sanity, if nothing else. For now, the only thing that was certain was that in the morning she'd have to get back up on that little horse and try to remain there whilst it stumbled and swayed its way down the side of a mountain. After that? Well nothing was at all clear. It was as if the life she was thinking about belonged to someone else and that thought helped her at least for the time being, to stop worrying.

The food was as good as it had smelled and the wine was, of course, excellent. The cabin was warming up and following their meal, they were all able to discard the blankets. Vanessa had gratefully clambered into her crappy jeans and a large woollen jumper, which Gianfranco had given her. Her mind had begun to work properly again and she wanted to quiz Maytham some more but she still wasn't sure what to make of Gianfranco. Caroline clearly trusted the laconic servant implicitly and in spite of the fact that he may well have saved her life, that was almost enough for Vanessa not to trust him at all.

She had no doubt that he wouldn't go to sleep before she did and so any conversation with Maytham would have to wait until morning. Once she had realised this, there was no longer anything stopping her body from wresting control away from her failing consciousness and in spite of her best efforts, she slept deeply until the shooting began.

## The Girl

It wasn't unexpected that Gianfranco would have a machine gun, although the fact that Maytham had one as well had thrown Vanessa slightly. The noise was extraordinary. Her body, doubtless just to be on safe side, flung her to the ground the instant that consciousness returned. Her hands clamped fruitlessly over her ears, she edged forwards on her elbows and belly until she had the solid stone chimney breast between herself and the shattered windows. When she heard one of the guns cease its chatter, she chanced a look. In the moonlight, she could see Gianfranco, his face calm, his movements measured and looking as unhurried as he had been when preparing dinner earlier that evening. Now, though, he was loading a gun. She couldn't see Maytham from where she was hiding but she heard him yell,

'Almost out!'

A second afterwards, Gianfranco, with a shout of 'OK!' resumed his firing position as Maytham took the opportunity to reload his own weapon.

As the Englishman was about to rejoin the fray, Gianfranco signalled with his hand and Maytham halted. Vanessa could hear nothing save the ringing in her own ears. Slowly, Gianfranco laid the machine gun on the floor and still looking out of the window, reached behind him and drew out a long rifle. With infinite care, he raised the gun until the very end of the barrel rested on the window sill. Neither he nor Maytham moved nor made a sound for what seemed an age.

Then another sound. A motorcycle? A smoke-filled cone of light swung rapidly through the room, as a headlamp passed across the far wall. Gianfranco shot twice and the light vanished. Silence once more. Then, in the distance, another bike. But this one was definitely bigger… and faster, for the sound grew rapidly until the note became one that Vanessa recognised. It was a sound she had heard only hours before, as she had crouched in freezing water beneath Pont Sacre.

Rotor blades; punching the air at almost four hundred times per minute sent debris flying in through the windows. Slate, stone, ice and snow swirled around the room. Seemingly oblivious, Gianfranco knelt by the window, sighting along the barrel of the rifle.

The sound, against all reason, became even louder until (no metaphor, this) the walls shook. It rose in a crescendo and once more, Gianfranco fired three times in rapid succession. Finally, the cacophony began slowly to diminish. Maytham asked,

'What are they doing?'

'Wait,' said Gianfranco, simply. He looked over at Vanessa and with his eyebrows and a gesture of the head asked her if she was all right. Vanessa nodded. She was shaking and felt sick but as far as she could tell, remained uninjured. Both men turned their attention to the window once more.

Then the whole room was ablaze with orange and yellow light followed a beat later by a tremendous explosion. Vanessa saw the two men duck below the window and she turned and flattened herself against the chimney breast. There was a slight tremor - that was all. When she dared to look once more, she noticed only a modest flicker of flame through the window. Gianfranco gestured, 'Stay there'. He remained at his post for a full minute then he beckoned to Maytham, who crawled over to his side. There was a whispered conversation and Maytham took over the rifle and assumed Gianfranco's position, as the Italian moved away from the window and crawled into the kitchen.

Through the open doorway, Vanessa saw him take hold of a small brass ring in the centre of the floor. With a gentle tug, a trapdoor rose silently. Beneath the kitchen, Vanessa knew, was a woodstore and adjacent to that the stable but surely, they'd have no chance of escaping on the horses. She didn't know Gianfranco well enough to realise that escape was not on his mind. She saw him give a wave and to her horror, Maytham, in response, struck a match and slowly and deliberately, lit the tilly lamp on the table. He walked over to the front door of the cabin and unlatched it. The bolts made a clatter that almost made her jump. What the hell were they playing at? Vanessa turned to see what Gianfranco was up to but he was no longer there. The trapdoor was closed.

'It's all right, Vanessa!' Maytham called out. 'We got the buggers. You can come out, now.'

'Bloody hell,' she said to herself, through gritted teeth, 'what the hell is he playing at?'

'Come on; it's fine. Let's get this mess cleared up.' Maytham said. 'Help me with this front door.'

Not a chance. There was no way she was going to leave her little alcove, at least not until she knew what the hell was going on.

Maytham leaned the rifle against the wall and to Vanessa's horror, he lifted the latch and the door swung open. There was a sound – utterly unidentifiable – that she decided was outside and after a moment or two of silence, Maytham stepped to one side and a black-clad figure stumbled in through the open door and lay sprawled at his feet.

As Gianfranco re-entered the cabin, he tucked one of the guns he was carrying, under his left arm. In one smooth movement, he grabbed the fallen figure by the collar and dragged it towards the fire. Lifting his captive into a kneeling position, he grabbed a handful of dark hair and tugged. With a squawk, more of defiance than pain, a face was revealed and Vanessa saw that it belonged to a young woman; early twenties, possibly; lithe, certainly; pissed off, definitely.

Gianfranco took out a pistol, cocked it and pressed it to the woman's temple. Maytham, grim-faced, took a step forwards but a glance from Gianfranco, stopped him dead. Gianfranco turned back to the woman and barked,

'Parlare!'

The girl had a slight accent, unplaceable, but her English was fluent.

'Fuck you,' she said.

Gianfranco's eyes widened and his lip curled. '*Parlare! Ora! O morire,*' he said and pressed the gun hard into the woman's head. She closed her eyes, tightly and set her jaw. Gianfranco tensed.

'Oh God, he's going to do it!' Vanessa felt sick. She screamed,

'Gianfranco! Stop it! She'll tell you what you need to know –won't you?' She looked the girl in the eyes. Gianfranco relaxed a little and drew the gun back a few centimetres.

'Well?' Gianfranco said, in English. The girl looked up at him and Vanessa could see clearly the mark Gianfranco's gun had made.

'Fuck you.'

Gianfranco's arm swung upwards and together, Maytham and Vanessa jumped forward, simultaneously crying,

'No!'

Gianfranco paused. His mouth trembled but then he relaxed. 'You are making a mistake,' he said to Maytham.

'Nevertheless,' Maytham said, 'Come; let me try. Please?'

Gianfranco turned his attention back to the girl.

'Hold her while I remove her boots,' he said. Maytham didn't move. After a dangerous moment, the Italian said, 'Then, after; you can speak with her.' As Maytham knelt down and took her arms, she shrugged herself free and her eyes blazed at him.

Gianfranco jerked his head towards Maytham and his eyes towards Vanessa.

'Help him,' he said. Vanessa knew she had little choice but felt the need to assert to Gianfranco the fact that he might well be in charge but he'd need to think twice before giving her orders of that kind. She steeled herself but made no move. To her surprise and relief, his eyes seemed to soften and he said, 'Please?'

Vanessa knelt at the girl's side and held her left arm in both hands, gripping it, (as her sister would do to her when they tussled together as children), with a slight twist and sly dig of the nails. The girl turned angrily and was about to remonstrate when Maytham grabbed her right arm. To a crescendo of profanities, the pair of them tipped her on to her back and her legs became trapped beneath her. Gianfranco sat on her left thigh and dragged her right leg out from beneath her. Her curses became unintelligible cries of pain as Gianfranco tugged the calf-length boot off and by the time the left boot had landed alongside it, the cries had given way to choking sobs.

It was too much for Vanessa who relaxed her hold just enough for the girl to drag her arm away, swing it around and rake her fingernails down Maytham's face. To his credit, he made only a sharp sucking sound between his teeth and refused to relinquish his grip. Gianfranco had clearly had enough. He hit the girl, hard, with the back of his hand and she sagged, her exhausted body heaving in time with her angry sobs.

Vanessa was torn. This girl had obviously been one of the party who had been shooting at the cabin and may have been willing to kill without a second thought. Christopher Maytham's face bore three broad streaks of red that could easily have graced her own, had it been he who had let loose his grip on the girl. And yet the anger she felt boiling up inside her was not directed at the girl but towards the man who had been appointed her guardian. Gianfranco took a single step towards the girl and in an almost balletic movement, swung his knee hard into her cheek. She went down, heavily and awkwardly and lay still.

'There was no need for that you bastard!' Vanessa cried.

'No?' Gianfranco said. He reached down and turned the girl over. Her left hand was thrust deep into a forward-facing pocket in the sleeveless jerkin she was wearing. As he pulled it out, Vanessa saw that it held what looked like an animal claw made of steel. She had clearly gone for it immediately after raking Maytham. Gianfranco wrenched it from her. As he did so, he winced and placed the side of his hand into his mouth.

'It's called a "crouchet", I believe,' said Maytham in answer to Vanessa's unspoken question. 'They use them in French bullfighting, to cut the ribbons that they tie between the bull's horns.'

'That is so. And killers use them to gut their victims and leave them to die in agony.' Gianfranco's face had darkened. There would be no more chances for the girl. As he reached into one of the boots, Gianfranco kept his eyes on Vanessa and as he removed a thin blade, some 20cm in length, she thought she saw him smile, bitterly. As he stalked off into the scullery, he tossed it towards her and it landed between her knees.

Once again, uncertainty began to overtake her. Lying next to her, looking like a discarded toy, a young woman lay bleeding but each time she thought about helping her, the same image flashed into her mind: something shiny and pointed sticking out of her chest. Maytham must have seen the despair and horror in her eyes for he took the girl's twisted legs, straightened them out and pulled her arm from beneath her. He laid her on her back and placed a cushion behind her head. If he signalled Gianfranco, Vanessa didn't see it but the Italian knelt beside the unconscious girl and tied her hands and feet together.

'Come along,' Maytham said, placing an arm around Vanessa's shoulder, 'it's over – for now. I don't know about you but I could do with a brandy.' To her shame, Vanessa Aldridge began to cry. Maytham helped her to her feet and as soon as she was upright, she shrugged him off and pushed him away from her with such force that he staggered backwards and fell into the table.

'Get away from me!' she screamed. 'Just leave me alone! Everything was fine before you showed up! I had a job! I had a life! I've done nothing! I don't understand any of this! Who are you people? How can you take all of this like… like it's… normal? You're fucking insane!'

Maytham, British diplomat, held up his hands in supplication.

'Why?' Vanessa yelled. 'Why am I here? Who is trying to stop me getting back to England and why are they doing it? Answer me!'

Maytham made no attempt to answer. Vanessa swept past him, opened the cabin door and went outside.

## PART 4 THURSDAY
## The Mountain

The night was bitterly cold and the tears on her face made it almost unbearable. Nevertheless, dragging her sleeve across her cheek, she walked down the small flight of steps onto the rock-strewn mountainside. She stood with her hands against her freezing face, her mind in turmoil. A few seconds later, Maytham was at her side, clothed in an anorak and a hat and offering similar ones to her. She donned them without a word and the pair stood, in silence. There was no trace of the helicopter but the smell of burnt fuel lingered on the still air. She would have thought that the thing would yet be ablaze but she could see nothing. Then she remembered the gorge. Vanessa speculated that the aircraft, its pilot flying blind after the searchlight was shot out, had simply flown into the mountain. The pilot may even have been shot, she didn't know. Whatever had happened, she felt sure that the machine was now lying at the bottom of the chasm.

Far off, thunder grumbled away and occasional gashes of light showed the teeth of mountains, many miles distant. Closer to, she could make out the line of some of the nearer mountains, cutting a deep violet gash into the indigo of the sky above them. Maytham spoke.

'Look, believe it or not, we all have your best interests at heart although, if I'm honest, they are not our primary concern. What is our primary concern, however, is to ensure that you arrive back in England as soon as possible, and as discreetly as possible.'

'You handled that machine gun like you knew what you were doing. You're no diplomat.'

'Well, I have been in the army. It's a not-uncommon route to the diplomatic service.

'You're a bloody liar!'

Vanessa was pleased that he appeared a little taken aback. It seemed to shut him up and there was a long silence as the two of them stood, their condensed breath whipping away within an instant of exhalation.

Vanessa watched the lightning for a full minute. She breathed in the icy air that tipped over from the northern slopes. Winter was not too far off. Probably never too far off up here.

'You're not going to tell me anything, are you?' she asked, without turning around.'

'It would place you in too much danger.'

'Oh really? It can get worse than this, can it? Practically freezing to death on horseback and being shot at by motorcyclists at the top of a mountain?'

'Yes. Yes it can. Believe me. You know, I really could do with that brandy. What do you say?' Vanessa swung her head back for one last look at the storms raging in the distance and said,

'I'd prefer to know more about Geoffrey Wittersham but I guess you're not going to tell me, are you?'

'I'm really very cold.'

'Yes, I believe you are,' Vanessa said, turning to face him. After a long moment, she looked back at the cabin. She could see Gianfranco closing the shutters. 'I don't trust you, Christopher. I can't. I don't trust him,' she said, jerking her head. 'And I certainly don't trust Caroline. But at least you have shown what a normal person might recognise as "decency" and for that reason I choose to give you the benefit of the doubt for the moment. But I deserve some answers, Christopher. Don't you think?'

Maytham showed no sign of relenting.

'I'm sorry,' he said. She turned to him again.

'Not as sorry as I am.'

She turned and walked back to the cabin. Maytham watched until she mounted the steps and disappeared inside. He clutched his jacket at the throat and whispered,

'Bugger it all to buggery.' And followed after her.

Although desperate for answers, Vanessa knew there was no point in trying to question Gianfranco. Even had he known anything, there would have been no more likelihood of him telling her than there had been of Maytham doing so. She decided, on balance, that the best thing she could possibly do at the moment would be to sleep. She looked down at the young woman who lay unconscious before the fireplace, her face red and beginning to swell, although there was, as yet, no sign of the livid bruise that must surely come by morning. As testament to her state of mind, Vanessa was, in spite of herself, grateful that Gianfranco had tied the girl up.

'You had better sleep.' It was Gianfranco. Carrying an armful of logs, he entered the room and as he passed her, Vanessa noticed that between two fingers, he was holding a small bottle of brandy. He indicated that Vanessa should take it. She did so and Gianfranco laid the logs in the fireplace.

He stood up, disappeared again into the kitchen and just as Maytham walked into the cabin once more, returned with three glasses and a polythene bag. Vanessa's stomach lurched. God, what was the bastard going to do, now? He set the glasses on the table and indicated that Vanessa should pour, before walking past Maytham and stepping outside. After a moment, he returned and Vanessa saw that he had filled the polythene bag with snow. He knelt down beside the girl and laid a tea towel over her jaw. Then, he gently placed the bag of snow upon it.

Vanessa began to weep, silently. Turning to them, Gianfranco said,

'This has been a very difficult day for all of us.' He raised his glass. 'Let us hope,' he said, 'that tomorrow will be better. Tomorrow.'

'Tomorrow,' said Maytham. Neither man drank until Vanessa had raised her glass, smiled weakly and said,

'Tomorrow.'

## Captain Flint

Arthur was pleased that he had decided to spend Wednesday night at his club. It had been late when he'd finally left Century House. There hadn't been an internal murder in a long while and a number of high-level meetings had been convened. He was due to attend one of them tomorrow. On the plus side, his involvement in the investigation meant that he was not likely to receive any new jobs until it was over with. Right now, he was in the dining room.

'You were the toast, Mr. Shepherd, weren't you?' said the waitress, as she laid it before him. He glanced up.

'Ah, yes, Genevieve, I was once the toast of all London!' She laughed and said,

'I just bet you were!' She'd got his feeble play on words and that cheered him enormously. She was obviously an indigent student of some species who was financing her studies. He must leave a generous tip. Not too generous, of course. He didn't want to be flattered for tips. The girl reached into her apron.

'Oh, and I was asked to give you this. Apparently, it was brought round earlier.'

She handed him a small package. He opened it and found his mobile phone, which he had given over to the Constables the night before.

'Blimey, that was quick,' he said. Stainforth glanced up from his Telegraph.

'Your phone? Yes we don't need them long nowadays. Get all you need in minutes. But looking at that thing, seconds would be nearer the mark.'

Arthur looked across at Stainforth.

'Sleep well?' he asked, refusing to rise to the bait.

'Always do, these days, old chap. Except for getting up for the lav every couple of hours. Expect you know how it is.'

'I don't, as a matter of fact.'

'Ah. Hidden from you are the delights of the enfeebled prostate, eh? Lucky sod. I say, isn't that Ricketts over there? I wonder if he knows about his oppo biting the dust?'

Arthur turned around. At the table by the window, Ricketts sat eating breakfast. Or rather, looking at breakfast. Around him, three men. The grey suits said it all.

'Probably,' said Arthur.

'What with that and the Paris business; too many slip-ups round here, if you ask me.'

'Paris business?'

'Ah yes, you were otherwise engaged on Tuesday weren't you? Well, there was this do in Paris – something to do with the D.P.S.D.; I don't know. Anyway, two of our bods copped it there. One of your chaps, and another from Clerical; name of Kirkwood. Right mess, by all accounts.'

Another one? Arthur wondered whether he should tell Stainforth about his adventure yesterday: but only for a moment. He turned back to Stainforth and as he did so, caught sight of Grafton in the doorway, obviously looking around for someone.

'Grafton!' Arthur called out. Grafton spotted Arthur and raised his hand somewhat hesitantly. 'Looking for me?' said Arthur, as Grafton approached. 'Don't tell me you've sorted out my little problem already?'

'Arthur! Erm, yes, as a matter of fact, we did – up to a point.'

'How sharp a point?'

'Not terribly, I'm afraid. Drop by tomorrow and I'll explain.'

'Can't you tell me now? You wouldn't mind, would you Stainforth?'

'Not at all,' Stainforth said, indicating a vacant seat. 'Make yourself at home, Grafton. How are you, by the way? Didn't know you were a member.'

'I'm fine, Rupert, thanks for asking; and I'm not, actually. I'm here to meet someone. Shepherd, are you quite sure that...'

'Grafton, if I trusted Bracewell, I'm sure as buggery going to trust Stainforth. Besides, it doesn't sound as though you've come up with anything especially earth-shattering. Now do sit down, there's a good chap.' As Grafton eased himself into the chair, Arthur said, 'Grafton and his chum have been trying to help me solve a little puzzle, Stainforth. Now, Grafton...'

'Well, I'm sorry to disappoint you, Arthur but it's just gibberish, I'm afraid. Random numbers and letters. I suspect the original message was corrupted in transmission. Poor old Bracewell worked on it for hours before he realised.'

'Oh,' said Arthur. 'That's a pity.'

'Yes, sorry to be the bearer of bad news but... well, there it is.'

'Transmission from where?' Arthur said. Grafton's hesitation told Arthur all he needed to know.

'Er... well, I suppose I just assumed it was sent to you.' Arthur waited. 'I mean, most things are, aren't they? *From* somewhere; *to* somewhere.' Arthur waited some more. Down phone lines or wirelessly or whatever.' Arthur presented Grafton with his cheeriest smile.

'I suppose you're right,' he said. 'Bloody electronics, eh?' Grafton laughed uneasily, as Arthur went on, 'Never had this trouble in the old days, eh, Stainforth? We'd be better off with pen and paper, wouldn't we? Even typewriters... or teleprinters, eh? Ah, well, no help for it, I suppose. Thanks for trying, Grafton and tell Bracewell I owe him a drink.'

'Yes, yes I shall,' Grafton said. 'Er, I'll have another look at it for you if you like – when I get the chance. You never know, eh?' Rising, he said, 'Anyway, I'd best be off. Nice to see you again, Stainforth.' With that, Grafton scurried away.

Neither man said anything for some time. Stainforth broke the silence.

'Want to tell me what that was about?'

'Not really but since you ask: for reasons best not gone into, I have determined to see if I can't track down the originator of a Cleaning request.' Stainforth thrust out his lower lip and forced his jowls to sink even lower than their usual saggy station.

'Going off piste again, Shepherd? You'll come unstuck one of these days,' he said.

'Your concern is noted, Stainforth but I think this is worth getting a bit of stick over.'

'That's probably why he's lying,' Stainforth observed

'Oh, you noticed that?'

Stainforth chuckled and said, 'I know I've not been in the field for a long while, Shepherd but I'd have to be an utter arse not to notice it!'

'The only people who lie as badly as that are scared people,' Arthur said. 'I'll have to have a bit of a think.'

'You mentioned Bracewell? Would that be Stuart Bracewell?'

'I believe so. Do you know him?'

'Yes. Odd cove: bit of a boffin: but I'd be surprised if he were messing you about.

'Stainforth?' said Arthur, 'I need a little favour.'

'Gladly, old chap, if it's in my power.'

'If you get a moment, would you mind running into Bracewell on some pretext or other and telling him what Grafton told me?'

'Oh, I think I could manage that. Rather flattered to be asked, to tell you the truth. Not much opportunity to play the Old Game proper these days, what?' Stainforth, still smiling, went back to his boiled egg and Arthur picked up his Guardian. The papers were still feeding off the Knightsbridge bomb, of course. Page after page of speculation but little in the way of information. In terms of facts, there were none of which he was unaware but he read the articles, anyway. It was with some satisfaction that he noted on page 14, that following a fatal accident at Tate Modern yesterday, the installation by Carsten Holler had been closed on health and safety grounds. There was, however, no mention of the demise of a "Supervisor: Permanent Exhibits". Arthur was not surprised. Someone would have put a lid on it good and proper.

'Shepherd?' It was Stainforth. He peered at Arthur over his glasses. 'You had a look at the Telegraph crossword this morning?'

'No. I don't do it as often as I used to – now that I don't have to. Why, what's up?'

'I think we might have a little Treasure Island going on.'

'Really?'

Arthur folded the Guardian and picked up the Telegraph. Many years ago, before more sophisticated techniques had evolved, both M.I.6 and the Council would sometimes hide messages in the Times Crossword. There would be certain clues that would be of significance to those who knew what to look out for. Patterns and themes would indicate, for example, who the message might be aimed at or where meetings might take place. All Council Workers had been required to complete the Times Crossword each day.

But as soon as that venal Aussie twat had taken over, things had altered. Some of the writing became barely literate for a start and even Council employees weren't paid enough to wade through that. So gradually, the Telegraph had taken over as message-board of choice. As far as he knew, though, the Intelligence Services had stopped messaging this way in the nineteen nineties. Now, according to Stainforth, there appeared to have been a posting.

'Have a look Shepherd. Could be a co-incidence or I may even, God forbid – have got it wrong. See what you think.'

Arthur took out his pen and folded the paper back on itself. The clue offering the most words was: 4 & 13 Down: 'Carriage-clock, gone a bit flat?' (7, 9). Arthur wrote in: "RAILWAY TIMETABLE". Next longest was: 6 Across: 'He's a hard skipper!' (7, 5) Arthur froze, his pen poised over the page.

'Well, I never,' he said, as he filled in each square: "CAPTAIN FLINT".

Stainforth was right: it could always be coincidence. There would have to be at least two other pertinent clues within this puzzle to be sure a signal was being sent. In addition, he would have to identify the person for whom the message was intended and that would come in the form of a coded answer. The answer that would signal that it was for him was "BARKING". He settled down. 7 Across: 'Slightly twisted shard of precious metal, maybe?'(6); 17 Across: 'They're not damp so Ezekiel will nab one, surely?'(5) and the real giveaway; 17 Down: 'Dark cur! Back gold for a good return.'(5, 3). There could be no doubt, now. Something wasn't quite right, though. Not only were the clues very easy, the answers were far too obvious. Even someone who wasn't looking for them could spot the relationship, easily.

'This is pretty amateur stuff, Stainforth. Or at the very least, bleeding obvious stuff.'

'I agree.'

'How far do think the rot has gone?'

'Sorry, old man?'

'What you were saying the other day about the quality of new recruits; surely it can't be as bad as you say.'

'I'm afraid it is, Shepherd. The whole of Box Standard is full of these people, now. They leave documents on trains and CDs in taxis and (probably so busy with their i-pods) lose data pens on the Tube. They give interviews to newspapers and take their employers to tribunals. They even go on telly, for God's sake! Documentaries, the lot! You were right in the middle of their latest cock up. You of all people should be aware of it after what happened the other day.'

Stainforth stopped suddenly and his eyes began to sparkle. Stifling a chuckle, he said,

'I say, Shepherd; I say, the only thing that would get you to notice… would be… if they were put a bomb underneath you! What!? What!? Eh?' He roared with laughter until he choked on a breadcrumb. Arthur passed Stainforth a glass of water and resumed the crossword. There had as yet, been no indication that the message was for him. And then: 27 Across: 'The sound of 17 Down, perhaps, may stop his majesty from entering East End borough.' *(7)*

There was no real information in a Treasure Island pointer, it was just a flare going up over a choppy sea, but one of the other answers (STRAND) did tell him where to find the information. He had to get to the toilet within the hour.

## The Dam

The little party stood before the cabin as Gianfranco locked the door. They had arisen only an hour before and the sun was bringing welcome warmth to Vanessa's limbs. She could barely believe, on waking, how much her body ached. Every move sent shards of agony through her legs and across her back and she had actually collapsed on several occasions, her calf muscles apparently unable to support her tottering frame.

'The next day's always worse, isn't it?' Maytham had asked, as he'd limped into the small sitting room with the coffee pot. 'I don't ride nearly enough,' he'd said. After breakfast, they'd noticed that even Gianfranco had seemed a little unsteady, as he'd worked to return the cabana to the condition that Caroline would no doubt have expected and so they'd helped. He'd seemed grateful.

Vanessa looked over to the girl. She hadn't eaten with them that morning and this was the first time she had managed to get a good look at her. As she'd thought, the girl's face looked a mess. Her jaw was swollen and a yellow-edged purple bruise had blossomed across the lower half of her face. Her lip was split and there was a heavy and bloody plaster over one eye. She clearly hadn't been allowed to bathe, either and her dark hair was lank, greasy and here and there, stiff with blood. She seemed to be moving with some difficulty. Her right arm was tethered to the pommel of Gianfranco's horse by means of a thin leather strap, which allowed her very little movement. She would be spending a good deal of energy and concentration trying to keep clear of the horse's hooves, Vanessa noted; and that was probably Gianfranco's intention.

'Now,' Gianfranco was saying to the girl, 'if you try anything foolish, I shall tie that other wrist... to that ankle and you will walk down the mountain like that.' He turned to the others. 'We must lead the horses down the steepest parts. In maybe one hour, we will be able to ride for a while.' He clicked his tongue and tugged on his horse's rein. 'Stay well in front and don't let the horse step on you,' he said, as he led them forward.

It wasn't as easy as Vanessa had thought it would be. As Abri made her way downhill, all plodding resignation, Vanessa stumbled, slid and fell before her. Where it wasn't snow-encrusted and slimy mud, the way comprised slivers of grey shale, which rode across one another as if lubricated, so that each step was an adventure. The stress of simply staying upright gave Vanessa no time to contemplate her situation and in that wonderful way in which humans deal with things, her situation didn't seem half so bad as it had the night before. Although the sun was shining brightly on the southern slopes, here, on the north side of the Alps, only occasionally did it knife through the odd cleft to provide a little warmth and even that was not always appreciated, as the strain of the descent generated more than enough heat within Vanessa's aching body.

As he had promised, within the hour they came upon a valley and were able to mount. All except the girl who walked, a little more strongly it seemed to Vanessa, close beside Gianfranco's horse. Vanessa spurred her little mount forward until she came alongside the girl.

'What's your name?' she asked. There was no response and Gianfranco turned his head towards her. She saw him smile and shake his head, obviously amused at Vanessa's naïveté. When he looked ahead once more, Vanessa said,

'Why did you come after us?' This time, it was the girl's turn to look. She did not smile. 'Look,' Vanessa went on, 'I haven't the faintest idea what's going on and these two won't tell me. I just thought you might be able to help me out, a little. That's all.' This time, Gianfranco's expression was less benign. He tugged on the leather strap and urged his mount forwards at a slow trot. The girl staggered a little but quickly and without complaint, took up the pace. Vanessa saw her glance back in her direction, an expression on her face that she couldn't readily identify.

The valley began to broaden out and at its far eastern end, Vanessa realised that the natural curve of the slopes was giving way to something altogether more straight and artificial. As they neared it, she could see that it was a wall. Before they reached it, however, Gianfranco indicated a track to their right, which rose for a short distance and then disappeared behind a hill. The girl had a little more difficulty with the climb but still said nothing as she clambered upwards. Ahead of her, Vanessa saw Gianfranco and the girl top the ridge and begin a descent down the other side. For a few seconds, they were out of sight before Vanessa herself gained the ridge.

On the other side was one of the most beautiful and terrifying things she could ever recall seeing. Some two hundred metres below lay a lake of blue-black water. The line of the mountainside was all that she needed to tell her that it must have been astonishingly deep and although the far end, over a kilometre distant, shimmered in the sun, for most of its length it was dark, desolate and forbidding. They had not yet encountered the tree-line and vast, blue-grey scree slopes bound the lake on all sides. This, combined with the very unlikeliness of it being there at all, lent it an air of unreality. It was impressive but not, Vanessa decided, in a good way.

'This is one of those hydro-electric dams, I was telling you about,' Maytham said, as he too, crested the ridge.

'Who does it belong to?'

'Anyone's guess. If we go past the plant itself, we may get a better idea.' Maytham looked around. 'It's only mid-morning but you'd think it was dusk.' He was right. The darkness that surrounded them was palpable and Vanessa had to admit to herself that the whole place made her feel uneasy. The thought that kept running through her head was that this would be the perfect place to dump a body. As far as she could remember, no place she'd ever visited before had caused her to muse upon its potential as a site of corpse disposal.

A quarter of an hour later and she was feeling rather better. They were in sunlight once more and the lake had taken on the familiar blue-green of others she'd encountered. It had been apparent for many metres that the head of the lake was bounded by a vast, concrete wall and as she drew nearer, Vanessa was able to estimate that it rose some ten metres from the surface of the lake. In the distance, she could hear a roaring sound that was impossible to place. The nearest she could manage was the M23.

Intellectually, she had known that the dam would have had to have been enormous but it was not until she had followed Gianfranco across the narrow service road that led, ultimately, over the structure and had begun to head down into the valley, that its immensity was revealed. The roar, it turned out, was caused by a jet of water, which shot out in a great arc from the face of the dam, some eighty metres below them. To her left, Vanessa was relieved to see a chain-link fence designed to prevent wayfarers from stumbling into the gorge. The top of it, however, was at the level of her saddle and she steered Abri as far away from it as the track would allow, her boot scraping along the granite wall beside her.

About twenty minutes of this and then the track appeared to widen out to accommodate what was clearly a view point. Whether it was a natural feature or whether the granite had been cut away, Vanessa couldn't tell but it had the appearance of a small amphitheatre, graced by two low benches, which were set into the ground. To her left, and slightly above, there was the great gush of the dam outfall, jetting many metres out into the gorge, disappearing into the gloom.

Squinting against the spray that was drifting away from the jet to drench the bleak landscape, Vanessa was able to glimpse, beyond the cliffs that formed the far side of the gorge (and God knew how far below), a broad sunlit valley. There was a railway line and a road and buildings and although they must have been many hours distant, the sight of them lifted her heart.

Gianfranco raised his hand and they all came to a halt.

Whether he said anything or not, Vanessa couldn't tell. The noise from the outfall was deafening. She saw him unwind the tether in order to give the girl a little slack. He tugged on it and she reluctantly moved around to the horse's right, leaving him space to dismount. As he lifted his right leg, placing his weight on his left, Vanessa saw the girl perform a series of frantic movements and suddenly, Gianfranco was on the ground.

His saddle, to which the girl was still tied, span above him, as she took the strain. Immediately, Maytham dismounted and ran towards the girl. Not quickly enough. She let the saddle fall and it landed on Gianfranco, even as he was trying to raise himself. He was caught off guard and stumbled a little. In a trice, the girl leapt onto the back of Gianfranco's horse.

For a moment, it looked to Vanessa as though she was going to try to get away on horseback but as Maytham made a grab for her, she threw her full weight on top of Gianfranco, her elbow smashed him in the face. The horse was now rearing, wildly so that Maytham could not get around it. He smacked the animal hard on the rump and it took off down the track. Only for a fraction of a second, Maytham's eyes followed it and when he turned back, the first thing he saw was Gianfranco's rifle pointed straight at his chest.

## In the Cubicles

Where else would you install the country's first fully functional electrochemical biosensor device, but in the lavatories at Charing Cross Station? It was in stall six and most of the time looked like a perfectly ordinary advertisement for flavoured condoms. However, when certain people entered stall six, they would be detected and the advertisement would become a message-board, capable of displaying any visual information whatsoever.

Arthur had had the implant for about two years and had used it in earnest, as it were, only twice before but this time, as he sat there, trousers around his ankles for the look of the thing, the advertisement steadfastly refused to reveal anything beyond the assertion that the flavour would last and last... come what may. Thoroughly emptied and increasingly concerned about his haemorrhoids, Arthur decided it was time to exit stall six.

Usually, and before now, he would have realised that he was not the expected recipient and would have left and gone about his business but in light of recent events, he determined that he was not going to let it rest, just yet. Trouble was – and this is one of the reasons the secret services had always liked lavatories - it was unwise to loiter too long.

Of course, as a younger man, he had spent quite a bit of his spare time in this and other lavatories throughout the capital but then, unlike today, one would have known which had the less zealous and occasionally (what would one say?) more *"pro-active"* attendants. A couple of pence and one could stay in there practically all day. Now it was all C.C.T.V. and counting turnstiles and frankly, nowhere to hide.

This morning, In order to avoid being disturbed, he had opted for major ablutions. No-one wants much to do with a man who has to wash his entire body in a public toilet and as he stood, stripped to the waist, shaving for the second time in four hours, he kept a close watch on stall six.

The first occupant had been a young man who had appeared to be a student. On balance, Arthur reasoned, it was unlikely that he was an agent, owing to the fact that however deeply under-cover one might be, one wouldn't walk through a lavatory playing Super Mario on a Nintendo DS and then fail to wash one's hands afterwards. The second man was a little more difficult to eliminate. Expensively suited, Telegraph on board, he strode directly for stall six without trying any of the other doors. After only a couple of minutes, he exited and made his way to the wash-basins, choosing the one immediately to the right of Arthur who, by this time was washing his hair.

Arthur tensed ever so slightly as the man looked into the mirror and caught his eye. He gave Arthur a pleasant enough smile and nodded a non-committal greeting. Arthur reciprocated in like manner and returned his gaze to his own reflection; or rather, beyond it, to the mirrors on the opposite wall where, from his position, he was able to watch his own and eight other backs. With his left hand, the man turned on a stream of warm water and with his right, slotted his folded Telegraph behind the taps. Both hands now free, he washed them, not in the brusque, peremptory manner of your average toilettier, but thoroughly and methodically. Arthur was beginning to think he had his man, when his eye fell on the folded newspaper. The crossword was clearly visible and was, most assuredly, letter-free.

Arthur breathed out through his nose and just to make sure, put his soapy head into the basin and ladled several handfuls of water over it. The man had a perfect opportunity. However, the fellow moved to the dryer, spent a full minute wringing his hands before reaching back around Arthur and retrieving his paper. Then, having bought a packet of flavoured condoms from the machine, he left.

Arthur had finished his armpits, had dried and was beginning to do up his shirt, by the time the lad from M.I.6 turned up.

Early twenties, green corduroys and brown brogues; Charles Tyrwhitt shirt, check jacket and honey-coloured waistcoat. He was topped off with clear skin, public school haircut and if that were not enough, he carried a small slip of paper, alternately scrutinising it and the stall numbers until he came to a halt outside stall six. It was occupied by a railway worker at present but instead of busying himself with some toilet-related activity, as Arthur had been, this chap simply stood outside stall six and waited. Arthur felt ashamed of his profession.

His tie now arranged and his jacket back on, Arthur was ready just in time. The railway worker, all hi-vis jacket and CAT boots, emerged and laddo was in. Before he had time to lock the door, Arthur barged into stall six. In one movement, he grabbed the young man by the upper arms, twisted him around and forced an arm up his back – not too far; he didn't want a scream. Arthur bashed the door closed with his bottom. A number of eyes swivelled around at the bang, saw nothing and refocused on the urinal.

'Good morning,' said Arthur.

'What on earth do you think you're doing?' said the young man, over his shoulder. 'I'm not gay, if that's what you're thinking.' Arthur was offended. He said,

'Oh, is that how homosexuals introduce themselves nowadays? They barge into other men's lavatory stalls, do they? "Hello, I'm a homosexual and I hope you don't mind if I watch you defecate" sort of thing?'

'Well...what are you, then?'

Arthur patted him down and removed a gun and a wallet from an inside pocket. He put the wallet into his own jacket pocket and the gun into the young man's back. He checked the other pockets. Nothing.

'This is a dart gun,' Arthur said, turning the weapon in his hand. 'Why do you have a dart-gun?'

'I... I'm not telling you anything,' the boy said, uncertainly.

'Fair enough. I'll just unload it into your arse then, shall I and sit back and watch the fun?'

'Please... I...'

'Guards?' asked Arthur.

'Eh?'

'I'll bet you're with a Guards Regiment. Blues and Royals, I'd say.'

'How...?'

'Oh, bit of a toff, not too bright.' Arthur grabbed the young man's buttocks. 'Ooh, fine seat. Yes, definitely Blues and Royals. Now just let me find a decent spot and we'll soon see what this thing's loaded with.'

'All right!' the boy said, 'It's a tranquiliser gun. I'm supposed to... tranquilise somebody with it.'

'Who?'

'I don't know.'

'You don't know?'

'Not yet. I have to wait in here until I get a message. Why are you smiling?

'Put your hands on your head. Now, slowly turn around and keep your eyes on the knot in my tie. If you see my face, I shall have to kill you. That's it; now, sit.'

He sat, bringing his face level with Arthur's crotch.

'Oh God!' he moaned, 'you *are* a homosexual, aren't you? Look, I have to tell you, I'm expecting someone. He'll be here any minute!'

'Ooh, a threesome!' said Arthur. He looked pensive. 'Although, it's been a while. Hope I'm still up to it.'

'Oh God!!' the young man wailed. 'Look, just tell me what you want!'

Arthur pointed behind the young man's head. Terror flooded back into his face as he read the advert for flavoured condoms.

Arthur looked at his watch. About now, he reckoned.

With no sound, nor any alteration in light intensity, the advert slowly faded and in its place, three words:

ID CENTAUR CONFIRMED

This in turn faded, to be replaced by a picture of Arthur beneath which a label read:

CODENAME: "RATTY" TWEP.

Arthur watched the image fade and then, flavoured condoms back in their allotted slot, he hauled the young man to his feet. As he did so, their eyes met.

'Oh no,' said the young man, jaw dropping, eyes widening etc.

'Oh dear,' Arthur said, 'now that is a pity.'

'I mean, no! No, now I come to think, it's not you at all; it's someone else!'

'No. It's me, I'm afraid.'

Arthur slipped his hand into his pocket, removed the young man's wallet, extracted a card from it and read aloud:

'Alan Hesketh-Macgregor. Did no-one suggest you leave this behind, Alan?' Alan bridled. Arthur's telephone rang. He listened for a moment then said, 'In a toilet… Charing Cross… Yes, that one.' He listened for a few more seconds before looking at Alan and saying, 'Fine. Oh, I have someone with me… Yes, yes, in the toilets, Jennifer… No, no I haven't. I'm far too old and ugly… Yes, I'm sure you'd like to meet him. See you soon.' He put the phone away.

'Come on. Almost lunchtime,' he said. 'I know a little place.'

## The Track

The girl stood up, all the while keeping the rifle aimed at Maytham. As she rose, she placed a foot squarely across Gianfranco's windpipe. He was clearly in pain. Nevertheless, he grabbed the girl's ankle. She increased pressure until he let her go and lay still.

'Over here!' she shouted above the roar of the water. Maytham, his hands above his head walked slowly towards her until she called out,

'That's far enough!' She took a step or two back and said, 'Now, his knife.'

The rifle barrel described an arc as Maytham stooped down. He retrieved Gianfranco's knife and as he stood, she took the rifle in her left hand. Keeping it levelled at Maytham, she held out her right arm and moved away from the saddle.

'Cut me loose!' Slowly, Maytham bent down. He took the leather strap and formed a loop. He placed the knife in the loop and tightened his grip on the strap. Suddenly, the rifle barrel wheeled around and the girl took aim at Vanessa. She raised her voice so that Vanessa might hear.

'You look to me like a man who might risk his own life but are you willing to risk hers?' Maytham swallowed. With a single stroke, he severed the tether. Immediately, the rifle was on him again.

'What now?' he asked.

'Now, she gets off that horse and she ties it to the fence!' She jerked her head to the right. 'Then, she ties you to that bench.' She jerked her head to the left. 'And she does it properly...' she turned to Vanessa. '...doesn't she? Because if she doesn't: I might just decide to make my life a lot easier and kill you now, Mr Maytham. And believe me; it will take a good deal less than that to make me kill this one.' She sent a hefty kick into the ribs of the unconscious Gianfranco.

'Do as she says, Vanessa!' Maytham called over.

Vanessa dismounted as Maytham sat on the bench.

'Give her the knife,' the girl said. Vanessa approached the girl, who still held out her arm. Vanessa cut the bond close to the girl's wrist and, as instructed, handed over the knife. Taking the length of leather, Vanessa, knelt down beside Maytham.

'I'm so sorry,' she whispered.

'Don't worry about me,' Maytham replied. 'Make it as tight as you can. She'll check, so do a good job.' The girl threw across another strap.

'Feet, as well,' she commanded.

Once Maytham was bound fast to the bench, the girl bade Vanessa do the same to Gianfranco, who appeared to be coming to until his own rifle-butt caught him right across the bridge of his nose. There was a great deal of blood.

As she finished the last knot, the girl ordered her to sit at Maytham's feet, which she duly did. The girl then went around checking the bonds and when she had finished, turned the rifle on Vanessa once more and said to Maytham,

'Money.'

'My jacket,' he said, 'over there.' The girl indicated that Vanessa should get it. As she removed the wallet, the girl said to her,

'Here.'

On the girl's instructions, Vanessa proffered the open wallet and girl took hold of the notes. She shook them free and let the wallet fall the ground. Having briefly counted the notes, she folded them and stuffed them into her jerkin. She did the same with Gianfranco's wallet.

Next, she checked both men and horses for weapons, finding a handgun on Gianfranco as well as the machine guns that Vanessa had seen used the previous night. She stuffed the handgun into her belt and hurled the other weapons into the gorge, along with anything she didn't appear to want to take with her. She undid the rifle holster from Gianfranco's saddle, attached it to Maytham's and slipped the rifle into it.

'Now, get back on your horse and continue down the track - slowly.' Vanessa did so. As she rode past her, the girl picked up the reins of Maytham's mount, swung herself into the saddle and urged the horse forwards. Vanessa turned to see the girl, the rifle now across the saddle in front of her, following close behind. Beyond, she could see the figure of Christopher Maytham, bathed in mist from the outfall, bound to the bench and tugging at the now-soaking leather thongs, tightening them with every movement. On the opposite side of the track, tied to a concrete fence-post, lay Gianfranco. Vanessa thought she saw his leg move.

'Hey! We're going that way,' said the girl. Vanessa faced forwards, once more and tried to adjust to this new development. She was amazed how calm she felt.

When the roar of the outfall had faded somewhat, Vanessa turned in her saddle, once more.

'Gianfranco said we should dismount, back there,' she said.' It looks a bit steep to me.'

'Does it?' The girl said, flatly. 'Had much experience riding in the Alps, have you?'

'Not really. Have you?'

'Concentrate on the path.'

Vanessa remembered back to the capanna and how the girl had been beaten into unconsciousness rather than give anything away and realised she was unlikely to get very far. But then, a thought occurred to her.

'Why have you taken me?' she asked. There was no response from the girl. 'Do you know why you've taken me?' Again, silence. 'You don't know, do you? I think…'

'No-one cares what you think.'

'I think you're under orders from someone and they've told you…'

'Be quiet.'

'…They've told you that I'm valuable and they've paid you a lot of money to…'

'I said, be quiet!'

Vanessa decided to shut up. She'd seen what the girl was capable of. Even so, in some strange way, she felt safer coming down the mountain with her than she had going up the mountain with Maytham and Gianfranco. Abri stumbled but the effect on Vanessa was little beyond a mild jolt. Nevertheless, she decided she had better pay closer attention to the track. It glistened and a small rivulet trickled down between the myriad flat shards of shale. Even on foot, this might be a bit tricky but swaying atop a horse, however used to the terrain it might be, and this close to the edge of a mountain was not fun. Behind her, she could hear that the girl seemed to be faring not much better. As she glanced over her shoulder, Vanessa saw her attempting to shorten her stirrups, no easy task in these circumstances. She was leaning far over to her left, tugging on the straps.

'Don't even think about it,' said the girl, without looking up. Vanessa faced forwards once more.

'Actually, the only thought in my mind was whether I could help you to adjust those stirrups,' she said.

'Right,' said the girl.

'Suit yourself. Strange as it may seem, not everyone goes around looking to attack people.' They walked on in silence. The path flattened out, somewhat and Vanessa felt a little less anxious. 'So, er... where are we going?' she asked.

'Down,' said the girl.

'Good, good. And erm... once we are... down, as it were, what then?'

'Have you forgotten that I have a rifle?'

'You know, I'd never even seen a gun before... what is it today? Er... Thursday is it? Blimey, Thursday, eh? Doesn't time fly when you're having fun? Anyway, before Monday I'd never even seen a gun. Since then, I've seen two men shot dead, been in a gun battle and tied up two other men. And not in a good way.

'Don't you ever shut up?'

'Oh, it's just nerves, I suppose. Don't mind me. Should be getting used to being abducted at gunpoint by now. Foolish to let it bother me, really.' She turned around in the saddle, once more. 'Have you thought about what happens once we hit civilization? I mean, you have a rifle and your face looks pretty awful – bound to attract attention. Oh, no offence, I think you're really pretty but... well, having been kneed in the face by that psycho last night... well. Of course, I don't suppose you've seen yourself, yet, have you. It's a right old "shiner" as we say in England. Do you know that word? Your English is very good, by the way, so I wouldn't be surprised.'

'I appreciate your concern. Let me worry about that.'

There was no more talk. Slowly, carefully, the mountain horses picked their way down to little accompaniment, save the skitter and scrape of hooves. At one point, the backbone of the mountains above bowed to allow the warm September sun to bathe them.

'Getting a bit hot,' Vanessa announced, over her shoulder. 'D'you mind if I take off my jacket?'

'Go nuts,' said the girl.

'Er… is that a "yes",' Vanessa asked, turning in her saddle to see that the girl was already down to her black jerkin, her own jacket wrapped around her waist. She did not reply. Vanessa shrugged off the jacket and tied it to her pommel.

At that moment, the foreleg of the girl's horse slipped away in front of it. It staggered and, her stirrups still too long, the girl was unseated. Clutching at the horse's neck, her feet easily came free of the stirrups and she tipped to the left, her hips scraping along the top of the chain-link fence. Reins lost, she managed to catch hold of the bridle and the horse's head twisted with her weight. Then it bucked. Vanessa saw the girl's legs flip over to the far side of the fence and as the animal, wrong footed, slammed into it, the girl swung out over the chasm.

There was a scream. It was not the girl, however but the horse. Struggling to free itself of its burden, it dragged the helpless girl along the fence, the twisted ends of the wire ripping the flesh of her arms and tearing the fleece jacket from around her waist. Vanessa saw it balloon out as the breeze lifted it momentarily only to collapse it seconds later, dragging it down into the shadows many metres below.

Then, the horse barrelled into Abri and for a stomach-churning second, Vanessa was sure that her mount would go down. But Abri held her ground and the girl's horse finally came to halt. The terrified animal lifted its head and let it drop over the far side of the fence and Vanessa could see the girl, holding fast to the bridle, trying to swing her legs forwards to gain purchase on the slippery walls of the cliff. But the horse's head still jerked up and down and the girl swung and bounced like a Victorian acrobat toy. She wouldn't be able to hang on for much longer.

Vanessa practically fell off the back of her horse and scrambled over to the fence. She knew that she would have to calm the horse down before it forced the girl to leave go. She made what she hoped were comforting, horse-friendly sounds and gradually, the horse's head ceased its frantic bucking and stood panting but seemingly calmer. Vanessa stroked its neck, feeling the sweat beneath her hand. She was afraid that once it recovered its breath, it might resume its frantic attempts to rid itself of the girl.

Positioning herself as close to the horse as she dared, Vanessa placed a foot in one of the diamonds of the fence and hoisted herself up. Reaching out, she was able to grab the girl's left wrist but it was slick with blood and she realised that without something solid against which to brace her own arm, there was no way she'd be able to support her weight.

And what would be so awful about that? Wasn't this a gift? It was her chance to get away. Maytham and Gianfranco were only a couple of hours up the track. She'd wait until the girl tired, fell and then walk both horses back up to the spot where she'd left the two men and that would be that. She forced herself to look at the girl's face. Her teeth were clenched, her lips drawn back; her eyes became narrow, dark slits as she strained to raise herself. Her determination was extraordinary but she had clearly run out of strength. It wouldn't be long, now.

'I'm going to try something else,' Vanessa said. 'I'm going to let go, OK?' Vanessa could see the muscles in the girl's arm tense, as she once more let the bridle take the full strain. The horse gave a token jerk of its head but remained standing still.

Almost before she realised it, Vanessa had retrieved the fallen rifle. For the first time, it seemed, the girl noticed her. As Vanessa lifted the weapon, the girl's face became impassive. For a long moment, Vanessa held the girl's eyes. She brought the rifle level with the chest of the helpless figure then she knelt down and thrust the barrel of the rifle underneath the link fence. When it was through as far as it could go, Vanessa stood up and put her full weight on the stock.

'Hurry,' she said, 'before he starts chucking his head about again.'

For a moment, it looked as though the girl was considering other options then she reached over with her leg and after a couple of false starts, managed to raise herself, gingerly, onto the barrel of the rifle. Vanessa heard the stock scrape against the shale and felt it lift a little from the ground. It only needed to hold long enough for the girl to pivot on it and swing herself over to the fence. For the first time in her life, Vanessa found herself hoping that she weighed more than another woman. The girl kicked off from the rifle and Vanessa felt herself lifted by a matter of inches before the stock crashed into the ground once more beneath her weight and the girl's shoulder made contact with the fence.

In an instant, Vanessa's fingers were between the links of the fence and she took hold of the girl's jerkin. The girl threw out her left hand and then she too gripped the fence. Her left foot made contact with the edge of the cliff as the horse, noticing the shift of weight, reared its head once more. This time the effect was to bring the girl's right hand within reach of the top of the fence. She made a grab for it and held on. Vanessa grabbed her wrist and they stood there, face to face: Vanessa on one side of the fence and the girl on the other. They were both gasping for breath but they realised that it was over and Vanessa laughed with relief. The girl was shaking and it was some moments, before her composure returned and gathering her strength, she lifted herself up and over the fence, landing beside Vanessa, who was still wasting adrenalin.

'God!' she laughed, 'I thought you'd had it, then! Are you OK? My heart's pounding like a...' The girl said nothing. Her eyes still on Vanessa, she knelt down and pulled the rifle back under the fence. Vanessa's face fell as she once more stared down the barrel.

'I think perhaps we should walk for a while,' the girl said and used the rifle to tell Vanessa that she should gather her things together and lead Abri on down the mountain.

'Oh, don't mention it,' Vanessa said, her face reddening. 'Perfectly all right. Any time. Bloody *hell*!'

'Finished?' said the girl.

'No, I bloody well haven't! I'm not moving another inch until you tell me what the fuck this is all about!'

The girl took aim.

'I'm not going to tell you again,' she said.

For an instant, Vanessa felt sick. But only for an instant. Perhaps it was the adrenalin; whatever it was, she was thinking quite clearly. It was not only the fact that she refused to believe that someone whose life you had just saved would kill you in cold blood, it was also that she appeared to need Vanessa alive.

'I don't think whoever's paying you would be terribly happy if you turned up empty handed,' she said. The girl shrugged.

'I could live with it,' she said.

'Then go ahead!' Vanessa yelled.' I've had all I can take of this fucking madhouse! Go on! Shoot me!'

And there it was: the hesitation. Vanessa knew then that the girl would not shoot.

'Look,' she said, 'all I ask is that you tell me what's going on. What do you want with me?' She pointed back along the track.' What did *they* want with me? All I did was pick up the wrong man at the airport. He told me nothing; he gave me nothing – well, apart from a gun but only to throw the police off. Oh, and he put a SIM card in my phone, which anyway Caroline what's-her-face took before I even saw it.' She held out her hands in a gesture of helplessness. 'So please; I'd like to help, I really would. Please. Just tell me what you want.' The girl lowered the gun and said,

'I'm under orders to take you to London.'

Vanessa, exasperated, threw out her arm and spluttered,

'They were taking me to London! God! I thought you people were supposed be clever!'

'What "people"?'

'Well... you lot. Spies, S.I.S., em eye bloody six, or whatever the hell you call yourselves. I don't know.' She rubbed her forehead.' Look, I've got a headache and to tell you the truth, I really need the loo.'

'I think I may have underestimated you,' said the girl.

'Eh?'

'You really are very good at this.'

'At what – getting really pissed off?'

'I think it must have been your age that had me off guard but I suppose you don't get to work for the Council unless you're pretty special.' Vanessa was nonplussed.

'Work for the Council?' she said.' I once had a summer job filing for Guildford Planning Office but they didn't seem to be a particularly difficult outfit to get into. Margo Winfield had been there eight years and she'd left school at sixteen.' The girl said nothing but continued to eye Vanessa who said, 'What!?' then threw up her hands and let them fall to her side. 'OK. OK, fine! I give up.' She skidded over to Abri, took her reins and commenced leading the little Haflinger down the track saying, 'Let's get going. The sooner we get where you want to be, the sooner it'll all be over, one way or another.'

## Moley

'Ratty!?' Arthur was really quite cross. 'How the fuck do they get that?'

'I don't know,' Alan answered, 'something to do with old kids' books, I think. You all have them. They're just code names... it... it's nothing... personal.'

'Well, it sounds pretty bloody personal to me.' Arthur said. 'I mean, what's wrong with "Aslan", or "Bagheera"? I mean, they call you fucking "Centaur"!'

'Well, Blues and Royals *is* a Cavalry Regiment.'

'I know but personally, I'd have gone with something like, "Horse's Arse". I mean, "*Centaur*" for fuck's sake!'

'Look, I don't know why you're having a go at me. I didn't choose it. And it's not necessary to swear.'

'It's not swearing! How many times...? At worst, it's a profanity. Didn't they teach you anything at Radley or Harrow or wherever the fuck your inbred twelve-toed parents sent you?

'It was Eton, actually. And I can't think why you're being so unpleasant.'

'Eton! Of course it was. How could I have been so stupid?' Alan leaned in towards him and whispered,

'You're causing a scene.'

Arthur had led him to the St. James' Tea Rooms in Piccadilly where you could get a pretty good pot of tea and a decent sandwich for under a fiver. It also happened to be just around the corner from the original headquarters of the secret service and over the years, had become something of a haunt of Council Workers, being close to both the centre of town and the clubs off Piccadilly. They were sitting at a white-painted, wrought iron table awaiting the return of the waitress. To Alan's disappointment, however, it was not the lovely Jacqueline, turning up laden with tea and sarnies but some wizened old bint. She placed the bits and pieces expertly, however and asked,

'Got that off your chest, then, Arthur?'

'Jennifer,' Arthur said, nodding politely.

'Apparently, it's "Moley", at the moment.' Alan was staring, his bulbous lower lip, twitching ever so slightly.

'So... you're... an operative?' he asked, querulously.

'Who is this?' Jennifer asked.

'His name's Alan,' said Arthur.

'Of course it is. Scuse me, I must take the weight off. This thigh's giving me gip, this morning.' She removed her pinafore and hat and sat down beside Arthur and Alan. Instantly, Jacqueline reappeared and began taking orders from other tables. Jennifer looked at Alan but spoke to Arthur.

'So what's his story, then?'

'No idea. I met him in a toilet. He had a dart-gun.'

'And what do you suppose he planned to do with that?'

'Kill me, I think.'

'Jacqueline's running an analysis on the darts. We'll soon find out.'

'No, no; they wanted me to tranquilise you. *Tranquiliser* gun,' said Alan. Remember?'

'Codename: "Ratty" TWEP,' said Arthur. 'Remember?'

'What's "TWEP".'

'It means "Target With Extreme Prejudice", dear,' said Jennifer helpfully.

'What's that mean?'

'Is he taking the piss?' she said to Arthur.

'I'm really beginning to wonder, to tell you the truth.' He looked up to see the waitress, Jacqueline. She handed a slip of paper to Jennifer.

'Tetrodotoxin. Nasty. So why didn't he TWEP you then, Arthur?'

'Oh, I got there early. Or rather, he got there late. He got lost, apparently. And his Oyster card had run out.'

'Wait,' said Alan. 'That thing you said: tetero... tetrotoxin... or whatever? Is that not a tranquiliser, then?'

'No, Alan, it isn't,' said Arthur. 'It's a particularly unpleasant nerve agent.'

'Oh,' said Alan. 'I'm really sorry.'

'Oh, that's all right, Alan. No harm done,' Arthur said, dangerously.

'Arthur...' Jennifer said. 'We might need him alive.' Arthur held up his hands in supplication.

'All right, all right. Just joshing, that's all. So what are you doing here?'

'Waiting tables, what's it look like?'

Arthur scanned the room. Is it my imagination or are there even more Council Workers in here than usual? If I didn't know better, I'd say you had me under surveillance.'

'What?' Jennifer said, with exaggerated disbelief, 'course not, silly. It's just that... well... one or two people are saying...'

'Yes?'

'That you were the last person to see Mulberry alive.'

'I was the first person to see him dead; and that's not the same thing at all.'

'Er... the second,' said Alan. Arthur and Jennifer looked at him. 'Well, technically, the killer would have been the first. Unless he was still alive when the killer left; in which case...' Alan seemed to lose his thread.

'Is it possible to keep him quiet,' said Jennifer, still looking at Alan.

'I believe so,' said Arthur. 'Alan, if you say anything else, I will kill you.'

'Right-oh,' said Alan.

'As I was saying,' she went on, 'I don't really know what's going on... yet.' She squinted at Arthur.

'Oh, and you think I do?' he said.

'Possibly. But neither of us will until we each share what we know.'

'I agree.'

She said nothing more; simply looked at Arthur.

'What? Oh, you want me to go first?'

'Yes, I do. Begin with why you decided to do the Telegraph crossword today.'

Arthur's brow puckered.

'Telegraph crossword? He said, as though he'd never heard the term before.

'Arthur. You were either extremely lucky or you knew there was to be a message today.'

'I always was lucky.'

'You always were a bloody deceitful sod, actually.'

'Jennifer, I'm shocked, I truly am. I had no reason to suspect anything was up; I merely spotted the pointer, that's all. I went to Charing Cross; Alan, here, turned up and you phoned me.'

'All right,' she said, 'I'll buy that for now but doesn't it seem a little odd that someone starts sending crossword pointers again after what... eighteen years? And it just happens to be for you.'

'I have a question for you,' Arthur said.

'Oh?'

'Yes. How did you know I'd done the crossword this morning?'

'I'm not going to tell you.'

Arthur looked as though he were about to say something but stopped. He shook his head and said,

'Oh fuck it. I don't really care anyway.'

'Ooh,' Jennifer said, 'and I was having such fun. What's the matter?'

'Someone tried to kill me yesterday.'

Jennifer burst out laughing.

'Forgive me, Arthur,' she said, 'that can't have surprised you.'

'It did, as a matter of fact. I was lucky to get away with it.'

'Don't give me that' Jennifer said, dismissively. 'So come on... who?'

'Funny,' Arthur said, 'that's exactly what I asked her.'

'A woman?'

'And a man. I don't know how well they knew each other and neither of them talked.'

'Did you give them a chance to?' Arthur flung her his "What do you take me for?" look.

'She,' Arthur said, 'was killed by him before she could say anything. I'd been given to understand that he was some functionary over at Box Standard who had blotted his copybook but it was, as our American chums might have it, a "set up" of some species.' Arthur studied Jennifer's face to try to detect what effect, if any, this observation might have. He almost smiled at his own foolishness. 'I did manage to get a name: "Selam". Ring any bells?'

'Not a one. "Selam" is a Turkish word, though. It means "Peace", like "Salaam" or "Shalom". Three years in Istanbul,' she said to his impressed expression.

'It said "Mrs Yardley" on her name badge,' Arthur continued. 'The man called himself Edward Darlington. Nightingale claimed never to have heard of him.' Jennifer curled her lip slightly and shook her head. She looked over to Jacqueline, who scribbled something on her pad.

'So, Nightingale knows you were targeted?'

'He does. I mentioned it to him yesterday. Any of this mean anything to you?'

'Possibly,' said Jennifer.

'Well?' Arthur said. She looked at him.

'I'm sorry,' she said at last, 'but I don't trust you, Arthur.'

'Well, I know that; but it should be pretty obvious that I'm not going to set myself up to be murdered just so I can approach you without you suspecting my involvement in anything.'

Jennifer again said nothing.

'Oh, come on!' said Arthur. 'Jennifer...'

'I only have your word for it that someone tried to kill you, Arthur.'

Arthur fished his Guardian out of his coat pocket and thumbed through it. He flapped it inside out, folded it roughly and pinned it to the table with his index finger. Jennifer untangled her glasses from their chain and rested them on the end of her nose. Arthur's finger indicated the story of the closing of the installation at Tate Modern.

'I'm to take it this is you?' Jennifer said, eventually. 'Not terribly convincing evidence, if you don't mind me saying.' Arthur was thoughtful.

'No,' he said. 'No, I suppose not. What about Alan?'

'Ah, yes, Alan.'

'Miss Carlisle?' It was Jacqueline.

'What is it, dear?'

She handed Jennifer her notepad. After a few seconds, Jennifer tossed it across to Arthur, who read:

"Centaur fallen first fence. Ratty still scurrying about."

He gave a mirthless laugh.

'Bit pathetic,' he said.

'But it eases you off the hook a little. I take it this was an intercept?' Jacqueline nodded.

'This is getting stranger,' Jennifer said. She suddenly looked grave. 'Arthur, Geoffrey Wittersham was killed in Rome last week.'

Geoffrey had been Arthur's mentor and they had been on a number of outings together. Geoffrey was determinedly heterosexual but Arthur had been very fond of him. Although death was a fact of life on the Council, Arthur was sorry to hear the news.

'He was a good man,' he said, simply.

'Actually,' Jennifer said, 'he was the best. He was "Badger", we understand.'

'Ah,' said Ratty. He was silent for several seconds then seemed to draw himself together.

'Right,' he said. 'Your go, I think.'

Jennifer still appeared to be suspicious of him. Arthur wished he could convince her that he was on her side. But then, he wasn't entirely sure that she was on his. She poured teas all round, sat back in her seat and said,

'Couple of days ago, I was in Paris...'

'Was that the "foreign" job you told me about on Monday?'

'The same. I'd been asked to attend some sort of D.P.S.D. reception...'

'Eh?' said Alan

'French Secret Service. Do keep up. The cover for it is "Publishers' Convention" and so they hold it in this wonderful old antiquarian bookstore on the Left Bank. (It has a bit of history for them, apparently – a bit like the clock at Waterloo Station is for us - Typical French, of course; they all fancy themselves as intellectuals – even their Secret Service.) Anyway, at this reception is Graham Knox...'

'Cleaner, Alan, before you ask; based in Paris...' said Arthur.

'...who takes me to one side and says, "Follow me..." All cloak and dagger and French Resistance. "Where to?" I say. "Upstairs", he says. Well, he's a bit of looker and it's been a while, so I follow him.'

Alan's nose wrinkled in distaste. Jennifer saw but chose to ignore it.

'Well much to my disappointment, he just wants to talk. Apparently, according to him, Council Workers – particularly Cleaners, appear to be going down like ninepins. "Talking of going down..." I said...'

'Eurgh!' said Alan.

'...but he wasn't having any. He mentioned Jeavons in Berlin, Bartholomew; Vienna, I think. Ransome in Madrid and he'd just heard that Wentworth had copped it in Amsterdam.'

'Perhaps there's something going around,' Alan offered. The other two looked at him. 'I mean perhaps they contracted some sort of...illness.'

'Yes, Alan. The symptoms would appear to be associated with lead poisoning and massive trauma to internal organs,' said Arthur. Alan looked puzzled.

'They are being shot, Alan,' Jennifer said. And with increasing frequency.'

'I'd heard about Jeavons and Bartholomew but the other two are news to me,' Arthur said. 'Was it Knox who told you about Geoffrey?'

'No. I don't think he knew at that time.' She paused for a moment before continuing. 'So he tells me to be on my guard – even amongst friends – and we go downstairs...'

'...You adjusting your dress so as not to arouse suspicion,' said Arthur.

'Naturally... and I begin to mingle. I'm chatting away to Graham and another... person – pretty little French piece who he's flirting with outrageously. I mean, at his age! Anyway, suddenly, she goes down like a ton of bricks.'

Alan emitted an explosive snorting laugh. Arthur and Jennifer stared at him.

'Sorry,' he said.

'Then Graham, bless him, dashes me to the ground. Well, there are more guns in that room than on HMS Victory and they're all out by this time. A shot goes straight through poor old Graham's head and does for him instantly. I'm headed for the window, along with everyone else, when another shot whistles past my head and into a copy of Proust. I dive to the floor again and another one goes smack into Portnoy's Complaint.'

'Nasty,' said Arthur.

'For a bunch of secret agents, none of them seemed to have much nous and I alone found myself downstairs offering the gunman some of my less important bits.'

'Why did you do that?'

'Well, Alan, (if it has anything to do with you) if two people have been shot with a high-powered rifle and the shooter continues firing, it generally means that they have missed the person they were intending to hit.'

'That being the case,' Arthur interjected, 'the accepted procedure for the gunman is to target the exits. Jennifer's strategy appears to have been to attempt to draw his fire and see if she can't pinpoint him a little more accurately. Did it work.'

'No.'

'Oh.'

'When I'd decided that the shooting had stopped, 'I got myself round to Quai St Michel. Had I been the shooter and I'd missed my target, I'd hot foot it to the nearest Metro and see if I couldn't catch my panicked victim there.'

'Naturally.'

'Well, of course, the nearest station is an R.E.R. but I figured a sensible chap would be waiting there. I got there P.D.Q. and was able to get a good look at the subway entrance.'

'And?'

'Nothing, I'm afraid.'

Arthur's brow furrowed.

'Someone's out to get us, Jennifer.'

'Really? And there's me wondering if it mightn't have all been a co-incidence. ' Arthur smiled then asked,

'So any ideas?'

'Not a one. I think I can vouch for those of us here but beyond that, I wouldn't like to say.'

Arthur swept the room.

'That Jacqueline's a bit…' he began.

'A bit what, Arthur?'

'A bit… young, that's all.'

'Ha! You were much younger than she is when you joined the Council.'

'That's as may be but things were different, then.'

'Rubbish.'

'Think about it, Jennifer. Inexperienced, probably quite cheap youngsters: biddable and not very intelligent. I would imagine some folk – especially at Box Standard – might quite like things that way.'

'It was no different in your day, Arthur,' Jennifer told him.

Arthur was quiet for a moment. Then he smiled and said,

'Did I ever tell you about the time Geoffrey and I went to kill Franco?' Jennifer looked at him through narrowed eyes.

'No,' she said, slowly, 'I don't believe you ever did. I wonder why?'

'Eh?'

'Well, Arthur,' she said, 'I have heard so many of your stories; and so many times, each telling more exciting and eventful than the last but no. Not that one. Franco? No.' Arthur said nothing. After a moment or two of silence, Jennifer said,

'Well?'

'Well, what?'

'Are you going to tell us or not?'

'You know, I'm not sure that I shall, now, *Moley*. I wouldn't want to bore you and besides, you'd only think I was making it up.' Arthur was in dire danger of becoming sulky.

'I'd like to hear it,' said Alan.

'Alan would like to hear it,' Jennifer said.

'I don't give a toss what Alan would like. I've gone quite cold on the idea, to tell you the truth.'

'Ah well,' Jennifer said, perhaps some other time.

'Perhaps,' said Arthur.

'You're sulking.'

'I do not sulk.'

'Yes you do; you're doing it now.'

'Well it's not nice to tell someone you think their stories are made up. I didn't question you about that Paris tale, did I?'

'No, Arthur, you didn't. I'm sorry.'

'Well, that's all right then.'

'I'm glad.'

'Well, just so you know. And in fact, the story about Franco doesn't reflect terribly well on me. I thought it would please you to learn something new.'

'It would, Arthur. I was extremely fond of Geoffrey. I would so much like to hear your story.'

'Well perhaps one day, you shall. But not today.'

Jennifer smiled, Arthur smiled, Jacqueline smiled and Alan looked bewildered.

'We definitely need a plan,' said Jennifer

'You mean *General* Franco?' said Alan

'Yes, said Arthur, staring at Alan, 'a plan. First off: let's kill Alan.'

'Oh Arthur, now stop being so silly. We've got a lot of work to do. Besides,' she added, mischievously, 'we need to extract some information from him first.'

Alan made a little squeaking noise.

'Alan,' Arthur said, suddenly, 'You've heard Jennifer and me talking about "the Council" haven't you?'

Alan nodded.

'Do you have any idea what the Council is?'

For a moment it looked as though Alan was about to speak. However, he seemed to give the matter some thought and said finally, 'Erm... no. No not really: at all, in fact.'

'Alan,' Arthur said, as though speaking to a small child, 'is that a lie?'

'Yes it is,' said Alan, looking ashamed.

'So Alan, tell us; what is the Council?'

Alan looked around. No-one was paying the slightest attention.

'The Council,' he said almost mechanically, 'is a group of renegade secret agents who are plotting the overthrow of the British Government.' He paused and added, 'As if you didn't know!'

'And who told you that, Alan?'

'It was in the text.'

'The text?'

'Yes.'

'You got... a text... telling you that there was a bunch of renegade agents on the loose in London?'

'Yes.'

'Did it say anything else?'

'Yes.'

'And what was that?'

'It said we had to report to Vauxhall Cross and we'd be given our assignments.' Alan was looking decidedly anxious. He wanted to lie but he'd been brought up not to.

'Who else got this text, do you suppose?'

'I don't know.'

Jennifer leaned forwards.

'Alan,' she said, conversationally, 'can you tell us what happened when you got to Vauxhall Cross? Alan straightened, set his jaw and said,

'No. I am not going to tell you anything more.'

'All right,' said Arthur, 'fair enough. But that aside, what happened when you got to Vauxhall Cross?'

'Well, once I was through initial clearance, I... Alan paused, smiled and said, 'Ahh, you're trying to catch me out aren't you?' Arthur laughed.

'Yes,' he said. 'yes, I am. I should have known you'd see through me.' Alan smiled broadly; clearly immensely satisfied with himself. Arthur, still laughing, placed his hand on Alan's shoulder. He heard Jennifer's best matron's voice warn, '*Arthur...*' He removed his hand and then he noticed a shadow at his side.

'Those implants hurt though, don't they? I mean when they put them in?' It was Jacqueline. All three of them looked up to see her standing by their table.

'Gosh, yes! Alan responded, 'Goodness me! "Won't hurt a bit"? Ha! I should say not! Jacqueline laughed.

'Yes, that's what they told me. Was it Doctor Edwardes?'

'Oh, I'm afraid I didn't catch her name. She was terribly stern-looking. Bit scary.' Alan pulled a scary face.

'That sounds like her!' Jacqueline said.' We call her "Rosa Kleb".'

Alan managed to smile broadly and look blank at the same time. Jennifer stood up and Jacqueline sat down.

'Can I have a word with you, Arthur?' Jennifer asked, moving away. Arthur stood and followed her. He heard her say, 'Oh to be young and attractive to men again.'

'Happy days,' said Arthur. 'Happy days.'

## The Stream

It was a good four hours before Vanessa and her captor encountered the first real signs of life. They had been among trees for a while when they came upon a small building. There was no-one around but there was a solitary tractor parked on the bank opposite. Beyond this, the track began to widen. Shale had given way to mud and stone several kilometres back but now, the horses' hooves crunched on pebbles.

Vanessa, to the best of her knowledge, was thinking of nothing, merely watching the rippling patterns caused by the movement of her shadow across the pebbles, when she heard the girl hiss, urgently,

'Say nothing!'

She raised her head to see, just in front and heading towards them, another group of riders. There were three of them: an older man and two teenagers – a boy and a girl. Vanessa had no intention of saying nothing, indeed she was about to say a very great deal when she remembered the rifle. The last thing she wanted was to witness another bloodbath. So much so that she willed the other riders to drift by them with nary a word but as they came alongside, the rider at the head of the party, a man of about sixty, gave her a cheery greeting.

'*Bonjour! Il fait beau, aujourd'hui, eh?*' Vanessa spoke no French but from the inflection, she felt it would be safe to answer,

'Oui.'

Then he caught sight of the girl. Vanessa turned around and her heart sank. She looked awful. Her arms were swathed in the bloody remnants of improvised bandages made from a t-shirt that had been in Maytham's saddlebag. Her bruised face was also flecked with blood and her hair was still matted with the blood of last night's beating.

Vanessa understood nothing of what was being said, but understood the girl's gestures perfectly. It seemed she had taken a tumble high in the mountain yesterday and had gone face first into a rock. There were many sympathetic noises and Vanessa heard a word that sounded a bit like "hospital" a couple of times. There were resigned sighs and a little quiet laughter from the girl, several "okays" and finally, some good-natured "*au revoirs*" and the party continued on its way up the mountain. If they noticed the rifle, it clearly wasn't unusual enough to attract comment.

'What were you saying?' Vanessa asked and received in response, only a quizzical look. They set off once more and it was over half an hour before either of them said a word. Of course, it was Vanessa, who broke the silence.

'We need to rest these horses, soon,' she said. Although it was certainly true that the horses had begun to slow their pace considerably, it was equally true that Vanessa was once again suffering those effects of sustained travel by horseback, which they never seemed to talk about in the brochures. The girl came alongside.

'There,' she said, pointing with the rifle. A few metres off to the left, Vanessa could make out a narrow stream. She wheeled Abri round and made for it. Even before she had dismounted, the little horse had its head down in the stream and it was gulping down great mouthfuls. The girl didn't object as Vanessa removed Abri's saddle and indeed, she did the same with her own horse. Then, both she and Vanessa sat down on the bank.

'It's a pity you didn't take Gianfranco's horse instead of Christopher's,' Vanessa said, 'He was the one carrying the supplies. I don't know if there's anything in those saddlebags.'

The girl dragged Maytham's saddlebags towards her, undid them and fished around inside. She drew out a checked flannel shirt and a cloth-wrapped parcel that turned out to contain cheese and half a baguette. Vanessa noted that there was no appreciable hesitation on the part of the girl as she broke both bread and cheese and shared them equally.

'I don't suppose there's a bottle of wine in there?' Vanessa asked.

The girl fished in the other bag and pulled out a plastic bottle containing water. She took a long pull and handed it to Vanessa, who did the same. As she was drinking, the girl said to her,

'Why didn't you let me fall?'

Vanessa spluttered on the water-bottle and replied,

'What the hell do you take me for?' She swiftly lowered her gaze, as she realised that the thought had indeed crossed her mind. She gathered herself and said, 'Look, we're just not the same, all right?'

They lapsed into silence, once more.

'You were working with Geoffrey Wittersham.' The girl said, suddenly. Vanessa forced down the piece of bread and cheese she had in her mouth and said,

'No, I bloody wasn't!'

'You killed one of our agents.'

'What? That was Wittersham...!'

'His name was Sebastian Reynolds. He was twenty-eight years old. And he was my fiancée.'

The girl lowered her eyes.

'Oh God!' Vanessa whispered.

'23rd of May, next year,' said the girl. 'That was when we were to marry. At his family church in Newark.'

'I'm so... sorry,' said Vanessa.

The girl sniffed, lifted her head and pulled her matted hair clear of her face.

'Don't be,' she said. 'He was doing his job; you were doing yours. He got careless. And now, I'm doing my job; taking you to London to hand you over to the British authorities.'

Vanessa didn't know what to say. For the first time in four days of dwelling on her own problems, she found herself sympathetic to someone else's; someone who'd been leading her down a mountain at gunpoint for the better part of half a day. Looking at the dishevelled and bloodied young woman, Vanessa felt she wanted to do nothing more than give her a hug. Sensibly, she decided against it. The girl looked Vanessa straight in the eyes and seemed to be studying her face.

'I swear to you,' Vanessa said, 'you're wrong about me. So many people are doing so much lying that I'll admit, I have no clue as to who's on whose side but this much I can tell you: until Monday last, I was paid way too much money to be a personal assistant to a very rich man who, granted, only kept me on because he was desperate to sleep with me but that's as may be; I was just an ordinary, boring English girl, trying to make a living in Rome and then... then I picked up the wrong man at an airport. I screwed up; and believe me I've been paying for it big time ever since. I do not, have not, nor ever shall I work for anyone who goes around killing people. When Wittersham killed your fiancée, I was his prisoner.'

She was looking hard to see if she had managed to get through to the girl when the girl asked the question that Vanessa knew she couldn't answer and which would smash a hole clean through her story.

'So why did he let you go?' the girl asked.

'I... don't know.' She remembered Caroline's theory but thought it politic not to say anything. 'I... I think he just needed a diversion, that's all. He planted a gun in my bag, took my clothes off me and I had to walk through the streets practically naked until I found a shop that would take pity on me. I thought that was it, until Christopher Maytham turned up at my place that night and said we had to clear out of Rome. He said that some secret service people at the embassy were out to get me.' She paused and realisation dawning, said to the girl, 'Was that you?'

'Go on.'

'So Christopher drove us north to meet up with someone he said might be able to help us.'

'Who?'

Vanessa realised that was a stupid thing to have told her. She didn't trust Caroline but she didn't trust this girl, either. Would she put Caroline in danger and if so, did it really matter? She decided on a half-truth.

'He called her "Caroline". Apparently, she was some sort of relative.' There was no reaction from the girl and so Vanessa went on a little more confidently. 'Gianfranco is her... sort of servant, I suppose. He was to lead us into France and then Christopher was going to get me to Paris to pick up another passport and then on to London.' She paused but the girl appeared to be waiting for more. 'And that's it. I promise you; that's all I can tell you.' The girl appeared to be digesting what she'd heard. Eventually, she said,

'Those riders were heading towards the dam. They will come across your friends in a few hours. We need to be well away by then.' Vanessa sighed and shook her head.

'You still don't believe me, do you?' she said. The girl gave her a long, hard stare.

'My name is Ursulet,' she said.

'That's a nice name,' said Vanessa. 'Is it French?'

'I don't know,' said Ursulet.

'The fact that you've told me your name; does that mean you believe me now?'

'No.'

'Oh good.'

'I shall need to ask you more questions.'

'Fine! Fire away.'

'Where did you go to school?'

Vanessa wasn't expecting this. Suddenly, her head ached and her throat tightened.

'What?' she managed

'Your school. What was it called?'

Vanessa felt the colour drain from her face. She feared she might faint.

'I... I thought...' she stammered.

'Where did you go to school?'

Vanessa knew the answer, of course but, for some reason, it wouldn't come. It was lost somewhere in a jumble of sounds; words; letters; mere ideas. It was fog from which arose, at last, a name.

'Corehampton Girls,' she said slowly, the words slurring; sounding strange in her ears. And then, she passed out.

## Alan Must Die

'So as we thought, he knows nothing?'

'I'm certain of it,' Jacqueline said. Arthur peered at her.

'No offence, Jacqueline. I know Jennifer here has faith in your abilities but I have to ask myself, in view of your age and what have you.' Jennifer rolled her eyes. Arthur didn't see and he went on, 'Just how good are you?'

Jacqueline nodded over to where Alan was sitting, breaking off bits of candle wax, which had pooled and cooled on the table in front of him. He was holding them in the flame of the candle and watching the drips. He gave a little yelp and jerked his hand away from the flame.

'How good would I have to be?' she said.

'All right, Arthur, that's enough. I think I trust Jacqueline on this one. What did he say?'

'Well, sure enough, he was sent a text, telling him of a secret cell of agents. He was asked to report to Vauxhall Cross for a special assignment. He was then given an implant and what I'm sure he believed was a tranquiliser gun and told to await a message regarding the target in the toilets at Charing Cross. He has no idea where the text came from. He was ordered to delete it so he did.'

Arthur spoke to Alan.

'What were you supposed to do after you'd "tranquillised" me?'

'I was told that you wouldn't even feel the dart go in and all I had to do was follow you around and keep in touch until…'

'Until my tongue started to swell up and my lungs dissolved,' said Arthur. 'Because that's what would have happened.'

'Urgh!' said Alan, 'really?'

'Oh, yes, Alan. Biological weapons are very nasty, you know. That's why they usually drop them from aeroplanes. So much safer.'

'Arthur,' said Jennifer, irritably, 'let the boy finish. What did they tell you would happen?

Alan looked pale.

'They said you'd probably start to feel tired and then you'd sort of want to sit down a bit. Then you'd fall asleep and when you did, I was to call and tell them where you were. Then I was to return to Vauxhall Cross.' His voice had begun to grow a little faint and he was slurring his words. 'I don't feel terribly well,' he said. Jennifer poured a cup of tea and tipped four spoonfuls of sugar into it.

'Get this down you then breathe slowly and regularly. If you think you're going to faint, put your head between your legs.'

This was perplexing. M.I.6 had killers; oh, perhaps not so well-qualified as the Council's but good enough, surely, to sort Arthur out if he wasn't looking.

'I think that someone, somewhere,' said Jennifer, 'is playing silly buggers.'

'Miss Carlisle?' It was Jacqueline. 'Will that be all?'

'Yes dear, of course. Thank you for your help.' Jacqueline smiled, took out her notepad and went back to serving tables.

'So, what does Jacqueline *do*, exactly?' Arthur said.

'She's a waitress, Arthur. You can tell by the uniform.'

'Fair enough. Well, I've apparently got a meeting with Sir Auberon at two so I'd better start thinking about getting off.'

'Watch it, Arthur. If there's anyone I wouldn't put anything past, it's him.'

'I wondered about that but it occurs to me, you know Jennifer, that Nightingale was adamant that he wanted me at Legoland this afternoon. He could have been trying to lull me into a false sense of security, of course, but I can think of better ways of doing that. No, although it pains me deeply to say it, I don't think he knew anything about this.

'One more thing. You might want to keep an eye out for Grafton and Bracewell from Engineering. Nothing definite; just a thought. If I'm not back by four, I'll not be back at all.'

'I'll look after Alan then, shall I?'

'No need. He can come with me.'

'Now, Arthur, the boy is clueless. Most likely, he'll already have forgotten about what happened this morning. He's no threat.'

'Everyone's a threat at the moment, Jennifer. Christ, you don't even trust *me*. Someone knows who he is and why he was sent to "tranquillise" me and as long as he's alive, he's a link to us. Much better he has a little road traffic accident somewhere.'

'I suppose you're right. Still, it leaves a nasty taste.'

## Atop The 88

Crawling along Piccadilly atop the 88, Arthur was speaking.

'Look at that. Damian Hirst at the Royal Academy.' He made a sucking noise using his tongue and the roof of his mouth. Out of the corner of his eye, he saw that Alan was about to speak so he said, 'If you are going to tell me that you thought the shark was pretty cool, I remind you: I have a gun. With bullets.'

Alan leaned back in his seat. After a few moments, he said,

'Do you mind if I say something?'

'Not at all. But remember: if it's an opinion…' Arthur patted his jacket pocket and raised an eyebrow.

'I really didn't know that the dart gun would have killed you.'

'I know you didn't, Alan'

'Why do they hate you so much?'

'I don't think they hate me, exactly. One needs only to be a source of minor irritation to these people, Alan.'

'Who are they, then?'

'Well that was something we were rather hoping you could tell us. But since it was all done by text and you deleted it… well, you see our problem.'

'Yes, of course.'

'You see, Alan, M.I.6 and the Council, we're basically on the same side but over the years, M.I.6 has been much more co-operative with governments, the military, the police and whatnot.'

'But isn't that a good thing?'

'Like most things, Alan, it very much depends on your point of view. When the Council was set up, it was in order to ensure that such things didn't happen. There were a number of times during the war when things could have gone either way and Military Intelligence was, (how shall I put this?) not always as sound as we might have wanted. James Carlisle set out to make sure that his section – which is what came to be called the Council – was above all that. The Council is beholden to no-one save the Council. If the Council endures, the country endures. There are no deals, no nods or winks to dictators, no compromises with enemies of the state – even the ones in the military, the police, Parliament, the Civil Service and the House of Lords. There are no pay-offs, no backhanders, no freeloaders and no embarrassments. The Council is pure intelligence: The way it should always be.'

'Blimey,' said Alan. 'That's not what I was told at all. Wait until I explain all that to my chums. They'll be amazed.' Alan's smile was almost enough to make Arthur regret what he had to do. Almost.

'You must be very proud of what you do,' Alan said. That, Arthur had to admit, made him feel a touch uncomfortable.

'Well, even if I say so myself, I'm pretty good at what I do, years of sterling service and all that; never made a serious mistake, apart from Elvis, far as I know.'

'But that's just it, isn't it? You "know". You know a lot. You must practically know everything there is to know about the Council. You could be "The Man Who Knew Too Much".'

'Alan's eager expression was beginning to get to Arthur. He snapped at the boy,

'And you could be "The Man Who Knew Sod All Yet, Strangely, Wouldn't Stop Talking About It".'

Alan's face fell.

'I don't know why you're so down on me,' he said. It was an open goal, but Arthur wasn't in the mood. Instead, he said,

'Perhaps it's because you were sent to kill me, Alan. Just a thought. Anyway, I don't know as much as you might think.' Alan grinned.

'Oh, come on!' he said.

'No, it's true,' protested Arthur, 'that's how the Council is run. Each section is like its own little fiefdom and the less each knows about the others, the better. I might pass other M.I.6 agents or even Council employees in the street and never know it. I mean, I've never seen you before, have I?

'Well, you have, actually; you just don't recognise me. I recognised you as soon as I saw you.'

'Eh?'

'We've met before.'

Arthur was intrigued.

'Go on,' he said.

'No, it's true!' exclaimed Alan.

'I mean,' said Arthur, 'Go on.'

'Oh, right. Well I was there when Miss Gregson did your interview.'

Arthur needed no further prompting. The bloody bag carrier who was trailing around after that sharp-faced cow who'd spoken to him about his pension a couple of months ago. It must have been even more traumatic that he'd remembered, for Arthur seldom forgot a face.

'So,' he said, 'you were an intern with Personnel?'

'Human Resources,' Alan corrected. Somehow, Arthur stopped himself from killing the boy there and then and said,

'Rapid promotion. I'm impressed, I suppose.'

'Oh, no,' Alan said, blushing, 'not at all. I'm still an intern, I'm afraid.'

Arthur looked at him for a very long time and finally said,

'Not still with...'

'Oh, yes,' Alan interrupted with a grin, 'Human Resources. That's me. Training up. Learning the ropes. Well, you would know, of course. You probably did much the same thing, I suppose?'

Arthur's mouth was open but he could think of nothing to say. The boy wasn't M.I.6 at all. He was nowhere near it. He was working ... for free. And for the personnel section. And he'd been sent to kill Arthur Shepherd, the great "Ratty". He stared at Alan, who was fiddling with a bit of candle wax he'd taken from the cafe, a sheepish smile playing about his lips.

'This must be it,' Arthur said, at last.

'I'm sorry?'

'My nervous breakdown. Either that or the Secret Service is using half-wit interns from personnel as assassins. Please tell me it's a breakdown. I mean... they're not even paying you! Do you know how much they pay me?' Alan shook his head. 'A fucking packet! And of course, you'll know how much my pension is worth, being with "Human Resources" and all that.'

Alan raised his eyebrows, puffed out his cheeks and nodded vigorously.

'Yet you, Alan, are paid nothing. Why is that Alan?'

'Well, you know, jobs are scarce, not much money about... deficit and what have you. We have to take what we can get.'

'But you're a guardsman. Blues and Royals,' Arthur stammered, 'please tell me they pay you.'

'Well, not yet, of course. I have to prove myself, first. Then, when I've spent a bit of time here, they'll take me on. Full time.' Alan beamed at Arthur and nodded, as if to say "What d' y' think o' that eh?" Arthur was once more rendered speechless. He went over the whole thing a few more times in his head. The something came to him; something so outrageous, that scarce felt able to voice it. He must be wrong. Surely?

'Alan,' he said at last, 'Are you certain that no-one told you why they wanted me dead?'

Alan assumed his thinking face once more. Eventually he said,

'I really don't have a clue. They did say you were dangerous.'

'Did they? Well, they were right. But worse than that Alan, far worse in today's economic climate...' Arthur lowered his voice and beckoned Alan forward. The young man obeyed and Arthur said, in a conspiratorial tone, 'I am very, *very* expensive.' Alan looked puzzled and said,

'I'm afraid I don't...' Arthur interrupted,

'I get two hundred-and-fifty thousand a year as a Cleaner,' he said. 'Oh, of course, it doesn't compare with what I could get elsewhere (the private sector pays ten times that much). Oh, it's not a bad wage; but Alan, my pension... Oh, dear, my pension... My pension is now worth somewhere in the region of... well, you were there when I had my interview, weren't you? What was it?'

'Eight million pounds, said Alan.

'Yes. Eight million pounds. And why do you think it's such a generous pension, Alan?' Alan spoke slowly and eyed Arthur, looking for signs of affirmation.

'Because... the job... is... quite... dangerous?'

'... And...' prompted Arthur.

'... And... not many... of ... you...'

'Live to collect it,' said Arthur. 'Well done, Alan! Now, Alan...' Alan licked his lips, clenched his fists and settled himself in his seat. This was going to be hard. 'If I were to tell you that in my section alone, there are always twenty-five Council employees of whom the vast majority are now more or less my age, on more or less my salary, what sort of pension bill, Alan, are we looking at in say, ooh, fifteen years or so? Take your time. Alan's face undertook a long and thorough work-out. He closed his eyes, opened them again, looked up, looked down. He tapped his forehead with his finger and then pressed the bridge of his nose. He grimaced, he frowned, he smiled, he murmured and mumbled and when he thought he'd done enough, he said to Arthur,

'Phew! It must be sooo much money. Unbelievable!' He shook his head and said, 'Unbe-blooming-lieveable!'

'Almost two- hundred million, Alan. That's what it is,' Arthur said.

'Phew. Lot of money!' said Alan.

'Well, it's peanuts to the average Merchant Bank but no-one's looking to make savings in that neck of the woods. But for public servants; yes it is a shitload of money, Alan,' said Arthur, 'and there's you, working your balls off; sent out to kill an experienced secret agent; getting felt up in a toilet; kidnapped and held at gunpoint; and for what? For what, Alan? Bugger all; that's what. Now, who the hell would do something like that to a nice chap like you?' Before he could answer, Arthur said, 'I'll tell you, shall I? Someone who is not willing to pay for things, that's who. Someone who is trying very hard not to spend any money. In fact, someone who is trying to make savings. Do see where I'm going with this?'

Alan was thinking hard, Arthur could tell but input invariably exceeded output. It was a law of physics and of the English public school system. He tried a different tack.

'Has anyone at Human Resources made any suggestions as to how savings might be accomplished?'

'Well,' said Alan, 'Miss Gregson's always going on about "waste". She hates waste.'

'I'll bet she does,' said Arthur. 'I wonder what Miss Gregson might say to not wasting two hundred million pounds?'

'Oh, she'd like that. She reckons the Intelligence Services will need to save upwards of two hundred and fifty million within the next five years. Actually, I think they have a bit of a competition going on between Human Resources and Accounts to see who can save the most.'

'Do they really?' said Arthur. It was pretty much time to kill Alan, now. He realised he'd been putting it off a bit, like he had with Elvis. He liked the King but a job's a job. He'd kept the boy's wallet but had decided to return the dart-gun Finding a loaded weapon on the lad would keep the rozzers interested and off the scent for a few days.

Arthur had been hoping, he supposed, that Alan would twig what a chump he'd been before he died but it didn't seem as if it was going to happen. How could what seemed to be an entire generation be duped into working for free, as "interns" in order to gain experience? Working for people who could afford to pay but saw a chance to get free labour and make it appear as though they were doing the person a favour. God, no wonder people liked capitalism.

'Nearly there,' said Alan. He looked down at his lap and said, 'I don't suppose I'm going to be checking in, am I?' He suddenly smiled. 'More like "checking out", eh? Ha-ha.'

'Yes, I'm afraid so Alan. This is our stop.'

## The Tate Again

The two men stood. Alan let Arthur go first and Arthur, for the fun of it, allowed him to do so. As they made their way down the stairs, the bus gave a lurch and Arthur was flung forwards. Alan steadied him, though not before Arthur had nudged the woman on the step below with his knee.

'I do beg your pardon,' Arthur said. 'Terribly clumsy of me.'

'Oh don't mention it,' said the woman looking upwards and behind. 'Oh... Hello,' she said.

He saw the glasses, the nose, the hair. Arthur knew her immediately but thought it politic to pretend he had to think about it.

'It's Miss LaSalle, isn't it? From the Tate?' he said, frowning. They all wound up on the lower deck, waiting for the doors to open.

'You must be on your way to the "Old" Tate,' Arthur said.

'Tate Britain, yes. Are you?'

'Oh no, not today, I'm afraid. I have work to do.'

She suddenly looked awkward and said,

'I think I might owe you an apology, Mr...'

'Henley.'

'... Mr. Henley.'

'Oh yes?'

The bus pulled up with a jolt and the doors hissed open. They stepped out into the warm sunlight and the bus pulled away to reveal, on the far side of the road, the Tate Gallery. Arthur's Tate Gallery. He looked at Alan who was staring at the building.

'Yes,' Miss LaSalle continued. 'The Rothkos.'

'What about them?'

'They aren't going to Paris. They never were, actually. Mrs. Yardley, the new supervisor who spoke to you? She lied to everyone about it. It's quite bizarre. Perhaps she was mad. Why would anyone make up something like that?'

'I have no idea,' said Arthur.'

'I don't understand...people.' Miss LaSalle said.

'Who does?'

'Anyway, they have sacked her.'

'Good thing too.'

'So you can pop over and look at them any time you like. That's good as well, isn't it?'

'Yes. Yes it is. Thank you very much for telling me.'

'Perhaps,' she went on, 'we might go and look at them together? It would be nice to study them with someone who is as passionate as you are.' She opened her purse and handed him a card. He looked at it. The Bird Goddess was asking him out! Arthur didn't fancy her, of course; that would have been absurd and indeed, even had he been solidly heterosexual, he knew she couldn't possibly find him attractive. Nevertheless, he decided to flirt back a little.

'I've been called many things, Miss LaSalle, but "passionate" is not one I've heard in many a year.'

'Surely not! Anyway, I hope to see you again soon! Goodbye!'

She took advantage of a gap in the traffic to scuttle across the road. He was somewhat surprised and not a little disturbed to have been propositioned so blatantly. Still, a turn with the Rothkos with someone who understood might be fun. Arthur turned to Alan, who was still staring at the portico.

'You like the Tate, Alan?' he asked.

'No,' said Alan. Arthur was rather disappointed but not surprised.

'Not enough sharks, eh?' he said

'Oh no, it's not that. It's just... I remember, when I was small boy, we had school outing... there.' He nodded at the building.

'Boring, was it?'

'Oh, no. No. I was really quite enjoying it. And then I remember walking into a room: a dark, warm room. There was a black lady sitting on a stool and she smiled at me and then...'

'What?' asked Arthur, his brow knitted.

'Then I saw them. The paintings. Great acres of colour, massive, heavy, dark, formless, yet...'

'Yet what?'

'Yet they filled me with such utter joy that I couldn't speak.'

'That,' said Arthur, hesitantly, 'sounds... wonderful.'

'Oh, it was! They were so dark and yet beyond the darkness, as if... through a window... great streams of colour and what I can only describe as music – I know, it's mad, isn't it – but it just poured out of them. They... sang to me. I had never been so happy and yet I was... crying. And not weeping. Really crying hard, you know, as though I were being beaten. I couldn't help myself and even when some of the other boys came in, I couldn't stop and I couldn't move and...'

'Tell me,' said Arthur.

'I wet myself,' Alan said. 'I was wearing short trousers and it just flooded out of me onto the wooden floor. They all laughed at me, of course, even the teacher; but the black lady didn't. She came over, took me to the toilet and helped me clean up. She washed my pants and even sponged off my trousers and dried them on the hand-dryer. The boys called me 'Waterfall' from then on. I always wanted to go back there; to see the pictures again but I was always too afraid. I saw them in a book once but it wasn't the same. Funny.' Alan turned to Arthur and said, 'I don't suppose you could do it... in there, could you. In that room. With the paintings. I'm sure I could find it again if...' His voice trailed away.

Arthur took Alan's arm, turned him around and together, they walked towards Vauxhall Bridge.

'Are you going to throw me in the river?' Alan asked.

'No, I'm not going to throw you in the river.' Arthur replied.

'Under a bus?'

'I had considered it but no, not under a bus.' Arthur reached into his jacket pocket.

'Are you going to shoot me?'

'No. Look, Alan, you really aren't cut out for this game, you know. If I were you, I'd just cut my losses and, and... I don't know... become a painter or something.'

'A painter?'

'Yes. You know, pictures... sort of thing.'

'I wouldn't know where to start.'

'Try Tate Modern. Floor 3. Room 6.'

'Why?'

'You'll know when you get there,' He pointed over the road. 'Vauxhall Station. Victoria Line south to Stockwell, then Northern Line to London Bridge. Get a cab from there. Here's a tenner and you've already got your dart gun. If you come across Miss Gregson, you might want to try it out on her.'

'Oh, I couldn't do that.'

'No, I don't suppose you could. Perhaps you should just chuck it in the river.'

'So,' asked Alan tentatively, 'you're not going to "Clean" me, then?'

Arthur looked at Alan for several seconds.

'I think you're already clean enough,' he said.

## The Way of The World

By the time he reached Vauxhall Cross, Arthur still hadn't fully come to grips with what Alan had told him.

As he sat down to his meeting with Sir Auberon, he asked, in passing, 'You ever hear of interns?'

'I have heard the term before, Shepherd; why do you ask?'

'I mean: you ever hear of them being used here? At S.I.S.?'

'S.I.S.? My goodness, what has come over you?'

'I should have known.' Arthur muttered; then, a little louder, 'So what's so important that I have to be hauled out of my bed of pain to drag all the way over here?'

'A couple of things, as it happens,' Sir Auberon said, opening the file in front of him. 'Let's begin with the less important item, shall we?'

'Begin where you like.'

'Thank you. So, someone tried to kill you yesterday, Shepherd. That must have been upsetting for you.'

'Oh, do fuck off.' Arthur said, venomously, before realising that he needed to be a little less... himself. In the first place, anything concerning the nature of the relationship between the Council and M.I.6 was always a matter of extreme delicacy, particularly between himself and Sir Auberon Nightingale, and in the second, in spite of his earlier assertion that Sir Auberon was not likely to have been involved, he didn't want to reveal anything about Alan, Jennifer or Geoffrey Wittersham to the irritating sod. And finally, one thing seemed pretty clear: whoever was getting interns to try to off professional assassins was likely to be not very far away at all. It was only his faith in the incompetence of M.I.6 that had caused him to decide to even be here.

'Such repartee.' said Nightingale. 'Positively Socratic in its scope and execution. Anyway, no joy with your gallery woman, I'm afraid but I have something on this Darlington fellow. Been with M.I.6 three and a half years. Very clean and good at his job, on the up until, it appears, yesterday, when he met you. Was it he who lured you to the Tate?' Arthur said nothing. 'Oh, of course: you can't say, can you. Well, if you followed protocol and destroyed every trace of the job, there's not much more I can tell you.'

'Has anyone around here mentioned it? It was in the paper but no names, of course.'

'Can't say I've heard anything out of the ordinary. Perhaps it's Council business.'

'Possibly but I'd say not.'

'Well, you would know. As you are constantly pointing out, I have no understanding of (nor, God forbid, any say in), what goes on over at the Council.' He closed the file. 'Tell you what:' he said, 'if I were you, I'd have a look and see who doesn't like you over there. No, wait...' Sir Auberon smiled. 'How foolish of me. Sorry.'

Arthur smiled - a forced, mirthless affair.

'Thank you so much for all the obvious effort you've expended on my behalf. I only hope the second item on your agenda has been researched as thoroughly.'

'I'm sure you'll find it to your satisfaction, Shepherd.' He opened a second file and said, 'You remember the Parliamentary Under-Secretary of State for Foreign and Commonwealth Affairs?'

'I have a vague recollection.'

'Well, he remembers *you*, that's for sure. I think you may have made an impression. He would like another chat.'

'Would he? I trust you pointed out that I am currently in Singapore, deep under cover and likely to be so for a number of years?'

'More or less.'

'Which?'

'I think probably "less", since he has informed me that a ministerial car will be arriving at 14:25 for the express purpose of spiriting you off to Whitehall.'

'Oh, for Christ's sake,' said Arthur. 'I mean, isn't this what they pay you for – to keep people like me away from people like him?' Nightingale didn't respond immediately; Arthur knew he was giving him time to work it out for himself. The second that Arthur *had* worked it out, Sir Auberon twisted the knife.

'Does the phrase, "*You strike me as the sort of chap who, should he turn his hand to the matter, might manage to come up with something...*" mean anything to you? Ah, I see that it does.' Arthur had a hand to his forehead. 'Well, you'll no doubt be pleased to learn that the Minister appears to have responded admirably to the faith you showed in his abilities, since I now hold in my hand,' (he flourished an envelope) 'the express desire of... who is it, now?' Nightingale opened the envelope and read aloud, ' Ah yes, "Sir Harold Templeton Head of Her Majesty's Secret Intelligence Services, that you accede to the request of The Right Honourable Ashley Sullivan, Queen's Council and Member of Parliament for Banbury North, to meet him to discuss matters pertaining to the explosion in Knightsbridge, which occurred on Tuesday the blah blah blah..." You get the drift. Hoist, I would say, very much on your own, so to speak, petard. You can leave any weapons you have about your person with my secretary on the way out. They take rather a dim view of interviewees being armed to the teeth at the Foreign Office.'

Arthur, as he often did, refused to accept that any of this was of his own making. But since it was, he thought at least he might make Nightingale feel as uncomfortable as he himself felt.

'I don't know why you're crowing about this,' he said, 'you should be the last person to want me to have a private meeting with a Government Minister.'

'Shepherd! You insult me,' Nightingale said, with all the appearance of being hurt, 'I have every faith that you will uphold the values of the Service. Why, if one our most experienced officers cannot be trusted to keep operational secrets from the Government, I cannot imagine what sort of Secret Service we would be; can you?' Arthur was puzzled.

'I don't remember you being quite so sanguine about this yesterday,' he said. 'I was afraid I might have been called upon to separate the pair of you.'

'A day is a long time in espionage,' said Nightingale. 'Do have fun, won't you?'

'You do realise, don't you,' Arthur said, 'that I could have this order rescinded by any number of people on the Council?'

'I have no doubt; although I suspect that even you would be pushed to do so in the next...' he glanced at his watch, 'twelve minutes.'

Although Arthur quite enjoyed sparring with Sir Auberon Nightingale, he had reached a point where he had become not a little concerned. He said,

'What does Sullivan know of the Council, do you think?' Arthur was gratified that Nightingale had taken his cue. When he answered, it was with a seriousness that only added to Arthur's unease, raising, as it did, his level of respect for his phony boss.

'I hope a great deal less than he thinks he does. You need to make sure that it remains that way. You are simply Arthur Henley, M.I.6 officer. You will tell him only what Arthur Henley would tell him and Sullivan must respect that, however much he may threaten or bluster. Remember that the Foreign Secretary himself (regardless of what his advisors tell him), has no direct control over S.I.S. and an Under-Secretary should consider himself to have done very well indeed to have obtained a meeting alone with a serving field agent.'

To tell the truth, Arthur didn't know what to make of this. Nightingale had seldom sounded so earnest. However, he gave him no time to consider it further.

'Oh, and remember, Shepherd,' he went on, 'meetings are always a two-way street. I should be most interested to learn how Templeton was persuaded to intervene with such alacrity.'

Arthur rose and made to leave. Before he reached the door, Nightingale called out,

'We have several, by the way.'

'Eh?'

'Interns. There are a number. In fact, I understand that recently, a good proportion of new appointments have been of unpaid workers. Mostly very young, of course but it's the way of the world now.' He opened the folder in front of him and began underlining things. Without looking up, he said to Arthur, 'Please; don't let me keep you.'

## Whitehall

Never one to be impressed by what passes for democracy in the United Kingdom, Arthur experienced nothing of the concern felt by lesser beings upon receiving an invitation to Whitehall. ` Those who purported to be in charge of government, he realised, were even more deluded than those who voted for them. The healthy cynicism of the electorate preserves it from anything other than mild disillusionment when it turns out that the new broom is just a couple of old brooms held together with sticky tape. Sadly for everyone, however, politicians actually believe they possess power.

Arthur knew that since the end of the Second World War, the secret services and latterly the Council had been well and truly in the driving seat. A small and dwindling number of the older permanent civil servants in the Home and Foreign Offices, were the only people outside the secret services who had any idea at all.

Fortunately, for the stability of the realm, the Head of State was in on it as well. Not by design of course; it was simply that she'd been around for a very long time - long enough to have figured it out for herself. The train of Prime Ministers, who at intervals grovelled before her, firmly believed that they must show her deference at all times. Of course, they also believed it was all just some sort of feudal pantomime; of the kind that one might encounter in say, a light operetta.

Arthur often wondered how a Prime Minister who really got up her nose would respond if a troupe of Yeomen Warders or Grenadier Guards woke them up one morning and frogmarched them down to Tower Hill. She hadn't quite done it yet but by the look of her, there was still plenty of time. He was certain the Duke of Edinburgh had no idea, though. If he had, he would probably have tried it already. When she finally did drop off the twig, things could get a little difficult. Arthur hoped she would hang on until after he'd retired.

Terrorism always upsets people and Whitehall (as it did periodically), was trying to make itself as secure as possible. This meant that instead of one policeman standing outside Number Ten, there were two and there were no longer any disabled parking bays along Whitehall. Police leave had been cancelled so there was an inordinate number of size thirteens beating up and down the pavements on both sides of the thoroughfare, as well as in the side streets. Mostly, they posed whilst tourists took photographs and a number even returned the favour. As Arthur arrived at the Foreign Office, a Community Policeman asked him who he was.

'None of your fucking business,' he said and breezed past. It was wicked of him really but he couldn't resist it. The young lad had no idea what to do. Arthur glanced back to see him speaking on his radio. It was possible they would send someone more senior – a traffic warden, say – and he would be required patiently to explain away the misunderstanding by producing a variety of pass cards, most of which they wouldn't even recognise.

'Arthur Henley for Mr. Sullivan,' he told the woman outside the door of the vestibule that led to the ante-room, just before the reception area in which he would be forced to wait until the Parliamentary Under-Secretary of State had decided he'd suffered enough.

An hour and a half later, Arthur was admitted in to the presence.

'Sorry to keep you waiting, Mr. Henley,' said Sullivan expansively as he moved around the desk to intercept Arthur. A handshake later and Arthur was shown to a rather nice armchair by the fireside. The Minister sat himself down and, as if on cue, a flunkey brought some tea.

'Jolly good to see you again. How are you? Fully recovered now, I hope.'

'Yes, thank you.' Just because you didn't respect someone, it didn't mean you couldn't show civility.

'So what do you think of my strategy, eh?' For a second or two, Arthur couldn't make out what the Minister was on about. Then it dawned.

'I'm impressed, I'll admit, he said, 'Sir Harold must have owed you one.'

'Indeed,' Sullivan smiled, 'and I dare say I now owe him several.'

'Am I really worth ministerial favours, Mr. Sullivan?'

'I don't know as yet; but one must speculate to accumulate, isn't that the case?'

'So I've heard. How did you know I wouldn't just bugger off while you were playing your little "keep the bastard waiting" game?'

'Well, I suspect that Sir Auberon will have chosen to exploit your visit and, much as I realise you couldn't give two hoots about the pompous sod, you "buggering off" before you'd even met the Minister would have diminished the power you have over him. But more importantly, as you said yourself: you were impressed and I have, (admit it) piqued your curiosity. Tea?'

This was no mere politician. There was a mind at work here. Arthur made his brain move up a gear.

'What makes you think I have power over Sir Auberon? I may find him irritating and he's certainly pompous but he is an M.I.6 Commander and he is my boss.'

'He is Arthur Henley's boss; he's not yours.'

A small but significant portion of Arthur's brain immediately set about planning his escape from the Foreign Office after he'd killed the Parliamentary Under-Secretary of State.

'Your name,' said Sullivan, 'is Arthur Shepherd. You are one of a number of British agents who call themselves "Council Workers". Your designation is "Cleaner", which means that you carry out assassinations on behalf of the Council. Earlier this week, you went to the Al-Nimrah Hotel in Knightsbridge in order to kill Prince Muffarim ibn Abdallah. You were beaten to it, as you probably recall. Yesterday, an attempt was made on your life. Happily, you succeeded in turning the tables.'

The Minister smiled and picked up his tea. He sat back and took a sip. 'Do take a biscuit, Mr Shepherd, they are home baked.'

'I would prefer to hear the rest of your story,' Arthur said.

'Oh I think that's probably enough for now. Perhaps we can continue this another time. I am confident that your... skills could come in very handy at some point.'

'Oh dear,' said Arthur. 'You know, I was beginning to quite warm to you, Sullivan,' he went on, 'but if you actually believe what you've said so far, then surely you must know that I won't let you play silly buggers with me. And even worse, from your point of view, you will have to be persuaded to explain how you know so much.' The Minister's smile faltered a little. 'And that,' said Arthur, 'could get rather messy, I'm afraid.'

'Are you threatening me, here, in my own office; in the centre of Whitehall?'

'Well, it sounded like it to me. Did I miss something out?'

Sullivan burst out laughing.

'They told me you were a little unorthodox, Mr Shepherd, but they made no mention of insanity!'

The Minister brought his teacup to his lips, still chuckling. Arthur leaned forwards and picked up a sugar cube. He slowly guided the tongs over his own cup and let the cube fall. Almost before the "plop" had finished sounding, Arthur was up and had the sugar tongs at the Minister's throat, the serrated tips nipping Sullivan's skin. A half-dozen tiny red droplets appeared and Arthur began to apply more pressure.

Sullivan, his tea cup, inches from his terrified face, had stopped laughing. Arthur whispered.

'Listen to me, Ashley; you don't mind if I call you Ashley, do you?' Sullivan shook his head and his cup and saucer tinkled. 'Good, good. Now, the only reason I haven't used these, if I may say so, rather exquisite little things to rip out your jugular is because I believe you are a lot brighter than most of your ilk. I meant it when I said I was impressed; there's not many politicians can throw their weight around quite like you did and that leads me to believe you are capable of very deep levels of understanding. So deep, in fact, that I'm certain you appreciate that unless you tell me everything you know about me and about the Council, your life will come to a very red and gurgling conclusion in about twenty seconds time; and I'm told by those who know, that it will seem to you to be a very great deal longer.'

'Please, Shepherd…'

'Ah, ah.' Arthur chided, gently.

'All right. I…I'll tell you everything. Please just let me go!'

'Ah!' Arthur sighed, 'if I had a penny for every time I've heard that…'

'I… I mean it! I'll tell you all I know. Please believe me!'

Arthur sat down as quickly as he'd jumped up. It was almost as though the previous ten seconds had not occurred at all.

'Good,' he said, cheerfully. 'Can I top you up? You appear to have spilled a bit.'

The Parliamentary Under-Secretary of State for Foreign and Commonwealth Affairs was trembling and pale. He couldn't speak. So Arthur did.

'Whoever told you about me must have "bigged me up" and no mistake. Is that the expression: to "big someone up"? I think it is. I actually thought you were going to piss yourself, Ashley. I mean, honestly, did you really think I could rip out your jugular with a pair of Edwardian sugar tongs? Come on!' Arthur began to laugh, as he poured tea into Sullivan's cup. 'I don't know. People really do watch too much TV, these days, don't you think?' He finished pouring the Minister's tea.

'Now, I'd very much prefer it if you would finish telling me what you know about the Council. Of course, it's up to you. If you'd rather leave it, I could come back tomorrow…'

'No! No,' the Minister stammered, 'I… I think we can do that now.'

There was a tap at the door and it opened a notch.

'Your five-o'clock appointment is here, Minister. Shall I…'

'They'll have to wait!' snapped the Minister.

'But sir, you told me…'

'I don't care what I told you, Henderson! I am speaking with Mr. Henley! Now please leave us alone.'

'I'd quite like some more tea,' Arthur said, 'this lot was a bit stewed, I'm afraid. I didn't like to mention it but…'

'Yes, yes, bring us some more tea, there's a good chap,' the Minister said.

Slowly, Henderson's puzzled face disappeared as the door closed upon it. Sullivan dabbed his upper lip with a pristine cotton handkerchief, drawn from his top pocket.

Everyone reacts differently to the prospect of their own death, particularly if it promises to be an immediate and untidy one. Arthur had lost none of his admiration for Sullivan just because he hadn't been able to handle it terribly well. Very few in his experience did. And credit where it's due, it was quite something for a politician to have learned so much about the Council as Sullivan appeared to have done.

Arthur didn't consciously study body language but he appeared to be able to read the whole human form almost holistically. The Minister was rattled, certainly and that was only to be expected but not so rattled that he didn't smooth down his ruffled jacket, straighten his tie and shoot his cuffs before getting his breathing under control. The fact that he appeared to have his priorities utterly wrong, told Arthur that substance over style might not be Sullivan's order of business. The Minister removed his glasses and wiped them on the white handkerchief, which upon completion of the chore, he reformed and replaced faultlessly into his top pocket. He crossed his legs and shot his hand along his thigh, to remove invisible and possibly imaginary flecks.

'You may not believe this, Mr. Shepherd, but your actions just now have convinced me that I am about to confide in the right person.'

'Oh?'

'Yes. Despite my boast, I know little of the world you and your colleagues inhabit but I was sincere in what I told you the other day – I am in awe of you and the other agents who keep our country safe in the way that you do. Without fear or favour, you act on behalf of the realm with no recognition and precious little reward…'

'Oh I wouldn't say that. I do pretty well in the…'

'Believe me, Mr. Shepherd, your worth, from what I hear, is practically incalculable.'

'I bet Miss Gregson could calculate it,' Arthur murmured

'Didn't catch that; sorry.'

'Nothing. Do go on.'

There was timid knock and the door opened a crack. Seeing that the coast appeared to be clear, Henderson, armed with tea, insinuated himself into the room. He placed the tray on the table, removed its dead fellow and left without a word.

'I wouldn't mind one of those.' Arthur said.

'What, a biscuit?'

'No. A Henderson.'

'You know Shepherd; and this is coming from someone whom you have just terrified to the very brink of incontinence, I rather like you.'

'I've been buttered up by experts, Mr. Sullivan. Please don't insult my intelligence. Now, tell me what you want.'

Sullivan took a breath.

'I have it on good authority that someone is making active efforts to de-stabilise and possibly even destroy the Council. I know little of the workings of the organisation; only that the work it does is as valuable *to* as it is unrecognised *by* the state it protects. The way it has been explained to me, M.I.6 has over the years developed into something rather less benign than a mere friendly rival and circumstances have led to that organisation seeking actively to at least diminish and, some believe, destroy the Council.' He paused and this gave Arthur an opportunity to ask questions.

'Before you go any further, I have to tell you that my first instinct is to disbelieve anything a politician tells me. Unless you stop being obtuse, I may really have to kill you. Firstly, name your "good authority"; secondly, tell me who it was who "explained" all this to you; and tell me who "believes" M.I.6 is out to destroy the Council. While you're at it, you can also explain what all this has to do with me.'

'Hmm,' Sullivan said, 'He told me this might happen. Perhaps it's better if I show you something.'

He stood up and took himself over to one of the ornate looking-glasses that adorned the walls of the office. He pressed on a corner of the glass and it swung open to reveal a wall safe. Having opened, reached, extracted and closed, he replaced the glass and returned to his seat. He handed Arthur a manila envelope. It was addressed to him.

'Open it,' Sullivan said. For a moment, Arthur considered whether or not to obey what sounded suspiciously like an order but he had to admit, he was now beyond curious. He tore open the envelope and extracted its contents. It was a letter.

> *My Dear Arthur,*
> 
> *I know it might offend, but in the circumstances, I hope you'll forgive a little post-ironic indulgence. Here goes:*
> 
> *If you are reading this, then I am dead. Killed, probably in some ghastly continental shit-hole, at the hands of M.I.6. I know; I can't quite believe it either but if you are currently in receipt of a benign smile emanating from the well-scrubbed face of one Ashley Sullivan who is, (or was when I last met him anyway), something at*

the FCO, I am afraid that reports of my death have not been exaggerated at all.

Now if I know you, you are planning to take Sullivan off at the knee and strangle the truth out of him so before you do that, I need to say that General Franco passed away quietly in his sleep. And don't worry; this is the only copy of this letter.

I shall have to start at the beginning so if Sullivan hasn't offered you a cup of tea (or something a mite stronger, one hopes) by now, I suggest you get him to do so and sit back and heed my sorry tale.

Cast your mind back to 2005. You have a little more hair and I have a little less waist. The idiot Bush is crowned President for the second time; a former member of the Hitler youth becomes Pope and four nutters blow themselves to bits in London, taking 48 innocent people with them. It's this last event that is the most significant from our point of view.

You may recall that both M.I.5 and M.I.6 came out of it looking like a set of prize pillocks. While they were busy making air travel as unpleasant an experience as possible, they took their eye off the domestic ball. You may also recall that they were warned by the Council that it was on the cards but, never short of hubris, M.I.5&6 thought they knew better. Anyhow, Blair ditched the hapless Charles Pretty as Chief of M.I.6 and installed our old pal, Sir Reginald Bray-Renshawe

Reg isn't the ideal choice, being under the spell of syphilis and already a few looters short of a riot, even at that time but the P.M. has been told that he is not only uncommonly pliable but would have little compunction in offloading the blame for the whole cock up on the Pakistanis if possible or even the Americans, if necessary. Blair now feels confident in holding an investigation.

But things don't go according to plan. Pakistan and the U.S. rather selfishly manage to defend themselves and the French and Germans (for once) have got their stories straight. M.I.6 try the Russians and the Israelis but to no avail; even the Spaniards see them coming and so, by 2008, with no-one left to shift the blame onto, the whole sorry mess is lifted bodily back over the fence at Vauxhall Cross. Bray-Renshawe is livid and by now as mad as a balloon and convinces himself that the whole thing has been engineered by the Council to make M.I.6 look foolish and force a change in thinking in government circles that would see the Council usurping M.I.6. He determines to destroy the Council. Thankfully, it's now well-known that Reg is utterly Deolali and so he's relieved of command before he can do any real damage. But the spark has been lit.

It smoulders for a while but recently, it's begun to flare up nicely. For the past three-or four years, the Council has been *actively undermined in a very complex and sophisticated manner by S.I.S. They have insinuated themselves into many Council departments both inside and outside the country. How deep they are, I don't know but I've a horrible feeling it's a lot deeper than I imagined. There is no-one I can trust. In fact, I'm not even sure I can trust you. But then, I'm dead so what the fuck.*

*Templeton doesn't seem to mind how long it takes. His plan appears to be to target Council Workers in the field, gradually closing in on Lambeth itself. The next move is to be made in Italy. His agent there is a former Cleaner. You may well know her: Caroline Ransleigh. She and I worked together once or twice before she upped and married an Italian diplomat with an unpronounceable name. She's a key mover, by all accounts, organising agents in Paris, Berlin, Geneva and Vienna, as well as in Rome.*

*If the worst happens (which, obviously it has) she will get away from me and will no doubt be heading your way on the hurry-up. I was never one to hold a grudge, by the way, but if you find out it was her that did for me, do me a favour and put a fucking bullet in her head when you get the chance. Pity, really; she's still a bit of a stunner, by all accounts.*

*I'm assuming, of course, that you are as loyal to the Council as I am or if not, then at least loyal to the massive pension you have no doubt accrued over the years!*

*The Council may have her faults but I really don't see too much wrong with the old girl, myself. She's getting a bit wrinkly and spills the odd bit of soup down her blouse but by and large, she still does what she was designed to do – stops foreign governments taking the piss and stops the politicians fucking up the country too badly.*

*Now you will be having trouble believing any of this and I* **would** *say, "would I lie to you?" but you know I would. All I can do is say that, of all the people I could have taken this lot to, you were the only one whose name I could remember!*

*Seriously, Arthur; it's been terrific fun and wouldn't have wanted it any other way. Except it would have been nice to have been alive.*

*Avenge me, my son! (Croak)*
*All the best,*
*Geoffrey.*

'Oh, Geoffrey, you silly bugger,' said Arthur, quietly. He hadn't wept in many years and he was fucked if he was going to start now but it took every ounce of willpower to keep control of himself. Wisely, Sullivan said nothing but placed a large tumbler of whisky on the table in front of Arthur.

'He said you might need a drink, once you'd finished reading.'

## Ursulet

The next cogent thought Vanessa had was of her neck. It hurt.

'Drink.'

It was Ursulet. 'You'll be fine in a few minutes. Don't try to sit up.'

The nausea was diminishing and although her ears were ringing and her skin tingled hot and cold, she realised she was beginning to come round.

'God, I haven't fainted in a long time. How weird. Ow!'

'You fell awkwardly. It's not serious. It'll be sore for a while, that's all. Take another drink.'

'It must be the stress. Or thin air or something.' She took another swig and a puzzled expression crossed her face. 'What were we talking about?'

'I can't remember. We need to move,' said Ursulet.'

Vanessa's head was beginning to clear and in a very short while, she felt strong enough to mount once more. As she pulled herself into the saddle, another wave of nausea came upon her but it passed quickly. Nevertheless, she was feeling decidedly shaky as they set off.

'How long until we get to where we're going?' Vanessa asked. She felt a certain relief when the girl answered,

'Three hours, maybe four.'

Vanessa gathered the reins, took a couple of deep breaths and kicked Abri into motion. Gradually, the wooziness began to subside and soon she was feeling herself again. The September sun was giving its best shot but, as the mountains rose up around them once more and the trees became thicker around them, it began to grow cold. From behind her, she could hear the sound of the girl rubbing the tops of her bare arms. Vanessa knew that she was dressed only in stretch pants, boots, a vest and a jerkin.

'There's that shirt in the saddlebag,' she called out. She heard the squeak of a buckle and turned to see the girl pull out the shirt. It would help, but it wouldn't be enough. Vanessa had her duster rolled up on the back of her saddle. She untied it and offered it to Ursulet. To her delight and somewhat to her surprise, she accepted it and put it on.

'How do you feel now?' Ursulet called over, a short while later.

'Better, thanks. Must have been the altitude... or something.'

'Yes, that's probably it.'

'Ursulet?' There was no response. Nevertheless, Vanessa persevered. 'Ursulet?'

'What?'

'Tell me about him.'

'About whom?'

'Sebastian.'

'I don't think so.'

'Why not?'

'Because it's none of your business.'

'You…you don't really believe I had anything to do with his death, do you?'

'Do *you*?'

'What's that supposed to mean?'

'What did you do the day before you met Geoffrey Wittersham?'

'What?'

'You picked him up on Monday morning. What had you been doing on Sunday night?'

'I don't know… Sunday night?' Vanessa thought for a few seconds. Then it came to her.

'Hang on, I *do* remember! That was the day Jessie broke up with her boyfriend.' Ursulet didn't respond and Vanessa felt some explanation was necessary. 'My friend Jessie came over,' she went on. 'She said she'd come to see my new apartment and brought along a bottle of vodka as a housewarming gift. But it was all bullshit, of course. Turned out her boyfriend had dumped her, that afternoon and she'd really come round for a little cry. We stayed up late and drank the whole bottle between us. If I hadn't felt so hung-over on the Monday, I'd probably have been thinking more clearly. It wasn't 'til we got to the car that the penny dropped… about Wittersham not being Stephen Mosley.'

'What was her boyfriend's name?'

'Ursulet, what on…?'

'His name.'

'Erm… Oh God, it was Italian. Erm… hang on, let me think: I keep wanting to say "Vittorio" but… it's not that. "Vee… Vee…Vee… Vincenzo"! That was it! He was a designer at Carlucci Bros. Why's that important?'

'What brand of vodka?' said Ursulet.

'I can't remember that! It had a red label – some sort of cod Russian thing going on. All backward "R"s and "N"s. No idea. What on earth has this to do with… ?'

'Was the TV on? Or were you listening to music?'

'What the…? I can't… There was nothing on. We were just talking. "IKON…!" "IMPERIA IKON" it was called!' She turned around in the saddle, a delighted smile on her face. Ursulet's face was impassive. Vanessa faced forwards again, murmuring to herself, 'Rough as old boots as well. Never again.' After a few minutes walking in silence, Vanessa said,

'I don't suppose you're going to tell me what that was all about?'

There was no reply. Ursulet, it was clear, had lived a long time amongst liars. That they must frequently have been killers as well added up, in Vanessa's mind, to a couple of good reasons why the girl was so reluctant to give anything away and so determined to disbelieve all she was told. Had it not been for the fact that Vanessa had saved her life, even this odd and unsatisfying conversation would probably never have been happening at all. She decided not to press her any more; at least until Ursulet had had time to digest the answers she'd already provided.

Vanessa didn't know how long it had been when Ursulet called out, 'Stop.'

She turned to see the girl dismount. They had pulled up at a gate beyond which, a track led to a jumble of farm buildings fifty metres or so away. Beside the gate, a handcart and on the handcart, a variety of receptacles – ranging from old saucepans to plastic bowls and wicker baskets, containing eggs, cheese, fruit, leeks and onions; all manner of produce: They had passed two or three other dwellings with such stuff for sale but this one clearly promised a better haul. Vanessa also noted that the buildings were far enough from the road to render an unnecessary meeting with a farmer's wife far less likely.

Ursulet gathered a number of items and deposited them in her saddlebags. She then picked up an old enamelled pot containing green beans. Having inspected them, she took out a handful and tipped the rest into one of the wicker baskets. She then tied the pot to the pommel of her saddle.

To Vanessa's surprise and satisfaction, Ursulet stroked off several notes from the wad she'd taken from Christopher, and put them into the honesty box.

They rode on.

By the time their horses finally set foot on tarmac, the sky was an orange fan; the shadows of the mountains, the folds and Vanessa was utterly exhausted once more. She turned to see the girl, who was herself looking pretty beat, swaying in the saddle. It occurred to Vanessa that she might make a break for it. A number of cars passed by, any one of which, Vanessa imagined, might have offered salvation but she was simply too far gone. She realised that for the past hour or so, she'd again begun to see the world as little disjoined blocks and that idiotic tune was bouncing round and round in her head, once more. It was definitely time to stop.

The road wound steeply down and in the valley below, Vanessa would catch glimpses of roofs and gardens, farms and fields at each turn on the switchback. The anxiety that had been her companion for most of the past four days had all but gone although why, she couldn't fathom. All she seemed able to think about was the possibility of getting off the horse, into a shower and into a bed. If there was a meal in there somewhere, all well and good and a glass of wine wouldn't go amiss, either. The lights of the village had begun to show when she heard, from behind her.

'There, to your left.'

It was nothing but a passing point in the road that funnelled gently into the trees. Vanessa walked Abri across the road and pulled her up. In a moment, the girl was beside her, leaning on her pommel and peering into the gloom of the forest.

'If you want a wee, I'll hang onto your horse,' said Vanessa. Ursulet said nothing but jerked her head to indicate to Vanessa that she should follow the narrow pathway into the forest.

'What?' she asked, genuinely puzzled.

'In there,' said Ursulet.

## Corehampton Girls

'We stay the night in there,' said Ursulet.

'You what?'

'We cannot go into the village.'

'You're kidding.' Vanessa peered at Ursulet's, swollen, bloodied, expressionless face and realised she wasn't. That was why she had taken the provisions and the old enamelled pot. 'Oh God,' Vanessa groaned, as she kicked Abri in the ribs. The little horse plodded into the gloom. Although the sky above the trees still showed violet, amongst them it was dark and getting darker with every step. Vanessa's eyes gradually adjusted but there was little to see save the dark avenue of glowering conifers through which she moved, and the odd glow-worm.

'Your friend and the Italian will have been found by now.'

Ursulet had thought to favour her with an explanation. Vanessa wondered if that was significant.

'The riders we met were going to a youth hostel above the dam. Apparently, it's on the road we crossed over, about two kilometres from where we left them. Even if there's no phone signal up there, the hostel is certain to have a land line. I think there may be police looking for us soon; if they aren't already doing so.' The mention of police brought Vanessa back to reality. There was no reason to believe that the French rozzers would be any more sympathetic to her plight than the Italian ones had been. She remembered Maytham's desire to avoid the law on their drive through Italy.

'I don't think that Christopher would call the police; and I'm certain Gianfranco wouldn't,' she said.

'If your friends seem reluctant to involve the police, it will certainly arouse the suspicions of others. The police *will* be called. We'll be safer in here.'

'And colder; and hungrier...' She raised her arm and made a face. '...and smellier.'

Twenty minutes later, with the horses tethered and munching on low but plentiful moss and scrub, Vanessa was helping Ursulet make camp. She agreed that sounded a little more egalitarian than it actually was, since all she could do was follow instructions and lug stuff about.

'Who do you think I am; Bear Sodding Grylls?' she'd said to Ursulet's suggestion that she make a fire. However, she'd agreed to have a go at collecting some wood and stalked off muttering to herself. It wasn't long before she realised that if she ventured any further, she would be lucky to find her way back. So making sure she could still hear the shuffling of hooves and the tearing and grinding of ground cover, she set about gathering fuel. By the time she returned with her arms full of twigs, Ursulet had assembled piles of bracken and was setting about fashioning some sort of lean-to.

'You were in the army as well, I suppose?' Vanessa said.

'Girl Guides,' said Ursulet.

'And did you get your "Spying" badge, then?' For a moment, Vanessa thought she might have misjudged it but there it was, the faintest flicker of a smile twitched at the corner of the girl's mouth.

'So, you lived in England, then – as a child?' Vanessa said. Immediately, the smile disappeared.

'What makes you think so?'

'Well, "Girl Guides", for a start. Do they have them in other countries? I just thought... Oh never mind.' She set about piling up twigs for a fire. She had no idea what she was doing.

'We are not friends, you and I,' Ursulet said suddenly.

'No,' Vanessa heard herself say. 'But I'd at least like the chance to show you that I'm not your enemy.' Yet again, the pair lapsed into awkward silence and it was not until the fire had well and truly taken and the old enamelled pot had been pressed into a service it hadn't seen in many a year, involving a butter-fried melee of leeks, potatoes, and onions, that Ursulet spoke up.

'Tell me a story from your childhood,' she said.

'Why is everyone so interested in my childhood? First Wittersham; then Caroline and now you. What's that all about?'

Ursulet teased a number of smoking logs back into the centre of the blaze and said only,

'Indulge me.' Vanessa sighed and because she had been remembering it on and off since visiting Caroline's mansion, she told the story of her teenage expedition to the festival in Scotland. When she had finished, Ursulet asked her,

'What were the names of your friends?' It took a moment for Vanessa to recall them but she did so with little difficulty.

'Did they go school with you?'

'Yes. We were in the sixth form at the time.'

'Were they boarders, too?'

'Oh no,' Vanessa said, 'What? Boarders? No. There were no boarders at my school.'

'At Corehampton?'

Vanessa began to feel faint. The mosaic structure of her recollection began to fragment once more.

'Are you all right?' Ursulet asked her.

'I... I'm just tired and hungry, I think. When will it be ready?'

'You were a boarder, though weren't you?'

'Of course,' Vanessa said. Her ears had begun to ring.

'Where did you say your friends went to school?'

'What?' She was feeling really grim now.

'Which school were your friends at?'

'Er... Uckfield... St. Philip's Grammar School... What's the matter with me?' She could feel Ursulet's arm about her shoulder.

'They were at school with you, weren't they? Fiona, Claire and Sarah?'

'Yes, I just told you... leave me alone. I don't feel well.' Ursulet took Vanessa's head in her hands and turned it towards her.

'Look at me, Vanessa. You were never at Corehampton Girls School.'

'What? Of course I was... I was...'

'No! You went to St Philip's Grammar School with Fiona and Claire and Sarah and you went to a festival in Scotland with them. Look at me, Vanessa!'

Afterwards, Vanessa would describe it as being like watching a deep-red velvet curtain tearing in half before her eyes to reveal a checkerboard pattern beyond it. And as the tear reached her eye-line, in some way, it seemed to continue through her face, her neck, her chest. Pieces of her frayed and flew from her, drawn, along with the smoke from the fire, upwards into the black.

Her cry was stifled by the vomit. Ursulet thrust her aside and had the good sense to turn her away from the fire and cooking pot. On all fours,

Vanessa retched until there was nothing left. There hadn't been that much to begin with so it could have been worse.

With her usual stoicism, Ursulet used bracken, dirt and leaves to clear away the puke, as Vanessa lay on her side, gasping and sobbing.

'What... what the... fuck?' she managed, at last. 'What the fuck was *that*? God..! What the fuck *was* that?'

'I think *that*,' Ursulet said, was a little bit of Geoffrey Wittersham leaving your mind.'

'What do you mean?' A part of her sort of knew. 'He did something to me. What was it?' Ursulet began stirring the food with a stick. Vanessa put her hand over Ursulet's and said, 'Ursulet, please... I'm... I'm scared.' The girl removed the stick, tapped it on the side of the bowl and turned to face Vanessa. With something that might have been recognised as concern, she said,

'I don't know. Not exactly, anyway. It's a form of executive control technique that Wittersham has developed over the years into a very sophisticated method of manipulation; a sort of cross between stage hypnotism, NLP and regression therapy.'

Vanessa had of course, come across neuro-linguistic programming in her business studies and she'd seen stage hypnotists make people do daft things in front of an audience.

'Regression therapy?' she asked.

'Some claim they are able to cause subjects to "regress" and relive past lives. It's complete garbage, of course, but the techniques of suggestion that they use are very real indeed. A skilled practitioner might make you believe almost anything, given the right circumstances. From a history of child abuse to alien abduction. In your case, Wittersham used it to make you believe you had gone to Corehampton Girls School.'

'Why the bloody hell would he do that?'

Ursulet turned her attention to the enamelled bowl and began pushing the food around.

'It's almost done,' she said.

'Ursulet. Why did Geoffrey Wittersham do that to me?'

'I don't know.' She turned to her once more. 'But it may not have been the only thing he did.'

'What, you mean to say that... I might still be... I don't know... "programmed" or something?'

'It's entirely possible. The school days thing is apparently a way into the mind. Although, I've been wondering...'

'What?'

'Coming out of it was a more traumatic process for you than I was expecting. He obviously really wanted you to think you'd been to

Corehampton but I don't know why. Now you know that you didn't, the reason for his doing so may never become clear.'

'But you think... there might be something else? Something that has nothing to do with schools or anything?' Ursulet remained silent. 'Oh shit,' Vanessa murmured. 'What a bastard.' Her eyes began to fill with tears. She looked pleadingly at Ursulet. 'Is there no way of knowing?'

Ursulet shook her head. 'I don't know. I know so little about it; just what I was told.' Her voice tailed off.

'Told by whom?' Vanessa asked, her eyes narrowing.

'My superiors. The ones who sent me to get you.'

Vanessa's voice was almost a whisper.

'Who are they,' she asked.

'I can't tell you.'

'Why not?'

'Because I still don't know if I can trust you. Your answers about what you were doing the night before you met Wittersham were convincing but he might just be good enough to have planted those thoughts there.'

'You can't mean that...'

'Look, I'm no expert. I was briefed about it, that's all. From what I understand, a skilful practitioner can make someone believe almost anything to be true, provided it's within reason for that person to believe it.'

'But I know who I am. I know what happened to me!'

'Really? Look at it from my point of view. You picked Geoffrey Wittersham up at the airport; you were there when British agents died; you provided a diversion for the killer. We have only your word that he abducted you. If you two were working closely together, it's entirely possible that he primed you to believe you were an innocent party; that you worked as a P.A.; that you hadn't met him before that morning; that he forced you into helping him escape. Just because you think all those things are true, it doesn't mean that they are. Until five minutes ago, you believed you had been a pupil at Corehampton.'

'Oh, my God.'

'And what's more, you may have even agreed to let him do it.'

'What! Don't be so bloody...'

'...It would be no more than a committed agent would accept as a duty. Enemies could subject such a person to all kinds of interrogation techniques – there is no one more convincing than one who truly believes he has nothing to hide.'

Vanessa's mind was in turmoil. She could no longer be certain of anything, not even that her thoughts were her own. How much of her consciousness owed its existence to Geoffrey Wittersham? The thought was almost too much to bear.

'So you see: I cannot be certain who you are and…' she paused for a moment. '…neither can you. I'm sorry.'

Her attention turned once more to the food. Placing two pieces of birch bark lined with cabbage leaves on the ground, she doled the contents into them. She handed one of them to Vanessa, along with a twig to be used as a makeshift fork. Vanessa took it without a word and settling herself beside the fire, said,

'You know, I think you are; sorry, I mean. And that's… kind of a relief.'

'How so?'

'It means that on some level, you hope that my story's true.'

'I suppose it does. But if it's not, and if I am forced to do it, I am prepared to kill you.'

'Oh. Well, fair enough, I suppose.'

Against all reason, Ursulet got the irony and smiled. Vanessa laid aside the birch-bark plate and wiping her eyes on her jacket, said,

'I don't think I would like to be a fanatical agent working with someone like Wittersham. If I turn out to be, I really hope you *will* kill me.'

## A Noble Treachery

Back at Harrow Gardens for the evening, Arthur was listening to the CD he'd bought from Crawthorne Beasley and going over the events of the day.

On the arm of his chair, lay the letter from Geoffrey. He hadn't a clue what to do about it. Sullivan had not been able to shed any more light on the matter except to outline his involvement with Geoffrey. Whilst on the Intelligence Sub-Committee, Sullivan had got wind of the Bray-Renshawe business and had even visited him in the loony-bin. He had concluded that Bray-Renshawe was in the right place and thought no more about it until he met Geoffrey at some do or other. Believing Geoffrey was something to do with M.I.6, he told him the tale in passing. Fortunately, they had been at Charterhouse together and so, instead of killing Sullivan for the indiscretion, he'd listened with a rather less jaundiced ear and decided to investigate a little. Sullivan, true to his word as an Old Carthusian, had told no-one in the interim and, sympathetic to the Council cause, had sided with Geoffrey in trying to sort the whole mess out.

Recently, however, they had begun to find themselves out of their depth. Needless to say, Geoffrey had left instructions as to what Sullivan should do in the event of a catastrophe and so Sullivan had done it. The thought had occurred to Arthur that the catalogue of errors of the last few days could easily have had their origins in the internal struggle to which Geoffrey had referred. Reassessing events in the light of this new information was not going to be a simple matter.

There was a knock at the door. He was never normally concerned by knocks on the door but this particular evening he picked up his gun from the table and, keeping outside any potential arc of fire, he crossed the floor. Peering through the spy-hole made him feel like an old woman and he'd decided long ago that he'd rather die than do that and so he just opened the door.

'Bracewell? What do you want?'

'No, Shepherd. The accepted mode of address is: "Oh, how jolly nice of you to come over. Would you like a cup of tea?" I had expected more from you, frankly.'

Arthur was certain that Bracewell's colleague, Grafton hadn't been straight with him that morning. It could be that a reasonably friendly chat with Bracewell might prove fruitful but, on the other hand, of course, something considerably more important had now come up.

'It's been a "what do you want?" sort of day, as it happens, Bracewell, so stop pissing about and tell me why you're here?' said Arthur.

'On edge, Shepherd? That's not like you.'

'How would you know? We've hardly exchanged two civil words since we first met. And I am not "on edge".' Arthur thought for a moment and said, All right, Bracewell, you'd better come in. It's far too late for tea but I think I owe you a drink, so I suppose I'd better offer you a whisky.'

'I'm driving: best make it a small one.' Arthur went to the sideboard to do the honours, invited Bracewell to sit and made to turn off the music.'

'Oh, don't do that!' Bracewell said, suddenly. Arthur gave him a quizzical look to which Bracewell responded,

'John Cage. String Quartet. Don't often hear that.' Arthur raised an eyebrow.

'Today's been full of little surprises,' he said, as he sat down. 'I suppose it's the mathematics, is it?'

'Not entirely but he's a clever bastard and no mistake.'

'So, with marginally increased respect, I ask: what can I do for you, this evening?'

'I ran into a pal of yours earlier today, Rupert Stainforth.'

'Oh?'

'Yes. He told me that Grafton had spoken to you about that alphanumeric you brought down to us the other day.'

'*Good old Stainforth,*' thought Arthur before saying, 'Yes. As I say, thanks for the sterling work and all that. Drink's on its way...'

'What did Grafton tell you, Shepherd?' Arthur, his back to Bracewell, smiled. Turning, drinks in hand, he said,

'He told me that you'd managed to get a little way into the mystery, that's all.'

'Did he? What else did he tell you?'

'Bracewell, I'm grateful for the help you've given but that doesn't entitle you to quiz me like some dimwit plod.'

Suddenly Bracewell's manner changed.

'I'm sorry, Shepherd,' he said. I've had a bit of a shitty day myself, to tell the truth. Grafton lied to you.'

'I know he did.'

'How did you find out?'

'When you get lied to as much as I do, you develop a nose for it. What I'd like to know, I'm afraid, Bracewell, is why he lied.'

'I swear to you, Shepherd, I have no idea but he appears to be making a habit of it.' Arthur searched Bracewell's face for signs that he might be doing a bit of am-dram but could detect none. He handed him his whisky and said,

'What do you mean?' Bracewell took a gulp and said,

'Well, when you brought that code in (by God, that's nice!), I wasn't the least bit interested.'

'You wouldn't even look at it.'

'Shepherd. I'm up to my armpits in crap down at Lambeth, with no sign of it easing.'

'A depressingly familiar tale.'

'So the last thing I wanted was to do a favour for anyone.'

'Least of all me, eh?' Bracewell bridled a little.

'Well, that's as may be,' he said. Arthur had no interest in baiting Bracewell at this time of night.

'Go on,' he told him.

'Well, it was only when Grafton said he couldn't help you that I thought...'

'You thought it would be fun to get one over on him.'

'It's just professional pride, Shepherd. I'd have thought even you could understand that. And all right; yes a bit of rivalry.' Arthur remembered Mulberry saying much the same thing earlier in the week and look where it had got him. Bracewell continued.

'The instant I saw it, I knew what it was and (and here's the point) so did Grafton. It was the easiest thing in the world, in fact. I asked him why he went on about check digits and tracking individuals and why he didn't just tell you and he gave me some bollocks about not wanting waste our time and what have you. It was fairly plausible but I had a feeling he was lying; although even when Stainforth told me that Grafton had spoken to you I didn't catch on until he told me that Grafton said he'd take another look for you.'

'Oh?'

'Well, he didn't bloody need to, did he? A three year old with a passing knowledge of coding could have told you it was a fragment of hexadecimal ASCII.' Arthur tried to look as though he knew what that meant.

'Shepherd,' Bracewell said, exasperated, 'Grafton could probably have read the code in English as soon as he saw it. Hex is that simple!'

'So what does it say?' he asked.

'I don't really want to say, just yet.' Arthur put his glass down on the table beside him. He slapped his hands onto his thighs and stood up, briskly. He whipped Bracewell's glass from his hand and said,

'Well, thanks for dropping round, Bracewell. Been most enlightening. Did you have a coat? I forget.'

'Stop mucking about, Shepherd. I can help you, here.'

'Apparently, so could a three-year-old.'

'I may have exaggerated a little,' said Bracewell.

'So are you going to tell me or not?'

'I need some reassurances.'

'Such as?'

'Well it'd be nice if you didn't kill me, for a start.'

'Bracewell, do you not think the temptation to kill you isn't practically overwhelming every time I see you?' Bracewell's expression did not change. 'All right. I promise not to kill you. Now come on. What did you find out?' Bracewell sighed deeply then knocked back his drink. He reached into his pocket and removed a piece of paper, which he unfolded and lay on the table between them. Arthur looked at it.

**61 76 69 6c 6c 61 69 6e 6f 75 73 70 61 6c 73 79 74 69 73 61 6e 6f 62 6c 65 74 72 65 61 63 68 65 72 79**

*avillainouspalsytisanobletreachery*

Arthur read the line aloud. ' *"A villainous palsy 'tis a noble treachery"*. Is that Shakespeare? I don't recognise it.'

'Me neither but I ran it through Google and you're not far out with Shakespeare. It's an amalgam of two lines from early 17th Century dramas. The first, "a villainous palsy" is from John Webster's "The While Devill" and the second is from a play by John Ford called *"The Ladies Triall"*. Shepherd, have you ever come across something called a Jacobean Cipher?'

'Never. But then, I usually come in long after that sort of stuff is over with. Much more up your street than mine.'

'Quite so. However, this is the first time I've ever actually come across something that might be such a thing. They are extremely rare and used, I'm told, only at the highest level.'

'Well, one does get quality villainy and treachery at the highest level.'

'Oh, you mustn't fall into that little trap, Shepherd. Text that looks like plausible and pertinent information is often employed to distract the recipient from its real value. In other words, although it appears to make some sort of rational sense, it may well be meaningless. The probability, in fact, is that it's still encrypted.

'You mean the lines are just another step in the encryption?'

'Exactly. If we want to make any real headway, we're going to need a key and an algorithm. Now, the algorithm I can manage. It's what I've spent the last twenty years of my life doing – creating just those kinds of algorithms.'

'I'll take your word for it.'

'What you'll need to do is get hold of the key.'

'What does it look like?'

'That's the problem. It could be words, numbers, symbols – practically anything. You see, it's basically gibberish but when encrypted, it provides another sequence of numbers that can then be worked against the existing series in order to give you a third series. Are you with me?'

'I am,' Arthur said. We get hold of any two elements of the cipher; you do some sums and Bob's your uncle, we have the third and we hope, important bit.'

'Exactly.'

'But if this type of cipher is so significant, why is it so easily crackable?'

'I said only that the hex was easy to crack. Believe me, I don't expect deciphering the whole thing to be a simple matter. I've no idea how this element was created but you can bet your boots it wasn't simple.'

'So it's your feeling that this is something we ought to be looking into more closely? Only something else has…'

'A *lot* more closely.' Bracewell polished off his whisky and said, 'Could I... could I trouble you for another?' Arthur got the bottle from the sideboard and poured a shot for Bracewell.

'I thought you were driving.'

'I am.' He smiled. 'But I've got a little gadget in my car that tells me the whereabouts of every police car in London. I can probably sneak home unscathed.' Bracewell took a drink. He bit his bottom lip and lowered his head.

'Bracewell,' said Arthur, 'what else is on your mind? It's almost bedtime.'

'Did you kill Mulberry?' Bracewell asked.

'Certainly not,' said Arthur. 'Who would think such a thing?'

'Practically everyone.'

'Oh. Well they're wrong, as it happens. He was, as they say in the films, already dead when I got there.'

'He gave you the code, didn't he?'

'Against my better judgement, Bracewell, I shall tell you the truth... yes he did. Does that help?'

'Oh, I don't know,' he said. Suddenly he looked tired and drawn. The arrogance, which Arthur found so tiresome, had drained from him.

'What is it?'

'Look, I'm worried about Grafton, all right?' Bracewell said

The look on his face told Arthur all he needed to know.

'Ah,' he said. 'You and he...'

'Oh come on Shepherd! Surely you must have noticed?' Curiously, he hadn't.

'You think Grafton's in trouble?'

'I do. And I think it's got something to do with Mulberry.'

'What makes you think that?' Bracewell ran his hand over his cheek and chin.

'You know,' he said at last, 'we spend all day trying to discover other people's secrets, guarding our own, teasing out the truth from lies, we could be excused for being a little cynical about our fellow man. I suppose that's why so few of us have really successful relationships. I thought I'd found someone I could... trust.' He laughed. 'What an idiot!'

'Ah, so Grafton's been stepping out with other gentlemen has he?'

'No, that's just it. At first, that's what I thought and, believe it or not Shepherd, I think I could have handled it but no. I've spent most of today, (for want of a better word) spying on him. I've traced his movements over the past couple of weeks using his Oyster card, Credit Card transactions and what have you as well as his passwords through various buildings and rooms.'

'You sneaky bastard.'

'And I found out that he appears to have spent a good deal of his time in the company of one George Ricketts.' Arthur looked up sharply.

'Ricketts?'

'Yes,' Mulberry went on, not noticing Arthur's heightened interest, '...he was Mulberry's boss over at Clerical before he came over to us and before you ask, *he* is most assuredly not gay, as both his wife and his mistress will probably attest, so I suspect I have nothing to fear in that department...'

'Came over to *you*?'

'Eh?'

'You say, Ricketts came over to *you*... at *Engineering*?'

'Yes, he used to be at Clerical...as I say, with Mulberry... and then he was transferred to Engineering. Oh, he's a good cryptographer but...'

'...but it seems like too big a step?'

'Well, you know me, Shepherd; I'm no snob. I mean, Mulberry was no slouch when it came to coding either but it's not a skill that's in heavy demand at Clerical, is it? I'd have thought if Ricketts had wanted a move, something like Accounting would be more in his line, wouldn't you?'

'Possibly,' said Arthur, his brow creasing as Bracewell went on,

'But what does concern me, however, is the fact that the code was given to you by Mulberry and I think Grafton knows it. That's why he's been trying to throw you off the scent ever since he saw it and also why I think he's mixed up in something he oughtn't to be.'

So that was why Grafton had been at the Walsingham that morning. Arthur, around whom the world, naturally, revolved, had assumed Grafton was looking for *him* when he saw him peering around the dining room but he must have been looking for Ricketts. After he'd tried to fob Arthur off, he must then have seen that Ricketts already had company and made himself scarce.

Bracewell held out his glass.

'I think I'll get the bus home,' he said.

Arthur, absently, refilled the glass. He settled back in his chair and asked,

'Do you know where Grafton is now?'

'No.'

Arthur told Bracewell about Grafton's visit that morning.

'Random numbers and letters?' That's just bollocks,' said Bracewell. But I'm convinced he's up to something with Ricketts. What do you think we should do?'

Arthur was certainly curious about this whole thing but, in terms of import, Geoffrey's letter still trumped it. He'd have to leave this business on the back burner until he could get cracking with the task Geoffrey had set him and would get back to the other thing later. Provided, of course, he didn't get killed. Arthur thought for a moment, then said,

'This all started when I was given a job that didn't sit right. That's all it was. Crawthorne Beasley was the fellow's name and I wondered why they wanted him dead. Worse: I wondered *who* wanted him dead. Ever since then, things have been a bit mad. I forgot something that I once knew almost instinctively: it doesn't pay to ask too many questions when it comes to the Council, Bracewell; if you get my drift.' A lifting of Bracewell's eyebrows was all that told Arthur that he did indeed, get his drift. He said,

'So what do we do?'

'We do,' Arthur said, 'what it says on page one of the book: We wait and see what happens in the next few days.'

'But...'

'You'll only spook the pair of 'em if you start making a nuisance of yourself. Just act normally – normally for you, that is – and bide your time. If anything else comes along, you can let me know. I shall (and I can't believe I'm saying this) give you my telephone number. Now, how about another drink?'

'You know Shepherd, I was worried about coming here but now that I have... well, I'm glad I did. There's something about you that gives a fellow... confidence.

'No Bracewell. I think you're confusing me with twelve-year old single malt.

## PART 5 FRIDAY

The following morning broke bright, clear and cold. Until the sun had risen over the mountains, they would have an uncomfortable time of it. Vanessa had slept only fitfully but the fact that she'd managed to sleep at all was, she decided, a minor miracle. Ursulet looked as bad as she had done the day before. The swelling over her lips and cheek had diminished but the bruise was now a palette of blue, black and violet with a fringe of gold around its outer edges. Vanessa suspected that the girl's hair looked even worse than her own, since she had wound it up and hidden it under a hat. She was leaning against her tethered horse, studying a map.

'I think we both need a bath,' Vanessa said. Although giving the impression of not caring, Ursulet was, Vanessa believed, of the same mind. However,

'We can bathe in a stream' she said, without looking up.

'Oh goody. Look, is there any chance of, I don't know, finding an indoor swimming pool with a nice sauna or something?' To Vanessa's amazement, Ursulet said,

'There may be.'

Vanessa walked over and she noticed Ursulet turn the map so that she would not see. Vanessa shook her head and turned away.

'Here,' Ursulet called, 'I'll show you. This,' she said, her finger pointing to a small cluster of brown rectangles on the map, 'is where we are and this is the village of Alberges. It's over that way.' Vanessa looked but saw only trees. 'I expect your friends will be there by now and will have made arrangements to be picked up.' Vanessa remembered that Caroline was going to meet them all in Alberges but she didn't tell Ursulet. For a moment, an uneasy feeling that she might have a good reason for not doing so came upon her.

'Now this,' Ursulet said, pointing out a larger area of habitation on the map, 'this is Malons. It's still pretty rural but bigger than Alberges. I think we might be able to rest there tonight and I will be able to make contact with someone who can help us.'

'Us?'

Ursulet said nothing. She folded the map and put it into the saddlebag.

'It's over the mountain and we must stay off the main tracks but the terrain is not difficult. We will be there by about four o'clock, three, if we get a move on.' Vanessa groaned.

'I'm still in agony from yesterday,' she said, 'and the day before.'

'It won't be so difficult as it was yesterday.'

'Provided you don't fall into a gorge, eh?' Ursulet didn't smile.

'Saddle up,' she said.

Vanessa sighed, and groaned once more as she picked up her saddle. She walked over to Abri, said, 'Good morning, horse,' and tugged up a clump of fresh green grass from beneath a tree. Abri took it and Vanessa set about saddling the horse.

It was about five minutes later, that she walked over to Ursulet and said,

'I think something's wrong.'

'What, with the horse? What's the matter?'

'No, not the horse. It's me; there's something wrong with me.'

'What is it?'

'I... I don't know what to do...'

Ursulet led her over to a tree and sat her down.

'What do you mean?' Haltingly, Vanessa tried to explain.

'I... I got the saddle on and then I put the thing underneath but... it wasn't right. So I tried the other thing... for its head but I couldn't... and...' Her voice tailed off.

'You mean you've forgotten how to tack the horse?'

'I s'pose,' said Vanessa. 'I sort of remember but... What's the matter with me?' Ursulet's face brightened.

'Where did you learn to ride?' she asked.

'At... school, I think,' Vanessa said and then realisation dawned. 'No I bloody didn't! I never learnt to ride a horse at school! I never learnt to ride a horse at all!'

'That's why Wittersham wanted you to think you'd gone to Corehampton,' Ursulet said.

'But why? He couldn't have known I'd end up trekking over a mountain on horseback, could he?'

'Possibly. But then again...'

'How could he? Even I didn't know until...'

'...Until Caroline Gagliardo-Patricelli arranged it,' said Ursulet. 'I need to know everything, Vanessa. In as much detail as you can manage, I need to know everything from the very beginning.

## Jennifer's Kitchen.

'I am assuming that this is important, Arthur,' Jennifer said, opening the door to him. 'I'm not comfortable with this sort of thing, as well you know.' Arthur Shepherd had asked Jennifer if there was somewhere they might meet. She had reluctantly suggested her apartment, high up in Fortune Tower at The Barbican.

As he followed her through to the kitchen, he said,

'I appreciate it.'

'Tea?' she asked, holding up the pot. Arthur nodded. 'Jacqueline, do get Arthur one of the scones we made yesterday evening.' Arthur glanced up to see Jacqueline heading for the larder. She smiled at him.

'Good Morning, Mr. Shepherd. How was the traffic, this morning?' she asked.

'I don't know; I came on the tube. Jennifer, is there anyone else here I ought to know about?'

'No, Arthur. Bloody hell, you're suspicious. And what have you got against Jacqueline anyway?' He looked at the young woman who was preparing his scone. She smiled at him.

'Nothing, of course,' he said, sighing. 'It's just that one or two of my, shall we say, expectations have been challenged lately.'

'You sounded a bit odd on the telephone.'

'An odd thing has happened, Jennifer,' he said.

'Do tell,' she said. Arthur glanced at Jacqueline and then at Jennifer and then back at Jacqueline. Jennifer sighed deeply.

'It's all right, Miss Carlisle,' said Jacqueline, brightly. 'I have some work to do anyway. Tea's almost done and the scones are ready.' She placed the plate in front of Arthur and made to leave. Arthur slumped back in his chair and pinched the bridge of his nose.

'Jacqueline?' he said, as she took hold of the door handle. She stopped and turned. 'Of course you must stay. Forgive me.' Jennifer came over. She looked concerned.

'Arthur, are you all right?'

'No. Not really.' He smiled at her and then his phone rang.

'Oh, Sorry,' he said. 'Would, would you mind if I...? Only...'

'Arthur, for God's sake answer the bloody thing.'

Arthur fiddled for a second, listened for another, then said,

'Ah, Bracewell. How's the head?'

'Shepherd, have you seen the crossword today?'

'Not yet,' he said, 'Why?'

'42 Across is "Car follows commonplace American chap to Hollywood. To make Westerns, perhaps?" (4.4.)'

'Too easy,' Arthur said.

'Yes it is. But "John Ford", Shepherd.'

'Iconic director of Western films, Bracewell. Look, there's a phone line if you want help with…'

'…And Jacobean dramatist.'

Arthur remembered.

'The Ladies Triall,' he said.

'Shepherd, the answer to 53 Across is "Ladies", and 46 Across is "Trial". It's only one "l" but it's too much of a coincidence. None of the codenames I know have come up as an answer.'

'You know other people's codenames?'

'Come on Shepherd, I've worked in Engineering for fifteen years.'

'You know mine?'

'Of course!'

Arthur sighed, and wishing he hadn't told Bracewell that there seemed to have been a resumption of crossword pointers, said,

'I'll take a look and get back to you. Where are you?'

'I'm at work, Shepherd. You may have heard of it; it's what some of us do.'

'Give me half an hour,' said Arthur and hung up.

'Sorry, Jennifer. What was I saying?'

'I don't know; I'd stopped listening.' He smiled weakly and took out the letter, handing it to Jennifer. She placed her glasses on the end of her nose and read it, folded it, held it up and, with a tilt of her head, asked Arthur if Jacqueline might be permitted to read it. With a nod of his, he agreed.

'This answers a few questions, doesn't it? I don't fully understand where Sullivan comes in, though.'

'He may well be that rarest of animals, the honest Tory politician.'

'I'm glad I'm sitting down.'

'We're lucky he misremembered Geoffrey's involvement in *Spies-R-Us* or he might well be dead in a ditch as we speak. He knows a very great deal about the Council and supports it wholeheartedly. In fact, I think he sees it as a sort of private sector success story.'

'So why doesn't he just blow the gaff on M.I.6?'

'I said he was an honest politician, Jennifer, not the Dalai Lama.' This is far too big and mad to be placed in the hands of the Prime Minister.

'It would explain the botched attempts on us.'

'It would. By the way, that Knightsbridge bomb? Another pop at yours truly.'

'Go away!'

'Afraid so. I was working on the assumption it was a cock-up involving the Council not being aware that terrorists had also targeted the prince. That was why I agreed to meet Sullivan in the first place. He seemed to know a lot about it and he wouldn't keep his nose out. I assumed he believed that Box Standard had got its wires crossed and had sent Arthur Henley into a surveillance situation that turned into a massacre. I was wrong. Apparently, the whole thing was about getting shot of me and putting it down to terrorists. The Council would think I'd fucked up and blown myself up.'

'But Arthur,' Jennifer said, 'that bomb was massive. It took out half of Knightsbridge. They didn't need all that, even if they were trying to put it down to terrorists.'

'That's because, as we surmised from the Alan episode, they really are not terribly good. In fact they are rubbish. For the first time in our lives, I think we may have over-estimated our enemy.'

You can't over-estimate Caroline Ransleigh, though Arthur. I remember her – even worked alongside her in Rome for a while. She was a vicious cow and very, very clever,' said Jennifer. 'Never had her down as a wrong 'un though. I wonder what Templeton's offering? Caroline sure as hell doesn't need money.'

'And I wonder who else is involved,' said Arthur. 'One of those who copped it in Paris was called "Kirkwood"; is that right?'

'I believe so.'

'I knew it rang a bell when Stainforth said it: Kirkwood worked with Mulberry in Clerical. I remember Mulberry mentioning that he hadn't seen him for a few days. That was on the Monday…'

'The day before he was shot.'

'What was he doing at a D.P.S.D. reception in Paris, do you suppose?'

'Lord knows. I don't even know why *I* was there.' Arthur smiled.

'Well obviously you were there to get shot, Jennifer,' he said. 'When I bumped into you on Monday morning, you'd just received notice of the reception, hadn't you?'

'That's right. Well, actually I got notice that there was a job for me so I went to Floor D. It was a good opportunity to show Jacqueline round. But when I went to pick it up, it wasn't really a job at all; it was this invitation – well I say "invitation" but you know what these things are like.'

'I don't suppose you still have this "invitation"?'

'Course not! What do you take me for? I incinerated it like every other bit of paper I find in my pigeon-hole.' Arthur determined not to catch Jennifer's eye. For good measure, he decided to change the subject.

'I'd like to get a handle on this Caroline Ransleigh. I'm due at the inquest into Mulberry's death this afternoon so I'll get on it once we've finished.'

'Might be wiser to do it sooner rather than later, Arthur.' Arthur made a face.

'I know but…'

'*I* could do it,' Jacqueline piped up. Jennifer nodded slowly and looked at Arthur.

'Might be an idea, Arthur.' Arthur thought for a moment and said, 'Jacqueline?'

'Yes, Mr Shepherd?'

'It's Arthur.'

'Yes, Arthur.'

'You might well need a little help and you could do with access to some slightly more sophisticated equipment than we have in Cleansing. You'll need to get to Lambeth. When you do, wander down to Room 188. I'll arrange for you to be met by a chap called Stuart Bracewell. Between you, I think you should be able to give us a reasonable idea of where Ms. Ransleigh…'

'Her married name is Gagliardo-Patricelli,' Jennifer chimed in.

'… where Ms…. what she said, is around about now.'

'Of course Mr. Shepherd… Arthur… but I don't have clearance for floor 18.' Arthur scribbled a sixteen digit number on a piece of paper.

'You do now,' he said.

'May I have your phone number?' Jacqueline said to Arthur.

'Erm…yes, I suppose so.' He searched his pockets and eventually drew out his phone. 'It's on here somewhere,' he said, fumbling with the keypad. Jennifer plucked it from his hand and read out the number to Jacqueline, who keyed it in to her own phone. Jennifer handed the phone back to Arthur just as it began to ring. Arthur put it to his ear.

'Hullo?' he said.

'No, Mr. Shepherd… Arthur,' said Jacqueline, putting on her coat. 'That's just me giving you my phone number.'

'Is it? Oh. Thank you. Now, don't underestimate anyone down on 18 just because they work behind a desk. Bracewell can be a pain but he's pretty sound and very bright but if you come across anyone named Grafton or Ricketts it might do to remember your training.'

'Be careful, dear,' said Jennifer, as Jacqueline left the kitchen.

'I shall,' she said and was gone.

'She's worth her weight in gold, is that one, Arthur,' said Jennifer. 'Top of her class in marksmanship and covert surveillance; knows all there is to know about weaponry and poisons; absolute genius with a computer, and she plays the piano beautifully.' Arthur smiled.

'Is she training to be a Cleaner?' he asked.

'Of course. Why?'

'No reason,' he said, miserably.

'Now, Arthur: snap out of this, for goodness sake. I think you're letting Geoffrey's death get to you. He was just a man, in the end. Fallible and definitely far too cocky by half. We've both said that would do for him in the end. Neither of us should be surprised. What's come over you?'

'Do you know...? I have no idea, Jennifer. A couple of days ago I did something a bit silly. I'm almost ashamed to tell you about it but I'm beginning to think that it may have something to do with what's going on around here.'

'How silly?' Arthur looked sheepish. He had a lot of respect for Jennifer and, although marginally her superior, if he were being truthful, he would have to say that he was a little afraid of her.

'I... I failed to carry out an assignment. On purpose.'

'Well, we all have discretion to decide...'

'There was no discretion required, Jennifer; no question of turning the target to our side. I simply refused to do the job I was told to do.'

'Why?'

'Because... well, because it didn't seem... fair.'

'Fair?'

'Yes.'

'Arthur, you didn't carry out an order because you didn't think it was... fair?'

'And that's not the worst of it.'

'No?'

'No. I then made an effort to track down the person who gave the order.'

'Arthur, have you gone mental?'

'Quite possibly.'

'Why do you think there might be a link between that and what's been happening?' Arthur thought for a while then said,

'Kirkwood. He worked with Mulberry. Mulberry was helping me. Kirkwood's killed in Paris and the next day, Mulberry cops it in London.'

'But Kirkwood was killed by mistake.'

'Yes, he was. I'm prepared to believe in coincidence, as you know but there comes a point when it's just taking the piss. Have you got today's Telegraph?'

Jennifer tossed it over and Arthur set to work on the crossword. It took him about ten minutes to complete it, after which he spent a good half-hour checking it thoroughly – both answers and clues – for anything important and not obvious. Then he phoned Bracewell.

'Though it pains me to admit it, Bracewell, I think you're right. There's something in the crossword but I don't think it's a pointer. I think it's definitely related to that code. We need a confab, you and me. Is Jacqueline there, yet?'

'Jacqueline?' said Bracewell, 'Oh you must mean Ms Leamington.' He reduced his voice to a whisper. 'She insisted I call her that. Is she all right?' Arthur 's face shone with approval.

'Oh, yes, Bracewell, she's wonderful,' he said. Could you put her on for me, please?'

'Hello?'

'Jacqueline? Arthur. Any news at all?'

'Little at the moment, I'm afraid. Mr. Bracewell has written a number of very sophisticated spiders, which he has looking out for mentions of her name on several encrypted European networks.'

'I shan't pretend I have the faintest idea what you're on about but I presume that's a good thing?'

'Er, yes it is. It's very impressive, as a matter of fact. It appears that the Italian Police have been a little excited by her over the last couple of days and there are indications that she may be in France but no confirmation as yet.'

'Can Bracewell leave his spiders in your care for a couple of hours?'

'I believe so.'

'Good. I'd like you to tell him to get over here.'

'Would you like to tell him yourself?'

'No need. Just tell him to take care not to attract any attention. If he has the slightest suspicion he's being followed, tell him to go shopping or something until they get fed up and leave him alone.'

'Will do.'

Arthur put his phone down.

'For someone who isn't sure about Jacqueline, you put an awful lot of trust in her.'

'I am no longer not sure, Jennifer.' She walked over and placed her hands on his shoulders, massaging them, gently. He placed one of his hands on one of hers and squeezed.

'Arthur?' she said. 'Has there been any talk of a successor to Father?'

'If there has, I've not heard anything.' Jennifer gave a little laugh.

'What's that mean,' Arthur asked her.

'Oh nothing. I don't suppose his successor's heard anything either.' She sniggered again.

'What's wrong with you Jennifer?'

'Nothing,' she said, slapping him on the shoulders with both hands. 'Come on: let's have a look at this crossword, then; shall we?'

## To Malons

Ursulet had been correct about the ride that day: up to a point. Certainly, the terrain was far more forgiving and the climb, both upwards and down the far side, less severe. What had been a major concern for Vanessa, though, was the fact that she no longer knew how to ride a horse.

The first few hundred yards had been quite traumatic. Though she had been able clearly to recall the previous two days experience, there'd been none of the natural balance and poise, which she had possessed when she had ridden out of Amazas. She'd had to concentrate to try to bring to mind how it had felt and what it had looked like as she had crossed, on horseback, the greatest mountain range in Europe.

She'd begun to realise why Gianfranco had been constantly at her side, checking the harness and... the thing underneath... girth; that was it. She remembered all the instructions she'd been offered; instructions she'd thought utterly unnecessary at the time; but they'd known, hadn't they? All of them had known she had never ridden before in her life. But how had they known?

She had been wary of Caroline and Gianfranco from the outset but she'd felt that (although he'd been keeping secrets), Maytham had, after a fashion, cared about her. To be disabused so cruelly had been deeply upsetting. Plus, it had left her with a problem. Ursulet was now the only one it seemed that she could trust but the fact that Ursulet couldn't trust her had made it difficult. And the fact that she couldn't trust herself, had made it practically impossible.

They had followed, as far as Vanessa could make out, a high contour, which bypassed about twenty kilometres of valley road. It had taken several hours but they hadn't met a soul on the way. It was only on their approach to Malons that they encountered the police car.

They had just emerged from woodland and were watering the horses in a stream, when along the track came a 4X4. Both women spotted the red and blue lights on the top and both turned their faces away from the road. They held their breath until the vehicle had passed. It disappeared around a curve and they both scrambled to re-mount. Before they'd been able to do so however, the car returned. It pulled up about ten metres away and two officers emerged. To Vanessa's horror, Ursulet reached for the rifle. Then one of the policemen called out to them and Ursulet lowered her hands.

Of course, Vanessa could make out none of what was being said. There were a lot of "nons" and "O.K.s" even a couple of laughs. At one point, one of the officers wrote something down on a piece of paper whilst the other drew a line on Ursulet's map with his finger. The officer handed Ursulet the paper and with a wave, they got back in their car and drove off.

Vanessa had got to know Ursulet well enough to realise that there was little point in asking her what all that had been about. She had contented herself with the fact that the police hadn't shown any more concern than they might have done towards any two young women out riding alone through the forest. However, to Vanessa's surprise, Ursulet had offered her an explanation.

'They told us to be careful,' she had said. 'Apparently, two travellers were attacked and robbed in the mountains yesterday. The assailants were two powerfully built men on dirt bikes. Did we come across anyone like that?'

'Not that I recall,' Vanessa had said, laughing.

'The blond one gave me the address of his aunt who keeps a stable just outside Malons. She runs riding holidays.'

'Wait a minute; does that mean she has accommodation?' A broad smile had spread across Ursulet's face and she had winced with the pain of it.

It turned out that Mme. Chantier, the policeman's aunt, had already taken her horses down to their winter stables in the valley but had not quite laid all away before the snows arrived. She had housed the little Haflingers for the price of some feed and few euros for her son to groom them. The accommodation block was some way from the house and many of the rooms had been closed in order to be spruced up in time for when the skiers arrived. Fortunately Mme Chantier had been able to find them a double room at the back with a view over the meadows towards the mountains.

Vanessa had been surprised that Ursulet had not only agreed to lay up here but had in fact suggested it, saying,

'We are both tired and so are the horses. We all need to rest properly. We could carry on until nightfall but I don't think that will gain us much in terms of distance. If we stay here tonight, I can arrange for us to be picked up here in the morning.'

It had sounded perfectly sensible but part of her had balked at the idea of being "picked up". Vanessa may have been becoming used to Ursulet but she was far from sanguine at the prospect of encountering any of her colleagues.

## Note Row

'Knock, knock.'

'Oh, hullo, Shepherd. How did it go?'

'You can never tell with these things, Bracewell but I've a feeling the Inspectors might want me back.'

'Inspectors give me the creeps.'

'Yes, that's sort of their job, Bracewell. Now, how are you getting on?'

Bracewell shook his head. Arthur noticed the plethora of dog-ends in and around the ash-tray.

'A two-packet problem, eh?' he said.

'Almost three,' Jacqueline said, sniffing her hair and making a face. Arthur addressed her,

'Spiders behaving themselves?'

'Impeccably,' she said. 'Apparently, there's an aeroplane on an airfield in Southern France registered to a Luca Gagliardo-Patricelli.'

'Her late husband.'

'Correct. It's been cleared for take-off at 9:00 tomorrow, French time: 8:00 BST. Bound for Biggin Hill.'

'That's good work, Jacqueline.'

'Shall we intercept her?'

'I don't know. How easy will it be to track her once she arrives in England?'

'Well Mr. Bracewell has a very impressive range of surveillance equipment. Are you hoping she might lead us to someone?'

'I think it's worth a try, don't you?'

'I'll get on it right away.'

Bracewell sidled over to Arthur.

'Where did you find *her*?' he asked.

'I borrowed her from a friend. How are you getting on with the problem?' Bracewell shook his head.

'Whatever message it contains, it's bloody well-hidden. I've tried a number of things and...' He seemed exasperated.

'...And?' Arthur prompted.

'Look anything is possible, Shepherd! I said as much this morning. This could take a bloody long time.'

'I've a feeling that a bloody long time may be something we don't have,' said Arthur. He fished into his pocket and withdrew an old CD jewel-case. He handed it to Bracewell.

'Here,' he said. 'Track 3. I'd never heard it before – which is one of the reasons I bought this compilation in the first place.' Bracewell turned the CD over and read the listing out loud.

' "*Limns*" by Noel Lear. Hang on...' Bracewell picked up the paper. 'Those are three of the answers! LIMNS, NOEL and LEAR. Ha! And LIMNS is 3 Down! Fuck, Arthur! Where did you get this?'

'It was in a pile round at Mrs. Jempson's in Gloucester Rd.'

'Blimey!'

'I thought you'd be interested. He's got another piece on there.'

'Who has?'

'Noel Lear, Bracewell. Try and keep up.'

'Which one? Ah, here…Track 25. "*Reiterations*".' Bracewell was grinning fit to burst. He looked again at the crossword and said, '25 Across: REITERATIONS. Ha! You've listened to them of course?'

'Oh yes.'

'Well what do they say!?'

'They don't *say* anything – not to me at any rate. "*Limns*" is a serial composition. It's a bit quick, right from the off but I think I have the note row.' Arthur handed over a slip of paper and Bracewell studied it.

'Technically, it looks fine but I'll have a listen. What about the other one?'

'Atonal but not serial - as far as I can make out: more complex but a deal slower. I've written out the theme on the other side of that.' Bracewell turned the paper over.

'I'll look at that in a minute. First things first.' He placed the CD into the drive of his computer. Again, Arthur heard the now familiar staccato of the piano giving the opening note-row. Twelve tones, clearly picked out before being overlaid by the harmony. The marimba providing a clarity at the top of the scale, immediately countered by a low bassline on the piano. Arthur felt music much as he did art; that is: on an instinctual and visceral level and as without the technique, the art was nothing, so without the soul, the technique – whilst admirable, could convey only so much. Arthur suspected that Bracewell, on the other hand, was one of those fortunate people for whom the intellectual pursuits of logic and mathematics, provided an almost aesthetic experience.

However, if there was any beauty hidden in this piece, Bracewell had not appeared to have uncovered it. What he had uncovered, apparently, were numbers. Bracewell scribbled away as he listened over and over to the leaping, cascading, agitated note-row being moulded and morphed into music. Music, Arthur distinctly hoped, with a message. Presently, Bracewell leaned back.

'Well?' asked Arthur.

Bracewell looked at him. Arthur, being a good killer, was possessed of immense emotional intelligence yet he could detect nothing in Bracewell's expression. Until the first flicker of a smile.

'This is bloody amazing, Shepherd. This piece is a serial composition that breaks down into several hexadecimal patterns…'

'…Hexadecimal?'

'It may not be significant, Shepherd,' Bracewell said hurriedly. 'Many serial pieces are hexadecimal in nature. This one's in 4/4 time and the twelve notes in the note-row are arranged in three bars at the outset. Straight crotchet beats: couldn't be simpler. I'm convinced this note row is the key to unscrambling our little bit of Jacobean drama but it'll take me an hour or two to tease out the algorithm from the piece as a whole.

'The second piece is utterly different. It's not a serial composition; but that makes sense. A serial composition alone is not sophisticated enough to provide much more than a key but once I have the matrix of notes, I'd bet anything that "Reiterations" will unlock the numbers for me. From then on, it should be a relatively simple job to decode.' Bracewell drew his hand across his head.

'Frankly, I'm astonished,' he said. 'The chances of it going astray at any point must have been enormous.' Bracewell looked thoughtful. 'You know, the fact that you were given this CD on Tuesday makes me think…'

'I wasn't given it.'

'Eh?'

'I wasn't given it. It cost me eight quid.'

'…makes me think that was the real start of this whole thing. Someone wanted to tell you something very badly indeed but whatever it was had to be encrypted in such a way as to make sure that only *you* might figure it out. They created this composition, got someone to perform it and put it in this compilation, which somehow they knew you'd buy. It links to the crossword and it links to the hexadecimal baby-talk that Mulberry sent you. This one isn't amateur, I can tell you that. I suspect we may be getting a little closer to people who really know what they're doing. Where are you going?'

'I'm going to see if I can't have a word with Mrs. Jempson. Find out how much she knows. You stay here and carry on with this. I'll be about ninety minutes.'

Arthur had a sudden thought.

'This hexadecimal code stuff? Is it still commonly used in communication technology?'

'Not really. It's a way into simple machine code but most computers nowadays – and for many years since – use much more sophisticated stuff.'

'So it was used in early computers, then?'

'And their forerunners: teleprinters, early word-processors and the like.'

'Teleprinters?'

'Yes but there aren't that many in use nowadays; if any.' Arthur hesitated but quickly decided there was no alternative.

'What if I were to tell you, Bracewell, that the Council still makes use of teleprinters?' Bracewell looked into his tea cup for a while then said,

'I suppose it might make sense. If someone wanted to send an unhackable message, an old analogue phone line and a bit of ancient electro-mechanics might be a way of doing it. Yes, it sounds like something the Council might do. How do you know about that, then?'

'Mulberry worked it out from a despatch I gave him.'

'A *Cleaning* despatch?'

'Afraid so.'

'Fucking hell, Shepherd.'

'I know,' said Arthur. 'I know.'

## Genius

'Afternoon, Mrs Jempson.'

'Mr. Shepherd. Glad to see you up and about. Looking a bit better than when I last saw you, eh?'

'I appreciate what you did the other day, Mrs. Jempson. Thank you.'

'You're welcome, I'm sure. So what can I do for you today, then?' she asked.

'Well, I thought I might have another little look through your compact discs, if you don't mind.'

'Good Lord! Mind? Of course not. Did you enjoy the last one, then?'

'Most... enlightening, it was.' Arthur approached the rack of CDs and began thumbing through them. He half wondered whether to come clean and tell Mrs Jempson what was up. He tried thinking back to the conversation they'd had immediately prior to him buying the CD last Tuesday but he'd been in such a state that it was hard for him to recall anything much. Had she proffered it? He had no idea. He remembered only that he'd been swayed by the fact that he had never before heard those two pieces.

He glanced behind him. Mrs Jempson was busying herself straightening racks and replacing items in their correct places. He smiled. Mrs Jempson didn't just use this shop as cover; she really cared about Oxfam and even as Council Workers wandered in and out, picking up and dropping off bits and pieces, they would find themselves mingling with (and often waiting in the queue behind) regular customers, to whom Mrs Jempson gave every bit as much attention.

Arthur remembered the James Last album as it toppled beneath his fingers onto the rest of the ones that he'd already looked at. Other than that, there was nothing to jog his memory. There were few twentieth century classical albums and absolutely nothing atonal whatsoever – apart from Whitney Houston.

He sighed. He'd have to give it a go.

'Ah well, there doesn't appear to be anything to match that other album I bought. Was it erm… a regular customer, do you remember? Much to his surprise, she answered,

'Oh yes. Nice young woman often brings in some lovely clothes – evening wear, mostly. She buys the odd thing too. First time she'd brought in any CDs though, as far as I remember.'

'She's local, then?'

'Dunno. Perhaps she works round here.'

'Ah well. Perhaps the next time you see her, you might ask if she has any more erm… similar items that she wants to get shot of. I'd be most interested.' Mrs. Jempson stopped her pottering and turned to face Arthur.

'I don't think you quite understand how charity shops work, do you Mr. Shepherd?' Arthur tried to recover.

'Well, naturally I meant through your august establishment.'

Mrs Jempson turned back to her work. Either she knew nothing or she was one of the most competent Workers the Council had ever had and he knew for certain she was the latter. This had been a waste of time and he felt foolish. More to the point, he'd probably gone and let Mrs. Jempson see his hand.

By the time he got back to Century House, it was beginning to get dark. Jacqueline had spent a good portion of the day trying to pin down Caroline Gagliardo-Patricelli and despite her protestations, Arthur insisted she go home and rest. Once she'd gone, Arthur turned to Bracewell. He had his back to him and he was hunched over a table. A single desk-lamp illuminated the mess of papers in front of him.

'You too, Bracewell. We'll carry on tomorrow.'

'Just a mo…' said Bracewell.

'It'll still be there in the morning.'

'No it won't; because I've almost done it.' Arthur moved across and looked over his shoulder. He read,

va---sa—drid-et-cra--h-r-ebeas-ey

'There are gaps,' said Arthur.

'I know there are gaps. That's why I need a minute or two. The gaps are where there are no corresponding numbers to notes. Being hex, some of the codes consist of alphanumerics: 6a,6b,6c and so on.'

'If you say so. Just don't start giving me a lecture.'

'Now the "A" at the end of the first bar is an "L", as is the one at the beginning of the second, making that and that "6c"; that "B" gives us "L", which is a 6e… "C";"O","6f"…' He muttered on for a few more moments until:

'There,' he said. 'We have our message.'

'Bracewell, you're a fucking little genius!' said Arthur.

'I know. However, a little of the credit has to go your way.'

'Oh?'

'Yes. You wittering on about hex coding. I couldn't get it out my mind so I decided to try it and bugger me, it worked. Would you like to know what it says?'

'If you wouldn't mind.' Bracewell turned around and held out a piece of paper, then seemed to hesitate.

'Did I hear you mention the name, "Crawthorne Beasley" the other day?' he asked.

'You may have,' said Arthur, warily. 'Why do you ask?' As if in answer, Bracewell handed over the sheet. Arthur took it and read,

*vanessaaldridgetocrawthornebeasley*

Out loud, he said, 'Vanessa Aldridge to Crawthorne Beasley.'

'You were supposed to kill Beasley, weren't you?'

'Hmm,' Arthur answered.

'Do you know this "Vanessa Aldridge"?'

'No, I don't.'

'Perhaps you need to find out who she is.'

'Oh, really?'

'Poor, Shepherd, even for you.'

'So this thing is based on hex code as well, then?' Arthur said.

'Yes. Bloody amazing!' Arthur stroked his chin. Presently, he asked, 'Have you got a minute or two, Bracewell?'

'What for?'

'Just before he was killed, Mulberry told me that he'd found something on Floor 16. I went up and had a look but couldn't think what it might have been. I have an idea I might do now, though.'

## Floor 16

Having reluctantly agreed to accompany Arthur to Floor 16, Bracewell stood in the muck and gloom and wondered what he'd been thinking.

'So are you going to tell me what we're looking for?' he said.

'Something that doesn't quite belong here.'

'Well, there's me, for a start.'

'I think it's likely to be covered in a dust sheet. You start in the end rooms and I'll go round and start on the other side. We'll meet in the middle.'

'Shepherd, what am I looking for?' Arthur said nothing more and disappeared around the corner. It had been a bit unkind but he reckoned that Bracewell would be a little more alert if he didn't know exactly what he was looking for. Truth was that Arthur wasn't sure either. He tried to remember what teleprinters looked like. He couldn't even be sure if they stood on the floor or sat on a desk. He knew that he wanted Bracewell to lift any dust-cover he came across and not be put off by any preconceptions. He was certain that Bracewell was bright enough to twig if he came across one.

It was close on twenty minutes before he heard Bracewell call out. When he arrived at room 162, Bracewell was leaning against a desk upon which sat a pristine-looking piece of office equipment, a beaming smile on his stupid face.

'I'm having my own day of surprises, Shepherd.'

'Operative?'

'Fully.'

'I think this is where Mulberry received that code. Unfortunately for him, he received it before the person for whom it was intended.'

'Something must have led him up here in the first place. I think he traced the sending machine from that despatch. This machine is an "SR", Shepherd: send and receive. I reckon someone's been both intercepting stuff and putting out misleading stuff as well.'

'Including sending me and God knows how many others off to get killed.'

'I'm going to nip downstairs and bring up a few things. I can probably put a trace on that phone line if anybody uses it again.'

'Can you tell me what the ident code for this machine is?'

'Shouldn't be a problem. Back in a minute.'

Alone, Arthur went over a few possibilities. The Council was using teleprinters to thwart hacking. However, the strategy would only work as long as no-one knew about it since data could be intercepted relatively simply. Only real insiders would have known this. It had only been the fact of Arthur's appalling breach of protocol that had given Mulberry the clue. He wondered if anything other than despatches were being transmitted up and down the internal phone lines.

When Bracewell reappeared, it took him no time at all to fire up the machine and within seconds, Bracewell handed him a slip of paper.

'It's as if this machine was built yesterday,' he said. Arthur looked at what Bracewell had written.

'Selam,' he said. 'Turkish for "peace", I believe. This is beginning to make sense.'

'I don't see how, Shepherd. That's a "5", not an "S". "5ELAM"…terminal 5E, Lambeth is what that means. So that's your Turkish theory down the pan.'

'Hmm,' said Arthur.

## Someone's Dog

It was almost 7:00p.m., and showered and wrapped in a towel, Vanessa was lying on the bed, wondering at the extent to which her hands, arms, legs and feet were tingling. It was almost painful. Ursulet was busying herself with maps and various pieces of paper. Although remaining concerned as to what might happen to her, Vanessa was feeling rather more equable about Ursulet and was the closest she'd been to relaxed for a long time.

'When we get to London,' she said, 'Do you think someone might be able to help me?'

'I have no idea.'

'I mean there must be people who know how to… fix people who've had this.' She spun her index finger around her temple. 'I bet Derren Brown could do it,' she mused.

'Is he a friend of yours?'

'No, he's just a… I don't know what he is, actually. He's on the telly.' Ursulet stood up, folded the map and chucked it on the table. Pulling on her boots, she said,

'I expect the laundry will be done by now.'

'Would you like me to go?'

'Dressed like that?' Vanessa had put all her borrowed riding clothes and every stitch of her own awful wardrobe in to be washed. She had severe doubts about its chances of survival. She looked down at the barely adequate towel.

'Point taken. Mind you, you're not much better,' she said. Apart from her boots, Ursulet was wearing nothing but the checked shirt. She said only,

'This is France,' and left.

Vanessa was pleased that Ursulet now appeared to trust her enough to leave her alone in the hotel room but then again, she reasoned, all she had to dress in was a towel. To her surprise and relief, she found herself falling asleep. At some point, she came round, but only enough to notice that Ursulet had returned to the room and with her, the scent of freshly dried laundry. She felt herself being unwound from the damp towel and felt the warm softness of a duvet being laid upon her before sleep engulfed her once more.

# PART 6 SATURDAY

Although it had been many hours, to Vanessa it seemed mere moments before she became suddenly aware, even from behind her closed eyelids, that the curtain had been drawn back. When she opened her eyes, the milky light of an early Autumn dawn was easing its way into the room and picking out the smooth pistol barrel that was swaying, inches from her face. Beyond it, was an arm at full stretch and beyond that, as her eyes focussed, she was able to make out a tall, elegant woman whom she recognised but couldn't quite place. Though only for a moment. Caroline Gagliardo-Patricelli was not a forgettable woman.

'Oh my God!'

'How depressingly unoriginal,' Caroline said. 'Now, I shall give you two seconds to begin talking and unless you tell me where Gianfranco and Christopher are in the following three, I shall shoot you.'

'Eh? Aren't they with you?'

'Four.'

'Hang on, I need to...'

'Three.'

'Caroline, it was...'

'Two.'

'It was all a mistake!'

'One.'

'They were on the mountain! We left them on the mountain!' Vanessa closed her eyes tightly and waited.

'Alive?'

Vanessa began to babble.

'Yes, yes. They were both alive. She tied them up so she could get away. There were some other riders who would have found them, you see. They were going up to the dam. Where...where's Ursulet? Caroline frowned. From the direction of the bathroom, there was a click. Without looking round, Caroline said,

'You managed to take his rifle from him. I'm impressed.'

'Very, very carefully... drop the gun onto the bed,' said Ursulet.

Caroline's gun remained where it was.

'Vanessa,' she said, 'Why don't you tell your... companion that you'd very much not like to have your head blown off.'

'I'm guessing you'd not be too keen on it, either,' said Ursulet.

'You'd have to be very fast, darling and an extremely good shot,' said Caroline, without taking her eyes off Vanessa. And without, Vanessa could hardly fail to notice, lowering her weapon.

'I am... Darling. And you would have to be a lot faster.'

'I like a challenge.'

Vanessa said, 'Might I suggest...?'

'Shut up!' said both women, in unison.

'All right!' snapped Vanessa, 'all right. I'm just not used to seeing women waving their dicks at each other, that's all.' There was no response from either woman. Vanessa took a chance. 'I mean,' she said, 'we've all seen "Reservoir Dogs". This sort of thing is bound to end in tears. Look, I don't know either of you very well but Caroline, Ursulet will shoot you; you can depend on it and Ursulet, I don't believe Caroline would think twice about pulling that trigger. But what both of you really want are answers. And so do I.' She turned to Ursulet.

'Remember what I was saying about trust? Lower your weapon first, Ursulet. Please.'

'She will kill you.'

'She won't.' She *fucking might, actually. What the hell am I doing?* 'Please, Ursulet.' Vanessa wasn't expecting Ursulet to respond with such finality. There was no tentative and careful movement on her part, she simply brought the rifle to a vertical position and placed it at her side, almost as though commanded by a drill sergeant. Oh, shit!

Caroline did nothing.

'You know, she said, I think I'm beginning to realise what Geoffrey saw in you.' She raised the barrel of the pistol, uncocked it, and placed it in a holster inside her jacket. Vanessa thought for a moment, frowned and said,

'You know what he did to me, don't you?'

'Oh dear. I hope you didn't let him do anything to you.'

'Caroline, stop! You know that he... messed with my head.'

'Oh, he'll do that, believe me.'

'Tell me!' Caroline appeared genuinely surprised by the vehemence with which Vanessa said the words.

'Tell you what?'

'Playing innocent doesn't suit you, Caroline. Tell me what Geoffrey Wittersham planted in my head.'

'Or what?' The click from the direction of the bathroom gave Caroline her answer. Caroline sighed, heavily.

'Oh very well,' she said. She unzipped her jacket and sat down.

'On Monday afternoon, I received a telephone call from Christopher, telling me of a young woman who had been abducted and released by Geoffrey Wittersham and that he was going to interview her at a police station.'

'*Monday?*' Vanessa had assumed that Christopher's decision to take her to Villa Sangone had been made on the spur of the moment.

'After speaking to you and learning that not only had Geoffrey let you go, he had actually given you his real name, Christopher called me again. Rightly, he realised that Geoffrey would not normally be so careless as to leave witnesses – let alone witnesses who knew who he was. I told Christopher that Geoffrey must have had a jolly good reason for doing so and I think you now understand what it was.' Caroline tapped her temple and raised her eyebrows. 'Christopher read the situation perfectly and had the good sense to get you away as soon as possible.

'Go on.'

'According to what you told me the other night, Geoffrey spent a lot of time making all kinds of small talk on your journey, is that correct? Finding out little details about you and so on?'

'I suppose. Is that when…'

'Yes. It's a well known technique but Geoffrey has a real gift.'

'So, apart from the riding stuff, what else did he do?'

'Oh he didn't do "the riding stuff", as you put it. I'm afraid that was me.'

'You?'

'Yes. He'd primed you with the Corehampton suggestion. All I had to do was give you memories of wonderful hacks and riding holidays in the Algarve and such. Add in a few procedural memories via demonstration and you became a passable (albeit somewhat temporary) rider. You see, we had to spirit you out of the country and it seemed to be the best way. It's not a route for amateurs, as I'm sure you discovered. But I'm curious. When did it dawn on you?'

'Last night… No, the night before. What is the time, anyway?'

Caroline turned her wristwatch towards the window.

'It's almost six,' she said. 'So, the night before last? Hmm. Not bad, I suppose. I'm nowhere near as expert as Geoffrey.'

'You haven't answered my question,' Vanessa said.

Caroline was no fool.

'I'm not entirely sure,' she said. 'We know that he has implanted something; we believe it to be information that must be got to the Council at all costs. The information on Geoffrey's SIM card told me that you are very valuable and that you and I have to be in London by Monday morning.'

'So why did you threaten to shoot me?'

'If people are frightened enough, they'll usually tell you something. Even if it's not true, it's a start.'

'You violated me, Caroline. He violated me. It isn't right.'

'It's true. Geoffrey was a thoughtless bastard at the best of times but we (and I'm not making excuses, mind) we were left with little option. If it means anything, Christopher was appalled. I had to speak to him quite forcefully.'

'Why didn't you just bugger with his brain?' Caroline's face took on an aspect that Vanessa hadn't seen before.

'Vanessa,' she said, 'I have been retired for a number of years but Geoffrey and I were once colleagues. You talk of trust; I'd have trusted Geoffrey with my life and did so on several occasions. I believe that he has uncovered a very serious threat to the stability of Britain. Furthermore, he knew that he was unlikely to live long enough to do anything about it. You were the only chance he had and he took it.'

'You are lying,' Ursulet said. 'Wittersham was working *against* the Crown and that is why they tried to stop him. Vanessa may be an innocent party but it's entirely possible that Wittersham is using her in some way. I intend to hand her over to *my* superiors in London.'

'You have no idea what you're doing,' Caroline said.

'But what I do have,' said Ursulet, 'is a rifle.'

Caroline made an "Ooh, I'm so scared" face.

Vanessa held up her hands.

'Look, stop it! Shut up both of you! I'm even more confused now than when I had no idea what was going on! According to you,' she pointed at Caroline, 'Wittersham was some kind of heroic secret agent who had discovered a plot and British Agents in Rome (presumably a part of the plot) have killed him. Now, because of information he gave me, they're out to kill *me* before I can get to London and M.I.6 can unpick whatever it was he did to me.' Ursulet and Caroline looked at one another. 'Well, that's just mental!' Vanessa said. 'For a start, Ursulet was sent by them and she doesn't want to kill me... *Do you*?' she added, anxiously.

Ursulet didn't answer.

'OK, then.' She went on:

'But according to Ursulet, Wittersham was part of a group of renegade agents, intent on de-stabilizing Great Britain. And because of what he did to me, I am now in possession of information, which will... do what? I don't know. But I am to be got to London to be handed over to M.I.6 so they can make sure I don't do whatever it is he wants me to do.' She paused as if in thought then said,

'And that's mental as well!' She fell back on the bed.

Caroline turned to Ursulet.

'Who are you, anyway?' she asked, 'Not M.I.6, surely?'

Still lying flat on her back, Vanessa said,

'For goodness sake tell her, Ursulet or we'll be here all day.'

Caroline smiled sweetly; Ursulet did not.

Raising herself onto her elbows, Vanessa said,

'Ursulet?'

'Something is wrong. I need to think.'

Vanessa, frustrated said,

'Well, perhaps you should have thought before you turned up at the cabin with a helicopter gunship!'

'Perhaps you should shut up!'

'Ursulet, we're all trying honesty at the moment. Please give it a go.'

'Honesty? From the Council? Huh.'

'You mentioned the Council before... and so did you, Caroline, just a moment ago. What does any "Council" have to do with anything?'

'I'm sure I didn't.'

'Oh, this is bloody ridiculous! Look, why don't you two just fight it out between you, and the winner gets me. It doesn't matter to me one way or another. As far as can see the shit's just as deep on either side of the fence.'

'I hope this "gunship" of hers didn't do any damage to my cabin.'

'No,' Vanessa said, waving her hand dismissively. 'Not really. Well, a bit.

Caroline sighed.

'All right. What happened?'

'Oh I was asleep. It was after midnight and I woke up to find Gianfranco and Christopher blazing away at something outside. Then all hell broke loose. Gianfranco must have shot the helicopter pilot or something because it crashed.' Caroline looked dangerous. Hurriedly, Vanessa continued, 'Oh it was a long way from the cabin when it went down. I think it ended up in that great gorge. Gianfranco went out and found Ursulet, dragged her in, beat her up like a bastard and that was it.

'In the morning, we set off and somewhere along the way – up by a big dam, as I said, Ursulet managed to tip Gianfranco off his horse and get his rifle. She tied him and Christopher up and she and I came down the mountain. Spent the night in the woods near Alberges and then over the mountain again to end up here. Ursulet was certain at first, that I was with this "Council" but then she realised I'd been... "*Geoffreyed*". Frankly, I'm not sure what she thinks now. She's just determined to get me to London.' Caroline looked at Ursulet.

'They lied to you, didn't they? You know that now. They told you that Vanessa was in league with Geoffrey and now you know that she was nothing of the kind, you're wondering if they lied about other things: correct? You are a gifted operative. It would have taken nothing less to have bested Gianfranco, I can assure you, but you have been despatched on a fool's errand.'

'And whose word do *you* have, Mrs Gagliardo-Patricelli? The word of a... Council Worker.'

'I should trust the word of a Council Worker over an M.I.6 functionary any day of the week.'

'And I would not. So we still have a problem, don't we?'

'Look, what is all this "Council" business anyway?' asked Vanessa.

'You've heard the phrase: "*I could tell you but then I'd have to kill you*?" Well, guess what?'

'They are renegades,' Ursulet interjected. 'For fifty years or more they have infiltrated all sectors of the British Establishment and recently, they have made a bid for power. Fortunately, we now have them on the run. Your friend here used to work with them and so did Geoffrey Wittersham. Whatever he put in your head, I can assure you it will be of the greatest value to either side. That is why she wants you. There is no threat to your life. Do not forget how your "friends" lied to you when they forced you to ride over the mountain.'

Vanessa tried to digest this. She said,

'So Ursulet, can I at least take it you no longer believe I was working with Wittersham?'

'You may still not realise that you were.'

'What does she mean?' asked Caroline.

'Oh, she thinks I might be in cahoots with Geoffrey without realising it. She thinks I might have been made to believe I'm Vanessa Aldridge, whereas in reality I'm an International Super-Spy who's allowed herself to be brainwashed in order to make sure she can't betray anyone.' She laughed but stopped when she saw the expression on Caroline's face. 'I mean,' she said, 'that's ridiculous, right? I'd know, wouldn't I?'

Caroline didn't say anything.

'Caroline! I'd know, wouldn't I?'

'Not necessarily,' Caroline said. 'It would not be impossible for him to have managed to do that. It has a name: Confabulatory Inspired Delusion. May I?' she asked Ursulet, raising a hand to her jacket pocket. Instantly, Ursulet brought the rifle to bear.

'Slowly,' she said. Caroline removed a newspaper. She unfolded it and tossed it onto the bed. Vanessa switched on the small bedside lamp so that she could see it. It was Italian and so Vanessa was able to read:

**HOTELIER TELLS OF SHOCK OVER LINGERIE GIRL!**

Andrew Mosley, owner of the "Mosel" chain of luxury hotels has expressed his concern over the disappearance of his former secretary, Miss Vanesa Alrich. Said Mr Mosley, "Miss Alrich worked for me for a year and a half. I am very concerned for her safety." The police say there are no suspicious circumstances surrounding Miss Alrich, who is believed to have returned to her native England, having been cleared by police of any wrongdoing.' Asked about rumours that he had fired the young woman, who was forced at gunpoint to walk through the streets of Rome wearing only her underwear, Mr Mosley said that there was no truth whatsoever in the rumours.

'Not much of a story. It's just an excuse print another one of those (I must say rather fetching) photographs of you.'

'Oh God,' Vanessa said, her head in her hands.

'The good news is that in the last couple of days, along with the pictures, there have been one or two quotes from people who worked with you and who knew you. Unless Geoffrey was playing the longest of long games, I think you're you.'

'God, you're right! Caroline, you're right! Ursulet, look!' She held out the paper. 'I'm *me*! I'm really me!' If Ursulet was satisfied, she didn't show it. However, after reading the article and checking the date, she said,

'It still doesn't mean I would let you be taken by the Council.'

'Forgive me,' Caroline said suddenly. 'I think it's time we were going.' She stood up. 'Put some clothes on, there's a good girl.' Ursulet stiffened and re-steadied the rifle. 'Oh, do stop pointing that thing at me.' She stopped and put a hand to her ear. 'No, no. I'm fine,' she said. 'No, she's no idiot. I don't think she'll shoot. Particularly if you show yourselves.' Caroline stepped to one side and pointed at Ursulet. The girl looked down and saw the small red dot hovering over her left breast. Caroline gazed through the window, pointing with a casual gesture.

About twenty-five metres away in a scrubby vacant lot, Gianfranco stood up. He was peering intently through the sight of a large hunting rifle. By his side, stood Christopher Maytham, who took one hand out of his pocket and gave a cheery wave. Caroline held out her arm. Without a word, Ursulet handed her the rifle.

'Hang on,' said Vanessa, 'so you must have known what happened all along. This whole conversation has been a waste of time!'

'Not at all. I now know that you are telling the truth about what happened. And what's more, I know that Gianfranco and Christopher are, too. And I now know far more than either of them about young Ursulet. What I don't know is who attacked me in my own home, but we simply don't have any more time to waste.'

'We're not leaving,' said Ursulet.

'Oh? Well, what are you going to do, then?' Caroline retorted. Vanessa looked from Caroline to Ursulet and back again. Eventually, Ursulet said,

'We are going north.'

'Are you? And just how are you going to do that?'

'We have horses.'

'*My* horses. And if I'm not mistaken, very little in the way of provisions.'

'We have money.'

'Christopher and Gianfranco's money. Which incidentally, they are eager to have returned to them.' Caroline paused and her face, to Vanessa's astonishment, appeared to soften. She said, 'Look, *you* want to get Vanessa to London; *I* want to get Vanessa to London. *You* want answers; *I* want answers. *You* have two tired horses; *I* have an eight-seater Mercedes Benz Viana, a Platinum Amex Card and a private plane waiting on an airstrip near Lyon. How would you like to have lunch in London?'

Ursulet's face was impossible to read. After several seconds, Vanessa said to her,

'Erm... are you still thinking? Only, it sort of sounds like a plan to me.' Finally, Ursulet said,

'If I do not agree, you will go with them anyway, even though you don't trust them.'

'Yes I will,' Vanessa agreed. 'Ursulet, I just want to get this over with and if I can get to London today, I'll be one step nearer to doing that.' Before either of them had noticed, Caroline had removed her gun. She pointed it at Ursulet, who stood defiantly in front of her.

'I'm beginning to believe,' Caroline said, 'we're on the same side. I hope that by the time we get to Lyon, you will too. If you don't, you have my word that I shall let you go but I am taking Vanessa to London. No matter what you do.'

'Caroline, no!' Vanessa shouted. Trying to avoid the window and clutching the duvet to herself, she clambered awkwardly off the bed and placed herself between Caroline and Ursulet. Caroline smiled and flipped the gun around so that she was holding the barrel. She said,

'Give this to her. A sign of good faith.'

Vanessa took the weapon, turned around slowly and gave it to Ursulet. 'For God's sake don't do anything stupid,' she whispered to her.

'I am about to get into a car with her and those two. Does that count?' Vanessa smiled and squeezed Ursulet's arm. Ursulet thrust the gun into her waistband and said,

'I paid for it to be ironed. The laundry.' Vanessa almost cried out. She leapt on the bag and began to rummage through it. Then a thought struck her.

'Caroline, you'll have noticed Ursulet's face?'

'You're joking, of course?'

'Gianfranco did that. I know she got something of her own back but…'

'Let me worry about Gianfranco.' She looked at Vanessa and gestured towards Ursulet. 'You just keep your own dog muzzled.'

Ursulet stiffened and Vanessa jumped in.

'Caroline?'

'Yes?'

'She is no-one's "dog".'

To Vanessa's relief, Caroline smiled. 'Do you know Alexander Pope?' she asked her.

'Should I?'

'He's a poet, Vanessa,' Ursulet said, 'or at least he was.' She looked at Caroline and said,

'I am his Highness' dog at Kew

Pray tell me, sir, whose dog are you?'

'Eh?' said Vanessa.

Caroline looked approvingly at Ursulet.

'Everyone is someone's dog, Vanessa,' she said.

## Change of Plan

Ten minutes later, the three women were striding across the car-park towards the biggest car that Vanessa had ever seen.

'Vanessa! Are you all right?'

'I'm fine, Christopher. Oh by the way, Caroline has told me all about your little charade on Monday evening. Allowing the possibility that you've been telling *her* the truth, is there anything else I should know about?'

'Vanessa, I'm sorry. Wittersham is a dangerous man. I knew he'd worked with Linny and when I knew I was going to interview you, I thought it politic to find out as much as I could about him and your relationship with him.'

'We didn't have a relationship.'

'I know that now. But Vanessa, I couldn't possibly have known that at the time. Either you were a confederate of Wittersham's or a victim; as it turns out, you are both. I regret that I had to mislead you.'

Vanessa's expression remained one of lofty disdain as she said,

'Mmm. So, anyway; how are you?'

'Better now, thanks.' He looked at Ursulet. 'Now that I've dried out, thawed out and eaten.' Ursulet returned his gaze without showing the faintest glimmer of concern or remorse.

'Her name is Ursulet and she's coming with us,' Caroline said. Gianfranco, his head swathed in bandages, muttered something that Vanessa failed to catch. In Italian, Caroline said to him, 'She is my guest, Gianfranco, and you will treat her with respect or you will remain here. If I have cause to speak to you of this again, I shall dismiss you.'

Vanessa looked at the ground, unwilling to catch Gianfranco's eye. She heard his mumbled response, though.

'Si, Signora.'

'Good,' Caroline said, brightly. 'Now, let's be on our way, shall we? Gianfranco will drive.' Everyone stared at the Italian servant, as he miserably surveyed his left hand, three fingers of which were splinted and taped together. He looked almost plaintively at Caroline, who said,

'Don't be such a baby.' She tossed him the keys, which he dropped. He winced as he stooped to retrieve them. As Caroline walked around the car, she passed Vanessa and said, quietly,

'That takes care of Gianfranco, I think.'

Vanessa had softened a little towards Caroline during the conversation in the hotel room but the calculating coldness of the humiliation of Gianfranco who, for all his faults had displayed remarkable loyalty and courage on Caroline's behalf, made her feel distinctly uneasy once more.

The interior of the Mercedes seemed to Vanessa to be more like a small sitting room than a car. Maytham sat immediately behind Gianfranco in one of the rear-facing seats and Ursulet sat next to him. In the seat facing her, sat Caroline herself. She placed Vanessa to her left. Separating the two sets of seats was a small table. Maytham spread out his hands on the table and with a smile asked,

'Anyone care for a rubber of Bridge?'

No-one said anything until Caroline, ever the gracious hostess, said,

'That's a jolly good idea, Christopher but first I think we might discuss one or two small matters, if that's all right.'

'Of course, Linny. It was… only a little… joke, by the way.'

'Was it? Well thank you, Christopher, for attempting to lighten the mood.' Vanessa and Maytham exchanged glances. Each found it difficult not to smile. Ursulet looked bemused. 'However,' Caroline went on, 'I believe we're all a little (how shall I put it) less uncomfortable with one another than we were: do you agree?' Maytham was the only one who answered.

'I should like to know a little more about Ursulet,' he said.

'I daresay,' Caroline answered. 'I think we all would; but I don't think she's quite ready to enlighten us at the moment.'

'She's been through a lot,' Vanessa said. 'And frankly I don't blame her for not trusting any of you. I sure as bloody hell don't.'

'Now, she's wondering if you said that purely for her benefit,' Caroline said. Vanessa looked at Ursulet. Her expression told her nothing. 'Besides,' Caroline continued, 'I suspect she trusts us rather more than you might imagine. She wouldn't be here at all if she didn't. I'm guessing that my version of events holds rather more water than the version she was given by her own superiors. The people who sent her here are the same people Geoffrey was trying to avoid in Rome, not because he was part of a renegade cadre of agents, but because he knew that security had been compromised.'

Ursulet looked steadily at Caroline, who held her gaze. Without looking away, Caroline called out,

'Gianfranco? How long until we get to the airstrip?'

'About two hours, Signora.'

'Excellent. All being well, I estimate our arrival in London will be around nine-thirty, English time.

'Then what?' Vanessa asked.

'Then we go and meet with another old friend of mine and find out what Geoffrey wanted us to know.'

Vanessa heard this with a modicum of concern. From what she could make out, being an old friend of Caroline's was a commendation only if you were prepared to be lied to and treated like an idiot or worse. She glanced across at Ursulet, who was looking out of the window. Christopher appeared be nodding off already and Caroline had picked up a magazine. Vanessa settled back and looked out of the window.

Gazing out at the French countryside as the journey unfolded, it occurred to Vanessa that it would be nice to be in England again. Autumn was not really a season in these latitudes. It could remain hot until late October in the low-lying areas after which time, the leaves seemed to turn brown overnight and drop off within minutes of being hit by the Tramontaine, an event that was followed rapidly, depending on altitude, by heavy rain or snow. There seemed to be none of the fecundity associated with autumn in England. She began to think about what her life might be like once all this was over. That she hadn't really worried about work since Christopher had whisked her away from Rome was hardly surprising but as the prospect of an end to this madness drew closer, so the anxieties associated with the demands of earning a living began to make themselves felt once more. If there was a square, a strange proto-square out of which square one would eventually evolve, that was the square she was on.

But of course, things remained even worse than that. She was still it appeared, harbouring in her mind, a little package of thoughts and ideas that didn't belong to her; that was hibernating in the folds of her brain like a big old toad waiting for something to wake it up. What that might be, she could only guess but she remembered the feeling when Ursulet had released the last one and she felt a rush of panic. She shook herself and looked round for a magazine to read.

'Signora.'

'Gianfranco?'

'Polizia.'

Caroline turned in her seat and looked behind.

'How long have they been there?'

'Twenty-five, thirty kilometres.'

'Leave the autoroute at the next exit. Take any road you wish after that.'

The silence that followed was broken some four minutes later by the click of the right-hand indicator. At the T-junction, Gianfranco turned right and Vanessa glanced behind. The police van was still there. Around two roundabouts and then Gianfranco turned left. Sure enough, the van did the same.

'Pull into that filling station,' Caroline said. A few hundred yards later, Gianfranco did as he was bidden. As they pulled up at the pump, they noticed the police van drive past. The driver paid them no attention. Everyone in the Mercedes relaxed a little.

'There's no need to fill up, Gianfranco. If anyone needs the loo, now's the time.' Caroline was first out of the car.

Christopher awoke.

'Where are we?' he said.

'Hour or so from Lyon, I think,' said Vanessa. 'There was a police car behind us for a while.' Maytham looked concerned. 'It's OK,' Vanessa said, 'they've gone.'

'Where's Caroline?'

'Gone to the loo.'

'Ooh, if you don't mind, I think I'll avail myself of the facilities, too.' He opened the door and climbed out, taking a moment to stretch, then headed for the shop. Vanessa spoke to Ursulet.

'Oh what the hell, I might as well go. Will you be all right with... you know?' She raised her eyebrows and tipped her head in the direction of the driver's seat. Ursulet smiled, mirthlessly.

'Go,' she said. Vanessa returned the smile.

'Well, if you're sure,' Vanessa clambered out of the car and Ursulet sat back and closed her eyes.

In the filling station, Vanessa found the toilet engaged and so waited outside.

The toilet door opened.

'Oh,' said Caroline on seeing Vanessa, 'don't be too long, there's a dear.'

'I'll do my very best,' she said.

When she came out, Vanessa wondered if she might have time for a coffee but decided that she didn't want to give Caroline any need to complain. As she made for the door, she glanced over at the machine to see Christopher and Caroline feeding it with coins. She stepped out onto the forecourt and walked back to the car.

She opened the door.

Although in a French policeman's uniform, the stranger, when he spoke, appeared to be English.

'Come in quietly and sit down,' he said. A slight flick of the gun he was holding served to reinforce the order. Vanessa thought back to the moment she might have escaped from Geoffrey Wittersham; however, the gunman must have noticed her stiffen because he said, as though speaking to a child who was about to do something naughty.

'Ah Ah!'

'Do as he says, Vanessa.' Ursulet said. Her left arm was resting on the back of the driver's seat and her gun – Caroline's gun - was pressed hard against the back of Gianfranco's head. Slowly, Vanessa sat down.

'You!' Ursulet said to Gianfranco, 'get out!'

'No!' the stranger snapped. 'Wait for the others to return and we'll kill them all.'

'There's no need for that,' said Ursulet. 'We have the woman. All we need is to get rid of *him* and drive north. We'll call for an aircraft to meet us en route.'

'I don't think so.'

'But...'

'We kill them all. Including this one.' He jerked the gun in Vanessa's direction and his smile told her that he was looking forward to it.

'That's not the plan,' Ursulet said.

'The plan has changed.'

'Since when?'

'Since you allowed yourself to be captured.'

'I've told them nothing.'

'We can't be certain of that, can we?'

'I'm telling you…'

And I'm telling *you*! And *you* do as you are told!'

Vanessa heard Gianfranco say something but she couldn't catch it.

'*Chiuda in su!*' Ursulet said to him.

'English…! If you please,' the stranger said. Gianfranco spoke, once more.

'If he speaks again, shoot him,' the stranger ordered. Again, Gianfranco spoke, louder this time, yet Vanessa still could not make out the words.

'Shoot him!' the man yelled.

'Don't be a fool!' Ursulet yelled back. All three of them began shouting and cursing at one another until suddenly, the stranger pulled his gun away from Vanessa and aimed it at Gianfranco. Vanessa saw that this was her chance. She leapt at the stranger. In the same instant that Ursulet's right arm arced upwards and swung past the gunman's hand. There was a flash of steel, a startled scream and two fingertips spun through the air, their paths traced by two bright fountains of blood. Ursulet's arm swung down. Another scream, more blood, then her left hand appeared over the driver's head-rest and the barrel of the gun it held, came to rest between the eyes of the gunman, who was now pinned to the floor by Vanessa.

The car door opened.

'Right, coffee for everyone,' said Caroline, 'but we'll have to…' She took in the tableau. Gianfranco, kneeling on the driver's seat; Ursulet, on the floor; both with weapons trained on a whimpering stranger, and Vanessa, sitting astride him whilst he leaked crimson all over the cream-coloured interior.

'Oh, abso-*fucking*-lutely marvellous,' Caroline said. Have you any idea how much this will cost to have cleaned? Get him out of there! No, wait; search him first.'

Between them, they tumbled the man out onto the forecourt, the huge Mercedes ensuring that he would not be seen until they had driven away. Maytham tied a belt tightly around the man's ravaged limb, noting the extraordinary power and effectiveness of a crouchet in the hands of an expert. Vanessa was busy tipping the man's belongings into a carrier bag.

'You can't leave me here!' he called out. He was looking directly at Vanessa. 'You can't just let me bleed to death!' She stared at him and appalled at herself, said,

'There's a phone in the shop.'

## To London

'He will be OK, won't he?' Vanessa asked, as Gianfranco headed towards the autoroute.

'Oh, he'll be fine,' Caroline replied. 'His chums won't be too far away. In spite of his protestations, Ursulet is very skilled in the use of that nasty little toy of hers. She managed to steer clear of major arteries - just severed the tendons by the look of it. In fact, if he's quick, they'll probably even be able to stick those finger ends back on at the hospital. You did give them back, didn't you?' Vanessa's eyes widened.

'No! I didn't!' She began a frantic search of the blood-spattered car.

'It's all right. I erm... slipped them into his shirt pocket,' said Maytham.

'There you are, see?' Caroline said, reassuringly. 'Fit as a flea in a couple of months. Now, we weren't sure what everyone would like and so we got a variety. Let's see: "Skinny Latte", I believe this one is called. Espresso – that's for me, I'm afraid. There's a Cappucino, another espresso for the driver (there you are, darling) and I believe the Americano is Christopher's. I'm sure it will be perfectly ghastly but needs must, one supposes. There, is everyone catered for? Good. Now will someone please tell me who the gentleman was and what it was he wanted?'

'Ron,' said Maytham. 'He was the chap I knew as Ron.'

'His name was Somerset,' Ursulet said. 'It was he who despatched us to intercept your party on the mountain and to capture Vanessa.' This was the first piece of information that Ursulet had offered Caroline. Vanessa watched the older woman's face. That surely couldn't be genuine concern, could it?

'Go on, please,' Caroline said. Ursulet put down her coffee and began,

'We followed your trail to the cabin. We were on motorcycles.'

'We?'

'Just two of us. Our orders were to gauge numbers, ensure Vanessa's whereabouts and when we'd done so, send for a helicopter to lift her off the mountain. From our vantage point, we could see that there were just three people there. I radioed in and we were told to lie low. Unfortunately, my partner had other ideas.' She turned to Caroline. 'He decided to draw your men out of the cabin, dispose of them and capture Vanessa himself.

'Young chap, was he?' Caroline said.

'He was brave but foolish.'

'They so often are.'

'But before he could get close enough, they spotted him and opened fire. We merely retaliated.'

'What happened to him?' Vanessa asked.

'He... he ran out on me. The headlight of his motorcycle was shot out. He probably rode off the mountain in the dark.'

'I don't think he did,' said Caroline. 'Sometime in the night, I was awoken by the sound of a motorcycle. I went down to see and whoever it was, they were lying in wait. I was bashed over the head.'

'You are fortunate that he didn't kill you.'

'He didn't get the chance. While he was rummaging around, Signora Anna came in and shot him.'

'Your cook?' exclaimed Vanessa.

'Yes, she often stays the night if I'm out late in the evening.'

'But I mean to say... your... *cook?*'

'Well, she does other things, of course. She's very versatile. So this "Somerset"; M.I.6, I presume?' Ursulet gave a bitter little laugh.

'What else?' she said. 'You know, when D.P.S.D. in Paris told me I'd been seconded to M.I.6, I was delighted. I always thought they were amongst the best in the world. But six months on and I was beginning to wonder why it was that the British were not all speaking Russian. Even before I was sent to Rome, I'd decided that this was to be my final job for them.'

'And yet you called them from Malons?'

'What?' said Vanessa.

'Oh, didn't you know? Don't tell me she's been less than honest with you,' Caroline said. 'Ah well, we all make mistakes. I take it you told them where you were before we had our little conversation at the hotel?' Ursulet said only,

'I'm amazed they managed to find us on the road, frankly. They are idiots.'

'Oh, you mustn't be too hard on them,' Caroline said. 'They do the best they can in the circumstances. And we've always found them rather useful.'

'We?' asked Ursulet. 'You are talking about this Council of yours. Tell me about it. Tell me the truth.' Caroline only smiled. Ursulet's face appeared to soften and she said, 'No, of course you won't; because you are a professional.'

'True, however, it is in the nature of the Council that most people who work for it, know very little other than what goes on in their own area of expertise. And those of us who no longer work for it, know absolutely nothing. It is what they used to call a "Secret Service": unlike M.I.6, which appears nowadays to have the profile of a supermarket chain.'

'I was singularly unimpressed by the agents at the Embassy,' Maytham said. Could it be, do you think, that Ursulet was not actually lied to but simply misinformed through incompetence?'

'Anything is possible,' Caroline said. 'Now I wonder if Ursulet feels able to tell us who her contacts are in London. I shouldn't imagine they'll be best pleased with her at the moment, is that fair to say?' She smiled at Ursulet.

'I have no name, of course, merely an address.'

'Which is?'

'You first.'

Caroline smiled broadly and picking up her magazine, began reading again.

Vanessa sat back in her seat. She was still upset with herself regarding her attitude towards Somerset's injuries. The thought occurred that it might be a little bit of her "real self" leaking out and wondered again if she might not be who she thought she was. She picked up her own magazine and forced herself to read.

The airfield was smaller than Vanessa had been expecting and so, frankly, was the aeroplane. It had propellers. Andrew Moseley had a jet.

'As soon as we pull up, everyone onto the plane,' said Caroline. 'Gianfranco, you'll need to get the car valeted of course.' She wrote something on a slip of paper. 'They'll be expecting you,' she said. She handed the paper to Ursulet, who was still sitting behind the driver's seat. Pass this to him, would you?' Caroline asked.

Ursulet swivelled the chair around and held the paper over Gianfranco's shoulder. Instead of taking it, he took Ursulet's hand. She made to pull away but stopped. Vanessa heard the Italian say,

'You saved my life. Thank you.' He let her go and Ursulet slowly withdrew her hand. Vanessa wondered if the world would ever make any sense to her again. Gianfranco brought the car to the very foot of the boarding steps and Caroline opened the door.

'Wait,' said Ursulet.

'Yes?' said Caroline, resuming her seat.

'Have you forgotten our agreement?' said Ursulet.

'I have not. I gave you my word. You may leave us here and go about your business in peace,' Caroline said. Ursulet looked at Caroline, then at Vanessa and Maytham.

'I still need answers,' she said at last. Vanessa thought she actually saw Caroline's lips form a smile, as she said,

'Very well. Let us go to London.'

The pilot greeted the party and followed them up the steps. Inside the aircraft, in a small galley, a second man in a pilot's; uniform had clearly just finished preparing food. He was stowing the contents of the galley into a large trolley. In under half an hour, the aircraft was aloft, food had been eaten and Caroline was speaking.

'We land at Biggin Hill Airfield at a little after 9:30. There will be a car waiting and you two will be needing these.' She handed over passports. 'Just check the names and details in case anyone starts asking questions and Vanessa; don't forget to sign it in *that* name – rather than your own! In the wardrobe behind you, you will find two reasonably smart business suits in what I believe are your sizes. Please put them on after we've taken your photographs.' She handed passports to Vanessa and Ursulet. Vanessa appeared to be Paula Dean and Ursulet, Sandrine Ravel. Then, she passed Christopher a laptop and said, 'Be a dear and set this up for British and French photo requirements. Ursulet, it may help to apply a little make-up before we take your photo.' Within a few minutes, both women were dressing and smartening themselves up, whilst Christopher and Caroline busied themselves attaching the photos to the passports.

Eventually, all was in readiness.

'I'm off for a word with the pilot,' Caroline announced. I want to make sure everything goes as smoothly as possible once we're on the ground.

'So,' Christopher said to Vanessa, 'with a bit of luck, we're on the home straight.'

'Do you know what will happen when we get there?' Vanessa asked, tentatively.

'Linny's playing it a bit close to her chest but from what I understand, she's planning to take us to see someone who can help you out.'

'Are they to do with this Council, do you know?'

'I don't know, Vanessa. I'm not even sure what the Council is. frankly. I always thought it was... sort of... an even more secret arm of M.I.6. I overheard Linny mention it to my mother on a couple of occasions, although I'm certain I wasn't meant to. That's how I knew that she and Wittersham had worked together. Stroke of luck, really.'

'Yes, I suppose it was. I have a lot to be grateful for in you and Caroline, don't I?'

'Well, it *is* my job, you know and I think, between you and me, that Linny has sort of enjoyed it, actually. I don't think she found it easy to adjust in the first place – leaving... "the industry"... as it were and then once Luca – her husband – died, it must have been doubly difficult.

'Do you think it will still be your job when this is over?' Vanessa asked with a smile. 'Or will you be joining me on the dole queue?'

'There are certainly going to be a few questions to answer,' said Maytham, 'but I trust Linny and if she says I did the right thing, then I'm sure that I did. In any case, I wouldn't have done it differently so the point is moot. Perhaps it is time for a change: who knows? Anyway, you try to relax. I'm sure everything will be fine.'

## Luscinia

Just as the first forkful of Arthur's full English was about to touch his lips, the phone rang.

'Shepherd? Good morning. I hope I'm not interrupting anything important?'

'Not at all, Sir Auberon: how lovely to hear from you.'

'I was wondering how you got on with Ashley Sullivan.' Arthur laid his fork down. 'Only you weren't in yesterday. Is anything wrong?'

Arthur had absolutely no idea what to make of this. Since when had Nightingale cared whether he saw Arthur from one month to the next? Wary, he replied,

'Such as?'

'Oh, I wondered if you might have been lured into another trap, that's all. I know how careless you can be in that area of things. Still, so long as you're all right. So tell me: your conversation with Mr. Sullivan: enlightening at all?' Arthur didn't like this one little bit.

'Not really,' he answered.

'Oh, that *is* a shame.'

'Yes. Yes it is.'

'Well, if it's not too much trouble, I'd like to have a debrief with you at some juncture.' What a huge pity, Arthur thought, that the mood didn't suit a bawdy quip of some kind.

'I shall be in on Monday morning,' he said.

'I do so look forward to it. Enjoy your weekend.' Arthur listened to the dial-tone for a second or two then replaced the receiver. He gave a start as the thing rang again. He picked it up.

'What?' he said to it.

'Oh charming, I'm sure,' said Jennifer.

'Sorry. What's up?'

'Jacqueline rang. She's being trying you on your mobile but I told her it's probably switched off.'

'No it isn't.'

'Oh?'

'No. It's just run out of battery, that's all.' There was a silence. Eventually, Jennifer said,

'She said to tell you that Caroline's plane is due to land in half an hour and would you like her and Mr. Bracewell to track her when she lands?'

'Is she working on this already? I've not even had breakfast.'

'She's keen.'

'I'll call her. Thanks, Jennifer.' He pressed down on the disconnect and dialled.

'Morning, Mr. Shepherd... sorry, I mean Arthur,' she responded. 'Thanks for calling. Couple of things: first do you want Mr. Bracewell and me to follow Mrs. Gagliardo-Patricelli when she lands?'

'I think that would be most helpful. But don't get too close unless you really have to. She's not to be trifled with, by all accounts.

'Very well.'

'And what was the second thing?'

'I've run some searches on the two names in the message: Vanessa Aldridge and Crawthorne Beasley.

'Oh yes?'

'On Beasley, very little, I'm afraid. You'd think with a name like that, he'd be easy to find but not a bit of it. There are lots of references but they all pertain to one thing.

'And what's that?'

'He won the Victoria Cross in Malaysia in 1965.'

'Blimey.'

'I know he went to Harrow and then to Cambridge but that's about it for a first trawl. The other one - Vanessa Aldridge - returned about 5,000 hits. At first, my money was on a senior diplomat based in Bahrain but then I came across a story about a young Englishwoman who was abducted in Rome earlier in the week. By all accounts, she was abandoned in the centre of the city, dressed only in her underwear and carrying a gun. She was arrested but released into the custody of the British Consulate but she has since disappeared, along with the consular official who was in charge of her case.'

Arthur remembered Stainforth drooling over the picture in Tuesday's Telegraph.

'Can you check it out?'

'Yes, of course.'

'And cross reference with Geoffrey Wittersham and Caroline Gagliardo-Patricelli.

'Mr. Bracewell's spiders are already on it.'

'Jolly good.'

'Oh, and there's just one more thing,' Jacqueline said.

'And that is?'

'Luscinia,'

'Beg your pardon?'

'The name of the compiler of your crossword. Mr. Bracewell thought you might like to know…'

'Yes, yes. "Luscinia" I remember. Bracewell said that the compilers just choose some random name to…'

'No no, you see: It's a little hobby of mine, ornithology and I spotted it right away.'

'Jacqueline, you're not making sense.'

'I'm sorry, only I thought you knew…'

'Knew what?'

'Luscinia is the genus name of the nightingale. Mr. Bracewell seemed to think it was important so he said I should call you… Are you still there?'

'Yes, Jacqueline. Thank you.'

'Oh, Mr. Bracewell's just arrived. He seems a little agitated. He says he'd like a word with you.'

'What, he's there as well?' Arthur asked, feeling slightly guilty.

'Yes. Erm… Mr Bracewell would really like to speak to you.'

'Very well. Put him on.'

'Shepherd, listen. Nightingale was here.'

'Where?'

'At Century House.'

'You mean… in the Council Offices?' he asked.

'Yes. I spotted him coming out of a lift on the ground floor about ten minutes ago. What the bloody hell's going on?'

## A Nightingale Sang in Westminster Bridge Rd.

Arthur had thrust his plate into the microwave and had entered "two minutes". He'd leaned against his Welsh dresser and before the microwave had pinged his breakfast back to life, he had made up his mind to come and see Sir Auberon. But even though the fucker had wanted to see him so badly that he'd phoned him up before nine on a Saturday morning, he'd still had him waiting there for nigh on twenty-five minutes.

If you are a professional killer, it pretty much goes without saying that you don't let very much bother you, on the whole. Arthur wasn't exactly a stranger to unease but over the years he'd kind of forgotten what it was like. But he'd been reintroduced to it in the last forty-eight hours and now, as he waited for Sir Auberon, he began to recall why he hadn't bothered to stay in touch. Finally, the door opened and a bright young woman said,

'Sir Auberon will see you now, sir.'

'Shepherd, my dear fellow! How good of you to accommodate me. Do sit down, won't you? Tea? Coffee?'

'What's going on, Nightingale?'

'The kettle, I hope.'

'Pack it in and tell me what that crossword is all about.' Arthur never shouted; he never had to. Nightingale turned to his receptionist, who was waiting by the door for orders,

'Thank you Miss Petersen, I think that will be all,' he said. She closed the door more quietly than Arthur thought possible.

'I take it you've solved it, then?' Nightingale said. Arthur appeared not to have heard.

'I'll ask you once more: *what's going on?*' he said. 'Oh, and Nightingale…?'

'What?' Sir Auberon asked, with a heavy sigh.

'I never ask the same question three times.'

Arthur removed a gun from his pocket.

Nightingale was smiling and Arthur really wanted to kill him. Fortunately, he possessed a great deal of pride and seldom killed because he wanted to. That and curiosity held him back.

'We knew you'd gone to see Mulberry about the Beasley despatch,' Nightingale said, suddenly. 'That was when I first suspected you might really not be involved, after all.'

'Involved? I presume you're talking about the Templeton business?' Nightingale cocked an eyebrow and Arthur knew he'd fallen for one of Nightingale's favourite stratagems; begin an explanation by pretending to assume the other person knows what you're talking about. Wrong-foots them every time. Too late, Arthur realised he'd taken the bait.

'Templeton business?' he said.

'You are really beginning to annoy me… I mean, more than usual,' Arthur said.

'Perhaps you might let me continue?' A movement of Arthur's head was all the response he received. 'We still couldn't approach you of course, not until we were certain. The fact that you'd originally gone round to Clerical asking for Ricketts was enough to concern me. However, the next evening, someone tried to blow you up. Dreadful overkill: threw us off for a while, I can tell you.

'Then of course there was the episode at Tate Modern: that helped…'

'Do you want me to shoot you?' Arthur asked. He wondered why Nightingale still appeared to have the confidence to ride him.

'…and then Ricketts killed Mulberry.'

'Are you certain of that?'

'Oh yes,' said Nightingale, with a dismissive wave of his hand. 'The Constables were all for bringing *you* in until we put a bit of evidence in their way. Ricketts panicked and has gone to ground but it's only a matter of time. We believe he took that second despatch you'd left with Mulberry – much good may it do him.'

Nightingale, clever sod, was telling Arthur just enough to pique his curiosity. The aplomb with which he was doing it, confirmed to Arthur that that he had probably been held at gunpoint a number of times before. There would come a point in the interrogation where Nightingale would say something along the lines of… *"I won't tell you that; you're going to have to shoot me"*… but by that time, he would have woven more loose ends than a Gabbeh carpet-maker and if Arthur wanted answers he'd have to begin compromising. One thing was for certain: the cold-hearted killer routine wasn't going to work, this time.

Arthur put his gun away.

'Oh,' said Nightingale, laying the surprise on with a trowel, 'I haven't finished yet.'

'You win, you arrogant bastard,' said Arthur, with a sigh. 'I think I'd like that cup of tea now. And some biscuits.' Nightingale leaned over his desk and pressed a button on the ancient intercom.

'Miss Petersen?' he said. 'Pot of Earl Grey for two and some…' He looked at Arthur, raised an eyebrow and said, 'chocolate digestives?' Arthur was staring at the carpet. He nodded, absently and without looking up, said,

'I'm guessing that you don't work for M.I.6.'

'You noticed that? I am gratified. You're right, of course: I've been a Council Worker almost as long as you have. Came in on a different floor, naturally.'

'Naturally.'

'Yes, I'm sorry about the charade and subterfuge and what have you but you must admit; we pulled it off pretty well.'

'You keep saying "we".'

'Do I? Can't imagine why.' Nightingale then said, carefully, 'I wonder if it might be my turn to ask some questions?'

'You can ask; but it seems as though you know more than I do.'

'It's all part of the job.'

'What, knowing; or seeming to?'

'Both. Why didn't you kill Beasley?'

'It didn't seem right.'

'Good enough.'

'What did Mulberry do to cause you to put your trust in him?' Arthur had been wondering about that himself.

'He seemed a decent sort,' he said. He had no "agenda" - simply the desire to do some good for a fellow. And of course, he was sharp as a tack.'

'Why did you hang on to the Muffarim despatch?

'It was the first two-page despatch I'd seen in years and it had some code at the bottom of the first and the top of the second page. I thought it might be of use to Mulberry.'

'And was it, do you think?'

'I really don't know. I was trying to find out who was sending me on dodgy jobs; Mulberry seemed to think the teleprinter codes might help. When he sent me that text, I thought at first it was something to do with the despatches. I'm pretty sure it wasn't, though.'

Arthur had been toying with the idea that Mulberry's killer might have sent the text in order to throw him off the scent. But the information was clearly pertinent. Had it not, after all, led (however indirectly) to Nightingale? Ricketts, (if that's who it had been) could have distracted Arthur with any bit of old rubbish.

'You're correct. Jacobean ciphers are not new. They were devised many years ago by Sir James Carlisle. Decryption keys vary of course (both in nature and content) but use of a Jacobean cipher is a signal that something of great import is transpiring.'

'But unless you have the unlock key, it's of no use at all.'

'No indeed. Just frightens people.'

Arthur eyed Nightingale as though sighting along a rifle.

'You don't have the unlock key, do you?' he said.

'Yes we do,' said Nightingale, tearing apart a couple of the loose ends Arthur believed he had managed to hitch together. 'And I know that you have it, too. You bought it the other day at Oxfam in Gloucester Rd. I'll hazard a guess that Bracewell is working on it as we speak.'

Arthur was in danger of becoming awe-struck. He could not show it.

'But hang on: If you know the nature and content of the cipher,' he said, 'and where to find the unlock key, why did you need the crossword at all? And much more to the point; why did you need me?'

'I was rather hoping you wouldn't ask that. Ah, here's our tea.' Miss Petersen put down the tray and left. 'You don't take milk, do you?' Nightingale asked, lifting the pot.

'No. Thank you.' Nightingale poured and Arthur took the proffered cup.

'What lovely China,' he said.

'Do you like it? It was a gift from Lord Winstanley on the occasion of my... elevation.'

'Exquisite. Edwardian, I'm guessing.'

'Oh well done.'

'Williamson, by any chance?'

'Good lord! You certainly have an eye for this sort of thing'

'Oh no, I dabble, that's all.'

'I have a set of Minton which I must show you before you leave.'

'I should like that.'

Excellent! Now where was I?'

'Hoping I wouldn't ask why you've been buggering me about for the past couple of days.'

'Ah yes. But, you know, "buggering someone about" is (no offense) such an ugly term; I prefer to think of it as... assessing. We all know that Cleaners are amongst the most gifted of our employees but they can tend towards the more (how may I put this) traditional manner of undertaking their role. You are a thoughtful man (some have said too thoughtful – although not I) and your rather more baroque attitude to the job seemed to be just what we were looking for. When it became clear that our enemies wanted rid of you, we decided to let you run with it and see what transpired.'

'Why?'

'Two reasons: Firstly (to be quite frank), we were running out of options. We needed someone we could trust.

'Me?' said Arthur, using his best disbelieving voice.

'Yes you. You may be an insufferable git but you are a loyal git, displaying just the right quantity of gittishness to serve our needs.'

'I'm supposed to be flattered am I?'

'And secondly, we did not (as you appear to suppose) have the contents of the cipher.'

'So how did you compile the crossword?' Arthur suddenly realised that he knew the answer to that question. He smiled and said, 'Of course; you had information that the cipher contained lines from "*The White Devill*" and "*The Ladies' Triall*" but you didn't know which ones!' Arthur's smile turned distinctly evil. 'And you still don't.' he said.

'Somehow, Mulberry got hold of them before you could and sent them to me in that hex cipher.'

'Correct, I'm afraid,' Nightingale said, with a shrug. 'However, I have tremendous faith in Bracewell. I'm sure it's only a matter of time.'

'And what makes you think he'll tell you?'

'Well, I would imagine that he will tell you and then you will tell me.' Arthur pretended to appear as though he were considering this, then he said,

'No... sorry, I'm afraid you've lost me there, Nightingale.' Nightingale took a sip of tea.

'Mmm,' he said, as though he had not heard, 'Delicious. Now, come along, Shepherd; now that I've got you here, tell me what that shit, Sullivan had to say to you.'

'Now, you see, speaking like that about him isn't exactly helping your case.'

'Oh?'

'No.'

'And why is that? Surely not because he gave you a letter from Geoffrey Wittersham?' Arthur was beginning to get a little angry with himself, now. How was he managing to always be so many steps behind and yet still be alive? He gripped his head at the temples, between thumb and middle finger.

'Fuck me...' he breathed. Then, a little louder, 'You've read it, haven't you?'

'Of course.'

Arthur leaned back in his chair, closed his eyes and said,

'All right. Go on then; I'm listening.'

## Biggin Hill

The aeroplane came to a stop and at 09:45 BST after an agonising wait, the steps were deployed and two pilots saluted smartly as a British diplomat and his widowed aunt, on a visit to the country of her birth, left the aeroplane. The pair were closely followed by a representative of the company that had built the aircraft and her French secretary. All passed swiftly through the customs shed and into a waiting car.

As they headed towards the outskirts of South East London, Vanessa could hardly believe it had been so easy.

'I am to take Vanessa to Vauxhall Cross,' said Ursulet, suddenly. It was the second spontaneously-offered piece of information that she had gifted to Caroline.

'What's there?' asked Vanessa.

'The Headquarters of M.I.6,' Caroline said. 'I assume you realise that I'm not going to let you take her?'

'The thought had occurred.'

'I think we should try the F.C.O.,' Christopher said.

'What's that?' asked Vanessa.

'The Foreign and Commonwealth Office. I think I'd like a word with my superiors. There are a few things we need to straighten out. Caroline looked concerned.

'I'm not sure I want the government involved, Christopher,' she said

'Oh, I shall only speak to the permanent staff. We try and keep the government out of Foreign Affairs if at all possible.'

'I'm very glad to hear it. Very well. I'll drop you there. I'd like you to check in every hour.'

'Will do.'

'And where are we going, Caroline?' Vanessa asked.

'Gloucester Rd.'

'And what's there?'

'Oxfam.'

## Gunfight at the Gloucester Rd. Oxfam

Mrs Jempson was folding clothes.

'Good morning,' she said, as she heard the shop bell ring. 'Are you looking for anything in… Well, I never! Caroline Ransleigh. In an Oxfam Shop. What would your poor papa say?'

'Nothing. The shock would probably have killed him. How are you, Mrs. J?'

'I'm fine, dear. Sorry to hear about your hubby.'

'Thank you,' said Caroline.

'You never get over it but the pain eases with time. Trust me.'

'Trust you?' Caroline said, archly. Both women laughed.

'Now, who might this be?' Mrs. Jempson said, turning her attention to Vanessa.

'I can't say at the moment, Mrs J. but I'd be grateful if you would answer a number of questions *I* have.'

'If I can, dear. What's up?'

'I'll come straight to the point. Have you seen Arthur Shepherd, recently?' asked Caroline

'Now, you know that even if I had, I wouldn't be able to tell you. You've not been gone *that* long.' Before Caroline could respond, the door of the shop dinged open and a man stepped in. All eyes turned upon him and he smiled, moving over to a rack of clothes. Mrs. Jempson said,

'Er... are you looking for anything in particular, sir? Only, we're about to close for...' She looked at the clock. 'Tea-break.'

'Tea break? You close for tea break.'

'Yes, we do, sir. European Union directive, sir. Sorry.'

'Er... Well, I was looking for a suit.'

'Any particular style, sir?'

'Yes, as a matter of fact. Driver's uniform, slightly singed.'

'Oh bollocks,' said Mrs. Jempson.

Caroline flung herself and Vanessa to the floor, as the old lady pulled a large gun out from beneath the pile of jumpers she'd been folding. Vanessa was pinned firmly to the floorboards but was still able to hear a number of sounds reminiscent of someone pushing through the foil on a fresh jar of instant coffee, accompanied by a now-familiar smell. Once Caroline had released her Vanessa was able to look up.

Mrs Jempson was over by the wall, fiddling with what turned out to be the controls of an extractor fan, whilst on the floor, in a spreading pool of blood, lay the erstwhile customer, two holes in his forehead and pistol in his hand.

'Bugger,' said Mrs Jempson, stepping over the corpse, 'I'm going to have to lock up now. And Saturday's my busiest day.' She locked the door and turned around the sign before pulling down the blind. Closing the shutters on the large bay windows, she walked back to the counter, picked up her gun and turned it on Caroline. Caroline slowly raised her hands and Vanessa thought it politic to do likewise.

'Sorry dear but I've been in this business a bloody long time,' said Mrs Jempson. 'I may be a suspicious old cow but whenever I'm talking to someone I haven't seen in an age and then someone else fetches up and turns this place into Dodge City, I tend to assume the two events are related.'

'You don't think that we...'

'What would *you* think? Tell me who he was and what he wanted.'

'I have no notion of who he was but I think he wanted a suit. Although why it had to be slightly singed, I cannot fathom.' Eyeing Caroline warily, Mrs. Jempson laid the gun on the counter next to her own and put the pile of jumpers over it.

'That's very civil of you, Mrs Jempson.' Caroline surveyed the mess. 'Do you mind if we try and learn a little more about our friend before you call for the Constables.'

'Bloody Constables,' said Mrs. Jempson. 'That's all I need.' She stood for a few seconds then obviously reached a decision. 'All right,' she said. But be bloody careful. You know what they're like.' Gingerly skirting around the blood, Caroline knelt down. After a few moments, she looked up and said,

'Mrs. Jempson? Lily; I must know if we can trust Arthur Shepherd. Can we?'

'*I* can, Caroline; my problem is, I don't know if *you* can.'

'What do you mean?'

From the top of a small flight of stairs that led to the back-room, a woman's voice came. It was rendered worth listening to by the gun, which was aimed directly at Caroline but which from the look of its bearer and her vantage point, could be used to do for all three of them.

'I think she means, Mrs. Gagliardo-Patricelli, that she and Arthur work for the Council. No-one knows who you are working for.' Slowly, Caroline got to her feet.

'The Council!' Vanessa piped up. Yes! She's working for the Council. Tell her, Caroline.' Ignoring Vanessa, Caroline addressed the young woman.

'I'm afraid you have the advantage over me, Ms...?'

'Yes, I do don't I? And that's why, for the moment, *you* will answer *my* questions. Oh, and I'd like you to drop that gun you just picked up.'

'Goodness,' Caroline smiled. 'Well, if you'll forgive me, you look a little wet behind the ears to be giving orders, and frankly, I'm not even sure...' Before she'd finished her sentence, her arm swung upwards.

The sound of the shot was far louder than anything that had gone before. Caroline's head spun round to her right and her hand flew up to her ear.

'And if you'll forgive me; you look a little bloody behind the ears,' said the young woman. Vanessa ran to Caroline's side.

'Now see here, young lady,' said Mrs Jempson, sternly. There's no call to be blasting away like that. This is a respectable establishment.'

The young woman glanced over at the body on the floor.

'Yes, I can see that,' she said. 'Now unless you want a matching pair, Mrs. Gagliardo-Patricelli, I suggest you begin talking.'

'And *I* suggest,' Caroline said with a smile, 'that you kiss my arse...'

Caroline still had her right hand to her ear but Vanessa noticed her left hand renew it's grip on the gun. She already had her finger through the trigger guard when Vanessa launched her kick. The gun flew into the counter, shattering the glass. Guns, pullovers, cash register, indeed anything that had been resting on the counter, fell amidst a welter of shattered crystal and splintered wood. Caroline stared at Vanessa with a mixture of astonishment and fury. Vanessa, equally astonished nevertheless made certain that her face displayed only brazen nonchalance although her brain kept saying,

'Oh shit! O shit! Oh shit!'

The final tinkle of glass died away and the shop fell silent. Mrs. Jempson, open-mouthed surveyed the devastation.

'Oh for crying out loud!' she said, turning to Vanessa. 'Now look what you've done!'

'Don't move,' said the woman with the gun.

'Well who's going to clean this lot up if I don't?' said Mrs. Jempson. Suddenly, she stopped. Apparently, for the first time, she had noticed the woman's companion. 'Hang on,' she said, 'is that Mr. Bracewell you have there?' Bracewell peered over the young woman's shoulder and gave a little wave.

'Erm... Hello, Mrs. Jempson. Yes. Yes it is me, I'm afraid. Sorry.'

'And well you might be, too. What on earth is going on?' Although, like all Council Workers of old, he'd had a degree of military training, it had been a long while since he had been in the field. He was finding it difficult to concentrate.

'Erm... well, this is Ms. Leamington and er... well, she's a Cleaner, as you might have... erm... and she is under the impression that... you, I believe: the lady with the ear, as it were, pose some sort of threat to a colleague of hers.' He took a step back and whispered to Jacqueline, 'Have I got that right?'

'More or less,' she replied.

'What colleague?' asked Mrs. Jempson.

'Arthur Shepherd,' Ms. Leamington said. Mrs Jempson took a step away from Caroline.

'Is this true, Caroline?' she asked.

Caroline said nothing. Vanessa had now begun ministering to her damaged ear, with a handkerchief and she whispered to her,

'Tell her it's not true!'

'Be quiet.' She winced and jerked her head away.

Mrs Jempson caught Ms. Leamington's eye, raised a quizzical eyebrow and pointed at the first-aid kit on the wall.

'Go ahead,' the young woman said in response.

'Here,' Mrs. Jempson said to Caroline, gracelessly plonking the first-aid kit on a small table. 'Try not to get any more blood anywhere, please. Now; *are* you after Arthur?'

'Oh my God, it's Ricketts,' said Bracewell suddenly.'

'Oh, you know him?' Mrs. Jempson asked. 'Don't suppose you know why he tried to kill us?'

'Er…no,' Bracewell lied. From the corner of her mouth, Jacqueline said,

'Arthur told me to watch out for a Ricketts. Is that really him?' Peering a little more closely at the body, Bracewell responded.

'Yes it is.'

'You,' Ms. Leamington said, indicating Vanessa. 'Why did you kick the gun away?'

Where it came from, Vanessa had no idea but she heard herself saying,

'I was kidnapped in Rome by a man called Geoffrey Wittersham – it wouldn't surprise me if you knew him intimately. He used me to get some information out of Italy. Now, I'm not going to tell you anything else until you stop threatening us with that stupid gun!'

Bracewell stepped forwards and said.

'You're Vanessa Aldridge.' Vanessa was pleased that she retained the capacity to be surprised but, having made her threat, she didn't think it wise to confirm or deny anything. Ms. Leamington spoke again.

'Arthur Shepherd received a letter from Geoffrey Wittersham,' she said. They all turned to look at her. She still had her weapon pointed in the general direction of Caroline and Vanessa.'

'I don't suppose you're going to tell us what it contained?' Caroline said.

'All you need to know is that Wittersham also suspected he might die at your hands.' All eyes were now on Caroline.

'And did he, Caroline?' Mrs Jempson sounded dangerous.

'For what it's worth, Lily, no he didn't. But I don't suppose that's good enough?'

'You suppose right.'

Everyone looked at everyone else.

'Caroline,' Vanessa said, 'this is utterly ridiculous. You brought me here in a search for Arthur Shepherd; these people know him; they work with him. I think we should trust them.'

'Oh, really?' Caroline asked, removing a piece of blood-soaked cotton-wool from her ear and holding it out for Vanessa to examine, 'D' you think?'

'Well, you *were* quite rude,' Vanessa said.

'And where, Vanessa, in Debrett's Guide to Etiquette and Modern Manners, do they recommend that the correct response to a rude comment is to *shoot* the offender?' Vanessa placed her hand on Caroline's shoulder.

'Caroline, I know you must be in pain,' she said, as she peered at the wound, 'but please, for once, tell them the plain truth. No prevarication;

no obfuscation; no omission; no economy. Just tell them what you know. I'm sure that they want to help us.'

'*How* can you be sure, Vanessa? How?' I've told you before: *everyone* lies. The reasons may differ but believe me, it's the only way that the human race knows how to survive. If we told others what they want to know and if others told *us* what they really think, do you think everyone would be happier? Do you think the world would even function?

'If politicians and governments and law-makers told the truth, where would we be? It's the fact that they can't be trusted that gives us our starting point when choosing which lie to go along with. And it's the skill with which the lie is maintained that matters; the truth is irrelevant.'

Vanessa turned in exasperation to Mrs. Jempson.

'Don't look at me, dear,' she said, 'I think she's absolutely right.'

Vanessa addressed Ms. Leamington.

'I'm sorry. Caroline's a very stubborn woman and I suppose you did shoot her...'

'All right,' Caroline said, waving a hand. 'That's enough. I don't need you to make any case on my behalf. I can speak perfectly well for myself. After a moment of silence, she said,

'Vanessa, as she says, was taken in extremis by Geoffrey Wittersham. He supplied her with information, which would...'

'Yeah,' said Vanessa, '..."supplied"...'

'...which would both carry her back to England and (we fervently hope), clarify and possibly even resolve a confusing and dangerous situation that appears to have arisen. On the way to England, it became clear that M.I.6 – at least M.I.6 in Rome, are very keen that she should not succeed. The efforts they have put into preventing Vanessa from reaching this point are by themselves an indicator of how valuable the information is.'

'And where is this information now?' Ms. Leamington asked. Caroline looked at Vanessa and nodded her head.'

'In here,' Vanessa said, tapping her head, 'and I very much want it out. Can either of you two help?' Ms. Leamington and Bracewell glanced at one another then back at Vanessa.

'No,' they said almost in unison. Vanessa turned to Mrs. Jempson.

'Can you?' she asked her.

'Ooh no, dear. Not my line at all.'

'Fantastic,' Vanessa said. 'Bloody marvellous.' She began to do up her coat. 'Well I think we'll be off now, then. Thanks for all your help.' Caroline looked at her and instead of saying 'You are an idiot,' simply shook her head.

'Stay where you are for the moment, please,' said Ms. Leamington. Vanessa sighed and unbuttoned her coat once more. 'Sounds to me,' Ms. Leamington continued, 'like he used an advanced N.L.P. – type process.'

'Correct.'

'And you think Arthur Shepherd will be able to do what is necessary?'

'I don't know. In fact, I don't even know him. Most of those I knew on the Council are either dead or retired. The only one I was certain was still alive and kicking was you, Lily. That's why I came here.'

'Why would Wittersham tell Shepherd to be careful of you?' asked Mrs. Jempson.

'I have no idea,' Caroline replied. All I know is that there is no circumstance in which I would fail to carry out a request made by Geoffrey Wittersham.' There was silence until Bracewell said,

'I think I believe her. Ricketts was bit of a wrong 'un and if he came here after her then that works in her favour. Also, we have a message requesting that a Vanessa Aldridge be taken to…' He paused.

'Taken where, Mr Bracewell?' Ms. Leamington asked.

'Well, first things first. I think, all things considered, we should get this young lady to Shepherd as soon as we can.'

'Very well, Mr. Bracewell. I'll go along with your judgement. For now.'

'Well, whatever you decide to do, you'd better do it quickly,' said Mrs. Jempson, firmly. I'm going to have to get some Constables down here to sort out Mr. Ricketts and the fewer people in here when they turn up, the quicker they'll be gone.' She looked around on the floor and bent down. An expression of severe irritation graced her face as she straightened up, a shattered mess of black Bakelite, wires and bits of metal in her hand. 'Do you know how much that phone was worth?' she said to no-one in particular.

'I'll call them,' Ms. Leamington said, taking out her phone.

'Not on that you won't,' Mrs. Jempson said. 'This place is under so much mobile phone surveillance, I can't dial the speaking clock without someone shouting the time down at me from a helicopter.'

'She's probably right,' said Bracewell.

Mrs. Jempson tossed the remains of the phone into the shattered debris of the counter and strode over to the back room.

Ms. Leamington put away her gun and approached Caroline.

'May I?' she asked, pointing at Caroline's damaged ear.

'What, admire your handiwork?'

'No, I thought I might be able to help.'

'Oh why not?' said Caroline. 'After all, you've been a real Godsend so far.' Without taking her eyes from the girl, she slowly turned her head to one side. The girl peered at the wound for a few seconds and said,

'I think it'll stitch.'

'Really?' said Caroline without any noticeable sarcasm. 'Vanessa, please could you hand me that little looking-glass on the shelf there?' Vanessa reached over and handed the silver-framed mirror to Caroline, who tilted her head and began examining her wound.

'I think you may be right,' she murmured.

'Would you like me to do it for you?'

'Well, certainly; if you think you're up to it.'

'It's the least I can do.' She plundered Mrs. Jempson's first aid box and, improbably, turned up a sterile suture kit. She applied a little Dettol to the wound, eliciting only a barely audible intake of breath from Caroline, and set to work. Caroline viewed the operation courtesy of the small mirror.

'Excellent shot, by the way,' she said.

'Thank you.' Jacqueline paused for a second to pat beneath her arm. 'This little thing is great at short range.'

'A Walther, isn't it?'

'Yes. A bit of a cliché, I know but it's very light.'

'Yes, I have one myself. Perfect for the more petite figure, I find.'

'And they don't make too much of a mess, either,' Jacqueline said with a smile, pointing at Caroline's ear.

'Who is your mentor, my dear?' Caroline asked the girl.

'I'd better not...' she said, without offence.

'I quite understand; but male or female?'

'Oh, female.'

'Quite right, too. Men always tell you it's a professional relationship... but it never is.'

To Vanessa, it sounded like the sort of conversation she might have heard in the hairdressers about a million years ago.

'Thank you, Ms. Leamington,' Caroline said. The girl snipped some loose thread and dusted it away from Caroline's shoulder.'

'Good as new,' she said and proceeded to tidy away the first aid kit. She paused and said to Bracewell, 'I wonder what's keeping Mrs. Jempson? Without being asked, Bracewell went to find out.

'That fellow, Ricketts.' Caroline indicated the body on the floor. 'He turned up about a minute after we arrived. He may have a pal or two out front. It might not be so easy getting us to Shepherd alive.'

'Don't worry,' said Ms Leamington. 'If anyone's going to kill *you*, it'll be me.'

Mrs. Jempson and Bracewell emerged from the back room. Bracewell appeared lost in thought.

'Right,' Mrs. Jempson said, 'I'm about to send this message. They'll be round pretty sharpish. Have you decided what you're going to do?'

'Mr. Bracewell,' said Ms. Leamington, removing her jacket. Bracewell's mind still appeared be on other things. 'Mr. Bracewell?' she said again. This time, he looked up.

'Eh? What? Oh, sorry; miles away.'

'Are you certain no-one knows that *we're* here?'

'Absolutely. My little signal blocker will have confused them good and proper.'

'Then I should like you to take Ms. Aldridge round to Miss Carlisle's. Have her wear my jacket. My car keys and a key for the flat are in the pocket. Mrs. Gagliardo-Patricelli and I shall leave by the front door. I shall wear your jacket, Ms Aldridge, if you wouldn't mind? If Ricketts wasn't alone, his colleagues will be more than a little disconcerted to see anyone save him leave the premises. I'm confident that we will be followed.'

Vanessa shrugged and took off her coat.

'I'm not happy about letting you out of my sight, Vanessa but I think Ms. Leamington is correct. You would be in some danger leaving by the front door with me. I take it we will meet up later?'

'We will rendezvous at The Barbican in forty minutes. If we are "delayed" for any reason (she cast Caroline a meaningful look), don't wait, Mr. Bracewell; ensure that Ms. Aldridge gets to Mr. Shepherd as soon as possible.'

'Right then,' said Mrs. Jempson. One last thing: I will not lie to Constables. I won't offer them anything either, mind but if they ask for names, I shall give them eventually. Those are my bullet-holes in his bonce and they'll want to know why I put them there. Do you all understand?' It seemed to Vanessa that the other three accepted this condition without reservation. Bracewell took her arm and said,

'Right, Miss. Aldridge; stay close to me, please and do as I say. And remember: if anyone is on the case, they're likely to be after you and your friend who, as far as anyone else is concerned have just left by the front door. He smiled and Vanessa managed to smile back. It was getting complicated again.

First, she'd had to grow used to Maytham being in charge, then Caroline, then Ursulet; Caroline again and now this guy. It would be strange getting back to not taking orders. But now, (and really for the first time since this began), she could detect the first glimmerings of light at the end of the tunnel.

'So where are we going?' she asked.

'We're going to the home of a colleague of Shepherd's. As soon as we're able to phone safely, I'll arrange for him to meet us there.' He led Vanessa down a number of streets until finally he pointed Jacqueline's keys at a small Nissan.

Soon, they were on a wide road heading east. Vanessa was unfamiliar with London but she recognised the Natural History Museum as they passed it. Bracewell shoved an earpiece in and said,

'Shepherd.' A few seconds later, he said,

'Bollocks.' Then, a moment or two after that he said, 'It's Bracewell. On the off-chance that you pick this up sometime in the next week or two: I'm heading for Jennifer's with a young lady. Her name is Vanessa Aldridge and she has a message from Geoffrey Wittersham. Oh, and Mrs. Jempson has a teleprinter.'

## Eminence Gris

'A good way to mislead someone, as I'm sure you know,' Nightingale began, 'is to hide the lie in a muck-pile of truth and let the other person talk themselves into believing it. All that stuff about Bray-Renshawe is perfectly true but then a number of people in your position are privy to that information -which is precisely why it's there.

'Then,' Nightingale continued,' he utilises the paranoia, which you and every other Council Worker has about M.I.6 – that they are out to get you and that they have infiltrated the Council all over the world. He particularly mentions an agent whom he claims is active in Paris, Berlin, Geneva and Vienna. You know that Jeavons was killed in Berlin and Bartholomew in Vienna and perhaps others of whom I am not aware have been disposed of in the other places. Wittersham appears to be letting you make up your own lies.'

Arthur was thinking at this point both of Jennifer's close call in Paris and Geoffrey Wittersham's ability to manipulate people.

'Have you heard of this Caroline Ransleigh?' Nightingale asked. Arthur didn't answer. All he could think was that if Geoffrey was trying to set her up, he couldn't have done a better job. Arthur had already determined that he was going to do her in as a special favour to Geoffrey. Christ, had he really failed to smell such an obvious rat? Then there was that paean to the Council. Arthur had never heard Geoffrey say a poetic thing in his life, let alone about the Council; and the whole thing rounded off with that outrageous double-bluff about not believing him. Arthur felt rage beginning to stir.

'It's not true, is it? None of it is true. *Sodding Geoffrey*: he's done it again!'

'Now wait a moment,' said Sir Auberon, holding up his hand. 'That line about Franco; whatever significance it has, I presume it is meant to quell your concerns about the authenticity of the note? Are you certain that no-one else appreciates the significance?'

'Absolutely,' Arthur said, thanking God that he hadn't told Jennifer and Alan the story of Geoffrey and General Franco.

'Hmm. But, you know, that's the problem with the Secret Service,' Nightingale said, 'No-one can keep a secret. It could well have got out, you realise?'

'What are you saying? That Geoffrey didn't write the letter?'

'Knowing what I know about Sullivan and what little I've gleaned about Wittersham, I would say it was more than possible. Look, I'll tell you what I believe, shall I? Sullivan, having failed to have you disposed of, has decided to try another tack. He's after convincing you that the Council is under attack as a result of an age-old vendetta involving M.I.6. He's tried to convince you that Wittersham was with him because he wants you inside the tent pissing out.'

'Why?'

'Because you are a right pain in the arse, Shepherd; as well you know.'

'You really believe that Sullivan is the eminence gris behind all this?'

'I never said that. I would characterise his role as being more of an "eminence off-white-with-a-hint-of-blackcurrant". There are those a lot greyer, believe me.'

'So what do you think he's after?'

'In the first instance, you. As I say, if he can keep you onside long enough, a) you won't be doing any damage to him and b) you might actually be able to benefit his cause.'

'And what is his cause?'

'What is any politician's cause?'

'Self-interest and power?'

'A bit harsh. Many politicians have a vocation for public service; however, in this case, I'm afraid you've hit the nail on the head. Our friend Sullivan is as venal a piece of work as I've come across in Whitehall in many a year. Of course, a lot of politicians have turned the current financial crisis to their benefit but Sullivan appears to be attempting to outdo the lot of them.'

'Well, it was dream come true for the Tories,' Arthur opined. 'They could chop the stuff they've always wanted to chop with gay abandon and blame it on the last lot.'

'Indeed. Now, I'm no Bolshevik, Shepherd, but even I am of the opinion that the Conservatives have been a little over enthusiastic with the axe; particularly as it now appears to be being wielded rather close to home.'

'Ah! I see. The cuts beginning to bite around your nethers are they, Nightingale? Getting a bit too close for comfort?

'Oh, don't get your hopes up, Shepherd. I'm Council, remember. But the Secret Intelligence Service? Oh my, the poor old S.I.S. are rather feeling the pinch. The public sector is always the first to feel any pain arising from the need to save money and S.I.S. (though far from the usual target area) has clearly found itself in a bit of financial bother.'

'People have certainly noticed a falling off in quality as well as quantity over at S.I.S.,' Arthur said. They can't afford to replace and when they do, those replacements are not exactly *summa cum laude.*'

'Quite. However, it's worth remembering that the earlier cuts were made at the instigation of the Foreign Secretary – you know; no area of government is exempt – that sort of thing. These latest ones are courtesy of one Ashley Sullivan. You see, over at Westminster, they're all scurrying about trying to get themselves noticed as "saver –in-chief". Word is that the P.M. will look kindly on those who are willing to cut their own departments for the good of the country and Sullivan has sensed an opportunity.'

'He's gone behind the Foreign Secretary's back?'

'In a big way. The way I see it, Sullivan fetches up at S.I.S. and says to one of the accountants, "If you can find a way of scraping off a layer or two, I might make it worth your while". Johnny Accounts rises to the task and at some point notices that S.I.S. appears to be using far more money than it's been getting.'

'Not terribly unusual, I'd have thought.'

'No indeed. However, it also appears that it has little to show in the way of goods and services purchased.' To Arthur, (and presumably to Sullivan's pet accountant) this indicated only one thing.

'Money laundering,' he said. 'And I think I can guess who's Widow Twanky…'

'Bingo. Johnny Accounts then turns up the fact that there is this little-known bunch of chaps over at Lambeth who seem to be eating into the budget like rats in grain-store – that is: surreptitiously and at a prodigious rate. S.I.S. should have been able to sustain even the most massive cuts, were it not haemorrhaging cash through the bottom of the sack, as it were.'

'But money for the Council has always been sacrosanct, hasn't it?'

'So we all believe. Early on, a number of carefully-negotiated schemes ensured (purely for security reasons, you understand) that Council's revenue streams would be entirely untraceable. Over the years, with successive changes of personnel and governments, the whole thing sort of scabbed over, allowing said streams to glug along beneath it, hidden from prying eyes. So Council cash, (whatever its source), is filtering through the Foreign Office and S.I.S. who are inadvertently scrubbing it nice and clean...'

'Until Johnny Accounts starts digging up the pipes.' Arthur stroked his chin. 'Sullivan couldn't have believed his luck. He could appear to be cutting millions off the budget but without affecting the running of his department one iota.'

'Absolutely. However, you reckon without the greed of friend Sullivan. Certainly, several millions being sucked back into the exchequer looks like it might represent a sudden and swift advancement for Our Man at the F.O. but it would be peanuts compared to that which Sullivan could siphon into his own little offshore accounts. And because to all intents and purposes, the money never existed in the first place, no-one would be any the wiser.'

'From that smirk, I'd wager that Sullivan was soon disabused of the idea.'

'In fairly short order. You see, even Johnny Accounts found himself unable to untangle the Gordian Knot that is the Council accounts. Every time he teased open a strand and followed it, it would dip back into the melee and be lost from sight; each time he would tug on a likely thread, another promising loop would be sucked into the whole rat's nest. In the end, he had to go to Sullivan and tell him that his dreams of advancement had been interrupted by the bedside alarm of Very Creative Accounting.'

'And if his recent actions are anything to go by, it would appear that he's hit the snooze button,' said Arthur. Nightingale frowned a little, then his face brightened.

'Ahh, I see!' he drawled. 'Very good, Shepherd. Yes, very good. "Hit the snooze button". Well done.'

'It wasn't that good.'

'One likes to be encouraging.'

'So what's he up to now?'

'Well, it seems as if the only success the accountant had was in gouging a way through to a number of administrative budgets, causing little damage. But then, he appears to have had a breakthrough.'

'The Council Pension Fund,' said Arthur.

'My word! If I could bear to tell you that you've impressed me, I would.'

'It's amazing what you can pick up on a bus.'

'No doubt. I wondered why you were asking about interns the other day. Looks like some people may have priced themselves out of a job, doesn't it?'

'And one or two have priced themselves out of existence.'

'Yes. I suppose you realise that you were meant to be among their number?'

'It was beginning to dawn.'

Nightingale smiled a brief smile and said,

'You know; if that's all there had been to it, I think we might have been able to sort it out quite quickly.'

'I was waiting for the other shoe to drop,' said Arthur. 'The codes have absolutely nothing to do with this, do they?'

'Not *absolutely* nothing, no. But you're quite right; we do have a case of co-morbidity on our hands. Somehow Sullivan has got himself in league with someone – we don't know who – who is not only sanguine about killing Council Workers but is also canny enough to kill the right ones.'

'Ones approaching retirement.'

'Ah yes; but they also have something else in common…'

## Escape From Fortune Tower

'So I'd like to hang about here, if you don't mind, and wait for Shepherd to call.'

Bracewell reached the end of his account of the morning's events. Miss Carlisle looked thoughtful.

'So this young lady has to be put in the way of Crawthorne Beasley?' she said.

'That's right. She has some kind of message to give him. I've no idea what and neither does she.'

Although possibly a little older than Caroline, Jennifer Carlisle appeared to Vanessa to have been cut from similar cloth. She had greeted her and Bracewell warmly and had listened carefully to the tale Bracewell had given her.

'Geoffrey's bloody mind-games again, eh?' she said. 'Well I think we should get her to him as soon as possible, don't you?' Bracewell was clearly surprised by this remark.

'To Beasley?' he said, uncertainly

'Definitely. It sounds to me as though Vanessa has suffered enough, don't you think?'

'So… you know where to find him, then?' asked Bracewell

'Of course,' Miss Carlisle said. 'We used to work together.' She took out her mobile phone, saying, 'I still have his number, I think… here we are.'

'I'd prefer to wait for Arthur,' Bracewell said. 'I mean Vanessa seems like a nice young lady and if it's a trap, I'd never forgive myself.'

'Have you ever met Crawthorne Beasley?' Miss Carlisle asked.

'No,' said Bracewell.

'Well if you had, you'd know that Vanessa will be perfectly safe. She paused for a second and then mouthed at Vanessa, 'It's ringing...Hello? Crawthorne! It's me, Jennifer... yes, Jennifer Carlisle... I know; it has hasn't it...? Yes...Yes, well it's all a little bit mysterious. You see; a young woman has washed up on our shore claiming to have a message for you... Yes indeed. Apparently, it was given to her by Geoffrey Wittersham... Yes, I thought you might be. Would it be convenient to come over now...? Splendid! Within the hour? Yes... yes of course...'

'Just a moment...' Vanessa said suddenly. 'May I have a word?'

'What did you say, dear?' Miss Carlisle said, her hand over the mouthpiece.

'I said I'd like a word with Mr. Beasley... If that's all right with you?'

'Well, we'll be there very shortly. I'm sure you'll...'

'I want to speak to him.' She held out her hand for the telephone. Instead of handing it over, Miss Carlisle spoke into it.

'Crawthorne? Yes, I'm sorry about that but the young lady would like a word with you... Yes, I told her that but she's... most insistent... All right.' Miss Carlisle passed the telephone to Vanessa.

'Hello, Mr. Beasley?'

'Yes, my dear,' came the reply. An old voice, Vanessa thought, but kindly and intelligent. 'I must say this story sounds most intriguing.'

'That's one way of putting it,' Vanessa said and was gratified when Beasley chuckled. He said,

'You spoke to Geoffrey Wittersham, I understand? Can you remember nothing of what he told you?'

'I'm afraid I can't, Mr. Beasley but the people I've met here tell me that you will be able to help me. Is that true?'

'I'm certain of it. If Wittersham insisted we meet, it must be because he believed I could unlock whatever he put in your mind. Now I suggest you get over here as soon as possible and we can make a start. Please would you pass the phone back to Miss Carlisle now?' Miss Carlisle took the phone and after a few more words, she ended the call and said to Bracewell,

'Right, let's go. Shall we take your car or mine?'

'Mine's probably safer,' Bracewell said. Miss Carlisle smiled.

'Has lots of gadgets, does it, Mr. Bracewell?'

'Ooh yes; I should say so.'

'Very well, then,' said Miss Carlisle. 'After you.'

'Before we go,' said Bracewell, 'I'd better ring Ms. Leamington and tell her where we're going.' Before he'd finished dialling, the doorbell rang. Miss Carlisle was standing right by it so Jacqueline was a little taken aback when it opened so smartly.

'Oh!' she said.

'Jacqueline. Come in, my love,' said Miss Carlisle. 'Mr. Bracewell was just about to give you up for lost.'

'Thank you, Miss Carlisle.' She turned towards Caroline. 'May I present...' Jacqueline began.

'I know who she is,' Miss Carlisle and Caroline said, in unison.

Vanessa had never spoken of her emotional intelligence on any of her C.V.s and with good reason, but even she had no trouble detecting the waves of animosity pouring from each of them. The squall had already breached the sea-wall and was well on its way to flooding the car-park before either of them said a word. Bracewell looked at Vanessa, his face suggesting they put some distance between themselves and the two older women. Jacqueline looked crestfallen. Vanessa was astonished to see the young woman who had dealt so deftly with Caroline, redden with embarrassment.

Miss Carlisle came around first. She laid her hand gently on the young woman's shoulder and said,

'I'm sorry, Jacqueline, that was unforgivably rude. You weren't to know.'

'Indeed, Ms. Leamington, please accept my apologies too. Jennifer.' Caroline extended her hand. 'It is... good to see you again. How are you?' Miss Carlisle held Caroline's fingers lightly for a moment and let go.

'Caroline,' she said, 'We've been expecting you.'

'Well, that at least partly explains it,' Caroline said. Before Miss Carlisle could respond, she continued. 'You were leaving?'

'Yes,' Miss Carlisle said. 'I thought it best to carry out Geoffrey's wishes and take Ms. Aldridge to Crawthorne Beasley.'

'Geoffrey's wishes? Crawthorne Beasley?' Caroline said. She looked at Vanessa. 'Have you remembered something?'

'No, I don't think so,' Vanessa said, hesitantly. 'It wasn't Wittersham who wanted me to meet Beasley. At least I don't...' She turned to Bracewell for help but he looked as bewildered as she was feeling.

'Mr. Bracewell, where does Crawthorne Beasley come into this?' Caroline asked.

'We received a deeply encrypted message instructing us that Miss Aldridge should be taken to see this Beasley chap presumably so that he can… deprogram her, I suppose.'

Vanessa did not like the sound of that.

'If it's all the same to you, Jennifer, I'd prefer Vanessa to speak to Arthur Shepherd. That was clearly Geoffrey's intention. Is he on his way?'

'I'm not sure,' replied Bracewell. 'I left a message but he's not exactly reliable on that front.'

'Bracewell,' Miss Carlisle said, 'what makes you so certain the instruction about Beasley came from Geoffrey?'

'Well, nothing. I mean I don't recall saying that it did. Did I?'

'I'm sure you did.'

'I don't think I did.'

'Come over here, please Vanessa,' Caroline said. She was looking intently at Bracewell. Vanessa obeyed instantly. This didn't feel right at all. 'There seems to be a little confusion. I'm sure you'll understand if I ask that the situation be clarified before anyone takes anyone anywhere. Now Mr. Bracewell: the message you received suggested that Vanessa be taken to see Beasley?'

'Correct.'

'But you don't know who sent it.'

'No.'

'And you, Jennifer, believe it to have been sent by Geoffrey?'

'Look; the message came to Arthur. It was aimed directly at him. When Arthur gets here – more likely "*if*", he will take her to Beasley himself.'

'And if that's the case,' Caroline said, 'I believe there is little to be gained by jumping the gun. Now, either we wait for Arthur Shepherd or Vanessa and I are leaving.' She placed herself in front of Vanessa and began to back her towards the door. The other three stood stock still, as Vanessa felt around behind her and found the door handle. Bracewell spoke up.

'Look, I'll give Arthur another try and if he's still not picking up, I'll go out and find him. We'll get him here somehow.'

'That's very good of you Mr. Bracewell but I feel a little uncomfortable about this,' said Caroline.

'But it was just a little misunderstanding. Perhaps I didn't explain carefully enough…'

'You're wasting your breath,' Jennifer said. 'She always was a bit of an old drama-queen.'

'It's so interesting how the middle classes appear perfectly at ease with insulting their own guests,' Caroline said. 'I've never quite been able to manage it.'

'Jacqueline, stop them,' said Miss Carlisle and instantly, her protégé went for her gun.

Vanessa watched as the young woman's expression changed from determined to nonplussed. Caroline reached into her own pocket and took out Jacqueline's Walther.

'One forgets just how crowded the Tube is,' she said. 'All those people crammed together, jostling and fumbling. It's a thieves' paradise down there. Open the door, Vanessa. We're leaving.'

Vanessa did as ordered and without taking her eyes from the others, Caroline backed her out of the apartment and onto the landing. She slammed the door behind them, turned to Vanessa and said,

'Run!'

Down the landing they pelted. Vanessa looked up as they ran past the lift. There was a car on the tenth floor, apparently. They were on the twenty-fourth. Without breaking step, Caroline burst into the stairwell and the pair of them scurried down the stairs. They had gained the twenty-first floor before Vanessa heard, from above, the sound of the stairwell door crashing open and another tattoo of footsteps hurrying downwards.

Caroline pulled open a door on the twentieth floor and they ran through onto the landing. Gently, she allowed the door to close, taking its weight as the hydraulic closer released it, so that it closed without a sound. Caroline took in the lift. The arrow was pointing downwards and the indicator said it had just left the twenty-second floor. They'd obviously called it before sending one or even two of their number down the stairs.

Vanessa's throat was burning but she was trying to breathe as silently as possible. Caroline looked calm: almost serene as she pressed the call button for the lift. Vanessa's eyes widened. Surely Caroline must have worked out that the lift was most likely to contain one of their pursuers? Caroline placed herself on the wall opposite the lift. As the doors opened, she launched herself into it, catching Bracewell in the midriff and knocking the air out of him. He sagged to the floor.

'Get in!' Caroline called. Vanessa heard but did not see the stairwell door slam open, as she dived into the car and hit the mirrored wall at the back of it. In it, even as the doors closed, she saw the reflection of Jacqueline shudder to a stop and raise a weapon. Both Vanessa and Caroline instinctively flung themselves to the sides of the lift as three or four shots shattered the mirror, sending glass cascading down upon the stricken Bracewell.

'Jennifer's still up there. She's not as nimble as she was.' Caroline actually laughed. 'She'll have warned someone – probably the tower security that we're on our way. We can't go to the ground floor in this lift. We'll get out on the second floor and then take the stairs again.'

Vanessa was collapsed on the floor amidst shards of mirrored glass. She gulped in air and fought to steady her racing heart. Still without complaint, as the door opened on the second floor, she followed Caroline out of the lift and into the stairwell. Glancing above her, she saw to her horror the shadow that was Jacqueline, tearing down towards them. In less than two minutes, she'd be on them.

Out through the first floor stairwell and onto the exterior balcony just one floor above the ground. It was still much too far to jump. Nevertheless, Caroline leapt easily over the balustrade and gripping the base of a support, she held out her hand towards Vanessa.

'Oh Christ!' said Vanessa. But she climbed over. Caroline took hold of her wrist and then pushed her off the balcony. Vanessa felt Caroline take her weight and then experienced a sickening lurch as the older woman stepped off the balcony. The two of them hung there, Vanessa now within four feet of the ground. Caroline let her go she fell onto the soft grass, rolling to one side just as Caroline landed beside her. Immediately, Caroline was up and moving.

Vanessa lay on her back, willing her exhausted body to move. She opened her eyes and looked up. Just above her, on the same first-floor balcony from which she and Caroline had just leapt, Jacqueline stood. In an instant, she was over the edge and had jumped. Vanessa rolled once again and tried to stand. It was no use. She looked over at Jacqueline who was already getting to her feet and despair flooded into her.

Suddenly, a shadow flashed between her and Jacqueline. Caroline's foot crashed into the girl's side. A groan escaped her and gasping for breath, she hit the ground once more.

Caroline stood astride the supine figure of Jacqueline, the Walther pointed at her pain-distorted face. Vanessa heard herself gasp,

'Caroline, don't! Please don't.' The older woman's face was impassive. After what seemed an age, Vanessa heard her say,

'I still need more answers. If any of them bring me back here, I shall not hesitate to finish this.' She put up the gun and reached out a hand towards Vanessa, who took it, dragged herself erect and staggered off alongside Caroline. Only moments later, the two of them skittered down the stairs at Old St. Tube Station having bought tickets to Vauxhall.

On the platform, they sat together on a red plastic bench. Vanessa was close to tears.

'What are we doing now?' she asked.

'Christopher has missed his check-in. I'm going to find him and then we are going to find Arthur Shepherd: and we do it without that bitch,

Jennifer Carlisle.' Caroline shook her head. 'I knew as soon as I laid eyes on her that she'd bring trouble.'

'Well, to be fair, we had a bit of trouble before she came on the scene.' Vanessa sniffed and smiled at Caroline. To her surprise, Caroline took her hand.

'Don't worry,' she said. I promise you we can get this sorted.'

'Do you?' Vanessa asked. Caroline looked at her. Brushing a strand or two of hair from Vanessa's face and stroking her cheek, she said,

'Yes I do.' As a metallic screech rang out across the platform, she patted Vanessa's knee and said, 'Right: this one's ours.' The train pulled in, the doors opened and the two women stepped into the carriage and sat down. Neither of them noticed a very ordinary-looking man in an old grey flannel suit step into the carriage through another door.

## The Northern Line

Arthur studied the two women. The younger one looked tired and a bit frazzled. She blew her nose, crumpled her handkerchief and stuffed it in her pocket. She pushed her tousled hair behind her ears and studied her own reflection in the window opposite, turning her head this way and that and removing the odd smudge from her forehead. She had a pretty face – the sort of face that might well have caught Geoffrey's eye. The older woman, on the other hand, was beautiful. She had an air of continental elegance about her that most English women seem unable to achieve. He had never known her name but as soon as he saw her, even now, after what must have been over a decade, he recognised Caroline Gagliardo-Patricelli. He'd seen her only twice before and both times at a distance. On both occasions, she had been with Geoffrey Wittersham. She was not studying her reflection; for one thing, she didn't need to (even the wound to her ear seemed neat and well-kept) and for another, she was intent on studying her travelling companions.

Arthur averted his gaze a split second before hers attached itself to his face. He could afford a smile. Neither of them had noticed him as they had raced from Fortune Tower.

He'd gone there in response to Bracewell's message and, as he rounded a corner, had seen Jacqueline raise herself from the ground and Bracewell stagger to help her. Both had seemed relatively unscathed and so he'd latched onto the fugitives without another thought. He'd have bet his boots that the younger woman was Vanessa Aldridge and what with both of them having legged it from Jennifer's place, leaving walking wounded in their wake, they definitely needed keeping an eye on.

He began to think on what Nightingale had told him. It had taken the Council some time to conclude that the attrition rate amongst experienced workers was exceeding what might reasonably be expected because there had been something rather more serious occupying their minds: the imminent death of Sir James Carlisle. It had been imminent for about ten years but the Council, being what it was, dealt with matters only when other alternatives had been exhausted. Arthur was still trying to get it all straight in his head but one thing he knew for certain: little could be achieved until Vanessa Aldridge had met with Crawthorne Beasley.

He would have to get her away from Mrs Gagliardo-Patricelli: a task, about which he was not altogether sanguine. He'd learned that she had been a close confidant of Geoffrey's for many years and it appeared more than likely that Geoffrey had entrusted the young woman to her safe keeping.

He was now convinced that Geoffrey hadn't written the letter and that its author had intended for Arthur to do away with Mrs Gagliardo-Patricelli. He was not going to do that unless he had to but he couldn't risk confiding in her. Jennifer was certainly wary of her (and rightly, as today's episode appeared to confirm), and he trusted Jennifer's judgement almost as much as he did Geoffrey's.

Whatever the case, he needed a plan. Mrs Gagliardo-Patricelli had been a Council Worker so there was no doubt that upon leaving the train, she would take note of everyone in the carriage who left with her and keep an eye on each until they had all filtered away.

He continued to study her when the opportunity presented itself. When not eyeing her directly, he was able to see something of her reflected in the window between carriages and was impressed. In spite of her striking appearance, she was well able to pass for an ordinary member of the public, maintaining an expression as vacant as any bored commuter's. This was an aspect of the Cleaner's craft at which Arthur was thoroughly adept and yet he noted (with not a little concern), that she was rather better at it than he. He couldn't swear to it but was willing to bet that she had glanced at the line map once upon sitting down but had not done so since. When the time came, she would give very little indication that she and her companion were about to disembark and might even wait until the train had stopped completely before doing so, making the possibility of tailing her without being spotted even more problematic.

Arthur looked at the line map opposite his seat. For anyone wanting to anticipate Mrs Gagliardo-Patricelli's movements, there could hardly be a worse line for them to be on. Beasley lived in Blackheath and although there was no obvious connection along the Northern Line, there was the mainline station at London Bridge, which offered a regular service to the South London village. Then there was the Elephant and Castle, a couple of hundred yards from Century House; and Stockwell, a cough and a spit from Vauxhall Cross.

The only crumb of comfort came via the fact that as he'd passed through the ticket hall at Old Street, he'd noticed the poster proclaiming engineering works at Southwark station. That would give him time to think.

The train pulled out of Bank station. London Bridge was the next stop. Arthur glanced over at Vanessa Aldridge, who was studying the map. She turned to Mrs Gagliardo-Patricelli and this, (the noise in the carriage making it difficult to hear), gave Arthur some assistance in making out what was being said,

'Have you decided yet?' she asked. Mrs Gagliardo-Patricelli looked at her companion briefly and Arthur detected the merest flick of the head, denoting a negative. Vanessa spoke again.

'He sounded genuine on the phone,' Arthur believed she said. He neither saw nor heard Mrs Gagliardo-Patricelli 's response and nor did he throughout the next few exchanges. However, he saw Ms. Aldridge say,

'Have you ever met him?' and 'I suppose so.' And 'What's the Ministry of Truth?' and 'Bugger.'

The train pulled into London Bridge and a large number of people left the carriage to be replaced by a new batch, somewhat fewer in number. Mrs Gagliardo-Patricelli had obviously decided against (or indeed had not yet even considered) Blackheath for as the train slowly hummed out of the station, the two women remained in their seats. Arthur was relieved. He'd left it far too late to exit without attracting attention.

The next most likely exit point would be the Elephant. If he messed up, he might be able to stay on until Kennington and try as best he could to run back to Century House. It would be a pain but better than being shot. However, the chances of losing them would be extremely high. As they left Borough station, Arthur decided that he might benefit (as he had often been told by people who should have known better) from being a little more pro-active.

There were only a few minutes separating Borough from Elephant and Castle so Arthur needed to act. He stood up and walked down the carriage, which gave a substantial shudder. This gave him the perfect opportunity to reach for one of those ridiculous hanging balls that had replaced the much more effective straps many years before. He caught it easily and set about pretending to try to regain his balance. His efforts left him suspended at a crazy angle. He looked foolish and not in the least bit dangerous. Perfect. He landed himself heavily on the seat facing the two women.

'Blooming things always catch you off-guard, don't they?' He said to them, an affable grin on his reddening face.

'Yes, I seem to have rather lost my sea-legs as well,' Mrs Gagliardo-Patricelli said, smiling in a not unagreeable manner.

'Are you all right?' asked the young woman, concern in her voice.

'Oh, yes thank you. Happens all the flippin' time, these days. Partially the decrepitude of the Northern Line, but I don't exclude the possibility of it being my own failing frame.'

'Well, you look reasonably serviceable to me.' Mrs Gagliardo-Patricelli said.

'You are too gracious. I'll think I'll remain here "*until the vehicle comes to a standstill*", as they used to say ha ha.'

He glanced around. Everyone within earshot had wires dangling from their lug-holes.

'So what brings you to England Mrs. Gagliardo-Patricelli?' he asked.

The young woman's eyes widened and her companion placed a steadying hand on her thigh. Arthur was enormously impressed. Mrs. Gagliardo-Patricelli displayed no surprise whatsoever but said merely,

'I'm afraid you have the better of me, Mr...?

'Henley,' said Arthur, 'Arthur Henley. How do you do?' He held out his hand and after a delay of only a second or two, Mrs. Gagliardo-Patricelli took it. Arthur was prepared for her to drag him across the aisle and wrap his liver around poniard of some description but she didn't.

'May I ask, Mr Henley, how it is that you know my name?'

'Indeed you may but I'm sure you'll understand that it's a long story and we have so little time.'

'Oh?'

'Yes, I believe so. You see, the reason I have revealed myself to you is that I would rather you knew my intention than have you speculate upon it. Having studied you since you left Fortune Tower, I conclude that it would have been a foolish - even dangerous - enterprise on my part to try to follow you once you left the train. I didn't want to run the risk of losing track of you.'

'Flattery, Mr. Henley? Tell me: who are you working for?'

'I am employed by Lambeth Council.'

'Are you, indeed? And what is that you do for them?'

'Oh, this and that.'

'Mostly "that", I'll warrant,' she said. Arthur smiled: he liked this woman and hoped he wouldn't have to kill her.

'I couldn't decide where you would get off the train,' he said. I supposed you could be heading for Stockwell and Vauxhall Cross but thought it unlikely. I concluded that it would be here.' He said this, the instant the train rattled into Elephant and Castle station. It squealed to a standstill and as the door hissed open, Mrs Gagliardo-Patricelli stood up, followed closely by Ms. Aldridge. She looked down at Arthur.

'I think Lambeth Council is lucky to have you working for them, Mr. Henley,' she said, stepping unhurriedly from the carriage. She walked slowly to the inner edge of the platform, where she turned, Ms. Aldridge by her side and looked back at the train. Arthur arose and alighted and the train trundled slowly away behind him.

'You were right; but for the wrong reason,' Mrs Gagliardo-Patricelli said, as he approached. 'You see, we're not going to Lambeth, Mr. Henley…'

'No. Engineering works today on the Jubilee Line at Southwark,' said Arthur. He pointed down towards the exit tunnel. 'You'll need to change at Waterloo for Westminster. It's only a short walk from there to the Foreign Office. We have approximately eighteen minutes to reach some kind of accord.'

'I was wrong,' Mrs Gagliardo-Patricelli said. 'Lambeth Council is *very* lucky to have you. She turned and headed for the Bakerloo Line. Arthur indicated that Ms. Aldridge should follow and he himself brought up the rear.

## The Jubilee Line

The conversation would have been tricky enough for Vanessa to follow anyway but amidst the clatter and roar of the Bakerloo Line, it was almost impossible. Somehow, this Henley bloke had worked out that they were headed for the Foreign Office and appeared anxious to discover whom they were planning to meet. Caroline, of course, had no intention of telling him.

To be honest, Vanessa had been more than a little surprised that Caroline had responded to Henley's arrival on the scene with such equanimity in the first place. In "normal" circumstances, she might have expected her to simply kick him in the nuts and have it away on her toes. Something in what he did or said must have impressed her although what it had been, Vanessa could not fathom. He seemed reasonable enough but as she'd come to recognise, that didn't generally count for a great deal in this murky place that was now her life.

The first part of the dialogue between Caroline and Henley seemed to consist of him telling her what he knew about the pair of them and their journey from Rome, which, although there were many gaps, seemed largely accurate. He knew about Christopher, too (although not his name, nor his relationship to Caroline) but seemed to have no idea about Ursulet. He had a stab at guessing how they ended up at Jennifer Carlisle's flat but was quite a way off on that, apart from knowing that Bracewell and Jacqueline Leamington were involved in some way.

It was when he mentioned the name of Ashley Sullivan, that Caroline began to respond with a little less self-assurance than she had thereto. Arthur Henley noticed at once, of course, and asked what her dealings had been with him. She did not answer.

And then he spoke about Geoffrey Wittersham. At that point, Vanessa's ears began to ring. At first she put it down to the depth of the train line but soon realised it had little if anything to do with it. It was distracting however, and she missed some of what was said. It turned out though, that Henley and Wittersham had been very great friends and at one stage, Henley had believed that Wittersham had died at the hands of Caroline and had determined to kill her for it. Now he understood that it was likely he had been lied to about that.

Then it had been time to change trains. They'd walked in silence together through the tunnels beneath Waterloo, Vanessa idly looking at the posters adorning the walls and wondering what she might have missed in the way of music, theatre and film since she'd moved to Rome. Caroline had drawn Henley's attention to a poster for an exhibition of Damian Hirst at the Royal Academy. Had he been yet?

No he fucking hadn't, it turned out. He wouldn't piss on one of Hirst's "crappy little daubs" if it was on fire – *especially* if it was on fire. They'd wittered on about Art for a while after that and Vanessa had sort of tuned out.

It was after they'd sat down on the train from Waterloo to Westminster that things began to get a bit strange. Vanessa had wanted to know if Ursulet and Christopher knew they were on their way. She wouldn't have said their names, of course; she was beginning to get it, but she only managed to say,

'Caroline...?' When she'd been slapped down with a very sharp,

'Not now Vanessa!' after which, she had begun to listen a little harder to their conversation. They appeared to be discussing the Tate. Vanessa had never been to the Tate and hadn't even known that there had been another, different one, somewhere else. Henley and Caroline began to speak in what Vanessa could only describe as a "careful" manner. Short questions and short or even no answers batted back and forth on the subject of art. Vanessa hadn't a clue what was going on. Then Caroline said,

'This young woman (as I'm sure you have deduced), is Vanessa Aldridge. Geoffrey Wittersham sent her to me.'

'What?' said Vanessa.

'Oh he knew that Christopher would be sent to deal with your case and he knew Christopher would bring you to me.' Caroline said to her.

She turned to Henley once more. 'Before doing so, however, he put a SIM card in her phone on which were just two things: a photo of an old man tending sheep and an image of a painting by Mark Rothko.'

Henley looked intrigued.

'Go on,' he said. Caroline smiled.

'Some years ago, Geoffrey told me of a friend of his called Shepherd, Arthur Shepherd, who understood painting better than anyone he knew. In fact, this Shepherd's response to painting – and particularly the works of Rothko, fascinated Geoffrey. He said it taught him a great deal about visceral responses to stimuli and how such things can be used to manipulate the thoughts of others. He would often refer to it when he and I studied psychology together. He was very fond of you, you know. I'm sure he'd be very pleased that we have finally met.'

'This is our stop,' Henley said.

## Interrupting The Ambassador

It seldom took Arthur long to engineer a row, although he was sorry to have do so with Henderson, Ashley Sullivan's secretary, who seemed like a perfectly nice chap.

'You toadying little prick,' Arthur said to him. I'll bet that's not all you do for him, either. Now tell him I'm here.' He was unconcerned that Henderson might alert security, since the man would have had to have been possessed not only of a loyalty that would shame a spaniel, but also balls of pure titanium to have ignored the pistol that was pressed into his forehead.

'But he's with the German Ambassador,' Henderson protested.

'I don't care if he's with St. Michael and all his Holy Angels; tell him I'm here or I'll just walk in anyway and say you told me it was all right.'

'But you have a gun!' wailed Henderson.

'Oh, you noticed?'

'You'll have to leave it out here.'

'What?'

'It's the rules!!'

Arthur looked at Caroline.

'Do you believe this?' he asked.

'I suppose rules *are* rules,' she said.

Gratifyingly, the door to Sullivan's inner office was dragged open and the minister's reddening face appeared and hissed,

'What is going on out here?!' He needn't have asked; it was pretty obvious. Arthur gave him his best beaming smile and waved his pistol in Henderson's face.

'*Fuck!*' Sullivan managed to blurt out whilst still keeping his voice down. 'I mean... *Fuck! Fuck*!' He stepped back into his office and the door closed.

'Arthur?' said Caroline.

'Hmm?'

'You say that you saw us leave Fortune Tower?'

'Indeed.'

'Then I expect you saw our little... altercation on the small patch of grass outside the entrance.'

'I did.'

'That young woman, Jacqueline, is (I'm given to understand), a friend of yours?'

'She's growing on me.'

'And what about Jennifer?'

'What about her?'

'Let's just say that she seemed a little... too keen on holding us there.'

'I expect she was waiting for me to turn up. I'm totally unreliable.'

'That's what I thought.' Before she could continue, the door opened again and Arthur hurriedly put his gun behind his back. Equally rapidly, Henderson lowered his hands as the German Ambassador, the minister's palm in the small of his back, was ushered emphatically into the lobby.

'Forgive me, Hans. I'm sure you understand that when the P.M. calls, we lesser mortals must jump to it.' Henderson stood up and brushed past Arthur and Caroline in order to open the outer door for the ambassador who, looking grave, stopped, turned and said to Sullivan,

'Oh, Ashley. You know, things could be so much worse.'

'Oh?'

'Ja. You could have Merkel as your boss!' Both men laughed. The ambassador acknowledged Caroline and Arthur with a slight bow and left, followed swiftly by Henderson. Sullivan turned to face them. His hand went to his forehead and then down across his face. Arthur indicated Sullivan's office and said,

'May we?' Speechless, Sullivan waved them in. When he entered, he made directly for his sideboard. Arthur said,

'Is it too early for brandy?' Then answered himself. 'I don't think so. Just a single please, Ashley.' Sullivan turned.

'You should have called,' he said.

'Beginning to lose faith in telephones, Ashley,' Arthur said. 'May I introduce you to Caroline Gagliardo-Patricelli?' Sullivan's face brightened perceptibly.

'How do you do?' Caroline said.

'How do you do?' he responded, taking Caroline's hand. Arthur took out his gun once more and aimed it at Caroline.

'And that's the lot of 'em, I think,' said Arthur.

'Are you certain?' said Sullivan.

'You have the other two who arrived with her?'

'Yes.'

'And I have the girl. I'll need her for a couple more hours but you can do what you like with her after that. Well, aren't you going to thank me?'

'Thank you, Arthur,' Sullivan said. 'I'm most grateful.'

'I should bloody well hope so.'

Sullivan made as if to take Caroline's arm but hesitated.

'It's all right,' said Arthur, 'She's unarmed and she'll not try anything whilst I've got this on her.' Caroline turned to Arthur.

'I am most disappointed in you, Mr. Shepherd,' she said, 'although not so disappointed, I think, as Geoffrey would have been.'

'Geoffrey would have done exactly the same, had he known what I know.' Arthur smiled. 'I am genuinely sorry we didn't have a chance to get to know one another better.'

'And I am not.'

Arthur moved over to Sullivan's side.

'Here,' he said and handed him his gun. 'Oh, don't look so hopeful, Caroline,' he said to her, 'and don't let the ministerial veneer fool you. Ashley here is former military. He knows what to do.'

'You'd better leave now,' Sullivan said.

'I'll see myself out.' A slight nod at Caroline, which wasn't returned and Arthur left the way he'd come in.

## Room 188

For the first time in days (apart from a few brief minutes of wakefulness in a French hotel), Vanessa Aldridge was by herself. She could only assume it was testament to the confidence that Caroline seemed to have in Arthur Shepherd. They had left her in St. Stephen's Tavern, a bar opposite the Houses of Parliament and as she sipped a glass of wine and wondered again how people managed to afford to drink at all in this bloody country, she once more tried, unsuccessfully, to take stock.

She'd found herself agreeing to do as Caroline ordered and remain in the pub until they returned. If they did not return within the hour, she was to head off to an address in South London, which Arthur had scribbled down on the back of a beermat. Thankfully, after only twenty five minutes, she looked up to see Arthur standing beside her table.

'Where's Caroline?'

'She's gone to pick up your friends. She'll meet us later. Come on: finish that up and we'll get off.'

'Was everything all right?'

'Oh, yes. Caroline is very good, isn't she?'

'You know, I've had to re-define that word a number of times over the last week. What's good; what's right; never mind what's legal. But that sort of thing doesn't bother you, does it?'

'Never used to. In fact, I never really thought about it until quite recently. But the world has suddenly got very... complicated. One isn't really sure of anything any more.' Arthur gave a little chuckle. 'I think you probably understand that.' Vanessa smiled at him. This odd-looking little man with his once-expensive, now shabby, rumpled suit; his thinning hair and pale complexion, could have been anyone at all: bank manager, shop-keeper, school teacher; but he wasn't. He was a secret agent and a killer and at the moment, the latest in the line of those to whom she'd had to surrender her will in the hopes of awakening from this nightmare.

The journey to Lambeth was short and uneventful. Shepherd was amiable and Vanessa felt safe. Until they arrived at Century House. There was something about the place. It was just an ordinary apartment building; dull and unattractive, on a bustling London street, but the entrance was overlooked by nothing but a high brick wall and although only feet from a busy trunk road, it was strangely quiet. In spite of the fact that she was warming to him, Vanessa was not a hundred percent content about entering this building with Arthur Shepherd. Still, she'd come this far. They seemed to stand before the entrance for some considerable time until for no apparent reason, there was a buzz and Arthur opened the door.

The entrance hall was rather grand and the concierge, behind his impressive, walnut-inlaid desk, smiled at them as they made for the lift. Once inside, she felt it descend. She would have been surprised to see the indicator on the wall outside tell the rest of the world that they were heading up to the ninth floor. As she stepped out of the lift, the unease upgraded itself to deep anxiety as she surveyed the dank, dusty corridor that greeted them. This floor had not been inhabited for many years, if ever. Arthur smiled he must have supposed reassuringly, as they rounded a corner and entered another lift. Arthur ran a card through a card-swipe and they were delivered two more floors down.

Vanessa relaxed a little as the doors opened and the quiet buzz of office-work entered her ears. Here and there, through frosted glass doors and even the occasional open one, she glimpsed normal people doing what appeared to be normal things and her mood began to lift. Arthur stopped at room 188, knocked on the door and ushered her inside. This room (and the one beyond it, as far as she could see) was stuffed with Dexion shelving on which was arrayed a bewildering variety of electronic equipment. There were any number of computer terminals and monitors, two of which were being operated. Vanessa stopped dead in her tracks as Bracewell and Jacqueline turned around to face her.

'Oh bollocks,' she said.

To her surprise, though, Bracewell smiled at her. He had a large plaster on his cheek. Clearly, he'd received a cut from the shattered mirror but otherwise seemed to have come out of his skirmish with Caroline fairly unscathed.

'Hullo again,' he said, brightly. 'Thought we'd lost you for good. Jennifer was spitting nails.' Jacqueline gave him a look and returned to her work. She seemed less equable than Bracewell.

'Is Jennifer all right?' Arthur asked him.

'She's fine. Her leg's playing her up more than she lets on though. She tried to chase after Caroline and our friend here but she had to give up after only a couple of minutes. She said she was going to rest up for a little while.'

'I'll pop round later and see her. Meantime, we need to track down Beasley. I have his home address and an address in the country but no phone number. Mind you, the way things are, I'm not sure ringing him would be such a good idea.'

'Jennifer phoned him,' said Bracewell.

'Really?'

'Yes, she used to work with him, apparently.'

'And she spoke to him?'

'Yes. Vanessa spoke to him as well, didn't you? Vanessa was not yet quite inured to the ways of these people. She ignored his question and instead said,

'Mr. Bracewell, I am so sorry about your face.'

'We all are,' said Arthur, unkindly. Vanessa went on.

'I think Caroline was a bit hyped up.' She thought a lie might help. 'She told me she wished she'd paid a little more attention before barging into the lift. I hope you aren't badly hurt.'

'Oh goodness me no!' said Bracewell. 'It was all quite... stimulating as a matter of fact.'

'Now, now Bracewell,' Arthur said. 'You're beginning to worry the poor girl. You and your stimulating. Vanessa? Did you speak to Beasley on the phone?'

'Yes I did.'

'What did you speak about?'

'I just asked him if he could help me. He seemed nice.'

'Did you notice anything... unusual or... difficult about the conversation?'

'Unusual?'

'Yes. Did it seem a little... stilted at all?'

'Stilted?'

'Yes. I mean was there a (I don't know) a... time-lag between you speaking and him replying?'

'I don't believe so. Why?'

'Oh, nothing. Just had a thought, that's all.'

'Care to share?' Bracewell asked.

'My uncle Jack,' Arthur said.

'Sorry?'

'My Uncle Jack: deaf as a post, he was. Couldn't use a phone at all.'

'Arthur?' It was Jacqueline.

'What is it?'

'My mother is Deaf. She uses a telephone perfectly well.'

'Perhaps your mother isn't as deaf as my Uncle Jack was.'

'Hang on,' Bracewell chimed in, 'this Beasley's deaf then, is he?'

'Completely mutton,' said Arthur.

'Mr. Shepherd!' They all turned to look at Jacqueline. That was extremely rude of you!' Arthur looked puzzled, then realised what he'd done and had the decency to look genuinely abashed.

'I'm sorry, Jacqueline. I didn't mean to suggest that your mother was...'

'It wasn't just that,' Jacqueline said. My mother is, as it happens, profoundly Deaf. She had scarlet fever as a child. But you shouldn't use terms like "mutton". It's not nice.' Arthur looked even more abashed. As a gay man, he had suffered more than his share of abusive terms which, although he was content to use them about himself, still rankled when he heard others use them. He'd also recently come to realise that he felt much the same way about terms like, "old git" and "slaphead".

'I am really sorry, Jacqueline. I promise you it won't happen again. Tell me about your mother and her telephone.'

'An induction loop,' said Bracewell. 'She probably uses an induction loop.'

'She does, Mr. Bracewell. It works very well.'

'A very clever system,' Bracewell said, 'that delivers a signal directly into a separate circuit found in most hearing aids nowadays. No extraneous noise and the quality, I'm told, is quite excellent. Any residual hearing is greatly enhanced.'

'Beasley doesn't wear a hearing aid,' Arthur said.

'Neither does my mother,' Jacqueline interjected, 'for most of the time, but she wears it indoors so that she can listen to the radio and television and... answer the telephone.'

'But why...' Bracewell stopped, tapped the side of his head and said to Arthur, 'Ah, I see. You had an idea that the fellow Vanessa spoke to might have been an imposter eh?'

'It's possible. But I suppose if Beasley has this induction loop system, then phone conversations are not likely to be a problem are they?' Arthur smiled and clapped his hands together. 'So,' he said. 'Time for a cuppa, I think. Bracewell?'

'Yes?'

'Put the kettle on, there's a good chap.' Bracewell affected a puzzled frown.

'I wonder if you might recall,' he said, 'what it was your last slave died of, Shepherd, that I may avoid a similar fate. Anyway, you'll have to do it yourself. Whilst I've been running errands on your behalf, work has been piling up and I need to get some of it shifted. I'm sure you'll excuse me.' Bracewell picked up his IN tray and left.

Arthur sighed.

'All right. Jacqueline, where does Bracewell keep his kettle?'

'It's in there,' she said, indicating a ubiquitous frosted-windowed door. Shall I do it?'

'No, no; I'll manage perfectly well. Besides, you appear busy.'

'I'm running a couple of searches.'

'Well done,' Arthur said, absently and went in search of tea.

Vanessa caught Jacqueline's eye and smiled. To her surprise, Jacqueline smiled back.

'Sorry about all that back there,' she said. 'Jennifer – Miss Carlisle – is so desperate to find out what happened to Geoffrey Wittersham. She's not normally so... impulsive.'

'Wittersham seems to inspire tremendous loyalty,' Vanessa said.

'You met him, I understand.'

'Yes. He was most... unusual.'

'In what way?' Vanessa thought about this but decided she couldn't really answer in a way that would quite explain.

'He was... handsome... charming... quite ruthless and possibly a little cruel. I sort of liked him and hated him at the same time.'

'Every so often one comes along,' Jacqueline said. 'People like Wittersham; people like Arthur and people like your Caroline. Marvels, even in a Golden Age.' Vanessa's eyes widened.

'She's not *my* Caroline!' she said and hesitated. 'Did she hurt you?'

'I'll feel it in the morning,' Jacqueline answered with a smile.

'You people are… amazing,' Vanessa went on. 'I mean the way you seem to control your feelings; objectify practically everything. Do you not bear any grudge at all against Caroline?'

'Of course not. She simply acted as one would expect; as did I. In fact I'm grateful to her for exposing a number of my weaknesses.'

'You see now; to most people, that would appear a bit… weird. Do you know what I mean?'

'Yes I do. I've not been doing this job that long. But training… alters you; makes you see things differently.' She fell silent, presented Vanessa with an odd little smile, took hold of the mouse and turned back to face the monitor again. Vanessa could think of nothing else to say and so sat, in silence until Arthur Shepherd returned and handed round the tea.

'Jacqueline?' he said, 'when you've finished that, can you pop round to Jennifer's with this, please?' He handed her an envelope. 'It's just to bring her up to speed; she needn't do anything. Tell her to stay in bed and let that leg sort itself out.' Jacqueline took the letter and popped it in her coat pocket.

'So what were you two chatting about, eh? Girly things?'

'Mr. Shepherd… Arthur,' said Jacqueline. 'May I ask you something.'

'Of course, my dear,' said Arthur, the all-wise.

'Do you really say all these things without thinking?'

'How do you mean?'

'I think it's part of an act. It makes people think you're not as thoughtful as you really are; makes them a little less wary of you.' Arthur smiled.

'Jennifer was right; you're going to be an excellent Council Worker.'

'She said that?' Jacqueline asked. Arthur was suddenly serious.

'She did. But do me a favour, would you?'

'Of course.'

'Just promise me you won't put all your eggs in one basket.'

'What do you mean?'

'There are dozens of jobs besides Cleaner, you know.' Jacqueline looked nonplussed.

'But you… and Miss Carlisle are…'

'I know what we are,' said Arthur. 'I know what we are.' Vanessa, knowing better than to get involved and watching this exchange from behind her teacup, took another sip. Jacqueline put down her cup. She swung her coat over her shoulder and said,

'I… I'd best be off.'

'What about your tea?'

'Erm... yes. Perhaps later.' She smiled briefly at Vanessa and opened the door. Bracewell was standing there.

'Oh,' he said to Jacqueline. 'Are you off somewhere?' She brushed past him without a word.

'Cleared that lot up already, eh Bracewell?' said Arthur. 'They're not paying you enough.'

'What's the matter with *her*?' Bracewell asked.

'Jacqueline? She's in a rush. Why are you back so soon?'

'Ah! I've had an idea,' Bracewell said.

## The Paragon

If there is ever a good time to be lurking in the bushes that surround the duck-pond on Blackheath, Vanessa was pretty certain that two o-clock on a Saturday afternoon is probably not it. Especially not when accompanied by two middle aged homosexuals and a plethora of odd-looking electronic equipment.

'What do you mean you don't have the exact address?' Bracewell hissed.

'It said only, "The Paragon, Blackheath". This is Blackheath and that,' Arthur said, indicating the great crescent of enormous Georgian houses before them, '... is The Paragon. Now just give me a few seconds and I'll tell you which one to aim your little gizmo at.'

Bracewell prepared the eavesdropping dish, which he'd adapted in order to send a signal, whilst Arthur peered at each house in turn through high-powered binoculars. Four houses in, he stopped.

'This looks promising,' he said.

'What can you see?'

'A grand piano and... yes, there's music on the stand. Hang on...' He sagged a little.

'What is it?'

'Elton John's Greatest Hits,' said Arthur. Thicker than I would have imagined.' He resumed his survey. 'Here's another piano. No. Electric. That's no use. Ah ha!'

'What?'

'Number twelve. There's a Steinway and a 'cello. If I can just make out what's on the music stand...' Vanessa and Bracewell remained still and silent until; 'Bingo,' Arthur said, quietly. "Karlheinz". It says "Karlheinz".'

'Stockhausen,' Bracewell said. 'This may be our man.' He put on a microphone headset, fiddled with some buttons and checked some dials.

'Four-hundred milliamps per metre,' he said. 'At plus or minus three decibels. BS6083.'

'I take it,' said Arthur, 'that that gibberish means he has an induction loop?'

'It does.'

'Right. So can you piggy-back onto it?'

'No. I thought it might be nice to spend the day feeding the ducks of course I can fucking piggy back onto it.'

'None taken. Pass me that headset, would you?' Arthur climbed into the headphone/mike combo and nodded to Bracewell, who did what he had to do. He looked at Arthur, who suddenly gave a thumbs up. Bracewell handed Vanessa a set of earphones, which she jabbed into her ear.

'Mr Beasely?' said Arthur,

'Speaking. Who is this?'

'My name's Henley; Arthur Henley. You probably don't remem…'

'The B.B.C.' said Beasley

'Eh?'

'We call it the "B.B.C." recording. Beethoven, Babbit, and Cage.' He chuckled. 'Did you enjoy it?'

'I certainly did. They play beautifully.'

'Thank you, thank you. Now, what might I do for you?'

'I was wondering if I might pick your brains.'

'Ha! Much good may it do you! Anyhow, fire away.'

'Well, I've recently come across two pieces by a chap name of Lear: Noel Lear.' There was only the merest pause before Beasley answered,

'I *have* heard of the fellow, yes. To which pieces do you refer?'

'Well one of them is called, "Reiterations"; the name of the other escapes me.' Again, a pause.

'Would it be, by any chance, "Limns"?'

'My word, you're right. I knew I could count on you!'

'And where did you come across these two pieces, Mr. Henley?'

'Oh they were on a compilation disk, which I picked up at Oxfam in the Gloucester Rd. Do you know it at all?'

'It's been a while since I've patronised the place but yes, I do know it. My daughter dropped a few things off there for me a few days ago, as a matter of fact.'

Bracewell became aware of a movement behind them. He turned slowly and tapped Arthur on the arm. Arthur was about to tell Bracewell where to go in no uncertain terms when he too caught sight of the figure standing behind them; an intense-looking young woman with masses of red hair, tumbling in Pre-Raphaelite tresses across her shoulders and arms.

So much hair, in fact, that at first, Bracewell failed to notice the small gun she was holding in her delicate, pale hand. Arthur didn't. Beasley said,

'I'm sure you'll remember Annabelle, Mr. Shepherd. Would you care for a cup of tea?'

'I've only just had one, actually, Mr. Beasley. Wouldn't mind a gin and tonic, if there's one on.'

Vanessa had yet to catch sight of Annabelle Beasley. She made an urgent signal to Arthur that he should remove his headset, which he did.

'That's not him!' she whispered. 'That's not Crawthorne Beasley.'

'Oh, I assure you it is,' Annabelle said.

Vanessa practically jumped into the duckpond.

## Noel Lear

'I am very pleased to meet you again, Mr. Shepherd,' said Crawthorne Beasley, gripping Arthur's hand. 'That is: pleased to meet Arthur Shepherd. Although Arthur Henley seems a perfectly nice chap, I do so prefer it when we can dispense with pretence, so to speak.'

'And have we "dispensed with pretence", Mr. Beasley?' said Arthur. Beasley chuckled again as only old men can and he released Arthur's hand.

'Probably not quite yet,' he said. 'Ours is a peculiar profession.'

'I take then, that you are not retired?'

'Chance would be a fine thing, eh? No, I had fully intended to take advantage of the Council's pension scheme but events rather intervened.'

'Your wife?' Beasley tilted his head back slightly and peered at Arthur.

'I knew who you were when I told you about her. And I wondered why I'd done so, at the time. I remain none the wiser.' Beasley turned his attention to Arthur's companions.

'You are Mr. Bracewell, I take it? I believe I knew your father. Captain Henry Bracewell, Dragoon Guards? Fine officer. Greatly missed. He would be immensely proud of you, I'm sure. You did very well to find the key to unlocking our little problem.'

Bracewell, seldom lost for words, was. Beasely smiled at Vanessa.

'Mr. Shepherd? I'm afraid you'll have to introduce me to this young woman.'

'Crawthorne Beasely? May I present Vanessa Aldridge?'

Vanessa very nearly responded to Beasley's "How do you do?" with a curtsey. Fortunately for all concerned, she managed to stop herself in time. Arthur handed Beasley a piece of paper. Beasley retrieved his glasses, which were dangling around his neck and read, '*Vanessa Aldridge to Crawthorne Beasley.* This was the message revealed by my little compositions, eh?'

'*Your* compositions?' said Arthur. Beasley held out his hand once more. Arthur took it.

'Arthur Henley? Noel Lear. Pleased to meet you. The hex code came our way some time ago. We were wondering how we might get it to you in a suitably secure manner and then we learned that you had been despatched to do me in at the South Bank. When I realised the extent to which you understood serial music, I came up with the idea of encoding it in a couple of pieces and sticking them on a CD. Annabelle was kind enough to drop it round for me and Mrs. Jempson assured me that she'd make sure you got it when you popped in to drop off your disguise on the Wednesday.'

'She made me pay for it,' said Arthur. 'Eight quid.'

'Worth every penny, as it turns out.'

'So you knew,' Bracewell said, 'that the hex code that Mulberry sent to Arthur was a Jacobean cipher but you didn't know the detail. However, you had the key to unlock it; and you slipped it to Arthur in that C.D.? Forgive me but why didn't you just kill Arthur, take his half of the message off him and decode it yourself?'

'In part, because we didn't know where Shepherd had it stashed and in part because we didn't have you, Mr. Bracewell.'

'But there must be any number of people who could have decoded it for you.'

'No doubt. However, at that point (and still, I'm afraid), we had no idea whom to trust. Mr. Shepherd had sought your assistance and we thought that if he'd made an error in doing so, the only thing we would have lost would have been Mr. Shepherd.'

'I like that reasoning,' Bracewell said. 'Very sound.'

'Actually,' Arthur responded, 'I was seeking Ricketts' help and that *was* an error of judgement. Grafton then tried to mislead me and it was pure chance that Bracewell entered the picture.'

'God protects fools and drunkards, Shepherd,' said Bracewell.

'I'm presuming,' said Arthur, that the encrypted message was from Geoffrey?'

'I'm certain of it,' Beasley said. 'On Monday morning, I received a text from him. It contained nothing but a hex code. We had agreed that, should anything go wrong with his mission in Rome, I should expect to receive such a text. The other text – the other half of the cipher- he sent to Ricketts.'

'Ricketts?!'

'I'm afraid so,' Beasley said. We had brought him into our confidence and it was he whom we had engaged to assist with our key. We made the error that *you* had managed to avoid. Ricketts had already been compromised. We'll probably never know exactly what happened in Mulberry's office but I think that Ricketts tried to enlist Mulberry's help. Mulberry managed to fire off the message to you before Ricketts, realising that Mulberry was not to be turned, killed him.'

'Presumably, Mulberry saw to it that Ricketts lost the cipher entirely so he couldn't possibly come up with an algorithm to unlock it.'

'That might have been why he turned up at Gloucester Rd,' Bracewell offered.

'So everything was Geoffrey making certain that whatever he's put in Vanessa's head arrives safely at your door,' Arthur said.

'Correct,' said Beasley.

'Er... you wouldn't happen to know anything about where Grafton fits into all this, would you?' Bracewell asked.

'We suspect that he and Ricketts had been working together for some time. Both had put in for transfers to Accounts.'

'But he never mentioned... ' Bracewell looked crestfallen.

'When I fetched up in your office,' Arthur said to him, 'Grafton must have already known that Mulberry was dead. He probably couldn't quite believe his luck; me handing him that code on a plate.'

'Hmm.' Bracewell responded, gloomily.

'But it did him no good. He was obviously panicked by the time he got to The Walsingham. All he had was "a villlainous palsy and a noble treachery" and that wasn't anywhere near enough to go on. Ricketts was surrounded by Constables and Grafton couldn't get near him.'

'I know nothing of this,' said Beasely. 'I suspect I shall have to be "brought up to speed" - as our American chums have it.'

'Is there anyone else involved that we ought to know about?' asked Arthur.

'I don't believe so. Auberon told you about Sullivan, didn't he?'

'Yes he did. Hang on: *what?*'

'Sullivan is H.M.G.'s finger in this little pie. We're not entirely certain what he's after but he needs to be kept an eye on.' Arthur realised his mouth was open.

'Auberon?' he said,

'Yes,' said Beasely, feigning puzzlement. 'Sir Auberon Nightingale.'

'You don't mean that he's...'

'...My Second-in-Command. He speaks very highly of you, Mr. Shepherd. That was one of the reasons we ran with you. He wasn't certain that you wouldn't kill me but fortunately, I knew that you had cleaned a Cleaner once before and probably knew that the despatch was a fraud.'

'Who sent it?'

'Still no idea, I'm afraid. We were rather hoping you might get to the bottom of it. We're certain it's all tied up with what's going on.'

'And what *is* going on, Mr. Beasely?' asked Vanessa.

'Ah, Miss Aldridge; that is very much what I'm hoping you might be able to tell us.'

'There's a couple of things I don't understand,' Vanessa said.

'You're not alone, Miss Aldridge, I assure you.'

'The first is: if Wittersham was able to contact you, why didn't he just text you the information he put in here?' She tapped the side of her head.

'It would have been far less secure, of course,' Beasely replied, 'but you're right; he must have had a very good reason for acting as he did. However, I'm not going to speculate until we learn a little more.'

'And the second thing is: if you are Crawthorne Beasley, who was it I spoke to on the phone?'

'Fuck,' said Arthur.

'I take it there's a problem,' Beasley said.

'Arthur's old friend, Jennifer Carlisle,' Bracewell said. 'She apparently telephoned you this morning.'

'I'm afraid not. I know her, of course but we've not spoken for a long time; several years in fact.'

'What's she playing at?' murmured Arthur. 'Mr. Beasley,' he said, looking up, 'I'm afraid I have to leave. And may I ask that you do nothing until you hear from me? I'm sorry, Vanessa; you'll have to hang on a little while longer. I'm certain you'll be safe here. Bracewell? Can you come with me, please?'

'Please?' echoed Bracewell. 'Bloody hell it must be serious.'

## Legoland

Bracewell unlocked the car and made for the driver's seat.

'I'll drive,' Arthur said. Bracewell, without comment, tossed him the keys. As they drove over the heath, Bracewell asked,

'You think that Jennifer's involved in this?'

'I'm certain of it. But what worries me at the moment is that I've probably sent Caroline into a trap. I handed her over to Sullivan.'

'What?'

'Oh, it was a ploy. He's no match for her. And I gave him an empty gun to threaten her with.'

'You'll have to start at the beginning, Shepherd,' said Bracewell.

'Caroline told me that she and Vanessa, along with the diplomat who helped her escape and a D.P.S.D. agent arrived together this morning. She took Caroline round to Mrs Jempson's in the hope of tracking me down and the other two went to the Foreign Office.'

'Oh dear.'

'Precisely. They failed to check in and Caroline was on her way round there when I collared her. I told her I reckoned they may well have run into our friend Sullivan. She, of course, had no idea what had been going on lately so I gave her a brief run-down and she reckoned the best way to find out what had happened to her companions was for me to hand her over to Sullivan.'

'A bit risky.'

'I thought so. But she's a good Worker, Bracewell. If anyone could persuade Sullivan to see reason, as it were, she could.'

'By "see reason", I expect you mean spill his guts before she did something slow and painful to him.'

'Quite so.'

'So what's the problem?'

'Just before we left for Beasley's, I asked Jacqueline to pop round to Jennifer's with a note telling her where we were up to. Thankfully, it was before you came up with that induction loop idea but Jennifer now knows enough to put a crimp in Caroline's plan.'

'So where are we going?'

'I'm going to take a chance on the F.C.O.'

Arthur managed to get to Horse Guards Rd. from Blackheath in a little under half an hour. An ashen-faced Bracewell slid over into the driving seat as Arthur jumped out.

'Wait here,' said Arthur. 'And if any traffic wardens turn up, shoot them.' He ran up the steps, along King Charles St and into the F.C.O. building. By the time he arrived at Henderson's desk, he was a little out of breath and rather dishevelled. Henderson eyed him with something approaching terror.

'He's not in,' Henderson said, hurriedly. 'I don't know where he is.'

Arthur reached over, took hold of the open diary on the desk and turned it around. He read aloud,

'"Hold all calls. PUS at M.I.6." "PUS"? I take it that's an in-joke?'

'Might be,' Henderson said.

'You've been most helpful, Mr. Henderson. Thank you. However, if he finds out that I'm on my way to meet him, as it were, I'm sure you can imagine what I might do to spoil your plans for the rest of the day.' Henderson could and he set about erasing the conversation entirely from his memory. Arthur ran back out to the car and climbed in the passenger side.

'He's at Legoland. Let's go.'

'What are you going to do when you get there?' Bracewell asked.

'Improvise.'

Ten minutes later, Arthur was keying in the pass-code for Vauxhall Cross. The door opened and he and Bracewell entered, clipping on their S.I.S. identity badges as they did so.

'Afternoon, Lionel,' said Arthur to the man at the desk. 'Have you had a visitation from Ashley Sullivan today, by any chance?'

'The MP? I only came on at two, Mr Henley. Let me have a look.' He perused his screen for few seconds. 'Doesn't look like it.', he said at last. 'Shall I call someone for you?'

'No, that's all right. May I?' Arthur asked, indicating the monitor.

'Of course, Mr. Henley,' said Lionel. Arthur stepped behind the desk.

'Nightingale was here earlier,' he said to Bracewell. 'And a Mrs. Charlton has just arrived. Thanks very much Lionel.' Arthur and Bracewell made for the lift.

'That's Jennifer Carlisle's stage-name,' Bracewell said.

'I know, said Arthur.'

'Are we still improvising?' asked Bracewell.

'Fraid so.'

## The Bowels

'Mornin' Arthur! Don't often see you in the bowels these days.' Samuel Carnegie, Scotsman, twat.

'Try to avoid them as much as possible.'

'Ha ha. "Void". "Bowels", they should have you in the crossword section.'

Arthur didn't much like Carnegie and was a little miffed to have run into him so soon.

'Who do you have in here at the moment?' They were in the lowest section of Vauxhall Cross where M.I.6 and M.I.5 had a suite of cells. Contrary to popular belief, there was no torture chamber but there were several extremely creative members of the military on duty when it got busy.

'There's no-one in here, Arthur. Just as well; we're ridiculously short staffed.' Arthur's hand shot out and grabbed Carnegie by the throat. The movement was so swift that Bracewell gave a start. The Scotsman would have instantly felt the pressure in his head as the blood fought to leave it.

'Where are they?' Arthur said. He realised that Carnegie would be toying with offering variations on the theme of *"I don't know what you mean"* but he would already be feeling faint, unconsciousness only seconds away. He might pretend that Arthur was gripping him so tightly that he couldn't speak but even he would realise that Arthur was doing no such thing. Arthur really was very good. He loosened his grip slightly, enough to allow the ringing in the man's ears to ease a little and to give him back a sense of hope that he might yet be allowed to live.

'Sam,' Arthur said quietly, 'I know how these people work. I *am* one, for fuck's sake and you've been left in the lurch good and proper. You owe them nothing – least of all your life. Now I know you have a number of people in these cells and I'm certain that you'd very much like to see daylight again. So for once in your life, do the sensible thing and tell me who you have here and where they are.' Carnegie was about to speak, when Jennifer appeared. She took aim at Bracewell and asked,

'Where is Vanessa?'

'I don't know,' said Bracewell. Jennifer shot him. He went down and lay still.

'Where is Vanessa?' she said to Arthur.

'With Crawthorne Beasley,' said Arthur, instantly, his hands flying skywards.

'And where is that?'

'Blackheath. The Paragon. No 12.'

'Has Beasely found out what she's carrying?'

'Yes. It's a message from Geoffrey.'

'Why thank you, Arthur. You are being accommodating today.'

'I've been paying into that pension scheme for years. I'd be most upset not to collect.'

'Yes, about that.' Arthur glanced round. To his right, stood Ashley Sullivan. 'Unfortunately, Arthur, there have had to be… cutbacks. I'm afraid that a great deal of the Council's funding has been… made subject to review.'

'Careful, Ashley,' Jennifer said.

'Oh come now. I think we can pretty much call this checkmate, don't you? What harm could it do?'

'Yes, Jennifer,' Arthur said, 'Do let him gloat.'

'Ashley, Arthur is a very dangerous man. I'm minded to kill him even before we check out that address. Now don't say anything else. Carnegie? Get his gun.'

'What?'

'Get his fucking gun, Carnegie. I've got him covered.' Gingerly, Carnegie felt inside Arthur's jacket and removed his gun. 'Now,' said Jennifer, 'give it to me then go and get Grafton. Ashley, go with him.'

When they had gone, Jennifer lowered her gun and said, in an urgent whisper,

'Sorry about Bracewell. I've just winged him. Had to keep up appearances.' Sure enough, Bracewell stirred and groaned a little. 'Now we need to free Caroline and the others. Here.' She returned Arthur's gun to him.

'Right. Follow me.' She led him down a maze of corridors until they arrived at a steel door. It was open. Beyond it, evidently surprised to see them were Grafton, Carnegie and Sullivan. Jennifer held them all at gunpoint.

Grafton couldn't have signalled his intention better if he had used a set of semaphore flags and so, before the gun had cleared his pocket, Arthur had levelled his own pistol and fired twice. Too late. Grafton got off a shot and Jennifer staggered backwards. She crashed into the wall and fell heavily. Arthur fired again; two more shots. Grafton clutched at his chest and collapsed. The others raised their hands. Keeping his gun on them, Arthur knelt beside Jennifer and felt her neck. She stirred and opened her eyes.

'Fuck it,' she said.

'I'm sorry Jennifer. I had no idea...'

'It's all right, Arthur,' she said, weakly. 'Bound to happen sooner or later. Pity it had to be Grafton; a bloody pen-pusher.' She laughed and began to cough. 'Still, I'm glad Beasely got the message from Geoffrey. Was it worth it?'

'I don't know,' said Arthur, looking wretched.

'What?'

'I'm afraid I lied, Jennifer.'

'What?'

'Yes, you see, he hasn't yet done it.'

'What do you mean?'

'Beasley hasn't got the message from her... so you can get up now and stop pretending that Grafton shot you.' He called out, 'And you, Grafton, can stop pretending that there were real bullets in this gun.' He tossed over the Walther that Jennifer had given him and retrieved his own from Jennifer's pocket. For good measure, he picked up Jennifer's gun.

'It wasn't a bad switch, Jennifer,' he said, 'but you're right: you're not nearly as quick as you used to be. And the fact that I got off two clear shots at Grafton before he fired confirmed it. By the way, if that's you're idea of winging poor old Bracewell, you'd better go back to marksmanship training. He's going have a right old bruise in his chest and no mistake.'

As if on cue, Bracewell appeared, staggering a little.

'Fucking hell. You didn't tell me it would hurt that much, Shepherd?'

'Didn't I? I'm sure I did.'

'Thanks for making me wear that vest. Sorry I called you neurotic. Fucking hell: that hurts! Ow!'

'Stop complaining, Bracewell and open those cell doors. I'll keep an eye on this little lot.'

'Stuart?' It was Grafton. 'I'm so sorry.' Bracewell covered his astonishment well.

'So am I,' he said. Bracewell grabbed hold of Carnegie and sat him down at the computer terminal. Carnegie knew what to do. There was buzz and a click and every cell door opened simultaneously. Bracewell walked down the row.

'They're empty, Shepherd,' he said.

'What, all of them?'

'All of them.'

'All right, you got me,' Arthur said to his captives. 'Where are they?' Of course, no-one spoke. Carnegie and Grafton seemed the easiest to terrify. Arthur didn't want to use Grafton in case it upset Bracewell so it was Carnegie who copped it. Arthur fetched him a single smack across the jaw and he went down on one knee.

'Shepherd,' he managed, 'Please… I don't know where they are.' Arthur hit him again. He noticed Sullivan beginning to look worried, which was exactly what he wanted. He only had to make as if to hit Carnegie again and Sullivan made a bolt for it. Bracewell went for him and went flying against a wall. Arthur had tripped him up.

'Come back, you idiot,' Jennifer yelled, as Sullivan disappeared around the corner.

'What the bloody hell…' Bracewell began. Arthur tossed him Jennifer's gun. Lock these two up, Bracewell. I'm going after Sullivan.' He tore off after the Under Secretary of State.

Keeping his distance, Arthur was surprised when Sullivan, at one point, turned left instead of right. All became clear when the Minister thrust open a set of fire doors and ran outside onto the back terrace of Victoria Cross. From behind a pillar, Arthur saw Sullivan scurry down to the jetty and jump into a small motorboat.

'Aw, shit and corruption!' said Arthur and took off back indoors. He hurried back to the cell-block and to his dismay came upon two figures lying on the floor. Jennifer and Carnegie were nowhere to be seen. Bracewell was bleeding from a deep gash to his head. Grafton was dead.

'She killed him, Arthur,' Bracewell said. 'He got between us. He saved my life.' Arthur removed his handkerchief, pressed it to Bracewell's head and placed Bracewell's own hand on it.

'You're hurt badly. Hold that in place. I'll send someone down here. I'll need your car keys.' Bracewell fumbled in his pocket and handed them over.

## Scrabble

'That was Mr. Shepherd,' said Crawthorne Beasley as he resumed his seat opposite Vanessa. 'My turn, I believe. Let me see… If I use your "O" from "SOB" I have "JUKEBOX". That's 77 plus a triple word score, giving me…'

'What did he want?'

'Oh, he had a few things to tell me.'

'What things?' Beasley leaned back in his chair.

'Disturbing and… disappointing things,' he said, quietly. He was thoughtful for a while. 'He thinks we should go ahead and try to extract that message right away.' Vanessa felt her stomach heave.

'And what do you think?'

'I'm inclined to agree,' he said. He stood up and left the room, returning a few moments later with Annabelle, who was carrying a small, wooden box. Beasley picked up the Scrabble board and letters and placed them on top of the piano.

'We can finish that later,' he said with a smile. She knew he was trying to make her feel better. A "later" is a nice thing to have. Annabelle placed the box on the table and went over to the window. As she closed the blinds and the room darkened, Vanessa's sense of unease returned.

'Now, I know it may be difficult but I should very much like you to relax and try to clear your mind.' He sat on Vanessa's right, with Annabelle, on her left. Annabelle gave her what she thought must have been a reassuring smile.

'Now, Miss Aldridge, I have in this little atomiser, a dilution of oxytocin.'

'Oxy-what?'

'Oxytocin. It's a compound that makes a subject more susceptible to hypnosis.'

'It's probable that Geoffrey used it on you,' said Beasley, 'but if you'd rather not…' She wasn't happy about it, but this was what she had wanted ever since she'd learned what Wittersham had done to her and she wanted it to work.

'All right,' she said. Annabelle squeezed the nozzle once and a cool mist hit her face. As soon as it did so, she recalled the little spray that Wittersham had produced in the car in Rome; the one he said he'd been given as a freebie on the plane. She couldn't recall him having used it it but then, she couldn't recall a lot of things.

At the far end of the now gloomy room, a dim light came on. From Vanessa's point of view, it was a mere spot – a star in a twilight sky.

'Now,' Beasley said, 'I'd simply like you to look at the light and relax.' She did her best. After a minute, she had a sudden sense of anxiety and her eyes flicked over towards Beasley. He was still there.

'Please,' he said, 'try to concentrate on the light.'

'Mr Beasley,' Vanessa said. 'There was nothing like this going on when Geoffrey Wittersham put this thing in my brain.'

'No, indeed. However, *writing* a symphony and *playing* one require entirely dissimilar circumstances. I beg you: please be patient.' Vanessa took a deep breath and settled herself once more. This time, she reckoned it was a good five minutes before she spoke again.

'Mr Beasley?' There was no reply. 'Mr. Beasley, what...' And then she noticed that the light, which had been a mere pinprick, was slowly increasing in size. It grew bigger and brighter and for a second, she wondered if someone was moving it towards her. Very soon, it was almost too bright to look at and she had to shield her eyes. Suddenly, the glare diminished and she found herself sitting in her boss's Mercedes.

Outside the car, she could hear the muffled, yet clearly recognisable sounds of a Roman morning. As she looked round, she became aware that someone was in the car with her. Sitting in the passenger seat was Geoffrey Wittersham.

## Blackfriars Bridge

Arthur had reason to be grateful to Bracewell for a number of things. Right now, he was grateful that he'd chosen to buy an Audi. It was one of those chases where he knew he'd have to break the speed limit and pretty soon, there'd be a police car or two taking an interest; but he couldn't bother about that now. Along the Albert Embankment, left and over Lambeth Bridge. He glanced to his right. There was no sign of the boat. He did what he could to scour the banks of the river but he saw nothing. At sixty miles per hour, he hurtled down Milbank and Abingdon Rd, weaving in and out of traffic and occasionally on the wrong side of the road.

But the piece de resistance came as he set off the wrong way around Parliament Square. As he plunged onto the southern carriageway and the traffic heading towards him veered aside, Arthur recalled that, in 1868, the world's first ever traffic lights were erected on the corner that was rapidly approaching. He took some delight in completely ignoring them, whipping right, running straight through another set of lights and out onto Westminster Bridge. Again, he glanced downstream. There was a motorboat, certainly but it was currently passing beneath Hungerford Bridge and it was difficult to discern it clearly. Looking in his mirror, it appeared that he'd got away with Parliament Square. No doubt some zombie who has to stare at C.C.T.V. screens all day would alert someone somewhere. The Met might send a car if there was one nearby. Arthur made a snap decision. He would miss out Waterloo Bridge and run on down to Blackfriars.

Along York Rd and round the IMAX roundabout, he suddenly opted to take a back route. It was a good call. Being a Saturday, the roads were relatively clear and in no time, he was haring along Blackfriars Road and out onto the bridge. As always, there were roadworks. He swung the Audi in behind a dumper tuck and jumped out, clutching a couple of sheets of paper as though he knew what he was doing. He picked up a yellow hard-hat from the seat of the dumper and walked briskly over to the Eastern side of the bridge.

There was no sign of the boat. Arthur was about to run back to the Audi when from beneath one of the arches, Sullivan's motorboat appeared. He was coming to terms with the possibility that he might end up chasing Sullivan to Tilbury when a police launch glided beneath him. Instinctively, he pulled away from the edge. He heard the squawk of a single blast on a siren and saw the blue light come on, as the boat steered towards Sullivan's craft.

'Oh you've got to be kidding,' Arthur said to himself, as the launch pulled alongside. The tide was coming in and with their engines cut, both boats began to drift back towards Blackfriars Bridge. Arthur scurried back to the car and opened the boot. Inside was a whole plethora Bracewell's bits and pieces. Arthur wasn't sure how to work it but how hard could it be? He was able to identify the adaptations Bracewell had added to send the signal to the induction loop, which he untangled and discarded. What he was left with, he recognised as a pretty standard eavesdropping device.

Back at the rail, Arthur pointed the dish at Sullivan's little boat with the police launch still alongside. He pressed what he thought was the trigger but could hear nothing. In frustration he began fiddling with various switches and knobs until he realised that he hadn't put the headphones on. With the situation rectified, he was delighted to discover that he could hear voices. Focussing in, he was able to identify Sullivan, who appeared to be turning on the charm.

'Of course. Had I realised, I would certainly not have borrowed it.'

'Yes, sir, but ignorance of the Law is not an acceptable defence, is it? You must at least familiarise yourself with the basics of navigation before you can pilot any vessel in the Port of London, sir. That way, we avoid accidents. You're very lucky nothing was coming the other way through that arch.'

'As you say, officer, safety must always be our number one priority. As I was saying to the Prime Minister only yesterday...'

'I'm afraid we're going to have take your vessel in tow, sir.'

'But I'm only going over there!' Arthur saw he was pointing towards the Southwark side of the river at a point downstream of Blackfriars.'

'I'm sorry, sir. Thames By-Laws – Permanent Directions to Mariners 2011, Para 13 subsection 1 states that all vessels should notify London Vessel Traffic Services of their intention to navigate through a bridge arch against the prevailing direction of traffic flow. Any breach may result in a fine or the impounding of said vessel.'

'Sodding priceless!' Arthur chuckled. 'Nicked by the River Police.'

'Well, where are you planning to take me?' Sullivan asked.

'We'll take you just downstream of Southwark Bridge so that you can navigate to Bankside Pier in a safe manner, sir.'

'Oh, very well. Do let's get on with it!'

'Just a few formalities first, sir. Now, if you could read this form...'

There was a movement at Arthur's right elbow. He turned to see a burly man in hard hat and hi-vis jacket.'

'Wot you doin',' said the man.

'I was... er... checking the... um...fore and aft conduits,' Arthur said, tapping a bit of the rail with his knuckle. 'They seem fine. Well done.'

'Hang on. Don't I know you?' Arthur had already recognised the man whom he had felled at Tate Modern on Wednesday.

'You may have seen me at... Head... Bridge... Office... quarters,' he said.

'Wait a minute,' said the man, his fists clenching. You're the cunt that swore at my daughter. And put me in A&E for a day and a half. You wanker!' He lunged at Arthur, who stepped backwards, causing the man to stumble on some piping and twist around. Never one to look a gift horse in the mouth, he jabbed the man in much the same place and with much the same effect as he had at the Tate. As the man lay motionless on the ground in front of him, staring in mute disbelief at the sky, Arthur removed his own hard-hat and placed it over the man's face.

'Sorry,' he said, 'I'm in a bit of a hurry.'

Leaping into Bracewell's car, he sped away over Blackfriars Bridge and in a few minutes, he was re-crossing the river, this time via Southwark Bridge.

Sullivan had just been cast off by the River Police and was drifting, with the tide, towards the mooring at Bankside. Arthur had ditched Bracewell's car and now watched as Sullivan, clearly no expert, clambered out of the little boat and secured it to the pier. Tidying himself and even running a comb through his hair, to Arthur's puzzlement, he made for Tate Modern. Arthur followed him into the building.

## The Song

Geoffrey Wittersham held Vanessa's hand and smiled at her. As is the case in any dream, the fact that this was impossible didn't occur to her. She felt a calm and a contentment that she had seldom felt even before all this. She became aware that Geoffrey had his fingers in the palm of her hand and was tapping. She had no idea how long this went on but eventually he stopped, closed her hand and opened his mouth.

From miles away, she heard it. A clear, yet mellow keening. It took some moments before Vanessa realised that the sound was coming from Geoffrey himself. It was the most beautiful thing she had ever heard: familiar and yet breathtakingly fresh. Presently, Vanessa recognised that the pattern was repeating itself. The sound seemed to bore into her and her chest began to resonate in sympathy until she too began to sing. Her own voice displeased her. Compared to the ethereal nature of Geoffrey's song, hers was a poor thing. But gradually, as the song repeated, it seemed she became able to reproduce the tones more accurately. She knew that Geoffrey was singing at the higher end of his range and that she, to match it, was having to push her own voice lower. The occasional wavering dissonances produced by conflicting tones became fewer until at last, both she and Geoffrey were singing in perfect unison.

She wanted the song never to end and it seemed as though she might get her wish. For hour after hour, it felt, she and Geoffrey sang the ethereal duet, never tiring, always looking forward with bright expectation to each note, whilst the savour of the preceding one yet lingered.

And then it was over. She felt bereft; as though she had lost a lover. A great wallowing emptiness opened before her. She desperately wanted the song and the prospect of not hearing it again began to cause almost unbearable physical pain, as though her entire body had toothache. As had happened on the mountain, she began to sense the curtain being torn: the tear moving towards her and threatening to rip into her. And then a gentle, soothing voice eased through the pain. It was Crawthorne Beasely's voice.

When Vanessa finally came to her senses, she became aware that Beasley was still speaking to her.

'…you've done very well, Vanessa and now, I'd like you to rest. You have been on a journey; a journey of discovery, of pleasure and of pain but now, you are here with us and we will take care of you…'

'Is it done?' Vanessa asked.

'What do you think?' Vanessa half-remembered the dream but the more she tried to grasp it, the more it slipped away. Yet paradoxically, the more it did so, the less agitated she became. She smiled.

'Thank you so much, Mr. Beasley,' she said to him. I hope you got what you wanted.'

'We seldom get what we want,' he said. 'But I think, as a friend of mine once said, we may have just got what we need.'

## A Bit Theatrical, The French

Arthur glanced at the sign, which told him that the Carsten Holler exhibition in the Turbine Hall remained closed to the public and he smiled. Sullivan was making his way through the crowds and presently, he stepped into one of the lifts. Three others entered with him. One young man with a beard, who could have been going anywhere and a young couple whom he heard discussing Joan Miro as they entered. He gambled that they were going up to look at the Surrealists (more fool them). He watched the indicator on the lift. It stopped one floor above. Arthur ran up the stairs. At the top, he practically ran into the young man with the beard who was heading for the toilets.

The Surrealists were on the third floor so provided no-one else had got in on this floor, the next stop was likely to be Sullivan's destination. Arthur took the next flight two steps at a time, arriving at the landing just in time to see a grey-suited leg disappear through a door marked "Gallery Staff Only."

Slowly, he inched open the door. Beyond it was a corridor, at the end of which, a large window provided a fine view of the dome of St. Paul's Cathedral. Listening at each door in turn, Arthur edged along the corridor. At a door marked "Acquisitions", he stopped. On the other side, he could hear voices – male and female. After listening for some time, he finally drew his gun and stepped into the room.

'I'm sorry,' he said, 'but I can't hear a bloody thing through that. Quality door, is that. Must have cost a packet. Hello, Ashley, how are we after our little boat trip? And Miss LaSalle; I thought I recognised the voice. And tea as well!' he added gleefully. 'How civilised.' It was a good entrance; not one of his best but it had a satisfying effect. Neither party was expecting him and he liked it when that happened. Sullivan spluttered,

'Oh God! How did you...'

'Oh good grief, you silly man,' Miss LaSalle said to him. 'He's obviously followed you here.'

'But how?'

'Well what you do is,' said Arthur, 'you look where the person you're after is going and then you go there as well. It's quite simple, really.'

'I apologise for my associate, Mr. Shepherd. He really is not very good under pressure. Oh, he's smooth as you like and quite bright when he needs to be but well, he's probably not as used to this sort of thing as we are, eh? Tea? It's just made.'

'Not at the moment, thanks. I'm bursting for a pee, as it happens. Perhaps we might just get on?'

'As you wish,' said Miss LaSalle. 'Er, you do realise that you won't leave here alive, don't you?' Arthur felt a shiver. Miss La Salle – his Bird Goddess - was threatening his life. That wasn't worrying him over much but he was certainly discomfited by the fact that he appeared to be becoming turned on at the prospect. He tried to ignore it.

'That sounds like it's from page one of the textbook. You appear to have transformed from Gallery Assistant to Baddie.' Miss LaSalle laughed.

'You are a one, Mr. Shepherd and no mistake. My name is Louise de Sauveterre.' Arthur's nascent arousal diminished instantly. The Bird Goddess had flown.

'D.P.S.D./S.I.S. liaison, Paris,' he said, unable to disguise his disappointment.

'Oh, you've heard of me?'

'Don't sound too pleased. It just means I'll be doubly careful.'

'Ashley was just telling me how you captured Jennifer and the others over at Vauxhall Cross. A very lively tale indeed. And I suppose you now think our goose is cooked?'

'Well... simmering nicely, anyway.'

'I'm afraid not. You see, I received a telephone call from Jennifer several minutes before Ashley arrived. She has told me that she was able to escape your man with relative ease and is now on her way to Blackheath.' Sullivan heaved a sigh and sat down.

'Oh, thank God,' he murmured.

'Now, Mr. Shepherd, where would you like me to begin?'

Sullivan's head spun around.

'What?' he said.

'Oh come on, Ashley,' said Arthur. 'What happened to "checkmate" and "gloating" and what-have you?'

'Louise!' Sullivan hissed. 'Don't…'

'Oh, stop it, Ashley.'

'Yes, stop it, Ashley. Let the lady speak.' He addressed Mlle de Sauveterre once again.

'Was it your idea to ease the drain on the exchequer by offing venerable Council Workers?'

'It wasn't, as a matter of fact. Actually, I haven't really involved myself in that side of things – apart from getting some of my chums on the continent to kill some of your chums on the continent. It suited Ashley's little enterprise, as well as my own.'

'You mean you were after Carlisle's little insurance policy?' Mlle de Sauveterre smiled but only, Arthur noticed, after a faint shadow of uneasiness had crossed her face.

'I'm impressed,' she said. 'Don't tell me: it was Jennifer, wasn't it. I knew she wouldn't be able to resist telling you.'

It hadn't been Jennifer, as it happened. Nightingale had told him that alongside the attempts of Sullivan to appropriate money from the Council, there had been another little game unfolding, concerning the legacy of Sir James Carlisle. Arthur, naturally, lied.

'Yes. We're old friends, you see.'

'I know. We were rather hoping she might be able to persuade you around to our way of thinking but… ah well.'

Nightingale hadn't said what Carlisle's secret was, only that it was in imminent danger of being revealed. The implications of it being discovered would apparently be catastrophic for the Council and for the Country: with capital "C"s.

'So Carlisle had a little secret of his own, then?'

'Several, we believe, any one of which could unseat the governments of several world powers. Including, happily, my own. You see, Mr Shepherd, you probably think that you know all about secrets but there are secrets and then there are Secrets. And Secrets are kept secret even from the people who keep the greatest secrets of all. That is how secret they are.'

'So, we're talking secrets then, are we?'

'Oh, yes indeed.'

'A veritable treasure trove of secrets?'

'Precisely.'

'Don't tell me: "who really shot Kennedy"; "how Hitler got to South America" sort of thing?' He suddenly had a nasty thought. 'Oo, er… nothing about Elvis at all, is there?'

'Oh dear: you disappoint me. There are far more valuable secrets than that, Mr. Shepherd. I thought someone with your imagination might have had a more… considered outlook on the way the world is. Oh, of course, they *are* political secrets; but then aren't all secrets political? Why do you think I've thrown in with Mr Sullivan?'

'I was wondering…'

'I would say it was quite simple, but it isn't. Motives are so much more difficult to fathom nowadays, don't you find?'

'Louise, for God's sake…' Sullivan was almost pleading. She looked at him.

'Poor Ashley,' she said. 'Hubris, Mr Shepherd. Ashley thought he knew what he was doing. You see, he made the same mistakes all politicians make when dealing with those who protect their nation: he believed he was the one in control. You and your Council would have been able to tell him, wouldn't you?'

'Kill him, for Christ's sake,' said Sullivan.

'He's the one with the gun, Ashley. Or hadn't you noticed?'

That was the point at which Arthur realised he needed to be a little less casual about this. Sullivan knew that Mlle de Sauveterre had something up her sleeve that trumped his little handgun. She went on,

'Besides, isn't it something of a Council tradition that you aim to coerce your enemy into working with you, Mr. Shepherd?'

'We've already tried that, for fuck's sake!' Sullivan yelled

'Ah, yes,' said Arthur, 'the letter from Geoffrey. I presume you had a little help from Jennifer with that. You know, I'm ashamed to say that it almost worked. I was all set to kill Caroline Gagliardo-Patricelli and fight your corner, Ashley. Fortunately, my boss is an utter bastard and a lot cleverer than I gave him credit for.' Sullivan sneered,

'Pity for her you didn't speak to Nightingale before you handed Caroline over to me, eh?'

'Oh, I did. Sorry, did I not mention that?' Arthur watched with satisfaction as Mlle de Sauveterre's smile faltered ever so slightly and Sullivan's lip curled even more floridly.

'Don't give me that. Why would you hand her to me? And give me her gun?'

'Oh, she just wanted to find out where you were keeping her friends. And the gun wasn't loaded. I'm surprised you're still alive, frankly. She must have thought you posed no kind of threat whatsoever.' Sullivan's face fell. Arthur realised that the Minister was more scared than he was letting on. It had obviously all got terribly out of hand – as it often did when you played with the big boys. Sullivan said,

'Look, I really don't know where they are! I thought they were at Vauxhall Cross. I was as surprised as you to find those cells empty.'

'Oh, I wasn't that surprised. In fact, I'm fairly certain that Nightingale took them. He was signed into the system at 07:50 and out again at 14:37. There were three others signing out at precisely the same time. But the oddest thing; I searched and searched but to no avail. They hadn't signed in.'

'I don't believe you,' said Sullivan, clearly thinking he'd caught Arthur out. 'If you knew they weren't there, why bother going down to the cells.'

'Well, trying to smoke out Jennifer, I suppose. Then blow me if you don't turn up as well. Stroke of luck, really: led me straight here.'

'But you beat up Carnegie when he wouldn't tell you where they were.'

'Yes, I'm not proud of that. Luckily for him, you cracked and ran before I could do any real damage.'

'Oh, Ashley,' said Mlle de Sauveterre, with mock reproof. 'He flushed you like a pheasant and you led him straight here. Bravo, Mr. Shepherd.'

'Thanks. Anyway, mademoiselle, you were saying: secrets.'

'Ah yes. Since 1945, the Council has amassed an extraordinary number of (what do they call them nowadays…?) "Factoids." That's it.' Arthur was starting to get it.

'And Sir James found them useful, did he?' he asked.

'Oh yes. He kept many powerful people at bay with them, Mr. Shepherd. A fearsome blackmailer was Sir James.'

'Needs must eh?'

'Oh indeed. I don't judge him. In fact I plan to do much the same thing myself, once I have my hands on them.'

'Right,' said Arthur. 'Anyway, look: I'd like to wrap this up so what say we toddle off to Century House and I'll introduce you to the Constables. Awfully nice chaps.'

'Oh, no need for that, Mr. Shepherd. I happen to be very well acquainted with a surprising number of them. I believe you know Sergeant Bligh?' Mlle. De Sauveterre leaned to her left and focussed on a point a little way behind Arthur. He held up his hands and Sergeant Bligh removed the gun he was holding.

'Hello again, Mr Shepherd.'

'Sergeant Bligh. Thrown in with the baddies, eh?'

'Looks like it.'

'Before or after Mulberry?' There was no answer. Arthur reckoned it would have been after. The inquest may well have been getting a little too close for comfort and Ms. Bligh had been offered more than even a Constable could ignore. Arthur was deeply saddened by this turn of events. A Constable betraying the Council? Why, it was worse even than Jennifer's offence.

'Now,' said Sullivan, 'can we *please* kill him?'

'You know, you can go right off some people, Ashley,' said Arthur. 'Mlle. De Sauveterre,' he went on, 'may I ask a question.'

'Of course.'

'This place,' he said, looking around. 'Tate Modern, I mean.'

'Yes?'

'How long have you…?'

'French Secret Service? Oh many years, Mr. Shepherd. Although my… associates and I have been here only a matter of months. M.I.6 are in the d'Orsay, you know.'

'Really?'

'Yes. They wanted the Louvre but… well, I'm sure you understand.'

'Yes, yes, perfectly. I take it you're not acting officially?'

'No,' she said, with a smile. 'Now, I think that's enough questions. Sergeant Bligh? Would you mind?'

Arthur felt a shove.

'Let's go, Mr Shepherd. I think we'll take the back stairs.'

Despite his bravado, Arthur was utterly in the shit. Jennifer was on her way to Beasley's and may well already have arrived; Bracewell was hors de combat and Nightingale and the others had no idea where he was. As soon as Jennifer had the code, she'd be round to Mlle de Sauveterre and the pair of them would have the Council, not to mention a number of world powers by the sound of it, well and truly by the shorts.

They'd probably kill Sullivan, so there was a bright side but all-in all, things were not looking too good.

'So, how many of your lot have gone along with this?' he asked Sergeant Bligh, as they descended the stairs.

'Just because Mlle. De Sauveterre likes to run off at the mouth, it doesn't mean I will. The French have their way of doing things and we have ours.'

'Yes. A bit theatrical, the French, eh? It's something they've always done – explaining everything to their victims. They seem to think it's good manners. The Germans wouldn't dream of it of course.'

'Nor the Russians,' said Sergeant Bligh, almost admiringly.

'The Russians! God no! Er…Evelyn, - do you mind if I call you Evelyn?'

'Yes.'

'Oh. Well then: Sergeant Bligh. I'm pretty much of the opinion that I could overpower you. What do you think?'

'I think possibly you could. Provided I didn't have a nine millimetre automatic weapon pressed against your spine, of course.'

'Yes, there is that. And I suppose you've tidied away after so many of these things that you've seen pretty much every failed escape attempt?'

'Victim feigning a fall, and then grabbing the gun: that sort of thing?'

'That sort of thing, yes'

'We call it the "*Stumble and Crumble*".'

'Doesn't work too well, then?'

'No'

'How about distracting you, like I'm doing now?'

'We call that the "*Chatter and Splatter*".'

'*Do* you? I believe I'm sensing a theme. Any more?'

'There's the "*Rush and Crush*"; the "*Grab and Stab*"; the "*Pull it and Bullet*". Loads of 'em.'

'And I thought the Constables had no sense of humour. How about the "*Dagger in the temple, then run away*"?'

'There's no such...'

## Don't Shoot The Piano Player

'Did you get it all?' Beasley asked his daughter.

'Yes,' said Annabelle. 'But what does it mean?'

'It means we can begin to put an end to this sorry affair. Geoffrey may not (as I was beginning to fear), have died in vain. This young woman appears to have been the perfect vessel.'

He must have believed that Vanessa was asleep. True, she felt calmer and more serene than she had felt in... well, ever but she was awake; and listening.'

'The series itself is utterly banal. Are you sure that Geoffrey would have remembered it correctly? You always said he couldn't sing or play a note.'

'Nor could he. But he had an astonishing memory... and perfect pitch.'

'Not so good as yours, surely Daddy?' She laughed.

'Well, in all honesty, I should have to say not, but then... he could still hear, whilst I, of course...'

'Poor Daddy.'

'Oh most of the time it's no bother but being unable to hear a synthesised sound was in this case, a disaster.'

'You're far too old to go gallivanting around Europe, anyway. It could have been you coming home in a box instead of Geoffrey and no-one would have been any the wiser.' Both of them were silent for a moment then Annabelle spoke again. 'Are you certain that this will work?'

'I am. James had a real fondness for this sort of thing.'

There was knock at the door, which Vanessa used as an excuse to appear to have woken up.

'Ah, back with us, Miss Aldridge?' Beasley looked up as his daughter got to her feet. 'Something wrong, dear?'

'A knock at the door, Daddy.'

'Oh I do wish folk would use the bell. Most irritating.' Vanessa smiled and said,

'I'm so grateful to you Mr. Beasley. I…' She stopped, abruptly and her expression told him all he needed to know. He stood up and turned around. Annabelle was standing in the doorway and behind her, no doubt with a gun in her hand, was Jennifer Carlisle.

'That's why you didn't ring the bell,' Beasley said.

'It's just like riding a bike Crawthorne. Nice to see you again. Sit down, please. You too.' Jennifer released Annabelle, who rushed over to her father's side.

'Right,' Jennifer said. 'First of all; was Arthur telling me the truth when he said you hadn't got Geoffrey's message?'

'Probably,' said Beasley.

'What sort of an answer is that? Doesn't make any sense at all. Crawthorne, I'm really getting fed up with all this, to tell you the truth. Patience is wearing thin. Do you have the message or don't you?' Beasley sighed and said,

'Yes, I have the message.'

'Daddy, no!'

'It's all right dear. She'd probably have shot Miss Aldridge and threatened you until I told her, anyway. It's what I would have done.'

'I always was a good pupil, wasn't I, Crawthorne?'

'Indeed you were, Jennifer. Your father was very proud of you.' The smile froze on Jennifer's face.

'He had a bloody funny way of showing it,' she said.

'Is that what all this is about?'

'Crawthorne, I'm not going to tell you what all this is about. All you need to know is that I want that message. Now hand it over.' Bealsey smiled at Annabelle and nodded.

'Daddy..!'

'It's all right dear. Just give it to her.' Annabelle leaned forward and picked up a piece of manuscript paper. She passed it to Jennifer, wh o peered at it.

'What the hell is this?' she asked. 'If you're taking the piss…' She turned the manuscript this way and that; but clearly, it was beyond her comprehension. Vanessa wasn't surprised. From what she'd seen, it was a whole side of A4 comprising hand-written and very sketchy musical notes and terms, complete with crossings out, amendments and redrafts.

'That's what Miss Aldridge was carrying in her head,' said Beasley.

It seemed apparent to Vanessa that Jennifer had no idea what to make of the manuscript. 'Play it,' she ordered, handing it to Annabelle.

'But there's nothing to play! There's no form or structure. It requires more study.'

'Oh that's a bugger, isn't it?' said Jennifer. 'Now I'm going to have to shoot your poor old dad in the kneecap.'

'No! No!' Annabelle cried. 'I'll… try. I'll try.' Slowly, the young woman took the paper and went to the piano. She propped the music up on the stand and stared at it.

'I'm waiting,' said Jennifer.

'It isn't easy! The rhythm is separated from…' Vanessa saw Jennifer turn the gun on Crawthorne Beasley.

'You have five seconds,' Jennifer said. Only when Annabelle began to play, did Vanessa breathe again. She heard the music (if it could be called that) with mounting bewilderment. This was not the song that Geoffrey had sung to her in her dream. Far from it. This was a – a bloody racket. Surely, Jennifer wouldn't go for this?

Vanessa was right. For when Annabelle had evidently finished, Jennifer said,

'You know that saying: "*Don't shoot the piano player*?"…'

'Jennifer, stop!' Beasley said. Jennifer Carlisle's face was red and if ever Vanessa had seen murder in anyone's eyes, it was in hers.'

'Then tell me what it means!'

'I don't know what it means.'

'Then you're no use to me are you?' She took aim at Beasley, who said, staring her in the face,

'No, I suppose not.' For a long moment, Jennifer held Beasley in her sights. Then she took out her phone and dialled. 'Hello, Jacqueline? Would you come in here, please?' Vanessa realised that Jacqueline must have been waiting in the car and wondered why she hadn't come in with Jennifer. Had Jennifer not wanted Jacqueline to know what was occurring? Why had she asked her in now? Without hearing the question, Jennifer answered it.

'Beautiful piano player, Jacqueline,' she said.

## The Rothko Room

Arthur retrieved his dagger from Sergeant Bligh's head before searching her. He took her phone but there wasn't much else worth having. Annoyingly, she had let her gun fall to the foot of the stairwell so apart from the dagger, he was unarmed. Improvising again, he made his way back up the stairs. He wouldn't be quite so cavalier with Mlle de Sauveterre this time. He cautiously emerged from the stairwell. The office from whence he had been taken was one door away but it was what was beyond that door that caught his attention. Ashley Sullivan was striding down it towards the main gallery. As Sullivan exited the corridor, Arthur made a snap decision.

Mlle de Sauveterre was clever and dangerous and clearly the brains of the outfit whereas Sullivan was an idiot. The obvious thing to do would be to go in and settle her hash. However, being a pro, she would be far less likely to provide information than Sullivan would. In addition, the longer she went on thinking that Sergeant Bligh had polished him off the better and besides, he was already formulating a plan that might kill, as it were, several birds with one stone. He edged past the office door and went after Sullivan.

He spotted him on an escalator heading down to the third floor. He was almost at the bottom. Arthur hurtled onto the escalator and pounded down it. Ahead of him, Sullivan ran into a gallery and Arthur followed, a few seconds behind. A couple of indifferent and one positively rubbish installation later, and he was in something termed, inexplicably, Poetry and Dream. Oh, there was some Surrealist tripe in there: that could be it, he supposed. He glanced to his left and saw Sullivan run into yet another room. Arthur was after him. He ran into the room and stopped. Oh goodness, he stopped.

In the shadow-drenched far corner of the dimly lit space, Sullivan stood as it were, at bay. There was no way out save the door by which both had entered. But Arthur barely registered him. For on the walls were ranged "*The Seagram Murals*" 1958-59 by Mark Rothko. Arthur felt the breath leave his body.

'I remember,' said a voice, 'the first time I saw them they took my breath away as well; literally. I got a knot in my stomach, tingles in my feet that… that…'

'… that creep up your legs as though a thousand insects are crawling on them, said Arthur. 'An almost liquid… agony at your waist and your chest, that feels like you're entering an ice-cold pool; unable to catch your breath.'

Sullivan was all but forgotten as Arthur's eyes were drawn to *"Black on Maroon 1959"*

It had been nine years since he had seen this painting and it would lose little of its power even at the point when he was viewing it several times a month. The central rectangles, the colour and taste of redcurrants, began to shimmer and appeared to float above the black panel upon which they existed (for most of the time) and yet they were the colour field and the black, the smoking, congealing and electric black, was the interloping hue. Arthur heard the voice again. This time, it said,

'Hullo, Mr. Shepherd. I wondered if you might turn up.'

With a supreme effort, Arthur dragged his consciousness back into the room. On the low wooden seat in the middle of the room sat a familiar figure.

'Alan,' Arthur said. He blinked twice. 'How long have you been here?'

'All in all, a couple of days.'

'If you'll forgive me, it smells like it.'

'Shepherd!' It was Sullivan. In a shaking hand, he held a gun.

'That's not the one I gave you, is it, Sullivan?' Arthur said.

'No. It's the one the Constable took from you.' An awful smile spread across Sullivan's face. This one has bullets in it!' Arthur turned to Alan.

'Sorry about this, Alan,' he said. He hauled the boy to his feet, spun him to face Sullivan and held him, his arm across Alan's chest.'

'A human shield? And to think I once respected you! Anyway, what do I care for this idiot?' He took aim and Arthur reached inside Alan's jacket. His hand closed around the dart-gun. In an instant, he had drawn it, levelled it and fired. The dart hit Sullivan in the throat. The Under Secretary of State for Commonwealth and Foreign Affairs staggered a little and collapsed, his hands tearing at his shirt, his eyes bulging and his teeth drawn back in a rictus. Arthur moved quickly. He picked up his gun, took Alan by the hand and together, they left The Rothko Room. Behind them, the last gurgling second of the life of Ashley Sullivan M.P. sprayed blood onto *"Black on Maroon, 1959"*.

The Rothko Room was not a popular attraction for most of today's gallery-goers but it wouldn't be too long before someone came across Sullivan. However, Arthur urged Alan to walk at a leisurely pace. They took the escalator downstairs and latching onto a little clutch of students leaving the gallery shop, were soon outside.

'Who was that?' Alan asked.

'No-one,' said Arthur. Now I wonder if you might be trusted to do a little job for me?'

## Texting

Making his way to the open-air café in front of the building, Arthur sat at a table. It wasn't too difficult to work out where the stairs would have come out and he could see, by a set of double doors at the eastern edge of the frontage, two men whom he believed he recognised. They were some distance away but Arthur was pretty sure they were the Constables who'd cleaned up after Mulberry. He had no idea if they knew that Bligh had gone bad but whatever the case, they would still obey their Sergeant. He ordered a coffee and took out Sergeant Bligh's telephone.

He'd been trained in the use of the phone decrypter but it was the same with all this stuff: unless you used it regularly, you simply forgot. It took him a while but finally, he was able to read Sergeant Bligh's Contacts list. Unfortunately, there were dozens. How could anyone need so many? However, there was only one "Neville" - the name of one of the Constables in Mulberry's office the other day. He decided to send Neville a text. It took ages.

Eventually, he dialled Neville's number. Over by the double doors, one of the men reached into his pocket and took out his phone. As far as he was concerned, the text was from his boss. It read:

The frogs dble crossed us. go to her office, grab her + Sullivan and meet me at Lambeth. Don't use back stairs it's a trap. BE carful u no wot shes like.

Some of the mistakes were genuine but others were Arthur's idea of text speak. It was the best he could do but it looked as though it had worked. Both men dashed towards the main entrance and into the gallery. Arthur ordered another coffee.

It took the plod about twenty minutes to respond to the call regarding a body in The Rothko Room. The timing was perfect. As the police entered the gallery, they practically fell over two burly characters in black suits who were bundling a struggling woman out of the building. Arthur smiled as he watched the ensuing fracas wishing only that he were a little closer and able to hear Mlle de Sauveterre's attempts at an explanation. In the normal run of things, of course, he would never have wished to involve the police in Council-related business and so his pleasure at seeing the woman who'd ordered his death sitting in the back of a police car was tempered somewhat by guilt...and betrayal.

For with Sullivan dead and Louise de Sauveterre, at least for the time being otherwise engaged, Arthur realized he would have to begin considering how to deal with Jennifer. If Louise had been telling the truth, Beasley might well be dead by now: and whatever it was that Geoffrey had put in that young woman's head, would be in Jennifer's possession. He had to act in accordance with that assumption. She would almost certainly be headed for Lambeth and Sir James's private offices on the 20th floor.

Of course, Arthur had no idea if that was where Sir James had kept his little stash of incriminating evidence; nor did he even have the faintest idea how he might get down to floor twenty but try as he might, he could think of no other course of action save to try to do so as soon as possible.

## Music Lessons

The doorbell rang. All eyes turned to Jennifer Carlisle.

'Right, now as far as Jacqueline is concerned, we're all friends together. Let's not disabuse her, shall we? Go and let her in and remember: I'll be listening; I have a gun; and your daughter will be sitting right in front of me.'

Jennifer angled her head so that she could hear what, if anything, Beasley had to say to Jacqueline. Vanessa glanced over at Annabelle. It was dangerous and a long shot but she had to try something. She leaned across and began to whisper to her but had said barely three words before Jennifer shot her a glance. Vanessa sat back immediately. She knew she would get no other chance.

Jacqueline nodded a greeting to the people in the room. Recognising Vanessa, she smiled and said,

'I'm glad you two are getting along a little better.'

'Yes; sorry about all that malarkey at the Barbican, Vanessa. All sorted now, though. Now, dear we have a little puzzle here, said Jennifer, 'and we'd like your thoughts.'

'Puzzles, puzzles; always puzzles.' Jacqueline said. The others returned her smile.

'I wonder, Annabelle,' Jennifer went on, if you could explain our problem to Jacqueline.' The two women moved to the piano and sat down. Jennifer stood behind them, looking intently at Beasley, whilst Annabelle and Jacqueline spoke about the piece, gesticulated and studied it together.

'I think I understand,' said Jacqueline, finally. 'And all you want me to do is play it?'

'Yes, dear.'

Jacqueline began to play. If anything, it sounded worse than before. Jennifer's face hardened.

'Are you sure you have it correct?' Jennifer said.

'Well, I... I think so. It doesn't sound very nice, does it?'

'Serial music can take some getting used to,' Annabelle offered.

'That's true,' Jacqueline said. 'It's quite mathematical, isn't it? More... codified than other music.' Jennifer's ears pricked up.

'Codified?' she said.

'Yes,' Jacqueline replied. I don't think it matters what it sounds like. The important thing is the fact that it's a sequence of some kind. Rational and logical. Or am I just being a Philistine?' She laughed.

'All music is rational and logical if you understand the premises upon which it's constructed,' Beasley said. 'It's just signs and symbols conveying meaning.'

'Or hiding meaning, eh?' said Jennifer.

'Oh, music never lies,' said Beasley. Jennifer returned her attention to Jacqueline. Frowning, she asked,

'What is it, dear?'

'Erm… I'm not sure. I… As I say, I don't really know much about serial music, said Jacqueline, 'but if Annabelle here can… clarify, I may be able to do something.'

'I knew I could count on you, Jacqueline,' said Jennifer. However, as the minutes passed, Jennifer was becoming a little impatient with Jacqueline. She and Annabelle continued talking music and occasionally playing. Sometimes, Annabelle would take Vanessa's hands and place them on the keys and at others Jacqueline would place hers on top of Annabelle's as she played. Finally, Jennifer said,

'It's getting a little late, Jacqueline. I wonder if you've managed to…'

'Yes I have, Miss Carlisle. I think I understand it now.'

'Excellent!' She lifted the music from the stand, folded it up and handed it to Jacqueline. 'Now if you take this back to Lambeth, I'll meet you there in about half an hour. I have one or two more things to take care of here.'

'I'll show you out,' Annabelle said.

'Oh, she's a big girl,' said Jennifer. 'She'll find her own way.' Vanessa watched in dismay as Jacqueline made her goodbyes and left.

'Well done, Annabelle,' said Jennifer. 'I think that was a success all round, don't you.'

'What are you going to do with us?' Vanessa asked.

'Oh, Crawthorne, if we had a penny for every time someone said that, eh?'

'She's going to kill us,' said Beasley. 'Well, she's going to try, at any rate.'

'Daddy, please don't do anything silly.' Beasley smiled at his daughter.

'Don't worry. I taught her everything she knows.'

'That's what worries me,' Annabelle said. Vanessa was astonished to hear Jennifer Carlisle laugh: a genuine, joyous laugh.

'She's a chip off the old block and no mistake, Crawthorne. Do you remember telling me that the ambition of every pupil must be to outperform the master?'

'I do,' said Beasley. There was a movement over by the door and all eyes turned towards it.

'And *I* remember, Ms. Carlisle, when *you* told *me* the same thing,' said Jacqueline, her gun trained on Jennifer.

'Ooh! You gave me a bit of a turn there, Jacqueline,' Jennifer said. 'What are you doing?'

'At the moment, I'm wondering why you intend to kill these people.' Vanessa could tell that Jennifer knew better than to try to bluff Jacqueline. It was a mark of respect, she supposed.

'They know far too much; as I'm afraid, you now seem to.'

'Keep your hands where I can see them, please,' Jacqueline told her.

'How did you know?' Jennifer asked.

'You always told me never to explain.'

Beasley left the room.

Annabelle smiled at Vanessa, who puffed out her cheeks in exaggerated relief. Just before Jacqueline had entered the room, she had leaned across and had whispered to Annabelle,

'Jacqueline's mother's deaf.'

It had been enough. Using sign language, Annabelle had somehow managed, during their work at the piano, to explain their predicament to Jacqueline. Jacqueline's prevarications, Vanessa presumed, had been engineered in order for her to get as much information from Annabelle as she could.

'That was amazing,' she said to Annabelle.

'Yes, well done, Darling,' said Beasley, returning with a pair of handcuffs. He drew Jennifer's arms behind her back and put them on her.

'Was that your idea?' Jacqueline asked Vanessa, putting away her gun.

'It was a long shot.'

'It was brilliant. Now perhaps someone can tell me what all this is about.'

'I'll gladly tell you what I know,' said Beasley. 'However, I freely admit that there are…gaps. I think we need to get Jennifer to Lambeth and I'll fill you in as best I can on the way.'

## Once A Cleaner…

Vanessa looked over at Jennifer who seemed worryingly unconcerned by her situation. Despite being handcuffed and pinned by a seatbelt to the passenger-seat of the Land Rover Defender, she wore an expression of mild amusement. Annabelle Beasley was driving whilst her father and Jacqueline were sitting next to one another in the central seats. It was their conversation, on which Vanessa, alone in the very back, was trying to eavesdrop. Although she was listening as hard as she could, the pair were speaking extremely quietly; indeed they both appeared to be lip-reading at least some of the time. Much of what she did hear went over her head, but the early focus of Beasley's explanation appeared to be an individual by the name of Sir James Carlisle.

As far as she could make out, Sir James had maintained a sort of insurance policy against attacks by enemies of the Council. It appeared to be in the form of secrets that could be used, should the need arise and was kept in some sort of vault. Beasley either didn't know or he wouldn't tell where the vault was but Vanessa got the impression that the information she had provided would allow access to it. She wasn't sure she was altogether comfortable with this. How did she know that Beasley did not himself possess those "wrong hands" into which he was so insistent that the information should not fall? Jennifer had threatened them all with death, of course, so her hands must surely qualify as the wrong ones but frankly, who knew what to believe any more? Vanessa waited for a suitable moment then spoke:

'Mr. Beasley? Can you explain how the music is going to help you?' She'd quite forgotten about Beasley's deafness and it took an intervention from Jacqueline to get him to turn and face her. Vanessa repeated her question and Beasley said,

'I do hope you won't think me rude but I believe it's better that you remain in the dark on some matters. Better for you; better for us.' Before Vanessa could object, he continued. 'Now, I appreciate that you may feel you have a right to know after all you've been through but I believe that what you've been through might give you some inkling as to why it may be better for you to forego that right.'

'It's a key, Vanessa,' Jennifer called over. 'I should have realized that Father would come up with something like this.' Beasley hadn't caught all of this so it was Jacqueline who said,

'Miss Carlisle, please.'

'You know, I'm a little disappointed, Jacqueline,' Jennifer went on. 'I had very high hopes for you. It's not too late though. I'm willing to overlook this little... aberration should you conclude that you may just have backed the wrong horse this time.'

'Miss Carlisle, you were proposing to kill three people in cold blood simply so that you could lay your hands on Sir James's secrets.'

'That's what we *do*, Jacqueline. That's what *you* do; and once your training is complete and I have made my recommendations, it is what you will do for the next fifty years or more. And take my word for it: you'll do a very great deal worse before your career is over, isn't that so, Crawthorne?' By this time, Beasley had resorted to his hearing-aid. He stole a brief glance at his daughter, who was biting her lip. He said,

'Concentrate on the road, Annabelle. Jennifer is trying to upset you because she has no weapon other than her spite and a Cleaner will use any weapon to hand in a crisis. Annabelle has known for some time what I used to do for a living, Jennifer. She has never been comfortable with it but I believe she is reconciled.'

'Once a Cleaner, Crawthorne,' Jennifer said.

'Actually, Miss Carlisle,' Jacqueline said, 'I've been thinking about something Arthur said earlier. I'm not certain that I've chosen the right career path. There are many ways I can serve the Council other than as a Cleaner.'

'Indeed there are,' Beasley said.

'Oh come off it, Crawthorne, you sanctimonious bastard! You only jacked it in because you were losing your hearing and slowing down. You miss it as much as I would.' Beasley seemed to be thinking, then said,

'You're right. However, I also miss ski-jumping and sky-diving but I know it would be foolish to attempt either at my age and what I can't do anything about, I tend not to worry over. I'm more concerned as to why you would throw away everything on this doomed enterprise.'

'Who said it was doomed?'

Vanessa wondered why no-one seemed amused by this comment.

## Arthur's Mess

It was with some surprise that on entering room 188, Arthur found Bracewell hunched over one of his terminals.

'I thought you had a concussion.'

'What do you think this is?' Bracewell pointed to the bandage that was wound thickly about his head.

'Rosa Kleb's work, if I'm not mistaken,' said Arthur. 'How are you feeling?'

'I have a fucking headache; thanks for asking.'

'So why are you here?'

'Message from Beasley. He's on his way. With Jennifer in irons, apparently.' Arthur's face betrayed the feelings he had about Jennifer's betrayal. Noticing, Bracewell asked,

'Are you all right?'

'What? Oh, yes. Mind you, it's a right old bollocks isn't it?'

'Yes. Yes it is. So why are you here?'

'I need to get to the Constables down on the 19th floor.'

'Blimey. Did you get a bash on the head as well?'

'There's at least one Sergeant and possibly her team gone rogue. I stabbed her in the brain.'

'Bloody hell.'

'Quite. Any ideas?'

'I'm a genius Shepherd, as you know, but even I can't get you in there… Unless…' He appeared to mulling over an idea.

'Unless what?' Arthur asked, at last.

'Unless you give yourself up.'

'It's an odd thing, concussion, isn't it Bracewell?'

'I'm serious. They'll welcome you with open arms, I expect.'

'Arms of some sort, anyway.' Arthur thought for a moment, reached into his pocket and withdrew a phone.

'Here,' he said, handing it to Bracewell. 'Sergeant Bligh's phone. Have a look on that.'

'What for?'

'Names; numbers; that sort of thing…'

'Oh, very helpful.'

'Well I don't know, do I? I need a way of making sure that Louise doesn't squirm her way out of this.'

'Louise?' Arthur realized he needed to explain.

After he'd finished, Bracewell said,

'So you've involved the police?'

'Yes.'

'The Metropolitan Police?'

'Yes.'

'The same Metropolitan Police from whom the Council has taken great pains to hide its existence for nigh on seventy years?'

'Yes.' Bracewell looked at his watch.

'If you get a move on, I reckon you'd get to Heathrow in time for 22:00 to Anywhere The Fuck Else But Here.'

'Stop pissing about, Bracewell. Everything is in hand.'

A third voice broke in.

'I'm so glad to hear that, Shepherd,' it said.

Arthur and Bracewell turned to see Auberon Nightingale standing in the doorway. He was accompanied by a young woman: black hair, black suit, black shoes, black eye. 'Mr, Bracewell,' he went on, 'Shouldn't you be lying down or something?'

'Well, *I* think so,' Arthur said, 'but you know how much notice people take of what I think.'

'Indeed,' Nightingale said. 'Mind you, one can't blame him. It's all getting rather exciting now, isn't it? You know, I've rather missed this part of the job. Anyway: allow me to introduce Mlle Ursulet Dellisalde of the D.P.S.D.' Arthur gave Nightingale his beadiest beady eye.

'Are you going to turn out to be a baddie as well then, Nightingale?'

'Certainly not!' He did a very good "affronted". 'I'm a goodie of the first order. I thought that Mr. Beasley might have explained.'

'He did, as a matter of fact but I've given up believing anyone.'

'Yes. It's amazing how many lies it takes in order to arrive at the truth. Is that irony? I'm never sure.'

'I take it young Alan filled you in?'

'Yes. Strange lad. Not one of ours, surely?'

'M.I.6 intern.'

'Ah! I see. Well, he seems to think the world of you, for some reason.'

'May I ask what you've done about Louise de Sauveterre?' Arthur asked.

'About cleaning up your mess, you mean?'

'It was the least of many, many evils.'

'Mr. Maytham is exercising his prodigious skills with the Commissioner as we speak and Mrs. Gagliardo-Patricelli is making sure that the Prime Minister – a good friend of her late husband, I'm given to understand – appreciates how difficult it might be to try to explain away C.C.T.V. footage of one of his ministers threatening two unarmed art-lovers with a gun.'

'Unarmed?'

'Oh yes. We have a number of people with a thoroughgoing knowledge of C.G.I. you know, Shepherd. Mlle Dellisalde, here, asked if she might be of some use in...how did she put it? "Fucking over Louise de Sauveterre".' He pretended to speak conspiratorially to Arthur, saying, 'They have history, apparently.'

'So do I need to hack Sergeant Bligh's phone or not?' Bracewell asked, exasperated.

'Sergeant Bligh, you say? We had an idea that a Constable team had been compromised. I'm disappointed it was hers. Anyhow, do excuse me. When Mr. Beasley gets here, tell him I'll be down on twenty.' With that, Nightingale glided from the room.

'Was that a yes or a no?' said Bracewell.

'Buggered if I know. Best carry on.' Bracewell sighed, shook his head and went back to work. Arthur held out a hand to greet Mlle Dellisalde.

'Would you like a cup of tea?' he asked, with a smile.

'No.'

'Oh. Well, Bracewell is your man for computers and such. I take it you'll be wanting access ...or something... to... things.'

'Mr Bracewell?' said Ursulet. 'Can you get me into the system at Place Beauvau?'

'The Interior Ministry?' Bracewell said. Then he smiled. 'Sounds like fun!' He tossed the phone down and dragged a keyboard across the desk. Arthur chipped in,

'Er... Bracewell? Can I remind you that should the Met grant Louise her phone call and she contacts some more naughty Constables and tells them that I dobbed two of their number in to the rozzers, we may find ourselves knee deep in le merde at any moment.'

'*La* merde,' corrected Ursulet. 'And I really wouldn't worry. Maytham and Caroline are extremely... persuasive. Now, Mr. Bracewell, let's see if Nightingale was right about you.'

## A Whole New Level

Feeling like a spare part, Arthur decided he ought at least try to keep an eye on the Constables. He had no idea if Ursulet's faith in her companions was justified or not but relying on others had never been something he'd taken to naturally. He even chose to ignore the fact that he was about to draw heavily on Bracewell's plan for getting to the Constables.

They worked in three watches, so approximately one third of the Council complement ( less those out in the field), would be down on the nineteenth. Arthur estimated that there would be around nine individuals – three Sergeants and six Constables. If he was lucky, they would be clean but the way his luck appeared to be running, he might need to rely on something rather less capricious.

He had no access to the Constables' section but he could at least get himself down to floor nineteen. He had been given clearance some six years ago when on a job with a team of Social Workers. He'd been down there only rarely since then but clearance is clearance. Within the confines of Century House, Arthur reckoned it was highly likely that if the Constables retained an interest in him, his implant would be being monitored and his whereabouts known. It was even possible that cameras were on him at this very moment. This being the case, (even had he been able to access the Constabulary) a surprise incursion was out of the question. Perhaps, however, he might turn this to his advantage. The Constables may not know the limits of his clearance. Simply going down to Floor 19 may (if they were watching him), draw them out. He wasn't going to give himself up: he was going to make a nuisance of himself – something at which he was rather adept.

He was not happy being the bait in his own trap. As a Cleaner, of course, his training and experience had seen him encounter and indeed engineer many dangerous situations, but this kind of plotting and skulking was more the province of actual Social Workers and relied rather too much, for his liking, upon luck. However, he had walked into traps before and he knew the procedure.

He went into his act for the potential cameras. The less concerned he appeared, the less any observer would be anticipating trouble. As he stepped out of room 188, he practically bowled into old Fred Barnes. He greeted him with a cheery wave and even engaged him in some slight conversation before walking confidently towards the lift. He pressed the "down" arrow and glanced in the mirror, straightened his tie, patted his hair flat onto his head and scratched behind his ear. A quiet ding, a rumble of door and into the lift. Once inside, he made a play of noticing something uncomfortable in his shoe. He took it off, shook it, peered inside and put his hand in it.

As the lift came to a halt and the doors opened, Arthur shot out of it like a Catford greyhound. He rolled and took the legs out from beneath the two men who had been standing there, waiting for him. They tumbled to the ground. One of them, the larger of the two, lay spread-eagled and in one smooth motion, Arthur sprang to his feet and kicked him hard in the bollocks. He then dropped to his knee on the chest of the other and brought the heel of the shoe on his hand down hard on the fellow's nose. Ooh dear. What a mess, Arthur thought, absently as, with his free hand, he lifted the small automatic weapon from his trouser pocket and thrust it into the man's bloody face.

'Good evening,' he said. 'Take me to your leader.'

'Oh, Mr. Shepherd,' said a voice. 'There was no need for that. Look at poor Clive's face. Still, you didn't kill them; which means, I suppose, that you're not sure whose side they're on.' Arthur looked up as a figure emerged from the shadows. He was becoming used to being wrong about people but this went to a whole new level.

'I take it,' said Arthur, as calmly as he could, 'that they are on yours. And by the looks of that big fuck-off gun you're waving in my nose, you are probably not on mine.'

'I'm gratified,' said Mrs. Jempson, 'that even now, you remain unsure of what's going on. I must be doing something right.'

'That all depends on what position you take.'

'Well, the position you take, I'm afraid, is kneeling down with your hands on your head.' Arthur knew that he would get even less out of Mrs. Jempson than he had out of Jennifer so he didn't even try. He just did as he was told. Clive, the Constable, had got to his feet and had already re-set his nose. The other Constable was having a little more trouble and remained in a foetal position, whimpering quietly. Arthur winced in sympathy. Mrs Jempson spoke to Clive.

'Now, if I keep this gun on him, do you suppose you might manage him on your own?' Her voice was heavy with irony. Arthur made a mental note. Clive removed Arthur's hands from his head and dragged them, with no unnecessary roughness, behind his back. As the handcuffs went on, Arthur thought he might try to find out just how loyal Clive was to the Jempson regime.

'Sorry about the nose... Clive, is it?' he said, kindly.

'Not as sorry as you're going to be,' Clive said.

'So, pretty loyal, then,' said Arthur.

'What?'

'Never mind. Worth a try.'

'Oh, Mr Shepherd, you do make me laugh!' said Mrs Jempson. 'Now: on your feet. Time to get tortured.'

The handcuffs didn't bother Arthur as much as an uninitiated observer might expect. Oh, they made life a little difficult but by no means impossible. Mrs. Jempson and Clive knew that too and so they kept a very sharp eye on him, as they took him to the Constabulary. There was a keypad but Arthur didn't get the number. He was pushed from behind and stumbled into the room. There were rather more Constables than he had anticipated – approximately a dozen or so – and his heart sank as he saw them look in his direction with smiles of satisfaction on their faces. One of the Sergeants (a young woman, a foot or so taller than Arthur) walked over to him.

'Evelyn Bligh was my friend,' she said to him. What, he wondered, did she expect from him in response? He could think of nothing so that was what he said. She bent herself level with Arthur's face and said, 'She was a good Constable.' This time, he felt he might be able to offer a thought on the matter.

'No she wasn't,' he said.

It's easy for some Council Workers to believe that Constables are like the police and may have expected Arthur to find himself on the noisy end of a smack in the teeth. Instead, what he got was,

'What do you mean?'

He glanced at Mrs. Jempson's face. Her expression was unreadable. Nonchalance or concern, he had no idea. It was only when she jerked her head at Clive and Arthur was pushed forwards that he realised that perhaps not all the Constables had been compromised. The tall woman glared at him as he walked past and Arthur held her gaze until a shove from Clive caused him to turn away. Once through the door on the far wall, Arthur was manhandled into a chair. Mrs. Jempson went over to a desk, sat down and began busying herself. Clive stood by the door. After about a minute, Arthur spoke.

'I suppose I should be grateful for small mercies,' he said. Mrs. Jempson merely glanced up over the rims of her half-moon glasses. 'I mean, that you don't feel the urge to gloat. Everyone seems to want to gloat nowadays.'

'Nothing to gloat about, Mr. Shepherd. I won because you didn't suspect me; that's it and all about it.'

'You did a good job, if you don't mind me saying so. Tell me, though: did you know they'd tried to blow me up last Tuesday?'

'Look, Mr. Shepherd: you and I will have a conversation in a minute or two. Please be patient.'

'And by "conversation", you mean *what*, exactly?' Mrs Jempson shook her head and went back to her paperwork. Arthur was worried. If Mrs Jempson turned out to be half as good at torture as she was at managing her Oxfam shop in Gloucester Road, then he was in deep shit. There was only one thing for it.

He screamed at the top of his lungs.

Mrs. Jempson looked up. Puzzlement turned to annoyance as she realised what he was doing. Clive looked around to see if anyone else was in the room. Seeing no-one, he simply spread his hands in mute helplessness as Mrs. Jempson came out from behind her desk. Arthur screamed again and this time added a few choice words.

'Oh my God!! No! No! Please, no!!! Not the needles!!! I'll tell you everything. Sergeant Bligh killed Ricketts and Sullivan. And Mulberry, too. Probably!

'Shut him up!' Mrs. Jempson snapped. As Clive approached, Arthur, still screaming, jumped up, spun around and kicked him in the face. Clive fell against the door. Arthur seized his chance and screamed once more,

'Please...no!! You can't do this... not to a colleague!' Perhaps that one didn't quite work but he recovered quickly. 'She'd gone rogue, Mrs. J. She'd gone rogue!' Mrs Jempson had gone back to her desk and had picked up her gun. She pulled back the hammer and snarled at Arthur,

'Stop it!'

Arthur had no intention of stopping anything. She obviously wanted him alive – unless the torture was for her personal entertainment – and he gambled she wouldn't shoot. The look on her face told him that whatever she wanted from him, she had just decided she could do without it. His face fell and he knew she was going to kill him.

The door burst open and in piled the tall Sergeant followed by several Bobbies.

'What are you doing?' she growled at Mrs. Jempson.

'Don't you take that tone with me, young lady,' said Mrs. J. 'This man has some valuable information... and he killed Sergeant Bligh.'

The Sergeant indicated that a couple of Bobbies might like to pick up the stricken Clive. She also suggested that they might like to help him straighten his nose.

'Now, Mrs. Jempson,' she said, 'perhaps you might like to brief the rest of us on the progress of your investigation.'

## Party Piece

Vanessa suddenly became aware that she was having yet another new experience. There was a jolt and the Land Rover slowed perceptibly.

'Stinger!' Jacqueline called out. 'Try to keep driving, Annabelle!' It wasn't easy. Annabelle struggled with the steering as, tyres in shreds, the car's naked wheels dug into the tarmac. Sparks flew up on each side of the vehicle.

'They're behind us.' said Beasley. Vanessa turned to see, framed in the rear window, headlamps on full beam.

'Who are they?' she asked.

'Friends of mine, I expect,' said Jennifer, calmly. Vanessa rolled down the window and peered out. She had no idea what street this was but it didn't look like it was on any of the tourist routes. All she could see, in either direction, were railway arches that had become lock-ups.

'They picked their spot,' said Beasley. Vanessa was aware that the headlamps were overtaking. In a moment, their pursuers were in front of the Land Rover. Some thirty yards ahead, Vanessa saw brake lights and Beasley told Annabelle to stop the car. Without a word, Jacqueline opened the off-side door and slid onto the road. Vanessa watched in disbelief as Jacqueline rolled beneath the Land Rover. She heard the slamming of car doors up ahead and in the gloom, could see two figures walking slowly towards them.

'Annabelle,' said Beasley, quietly. 'Let me take the wheel.' Annabelle slipped into a rear seat and Beasley took her place.

'I hope you're not thinking of doing anything silly, Crawthorne,' Jennifer said. Beasley smiled broadly, revved the car and let out the clutch. With no tyres, it certainly wasn't a fast start but by the time he leaned over and unclipped Jennifer, he'd got it up to twenty five. The impact, when it came, thrust Vanessa and Annabelle forwards hard against their seat-belts and although both front airbags deployed, only Beasley stayed more or less where he was. Vanessa looked up to see a crack spreading across the windscreen and traced its origin back to a bloodstained spider web above just above where Jennifer's head now rested.

There were gunshots. She knew what they sounded like now; and behind her, muzzle flashes lit up the railway arches. Whoever had exited the car ahead of them had clearly not noticed Jacqueline slide out of and beneath the Land Rover. As Beasley sped off, she must have jumped up and was presently engaged in picking off the two attackers. It was now Beasley's turn to tumble out of the car. He lurched over to the vehicle into which he'd just slammed his Land Rover. To Vanessa's astonishment, he punched out the window, hauled the driver out onto the road and kneed him in the face.

A door opened and Jacqueline's head appeared.

'Come on,' she said, and indicating Jennifer, 'Help me get her out.' Vanessa and Annabelle scrambled from the Land Rover.

'Leave her,' said Beasley. 'We don't have time… or room by the looks of it.' Without hesitation, all three women piled into the car and Beasley drove away. In the back of the car, Vanessa whispered to Jacqueline,

'He punched the bloody window out!' Annabelle looked vaguely embarrassed.

'It used to be his party piece,' she said.

## The Secret Door

'It seems I can't leave you alone for a minute,' said Nightingale.

'If only,' Arthur responded. 'Do you think you can get Mrs. Jempson to talk?' he asked.

'Time was; you couldn't get her to shut up.'

Arthur leaned on his elbow. Across the table, Sir Auberon Nightingale was perusing a document. Every few moments, it seemed, he checked his watch. They were on Floor 20 and Arthur could still not quite believe it. He'd never been the ambitious sort; he'd simply risen through the ranks on the strength of an ability that couldn't be ignored. Never in a million years did he ever expect to be down here, in the Council Chamber, invited to be present when Sir James Carlisle's legacy was revealed.

Behind him was a bookshelf and behind that, Nightingale had informed him, was the safe itself. Truth be told, Arthur wasn't really that interested. He had no intention of blackmailing anyone so outside of a little natural curiosity as to why Jennifer and Lily Jempson had felt compelled to risk everything to obtain whatever was in there, he wouldn't have minded not being there at all.

After a period of silence, Arthur said,

'It seems strange that the two big fish in this are amongst the oldest, most long-standing Council Workers. Frankly, I find it a little disturbing. You'd think it would be the young and hungry who'd try something like this. Mind you, Mlle de Sauveterre is rather young, I suppose. She seemed to think whatever's in there would give her some sort of leverage at the Elysee. Strange bedfellows, those three. I think Jennifer has "issues" about her father and Lily… well, who knows? Of course, Sullivan's only motivation seemed to be to save money and raise his profile with the P.M. Are you listening to me?'

'Not really,' said Nightingale. Arthur knew what was wrong.

'Beasley's cutting it a bit fine, isn't he?' Nightingale looked up and said,

'You know Carlisle's daughter quite well, don't you?'

Arthur shrugged and said,

'I s'pose.'

'How dangerous is she?'

'She's unlikely to come quietly, that's for sure. And young Jacqueline could be a problem.'

It was a novel experience seeing Nightingale put out. Arthur, to his astonishment, sympathised. Nightingale's phone rang and he fairly smacked it into the side of his face. After listening for a few moments, he said,

'Tell him everything will be prepared for when he arrives.' He put down the telephone and said, 'Right, Shepherd; you and I have a little work to do.' Nightingale stood up, walked across the room and stood before the enormous oak bookshelf that filled the wall. Arthur always liked a good secret door and was curious as to how the safe would be revealed. Slowly, Nightingale ran a long white finger along a shelf. He stopped at a large, leather-bound volume and delicately hooked his fingertip over the spine. He pulled gently and gingerly removed the volume, placing it on a chair. He did the same to its neighbour, thus giving him room to insert his entire hand. He tugged his sleeve up his arm and with a look of intense concentration, Nightingale began to explore the gap.

Then, he swept his arm along the shelf and dislodged the entire row. The books tumbled off the shelf and crashed in a jumbled, dusty heap on the floor. Then, like a man possessed, he tore into the other shelves. There were books everywhere. He turned to Arthur and said,

'So I'm to do this all by myself, am I?' Arthur blinked and followed Nightingale's lead. In under a minute, the entire bookcase was denuded. As he stepped back, Arthur stumbled over volumes of expensive-looking literature, whilst Nightingale laid about him, kicking great tomes halfway across the room, clearly making for a large walnut dresser, which stood on the opposite wall. Having bashed his way through to it, he took the handles of the dresser in each hand and wrenched the doors open.

He reached in and removed a hard-hat, which he placed on his head and another, which he tossed to Arthur. In again and out with a couple of paper cover-alls, one of which he also slung across to Arthur. His last foray into the cupboard saw him emerge with pick-axe in one hand and a sledge hammer in the other.

'Ah,' said Arthur, flapping out the cover-alls and stepping into them, 'no intricate hidden mechanism, then?'

'You noticed...'

'Very little gets by me.' Arthur shrugged the cover-all over his shoulder, picked up the pickaxe and said, 'All right, where do I start?'

'Anywhere you like. All I know is that what we're after is somewhere behind this wall.' Nightingale swung the twelve-pound hammer in an upward arc and two of the oak shelves tore free of their mountings. Arthur followed this up with a straight blow to the plaster. As Nightingale continued to demolish the shelf and Arthur hacked away at the wall, they chatted.

'Sir James had decided who would be his successor after his death, hadn't he?'

'Finally. He found it difficult to let go, as I'm sure you realised. Although long retired, it was only when he was actually on his death-bed that he realised the council would need a proper leader once he'd gone.'

'He named Crawthorne Beasley,' Arthur said. Nightingale tried not to look impressed. 'It was something Jennifer said a couple of days ago: something about Carlisle's successor not having heard anything. She thought it was funny. I'm guessing Jennifer found out about Beasley and wasn't best pleased.'

'Sir James had chosen Mr. Beasley over ten years ago.'

Arthur raised an eyebrow.

'So why did Beasley retire two years back?'

'The same reason we all do: he wanted to spend the remainder of his time relaxing. He knew Carlisle couldn't last much longer but I think he'd just had enough.

'Funny; I never knew anything about Beasley,' he said. 'Geoffrey mentioned the name on a couple of occasions but never led me to believe he was anything special. Of course, that was before I realised that he had been Geoffrey's mentor.'

'He was always rather more than that. Wittersham was there when Mr. Beasley first opened the boxes,' said Nightingale.

'Boxes?'

'Yes. It was all a bit amateurish by all accounts. Carlisle had made plans up to a point but he had no precedents to go on. Basically, he was making it up as he went along. There was no formal hand-over procedure; no briefing; no settling in process; just a pile of boxes that the old boy had kept locked in his desk: that desk.' The heavy hammer poised to strike, Nightingale jerked it to indicate the large oak desk that stood in the middle of the room.

'Most of it was in the form of encrypted files in various formats – from hand-written vellum to MP3s - indicating where the actual material could be accessed. Mr. Beasley and his assistant worked on it for several months.'

'Kirkwood.'

'I beg your pardon?'

'Kirkwood. Worked with Mulberry in Clerical. Jennifer lured him to Paris to be shot by accident: presumably after she'd persuaded him to tell her what he knew.' Nightingale lowered the hammer and gave Arthur a Hard Stare. 'What?' Arthur said.

'Just how much do you know, Shepherd?'

'I got tired of always being surprised. I decided it was time I did a bit of thinking. However, I'm sure you'll be gratified to learn there are still one or two gaps.'

'Are there? I'm agog to learn whereabouts.'

'Why did Beasley come out of retirement?'

'You'd have to ask him that, I'm afraid.'

Arthur paused for a moment or two. He was still feeling the effects of the week's antics and as he rotated his shoulder muscles, there were a number of audible cracks.

## Very Little Time

'Ursulet!'

As Vanessa entered the room and saw her companion, her heart leapt. She rushed over and threw her arms around her. A moment before the embarrassment kicked in (and somewhat to her surprise), she felt Ursulet's arms around her own body.

'It's good to see you, Vanessa.' Ursulet pulled away, but as her eyes fell upon Beasley, Annabelle and Jacqueline, even what little smile there had been disappeared instantly. 'Who are these people?' she asked.

'They're friends, Ursulet. This gentleman got Geoffrey Wittersham out of my head.' Beasley smiled and gave a slight bow.

'Forgive me,' he said. 'There is very little time...'

'Nightingale said to meet him on the twentieth,' Bracewell said. Beasley turned to Annabelle, saying,

'You and Vanessa must remain here. Jacqueline? Could you take a team of Constables back to where we left Jennifer? We need her, obviously and we need a thorough disinfecting of the area.' Jacqueline nodded and left and Beasley continued, 'Mr. Bracewell? Would you mind coming along with me?' Bracewell looked a little nonplussed but Ursulet's head told him she could carry on without him and the two men departed.

'Annabelle,' Vanessa said, 'this is Ursulet. We rode over The Alps on horseback.' Annabelle and Ursulet exchanged handshakes and Annabelle said,

'Sounds exciting.' The briefest of smiles graced Ursulet's face.

'What happened to you?' Vanessa asked her.

'Christopher's Foreign Office contact introduced us to a man called Sullivan, who turned out to be a bit of a bastard. Before we knew what had happened, we were "arrested" by Council Constables. We were held in cells but I had no idea where until Nightingale let us out.' Ursulet delivered this in her usual matter-of-fact manner and it was left to Vanessa to emote for the pair of them.

'My God!' she breathed. 'Is Christopher all right?'

'He's fine.'

And what about Caroline?'

'She's having supper with the Prime Minister.'

'Of course she is. Will she come back here?'

'I doubt it. She suspects that he was involved in her husband's death.'

'Of course she does. And *you're* all right?'

Vanessa shrugged a very Gallic shrug. Vanessa couldn't think what else to say so she just smiled. Ursulet returned to her task and Vanessa stood there feeling foolish. She looked at Annabelle, whose expression was hard to read. A moment later, Ursulet stopped what she was doing and looked at Vanessa over her shoulder. She said,

'Do you remember when we on the mountain and I told you that we were not friends?' Vanessa's smile faded and she answered,

'Yes.'

'Well, I think that now, we are.'

## Opening The Vault

'Goodness Auberon; what a mess you've made,' Beasley said.

'Omlettes and eggs and all that, Sir,' Nightingale countered.

'Are you through yet?'

'Just widening the breach now, Sir. Be there in a moment.'

Arthur and Sir Auberon took a dozen more swings and managed to excavate a hole large enough to crawl through and soon all four men stood in the room beyond. It was completely dark but for the light coming through the hole. Unfortunately, all it illuminated was dust upon a white tiled floor. There was a click and the lights came on to reveal Beasley, standing by a large oak door.

'I have to ask,' Arthur said. 'Could we not have come in through there?' Beasley selected a key from the great bunch he was holding and inserted it into the keyhole. There was a solid click and he opened the door... onto a brick wall. 'Ah,' said Arthur.

'Sir James ordered me to seal the room three weeks ago,' Beasley said, 'as soon as he realised the key was lost. I think that for the first time in his life, he panicked. Without the key, he could not begin to imagine how the secrets of the Council could be secure.'

Arthur raised a tentative hand.

'Er... question?' Beasley waited. 'Could he not have had the locks changed?'

Beasley smiled and shook his head.

'In this case, I'm afraid, no.' You see, behind that door is a tunnel; and that tunnel leads to Vauxhall Cross. It's proved very handy over the past forty years or so. I'm hoping we can open it up again; Auberon feels a little "exposed" having to use the front door.' Beasley smiled and walked across the room and towards a large bureau, which none of them had noticed until then. It stood beside yet another large oak door. This time, Beasley had to select and use three keys, two of which, Arthur saw, fitted hidden holes on the same side as the hinges.

'Don't tell me he bricked this one up as well,' said Bracewell.

'Not quite,' Beasley said, as he swung it open. Beyond it was a featureless slab of grey steel.

'Blimey,' Bracewell said.

'So how does it open?' Arthur asked. Beasley stepped in front of the bureau and after using another four keys, rolled up the top. The sound told Arthur that, despite appearances, it was made of metal. Beasley turned to face the others and spoke.

'I joined the Council as a Cleaner in 1968 by which time, Sir James Carlisle's enterprise was twenty-three years old and he, considerably older. At sixty, he was already seeking a replacement. He had two deputies, both of whom were expecting preferment. Neither obtained it. Sir James could never quite bring himself to believe either of them was ready. The Council, you see, had had a very difficult birth and there were many still active in other branches of the Secret Services who believed that Sir James had betrayed not only his country (for which they might have forgiven him) but also his Class (for which they could not). This, coupled with his determination to remain immune from political advice and influence of all kinds, secured him many powerful enemies – the most prominent of whom, up until his death in '65, was Sir Winston Churchill.

'Churchill's failure to win the 1945 election was seen as a bitter blow by all those who had expected a brave new world of feudalism following victory in the War. What they now faced was the spectre of Communism under Atlee's Labour government. It isn't widely known that there was serious talk of civil war and Sir James always believed that had it not been for the fact that the country – meaning of course, the Establishment – was on its uppers, they would have gone ahead and fought Socialism with every bit as much vigour as they had Nazism.' Here Beasley paused and scratched his head. He smiled and said,

'But here I am giving a lecture and you probably already know most of this. I'll stick to the point. All of these early machinations served to teach Sir James that if creating the Council had been difficult, then sustaining it would be even more so. He decided, therefore, to take out insurance and the currency he used to purchase it was information – the very stuff of his business. Before long, he had amassed a very great deal of it and no, before you ask, I have never been privy to the contents of this vault; and nor has anyone other than Sir James himself.'

'But he retired; in '89, I think,' Bracewell piped up. 'His successors must have seen it.'

'Ah,' said Beasley. 'His successors.'

'Can you name any of them, Bracewell?' asked Nightingale.

'Well, only Benison, of course. He was a bloody disaster and nearly ruined the Council. After that, they were all referred to as "G".'

'That was an affectation of Robert Glendenning, the first of Sir James's successors. Sir James didn't think Glendenning was the right man. He had someone else in mind but it fell to "G" to run the Council for a while. He wasn't as bad as Benison but not by much. He soon realised that beyond these walls, his talents would not be recognised and he did not take well to the prospect of obscurity. He died in '97, having been thwarted, as he saw it (and quite correctly), by Sir James.'

'It always felt as though Carlisle's fingerprints remained on the council,' Bracewell said. 'So who was the next "G"?'

'Sir James Carlisle.'

'Eh?'

'At the age of eighty-nine, he came out of retirement and ran the Council for two years, using the time to make certain that his protégé would be bound to accept the post of leader when it again became vacant.'

Bracewell and Arthur looked at each other. Arthur said,

'It was *you*, wasn't it? *You've* been head of the Council since 1999.'

' ...and Sir Auberon has been my deputy since 2007.' Arthur and Bracewell glanced over at Nightingale, who acknowledged them with a slight nod of the head.

'Mr Bracewell?' Beasley said. 'May I have the music please?'

Bracewell fumbled in his pocket, eventually drawing out a crumpled sheet of paper, which he made a bold attempt at straightening out. Beasley took it and turned towards the bureau. He released a number of catches and the front of the bureau glided down into its body. Arthur took a step forward just to be sure he was seeing it correctly. Beasley noticed him at his shoulder.

'It's a Hammond L-100,' he said

'I know,' replied Arthur. 'I used to have one. Had to get rid of it when I moved to Harrow Gardens.'

'You were a serious musician, then?' Arthur smiled weakly, recalling that the inspiration for the massive purchase had been an Emerson Lake & Palmer gig at Hammersmith Odeon in 1972. Beasley went on. 'As you will see, this one has a very singular adaptation.' He pressed one of the red toggle switches and the machine began to hum.

'It's an electronic sonic security system,' Bracewell said, with something approaching wonder in his voice. 'The bloody thing is a keypad!'

'And this,' said Beasley, brandishing the sheet of music, 'is the code.'

'So why did Bracewell have it?' asked Arthur.

'Oh, merely safe-keeping, Mr. Shepherd. You see, the only person who knew the key, or so we thought, was Sir James himself. When he knew he was dying, he called me to his bedside in order to sing it to me. He knew it well and had done for nigh on fifty years, but hadn't realised that by the age of one hundred-and-four, his vocal cords were no longer capable of rendering it.' A pained expression crossed Beasley's face. 'He was dying and he couldn't impart his greatest secret to his successor. He handed me a letter and almost with his final breath, he gave me a name to write upon the envelope: the only other person in the world who knew the key.'

'Ah,' said Bracewell, 'Jennifer Carlisle.' Beasley laughed out loud.

'Good God no!' he said. 'He and she were estranged years before. She thought he was a stubborn and stupid old man and he though her flippant, lightweight if you will, and far too interested in sex to be trusted with anything so important.' Bracewell's face fell. 'No, Mr. Bracewell, the name he gave me was Graham Wainwright.'

'Who?'

'He had been the engineer who'd installed the system when the Council first occupied Century House in the 'seventies. He was a veteran of Bletchley Park and what he didn't know about musical codes wasn't worth knowing.'

'Hang on,' said Arthur, 'so it was here before the Council returned in 2000, having already been installed five floors below ground when M.I.6. was twenty floors *above* ground? That must mean that Carlisle built this office and the rest of the basement complex, around the thing.'

'Precisely.'

'So Geoffrey goes looking for this Wainwright?'

'Correct. He tracked him down to Rome and gave him the letter. Whatever he read must have convinced him to give Geoffrey the key because he handed over an old cassette tape. However, something went wrong. There were already agents in Rome trying to find Wainwright and Geoffrey was compelled to commit the code to memory before destroying the tape.'

'And, believing he was not going to make it back, he sang it to Ms. Aldridge,' Arthur said.

'...after first priming her, of course. As it turns out, she was an excellent choice.'

'Geoffrey always was a lucky bugger.' Arthur smiled.

'And then he got killed,' said Crawthorne Beasley.

There was a pause and a heavy silence, broken when Arthur said,

'Well, let's see what's in there, shall we?' He rubbed his hands together and continued, 'I will admit to being a little curious about Margaret Thatcher's serial affairs and her love-child with Ronald Reagan. Oh! And who adopted George Bush's clone.'

'I'd quite like to find out just why the Nobel Committee awarded the Peace Prize to Henry Kissinger,' Bracewell said.

Beasley and Nightingale exchanged glances and the old man sat down before the keyboards. He placed the music on the stand and began to play.

It was a short piece, only a couple of bars long, Arthur reckoned. It was atonal and clearly based on a note-row. Even to Arthur's reasonably trained ear, it made little musical sense but clearly it didn't need to. Before the final note had died away, there was a large metallic clunking sound from the direction of the steel door, followed by a grinding of gears and wheels. A long and sustained whirr and a gigantic thud and the door... remained steadfastly closed.

Nightingale let loose the breath he had clearly been holding in and Beasely too, relaxed.

'Well done, Mr. Beasley,' Nightingale said.

'Is that it?' Bracewell said, a moment or two later. 'Is it open?'

'No, Bracewell,' Arthur said. 'It's not open. In fact, it's well and truly locked. Isn't that right, Mr. Beasley?'

'Indeed, Mr. Shepherd. You see, Mr. Bracewell, the vault is designed to open automatically every seven years unless given the code within five minutes of the due opening time: not before that time, nor after it. Had we entered the key outside of our five-minute window, 300 tons of incendiary weapons would have reduced a half-mile radius to ashes. It was due to open in…' he looked at his watch, '…three minutes and twenty seconds. Now it's secure for the next seven years.'

'When presumably, the note-row will have changed, according to a preset mathematical formula,' Arthur said.

'Correct. We have the previous code and we now have this one; and we also have Mr. Bracewell…'

'…who ought to be able to work out the next sequence within… ooh, I don't know… the next seven years or so, don't you think, Bracewell?' Arthur smiled and slapped the bewildered Bracewell on the shoulder.

'And part of your duties, Mr. Shepherd, will be to see to it that Mr. Bracewell is allowed to get on with his work… unhindered.'

Arthur had wondered why he and Bracewell had been granted the privilege of witnessing the ceremony and now he knew. He wasn't altogether sanguine at the prospect but thought it best not to mention it just yet.

'A thought occurs,' he said. 'Did Jennifer and Mrs. Jempson know that the code was designed to *lock*, rather than *open* the vault?' Beasley pondered this for a moment.

'You know, I haven't the faintest idea,' he said.

## Bloody Police!

Ten minutes later, they were all back up on floor eighteen and Arthur was quizzing Ursulet about the state of play regarding Louise de Sauveterre.

'What do you mean, they've let her go?'

'Someone's obviously trying not to make too many waves,' said Ursulet. 'In any event, Louise de Sauveterre is no longer in custody.'

'Bloody police!' spat Arthur.

'Don't be too hard on them,' said Nightingale. 'Besides, it was I who arranged her release.' Nightingale obviously caught Arthur's look of angry disbelief, for he continued, 'We don't like involving the police, Shepherd, as you know; it only complicates matters.'

'You know, of course, she'll have no trouble getting back to Paris?' said Arthur.

'In fact,' said Ursulet, Mr Nightingale is helping her as we speak.' By this time, Arthur realised they were messing with him.

'You've arranged a welcoming committee at the Elysee, haven't you,' he said with a grin.

'Oh yes,' smiled Ursulet. 'She is now well and truly implicated in the killings at the Parisian bookstore earlier this week. My people were not happy to learn of her freelance operation at the Tate.'

'Anyhow, we have a more pressing matter to deal with,' Nightingale added. 'It seems the Constables found no sign of Jennifer Carlisle apart from a few flecks of blood. Rather worryingly, it seems she was driven away.'

'Carnegie,' said Arthur. 'He escaped with her from Vauxhall Cross. Personally, I wouldn't want Carnegie as my back-up plan. She must have been desperate.'

'I'll get someone onto it,' said Nightingale. 'In the meantime: Mrs. Jempson has been seen by the Inspectors.'

'Oh yes?'

'Yes. They'd like you to take care of it.'

'Now?'

'No. It can wait until morning.'

# PART 7 SUNDAY
## Royal Victoria Dock

It was one of those crisp, bright mornings. On the far side of the expanse of water, buildings were beginning to emerge from the early mist. The sun had not been up for long but even so, there was some warmth in it. Arthur watched as it teased wisps of vapour from the waters of the dock. He was sitting on a bench close by the Excel Centre and his task that morning was to supervise the death of Lily Jempson, who sat beside him. They had chatted for some time about this and that; old friends and old enemies; the strange lives each had led. Lily's chief concern was over the Oxfam shop. She hoped they'd get a replacement who wouldn't allow Council business to get in the way too much but she doubted it.

'No commitment, young people, Mr. Shepherd,' she said, sadly.

'Oh, I don't know, Mrs. J.' Arthur said. 'There are one or two I wouldn't mind at my side in a crisis. You might be surprised.'

'No more surprises for me now, though eh?' She gave a bitter laugh. Over to their right, an aircraft was coming in to land at Docklands Airport. Arthur always marvelled at the way the pilots managed to manoeuvre their charges through the skyscrapers at such a ridiculously steep angle. This one seemed even lower than usual.

'Mind if I ask you a question?' said Arthur.

'Not at all.'

'Why Sullivan? He was an arse. You could surely have managed without him?'

'Jennifer was convinced that his plan to pinch the Council's money and ingratiate himself with the P.M. would not only provided a handy diversion from our own, it would also mean that we could remove a number of inconveniently effective Council Workers from the scene and at the same time, fill S.I.S with incompetent agents. Louise and Jennifer would pin the lot on Sullivan and turn him in to S.I.S.'

Mrs. Jempson sniggered.

'Jennifer was looking forward to scaring the crap out of the Prime Minister,' she went on, 'by revealing to him that not only was one of his ministers a thief and a killer, but his intelligence services were in utter disarray. Chuck a few of her dad's little secrets into the mix and she reckoned she'd not only be in charge of the Council but within a year, she'd also have S.I.S. under her belt. And by then she'd have more than enough clout to get the government to do pretty much anything she wanted.'

Arthur was following the airplane as it buzzed over the tall buildings of the Isle of Dogs. At last he said,

'You killed some good people.'

'Well, of course. Otherwise, what would have been the point?'

'Here,' said Arthur and handed Mrs. Jempson a small capsule. 'It's completely painless.' Mrs. Jempson took it and held it between her thumb and forefinger.

'Highgate Cemetery?' she said

'Everything's in order,' Arthur said. He wondered if he should hold her hand whilst she did it but that would have been too weird. A shadow crossed his face, as the plane flew between him and the sun and as he glanced up, he saw that this was no executive flight inbound to Docklands Airport, but a seaplane; and it was banking, turning back towards them. They both watched it and it soon became apparent that it was going to set down in the dock itself.

'I didn't know they did that,' said Arthur. It tracked along, above the surface of the water and touched down. Spray kicked up in a huge arc and rainbows formed on each side of the little craft. 'Lovely sight, isn't it?'

'Yes it is,' Mrs. Jempson agreed. Together, they watched the seaplane glide past them and putter off down the dock.

Arthur would never hurry a job like this. Mrs. Jempson had been an exemplary agent until hubris and of course, Jennifer Carlisle took hold of her but he was not happy about prolonging the fateful hour either. He smiled at her but noticed she was paying him no heed. All her attention was on the seaplane, which had now turned at the western end of the dock and was approaching them once more.

Even before the first shot, Arthur had realised something was up; for standing on one of the floats of the seaplane was a figure and that figure appeared to be taking aim.

Although Arthur realised that the sun would be full in the shooter's eyes and the movement of the plane would make things even harder for him, both he and Mrs. Jempson instantly leapt over the back of the bench and crouched down.

'Sorry about this, Mrs. J.' said Arthur, sincerely. I've no idea who the fuck this is.' Mrs. Jempson tutted and said,

'I do wish you wouldn't swear like that.'

'It's not swearing! What is the matter with people?!'

'Well whatever it is, it's not nice. Anyway, I'd best be off.'

'Eh?' A shot zinged off one of the arms of the bench.

'Well, he'll hit *me* if he's not careful,' said Mrs. Jempson. 'You keep your head down. There's no telling where these shots are going.'

With that, she sprang to her feet, threw off her overcoat and dived into the dock. She emerged about twenty feet away and struck out for the plane. Arthur was seldom dumbstruck but as Carnegie held out a hand and Mrs. Jempson grabbed it, his brain couldn't quite take it all in. It was only as she was hauled onto the float, that Arthur began to pull himself together. He saw Mrs. Jempson and Carnegie clamber inside the cockpit.

Worried about being caught so flat-footed, he was relieved to note his lack of surprise on seeing Jennifer, her neck in a brace, piloting the plane. He drew his gun and took aim as it gathered speed. But the angle was narrowing and there was a considerable amount of spray, which fractured the sunlight into a million tiny, dazzling flecks.

There was no wind, so even running eastwards, Jennifer had no trouble getting off the water. As he followed the seaplane with his gun, trying to pick a target, the morning sun caught him full in the face. He winced and looked away. By the time he could see clearly once more, the plane was soaring up between the buildings.

'Bugger,' said Arthur. This was going to take some explaining. He plonked himself down on the bench once again and rubbed his eyes. He hadn't even got off a single shot. He stared up towards the eastern end of the dock. He could see the little seaplane and wondered if he ought to alert someone. Then he noticed it bank and turn westward once more.

The sound of the engine picked up and he shielded his eyes. There was no doubt about it; Jennifer was coming back. Within seconds, the plane was again over the dock. He drew his gun again and took aim. He had a clear shot at Jennifer. She turned, smiled and waved and took the aircraft into a steep climb. Arthur lowered his gun, shook his head and waved back. He watched until it was a speck in the western sky. He smiled ruefully and turned away.

As he walked up the rise, an odd sound caught his ear. It was a moment before he recognised that it was a scream; and it was growing louder. Arthur turned to see Carnegie hurtling to earth from God knows how high. He hit the water of Royal Victoria Dock with a smack, which reverberated off the surrounding buildings and sent a plume of water almost twenty feet in the air. As it hissed back into the dock, Arthur turned and continued his walk.

'Blimey,' said a man sitting on a bench at the top of the rise. 'That's something you don't see every day.' Arthur looked at him and said,

'Hello, Geoffrey. Fancy some breakfast?'

End

# Crossword No 2346

Compiled by *Luscina*

**Across**

10 Injured arms sorted out in emergency room. Possibly a bullet wound? (11)
11 Legendary knights of old didn't turn a hair, strangely. (9)
12 British Rail school outing from Windsor to Normandy? It's hard for us to understand. (6)
13 Split up from self-perpetuating organisation to rescue Bond. (4,5)
15 Perform Buddhist chant? It means the end. (4)
16 De-regulation leads to waste. (5)
18 ...or swim with style? (4)
20 Chickens getting along. (4)
21 I and a cutting from the end of the flower reveals discoverer. (5)
24 One stone lighter, relatively speaking. (8)
25 One irritates badly over and over again. (12)
26 Hat for schoolboy in 12? (4)

**Down**

1 Protect rant and avoid a fall. (9)
2 It's certainly not the Old Testament. (4)
3 Minerals are extracted and mixed to create drawings. (5)
4 Demotion for mad old king? (4)
5 I will work out how the land lies (4)
6 Gores emu horribly. Very nasty! (8)
7 We about hit the brilliant colour. (5)
8 Wife swapping for the workers? (5,6)
9 Sweeteners for California Highway Patrol? What a racket! (11)
13 To escape trouble, get out of this; but be careful not to get burned! (6,3)
14 A coded reference to Big Hearted Arthur? (5)
17 Wound caused by timber offcut? (4)
19 It'll blow up more than the tyres. (3,4)
22 Touched soft fabric. (4)
23 Playwright refused entry? (4)

Across (cont...)

27 Do Verdi badly? It was really too much. (7)
30 Cowardly Christmas? (4)
33 Caruso and this Goddess of Youth create herbaceous tangle. (4)
34 Bellows and won't shut up! (7)
35 Rebuild dome. It's the fashion, they say. (4)
39 I don't know what it is in French. (2,2,4,4)
42 Car follows commonplace American chap to Hollywood. To make Westerns, perhaps?. (8)
43 Sounds like protest singer will blow his own trumpet. (5)
44 Opt out of tapioca and turn up a berry. (4)
45 A ditch to stop livestock wandering? You're having a laugh! (2-2)
46 Test Gore's veracity again and again and again. (5)
49 I against an insect? (4)
50 Not an odd service at the end of the day. (9)
53 City of Angels passes over gentlewomen. (6)
55 They predict disaster from James' dire mix-up. (9)
56 Royal house sounds like its placing a small wildcat in a flowerpot! (11)

Down (cont...)

28 A nation turned up on shingle. (7)
29 Half of Cleese, Wayne and 42 Across? More than enough to get drunk on! (9)
31 Inform a typesetter? Even this is an obsolete form of communication. (11)
32 Britten's grubbiest opera? (5,6)
34 Northern English river causing destruction? (4)
36 Spicy writer of childrens' stories? (4)
37 A near thing? Just the opposite. (4)
38 Never bake badly before making a profit. (5,4)
40 Sounds like a bird needs a sharper beak! (8)
41 More than one. (5)
47 Lived diabolically. (5)
48 Change a place of worship? (5)
51 Conditions in place to trip you up, commonly. (4)
52 Its bite may result in a nasty tang. (4)
54 The day's end? (4)

## Serial Matrix and Note Row for "Limns"

|  | $I_0$ | $I_2$ | $I_4$ | $I_{11}$ | $I_7$ | $I_1$ | $I_3$ | $I_5$ | $I_6$ | $I_{10}$ | $I_9$ | $I_7$ |  |
|---|---|---|---|---|---|---|---|---|---|---|---|---|---|
| $P_0$ | G | A | B | F# | D | G# | Bb | C | C# | F | E | D | $R_0$ |
| $P_{10}$ | F | G | A | E | C | F# | G# | Bb | B | D# | D | C | $R_{10}$ |
| $P_8$ | D# | F | G | D | Bb | E | F# | G# | A | C# | C | Bb | $R_8$ |
| $P_1$ | G# | Bb | C | G | D# | A | B | C# | D | F# | F | D# | $R_1$ |
| $P_5$ | C | D | E | B | G | C# | D# | F | F# | Bb | A | G | $R_5$ |
| $P_{11}$ | F# | G# | Bb | F | C# | G | A | B | C | E | D# | C# | $R_{11}$ |
| $P_9$ | E | F# | G# | D# | B | F | G | A | Bb | D | C# | B | $R_9$ |
| $P_7$ | D | E | F# | C# | A | D# | F | G | G# | C | B | A | $R_7$ |
| $P_6$ | C# | D# | F | C | G# | D | E | F# | G | B | Bb | G# | $R_6$ |
| $P_2$ | A | B | C# | G# | E | Bb | C | D | D# | G | F# | E | $R_2$ |
| $P_3$ | Bb | C | D | A | F | B | C# | D# | E | G# | G | F | $R_3$ |
| $P_5$ | C | D | E | B | G | C# | D# | F | F# | Bb | A | G | $R_5$ |
|  | $RI_0$ | $RI_2$ | $RI_4$ | $RI_{11}$ | $RI_7$ | $RI_1$ | $RI_3$ | $RI_5$ | $RI_6$ | $RI_{10}$ | $RI_9$ | $RI_7$ |  |

# By the same author:

# The Circling Song

http://www.russellcruse.com

**Private Lawrence sees the world differently from those around him. Unfortunately, those around him are the British Army.** To Dr. Pennyworth, Private Henry Lawrence appears to be just another wounded soldier but slowly he begins to realise that Lawrence experiences the world in a unique and inexplicable manner. From the chaos of The Great War, Lawrence begins to create order. And Physics is struggling to keep up. Pennyworth and Dr. Caroline Charteris, a Cambridge mathematician, widowed by the war, work together to unlock the mysterious mind of Henry Lawrence and to determine how he intends to use it. Then, they must decide whether to assist him or stop him. The story of Henry Lawrence is told here through the correspondence, private papers and published works of those who knew him.

# Head Count

**It was never going to be easy taking twenty teenagers skiing in the Alps but it wasn't half so difficult as returning with only nineteen.**
When fifteen- year-old Carly Elliot parts company with an Alp, David Benedict, the teacher in charge of the ski-party is suspended from his job pending charges of negligence and possibly even manslaughter. His only ally is journalist Rebecca Daley and even she's trying to connect him to two teenage suicides. Polizeikommissar Kurz thinks David may be a murderer, D.S. Sands thinks he's an idiot and the others down the nick reckon he's a paedophile but it won't be until he finds himself tied to a chair in a run-down church, an automatic pistol in his face and trying desperately, through broken teeth, to speak German with a Swiss accent that he'll begin to suspect he may be in over his head. Could things get any worse? Of course they can; this is David Benedict we're talking about.
Daley wants a story, Benedict wants his old life back; if either gets what they want, the other will be seriously disappointed. In the event, each of them is going to get a bloody sight more than they bargained for.

Printed in Great Britain
by Amazon.co.uk, Ltd.,
Marston Gate.